P9-AEY-305

A CLASSIC NOVEL BY ONE OF AMERICA'S
MOST ACCLAIMED AUTHORS

WILD SEED

PRAISE FOR OCTAVIA E. BUTLER

"Butler is one of the finest voices in fiction—period. . . . A master storyteller."
—*Washington Post Book World*

"Butler's books are exceptional. . . . [She creates] some of the most fascinating female characters in the genre . . . real women caught in impossible situations."
—*Village Voice*

"Butler brings Toni Morrison to mind."
—*Publishers Weekly*

"She is one of those rare authors who pay serious attention to the way human beings actually work together and against each other, and she does so with extraordinary plausibility."
—*Locus*

"Her visions are strange, hypnotic distortions of our own uncomfortable world. . . . Butler's African-American feminist perspective is unique."
—*L.A. Style*

more . . .

"Superb . . . challenging and visionary."
—*Seattle Times/Post-Intelligencer*

"Well written, thoughtful."
—*St. Louis Post Dispatch*

"Clever, thoughtful, and engaging."
—*Ms.*

"Butler sets the imagination free, blending the real and the possible."
—United Press International

"Excellent, unique."
—*Knoxville News-Sentinel*

"There are few authors today who are as good as Butler."
—*Denver Rocky Mountain News*

WILD SEED

OCTAVIA E. BUTLER

WILD SEED

ASPECT®

WARNER BOOKS

A Time Warner Company

WARNER BOOKS EDITION

Copyright © 1980 by Octavia E. Butler
All rights reserved.

Aspect is a registered trademark of Warner Books, Inc.

Cover photo by Marc Yankus
Cover design by Don Puckey
Book design by H. Roberts Design

Warner Books, Inc.
1271 Avenue of the Americas
New York, N.Y. 10020

Visit our Web site at
www.twbookmark.com

W A Time Warner Company

Printed in the United States of America

First Mass Market Printing: 1988
Reissued: February 1999
First Trade Printing: April 2001

Library of Congress Cataloging-in-Publication Data

Butler, Octavia E.
    Wild seed / Octavia E. Butler.
        p. cm.
    ISBN: 0-446-67697-7 ISBN: 978-0-446-67697-7
    1. Afro-American women—Fiction. 2. Women healers—Fiction. I. Title.

PS3552.U827 W5 2001
813'.54—dc21   00-051339

To Arthur Guy
To Ernestine Walker
To Phyllis White for listening.

WILD SEED

BOOK I

Covenant

1690

1

D oro discovered the woman by accident when he
went to see what was left of one of his seed villages. The village was a comfortable mud-walled
place surrounded by grasslands and scattered trees. But Doro
realized even before he reached it that its people were gone.
Slavers had been to it before him. With their guns and their
greed, they had undone in a few hours the work of a thousand years. Those villagers they had not herded away, they
had slaughtered. Doro found human bones, hair, bits of des-
iccated flesh missed by scavengers. He stood over a very small
skeleton—the bones of a child—and wondered where the sur-
vivors had been taken. Which country or New World colony?
How far would he have to travel to find the remnants of
what had been a healthy, vigorous people?

Finally, he stumbled away from the ruins bitterly angry,
not knowing or caring where he went. It was a matter of
pride with him that he protected his own. Not the individuals, perhaps, but the groups. They gave him their loyalty,
their obedience, and he protected them.

He had failed.

He wandered southwest toward the forest, leaving as he had arrived—alone, unarmed, without supplies, accepting the savanna and later the forest as easily as he accepted any terrain. He was killed several times—by disease, by animals, by hostile people. This was a harsh land. Yet he continued to move southwest, unthinkingly veering away from the section of the coast where his ship awaited him. After a while, he realized it was no longer his anger at the loss of his seed village that drove him. It was something new—an impulse, a feeling, a kind of mental undertow pulling at him. He could have resisted it easily, but he did not. He felt there was something for him farther on, a little farther, just ahead. He trusted such feelings.

He had not been this far west for several hundred years, thus he could be certain that whatever, whoever he found would be new to him—new and potentially valuable. He moved on eagerly.

The feeling became sharper and finer, resolving itself into a kind of signal he would normally have expected to receive only from people he knew—people like his lost villagers whom he should be tracking now before they were forced to mix their seed with foreigners and breed away all the special qualities he valued in them. But he continued on southwest, closing slowly on his quarry.

Anyanwu's ears and eyes were far sharper than those of other people. She had increased their sensitivity deliberately after the first time men came stalking her, their machetes ready, their intentions clear. She had had to kill seven times on that terrible day—seven frightened men who could have been spared—and she had nearly died herself, all because she let people come upon her unnoticed. Never again.

Now, for instance, she was very much aware of the lone intruder who prowled the bush near her. He kept himself hidden, moved toward her like smoke, but she heard him, followed him with her ears.

Giving no outward sign, she went on tending her garden. As long as she knew where the intruder was, she had no fear of him. Perhaps he would lose his courage and go away. Meanwhile, there were weeds among her coco yams and her herbs. The herbs were not the traditional ones grown or gathered by her people. Only she grew them as medicines for healing, used them when people brought their sick to her. Often she needed no medicines, but she kept that to herself. She served her people by giving them relief from pain and sickness. Also, she enriched them by allowing them to spread word of her abilities to neighboring people. She was an oracle. A woman through whom a god spoke. Strangers paid heavily for her services. They paid her people, then they paid her. That was as it should have been. Her people could see that they benefited from her presence, and that they had reason to fear her abilities. Thus was she protected from them—and they from her—most of the time. But now and then one of them overcame his fear and found reason to try to end her long life.

The intruder was moving close, still not allowing her to see him. No person of honest intentions would approach so stealthily. Who was he then? A thief? A murderer? Someone who blamed her for the death of a kinsman or some other misfortune? During her various youths, she had been blamed several times for causing misfortune. She had been fed poison in the test for witchcraft. Each time, she had taken the test willingly, knowing that she had bewitched no one—and knowing that no ordinary man with his scanty knowledge of poisons could harm her. She knew more about poisons, had ingested more poisons in her long life than any of her people could imagine. Each time she passed the test, her accusers had been ridiculed and fined for their false charges. In each of her lives as she grew older, people ceased to accuse her—though not all ceased to believe she was a witch. Some sought to take matters into their own hands and kill her regardless of the tests.

The intruder finally moved onto the narrow path to approach her openly—now that he had had enough of spying on her. She looked up as though becoming aware of him for the first time.

He was a stranger, a fine man taller than most and broader at the shoulders. His skin was as dark as her own, and his face was broad and handsome, the mouth slightly smiling. He was young—not yet thirty, she thought. Surely too young to be any threat to her. Yet something about him worried her. His sudden openness after so much stealth, perhaps. Who was he? What did he want?

When he was near enough, he spoke to her, and his words made her frown in confusion. They were foreign words, completely incomprehensible to her, but there was a strange familiarity to them—as though she should have understood. She stood up, concealing uncharacteristic nervousness. "Who are you?" she asked.

He lifted his head slightly as she spoke, seemed to listen.

"How can we speak?" she asked. "You must be from very far away if your speech is so different."

"Very far," he said in her own language. His words were clear to her now, though he had an accent that reminded her of the way people spoke long ago when she was truly young. She did not like it. Everything about him made her uneasy.

"So you can speak," she said.

"I am remembering. It has been a long time since I spoke your language." He came closer, peering at her. Finally, he smiled and shook his head. "You are something more than an old woman," he said. "Perhaps you are not an old woman at all."

She drew back in confusion. How could he know anything of what she was? How could he even guess with nothing more than her appearance and a few words as evidence? "I am old," she said, masking her fear with anger. "I could be your mother's mother!" She could have been an ancestor of his mother's mother. But she kept that to herself. "Who are you?" she demanded.

"I could be your mother's father," he said.

She took another step backward, somehow controlling her growing fear. This man was not what he seemed to be. His words should have come to her as mocking nonsense, but instead, they seemed to reveal as much and as little as her own.

"Be still," he told her. "I mean you no harm."

"Who are you?" she repeated.

"Doro."

"Doro?" She said the strange word twice more. "Is that a name?"

"It is my name. Among my people, it means the east— the direction from which the sun comes."

She put one hand to her face. "This is a trick," she said. "Someone is laughing."

"You know better. When were you last frightened by a trick?"

Not for more years than she could remember; he was right. But the names . . . The coincidence was like a sign. "Do you know who I am?" she asked. "Did you come here knowing, or . . . ?"

"I came here because of you. I knew nothing about you except that you were unusual and you were here. Awareness of you has pulled me a great distance out of my way."

"Awareness?"

"I had a feeling. . . . People as different as you attract me somehow, call me, even over great distances."

"I did not call you."

"You exist and you are different. That was enough to attract me. Now tell me who you are."

"You must be the only man in this country who has not heard of me. I am Anyanwu."

He repeated her name and glanced upward, understanding. Sun, her name meant. Anyanwu: the sun. He nodded. "Our peoples missed each other by many years and a great distance, Anyanwu, and yet somehow they named us well."

"As though we were intended to meet. Doro, who are your people?"

"They were called Kush in my time. Their land is far to the east of here. I was born to them, but they have not been my people for many years. I have not seen them for perhaps twelve times as long as you have been alive. When I was thirteen years old, I was separated from them. Now my people are those who give me their loyalty."

"And now you think you know my age," she said. "That is something my own people do not know."

"No doubt you have moved from town to town to help them forget." He looked around, saw a fallen tree nearby. He went to sit on it. Anyanwu followed almost against her will. As much as this man confused and frightened her, he also intrigued her. It had been so long since something had happened to her that had not happened before—many times before. He spoke again.

"I do nothing to conceal my age," he said, "yet some of my people have found it more comfortable to forget—since they can neither kill me nor become what I am."

She went closer to him and peered down at him. He was clearly proclaiming himself like her—long-lived and powerful. In all her years, she had not known even one other person like herself. She had long ago given up, accepted her solitude. But now . . .

"Go on talking," she said. "You have much to tell me."

He had been watching her, looking at her eyes with a curiosity that most people tried to hide from her. People said her eyes were like babies' eyes—the whites too white, the browns too deep and clear. No adult, and certainly no old woman should have such eyes, they said. And they avoided her gaze. Doro's eyes were very ordinary, but he could stare at her as children stared. He had no fear, and probably no shame.

He startled her by taking her hand and pulling her down beside him on the tree trunk. She could have broken his grip easily, but she did not. "I've come a long way today," he told her. "This body needs rest if it is to continue to serve me."

She thought about that. *This body needs rest.* What a strange way he had of speaking.

"I came to this territory last about three hundred years ago," he said. "I was looking for a group of my people who had strayed, but they were killed before I found them. Your people were not here then, and you had not been born. I know that because your difference did not call me. I think you are the fruit of my people's passing by yours, though."

"Do you mean that your people may be my kinsmen?"

"Yes." He was examining her face very carefully, perhaps seeking some resemblance. He would not find it. The face she was wearing was not her true face.

"Your people have crossed the Niger"—he hesitated, frowning, then gave the river its proper name—"the Orumili. When I saw them last, they lived on the other side in Benin."

"We crossed long ago," she said. "Children born in that time have grown old and died. We were Ado and Idu, subject to Benin before the crossing. Then we fought with Benin and crossed the river to Onitsha to become free people, our own masters."

"What happened to the Oze people who were here before you?"

"Some ran away. Others became our slaves."

"So you were driven from Benin, then you drove others from here—or enslaved them."

Anyanwu looked away, spoke woodenly. "It is better to be a master than to be a slave." Her husband at the time of the migration had said that. He had seen himself becoming a great man—master of a large household with many wives, children, and slaves. Anyanwu, on the other hand, had been a slave twice in her life and had escaped only by changing her identity completely and finding a husband in a different town. She knew some people were masters and some were slaves. That was the way it had always been. But her own experience had taught her to hate slavery. She had even found it difficult to be a good wife in her most recent years because of the way a woman must bow her head and be subject to her husband. It was better to be as she was—a priestess who spoke with the voice of a god and was feared and obeyed. But what was that? She had become a kind of master herself. "Sometimes, one must become a master to avoid becoming a slave," she said softly.

"Yes," he agreed.

She deliberately turned her attention to the new things he had given her to think about. Her age, for instance. He was right. She was about three hundred years old—something none of her people would have believed. And he had said something else—something that brought alive one of her oldest memories. There had been whispers when she was a girl that her father could not beget children, that she was the daughter not only of another man, but of a visiting stranger. She had asked her mother about this, and for the first and only time in her life, her mother had struck her. From then on, she had accepted the story as true. But she had never been able to learn anything about the stranger. She would not have cared—her mother's husband claimed her as his daughter and he was a good man—but she had always wondered whether the stranger's people were more like her.

"Are they all dead?" she asked Doro. "These . . . kinsmen of mine?"

"Yes."

"Then they were not like me."

"They might have been after many more generations. You are not only their child. Your Onitsha kinsmen must have been unusual in their own right."

Anyanwu nodded slowly. She could think of several unusual things about her mother. The woman had stature and influence in spite of the gossip about her. Her husband was a member of a highly respected clan, well known for its magical abilities, but in his household, it was Anyanwu's mother who made magic. She had highly accurate prophetic dreams. She made medicine to cure disease and to protect the peo-

WILD SEED 🔊 11

ple from evil. At market, no woman was a better trader. She
seemed to know just how to bargain—as though she could
read the thoughts in the other women's minds. She became
very wealthy.

It was said that Anyanwu's clan, the clan of her mother's
husband, had members who could change their shapes, take
animal forms at will, but Anyanwu had seen no such strangeness in them. It was her mother in whom she found strangeness, closeness, empathy that went beyond what could be
expected between mother and daughter. She and her mother
had shared a unity of spirit that actually did involve some
exchange of thoughts and feelings, though they were careful
not to flaunt this before others. If Anyanwu felt pain, her
mother, busy trading at some distant market, knew of the
pain and came home. Anyanwu had no more than ghosts of
that early closeness with her own children and with three of
her husbands. And she had sought for years through her clan,
her mother's clan, and others for even a ghost of her greatest difference, the shape changing. She had collected many
frightening stories, but had met no other person who, like
herself, could demonstrate this ability. Not until now, perhaps. She looked at Doro. What was it she felt about him—
what strangeness? She had shared no thoughts with him, but
something about him reminded her of her mother. Another
ghost.

"Are you my kinsman?" she asked.

"No," he said. "But your kinsmen had given me their loyalty. That is no small thing."

"Is that why you came when . . . when my difference at-
tracted you?"

He shook his head. "I came to see what you were."

She frowned, suddenly cautious. "I am myself. You see
me."

"As you see me. Do you imagine you see everything?"

She did not answer.

"A lie offends me, Anyanwu, and what I see of you is a
lie. Show me what you really are."

"You see what you will see!"

"Are you afraid to show me?"

". . . No." It was not fear. What was it? A lifetime of concealment, of commanding herself never to play with her abilities before others, never to show them off as mere tricks, never to let her people or any people know the full extent of her power unless she were fighting for her life. Should she break her tradition now simply because this stranger asked her to? He had done much talking, but what had he actually shown her about himself? Nothing.

"Can my concealment be a lie if yours is not?" she asked.

"Mine is," he admitted.

"Then show me what you are. Give me the trust you ask me to give you."

"You have my trust, Anyanwu, but knowing what I am would only frighten you."

"Am I a child then?" she asked angrily. "Are you my mother who must shield me from adult truths?"

He refused to be insulted. "Most of my people are grateful to me for shielding them from my particular truth," he said.

"So you say. I have seen nothing."

He stood up, and she stood to face him, her small withered body fully in the shadow of his. She was little more than half his size, but it was no new thing for her to face larger people and either bend them to her will with words or beat them into submission physically. In fact, she could have made herself as large as any man, but she chose to let her smallness go on deceiving people. Most often, it put strangers at their ease because she seemed harmless. Also, it caused would-be attackers to underestimate her.

Doro stared down at her. "Sometimes only a burn will teach a child to respect fire," he said. "Come with me to one of the villages of your town, Anyanwu. There I will show you what you think you want to see."

"What will you do?" she asked warily.

"I will let you choose someone—an enemy or only some

useless person that your people would be better without. Then I will kill him."

"Kill!"

"I kill, Anyanwu. That is how I keep my youth, my strength. I can do only one thing to show you what I am, and that is kill a man and wear his body like a cloth." He breathed deeply. "This is not the body I was born into. It's not the tenth I've worn, nor the hundredth, nor the thousandth. Your gift seems to be a gentle one. Mine is not."

"You are a spirit," she cried in alarm.

"I told you you were a child," he said. "See how you frighten yourself?"

He was like an ogbanje, an evil child spirit born to one woman again and again, only to die and give the mother pain. A woman tormented by an ogbanje could give birth many times and still have no living child. But Doro was an adult. He did not enter and re-enter his mother's womb. He did not want the bodies of children. He preferred to steal the bodies of men.

"You are a spirit!" she insisted, her voice shrill with fear. All the while part of her mind wondered why she was believing him so easily. She knew many tricks herself, many frightening lies. Why should she react now like the most ignorant stranger brought before her believing that a god spoke through her? Yet she did believe, and she was afraid. This man was far more unusual than she was. This man was not a man.

When he touched her arm lightly, unexpectedly, she screamed.

He made a sound of disgust. "Woman, if you bring your people here with your noise, I will have no choice but to kill some of them."

She stood still, believing this also. "Did you kill anyone as you came here?" she whispered.

"No. I went to great trouble to avoid killing for your sake. I thought you might have kinsmen here."

"Generations of kinsmen. Sons and their sons and even their sons."

"I would not want to kill one of your sons."

"Why?" She was relieved but curious. "What are they to you?"

"How would you receive me if I came to you clothed in the flesh of one of your sons?"

She drew back, not knowing how to imagine such a thing.

"You see? Your children should not be wasted anyway. They may be good—" He spoke a word in another language. She heard it clearly, but it meant nothing to her. The word was *seed*.

"What is seed?" she asked.

"People too valuable to be casually killed," he said. Then more softly, "You must show me what you are."

"How can my sons be of value to you?"

He gave her a long silent look, then spoke with that same softness. "I may have to go to them, Anyanwu. They may be more tractable than their mother."

She could not recall ever having been threatened so gently—or so effectively. Her sons . . . "Come," she whispered. "It is too open for me to show you here."

With concealed excitement, Doro followed the small, wizened woman to her tiny compound. The compound wall—made of red clay and over six feet high—would give them the privacy Anyanwu wanted.

"My sons would do you no good," she told him as they walked. "They are good men, but they know very little."

"They are not like you—any of them?"

"None."

"And your daughters?"

"Nor them. I watched them carefully until they went away to their husbands' towns. They are like my mother. They exert great influence on their husbands and on other women, but nothing beyond that. They live their lives and they die."

"They die . . . ?"

She opened the wooden door and led him through the wall, then barred the door after him.

"They die," she said sadly. "Like their fathers."

"Perhaps if your sons and daughters married each other . . ."

"Abomination!" she said with alarm. "We are not animals here, Doro!"

He shrugged. He had spent most of his life ignoring such protests and causing the protestors to change their minds. People's morals rarely survived confrontations with him. For now, though, gentleness. This woman was valuable. If she were only half as old as he thought, she would be the oldest person he had ever met—and she was still spry. She was descended from people whose abnormally long lives, resistance to disease, and budding special abilities made them very important to him. People who, like so many others, had fallen victim to slavers or tribal enemies. There had been so few of them. Nothing must happen to this one survivor, this fortunate little hybrid. Above all, she must be protected from Doro himself. He must not kill her out of anger or by accident— and accidents could happen so easily in this country. He must take her away with him to one of his more secure seed towns. Perhaps in her strangeness, she could still bear young, and perhaps with the powerful mates he could get her, this time her children would be worthy of her. If not, there were always her existing children.

"Will you watch, Doro?" she asked. "This is what you demanded to see."

He focused his attention on her, and she began to rub her hands. The hands were bird claws, long-fingered, withered, and bony. As he watched, they began to fill out, to grow smooth and young-looking. Her arms and shoulders began to fill out and her sagging breasts drew themselves up round and high. Her hips grew round beneath her cloth, causing him to want to strip the cloth from her. Lastly, she touched her face and molded away her wrinkles. An old scar beneath one eye vanished. The flesh became smooth and firm, and the woman startlingly beautiful.

Finally, she stood before him looking not yet twenty. She cleared her throat and spoke to him in a soft, young woman's voice. "Is this enough?"

For a moment he could only stare at her. "Is this truly you, Anyanwu?"

"As I am. As I would always be if I did not age or change myself for others. This shape flows back to me very easily. Others are harder to take."

"Others!"

"Did you think I could take only one?" She began molding her malleable body into another shape. "I took animal shapes to frighten my people when they wanted to kill me," she said. "I became a leopard and spat at them. They believe in such things, but they do not like to see them proved. Then I became a sacred python, and no one dared to harm me. The python shape brought me luck. We were needing rain then to save the yam crop, and while I was a python, the rains came. The people decided my magic was good and it took them a long time to want to kill me again." She was becoming a small, well-muscled man as she spoke.

Now Doro did try to strip away her cloth, moving slowly so that she would understand. He felt her strength for a moment when she caught his hand and, with no special effort, almost broke it. Then, as he controlled his surprise, prevented himself from reacting to the pain, she untied her cloth herself and took it off. For several seconds, he was more impressed with that casual grip than with her body, but he could not help noticing that she had become thoroughly male.

"Could you father a child?" he asked.

"In time. Not now."

"Have you?"

"Yes. But only girl children."

He shook his head, laughing. The woman was far beyond anything he had imagined. "I'm surprised your people have let you live," he said.

"Do you think I would let them kill me?" she asked.

He laughed again. "What will you do then, Anyanwu? Stay here with them, convincing each new generation that you are best let alone—or will you come with me?"

She tied her cloth around her again, then stared at him, her large too-clear eyes looking deceptively gentle in her young man's face. "Is that what you want?" she asked. "For me to go with you?"

"Yes."

"That is your true reason for coming here then."

He thought he heard fear in her voice, and his throbbing hand convinced him that she must not be unduly frightened. She was too powerful. She might force him to kill her. He spoke honestly.

"I let myself be drawn here because people who had pledged loyalty to me had been taken away in slavery," he said. "I went to their village to get them, take them to a safer home, and I found . . . only what the slavers had left. I went away, not caring where my feet took me. When they brought me here, I was surprised, and for the first time in many days, I was pleased."

"It seems your people are often taken from you."

"It does not seem so, it is so. That is why I am gathering them all closer together in a new place. It will be easier for me to protect them there."

"I have always protected myself."

"I can see that. You will be very valuable to me. I think you could protect others as well as yourself."

"Shall I leave my people to help you protect yours?"

"You should leave so that finally you can be with your own kind."

"With one who kills men and shrouds himself in their skins? We are not alike, Doro."

Doro sighed, looked over at her house—a small, rectangular building whose steeply sloping thatched roof dipped to within a few feet of the ground. Its walls were made of the same red earth as the compound wall. He wondered obscurely

whether the red earth was the same clay he had seen in Indian dwellings in southwestern parts of the North American
continent. But more immediately, he wondered whether there
were couches in Anyanwu's house, and food and water. He
was almost too tired and hungry to go on arguing with the
woman.

"Give me food, Anyanwu," he said. "Then I will have
the strength to entice you away from this place."

She looked startled, then laughed almost reluctantly. It
occurred to him that she did not want him to stay and eat,
did not want him to stay at all. She believed the things he
had told her, and she feared that he could entice her away.
She wanted him to leave—or part of her did. Surely there
was another part that was intrigued, that wondered what
would happen if she left her home, walked away with this
stranger. She was too alert, too alive not to have the kind of
mind that probed and reached and got her into trouble now
and then.

"A bit of yam, at least, Anyanwu," he said smiling. "I
have eaten nothing today." He knew she would feed him.

Without a word, she walked away to another smaller
building and returned with two large yams. Then she led him
into her kitchen and gave him a deerskin to sit on since he
carried nothing other than the cloth around his loins. Still
in her male guise, she courteously shared a kola nut and a
little palm wine with him. Then she began to prepare food.
Besides the yams, she had vegetables, smoked fish, and palm
oil. She built up a fire from the live coals in the tripod of
stones that formed her hearth, then put a clay pot of water
on to boil. She began to peel the yams. She would cut them
up and boil the pieces until they were tender enough to be
pounded as her people liked them. Perhaps she would make
soup of the vegetables, oil, and fish, but that would take time.

"What do you do?" she asked him as she worked. "Steal
food when you are hungry?"

"Yes," he said. He stole more than food. If there were no
people he knew near him, or if he went to people he knew

and they did not welcome him, he simply took a new strong, young body. No person, no group could stop him from doing this. No one could stop him from doing anything at all.

"A thief," said Anyanwu with disgust that he did not think was quite real. "You steal, you kill. What else do you do?"

"I build," he said quietly. "I search the land for people who are a little different—or very different. I search them out, I bring them together in groups, I begin to build them into a strong new people."

She stared at him in surprise. "They let you do this—let you take them from their people, their families?"

"Some bring their families with them. Many do not have families. Their differences have made them outcasts. They are glad to follow me."

"Always?"

"Often enough," he said.

"What happens when people will not follow you? What happens if they say, 'It seems too many of your people are dying, Doro. We will stay where we are and live.'"

He got up and went to the doorway of the next room where two hard but inviting clay couches had been built out from the walls. He had to sleep. In spite of the youth and strength of the body he was wearing, it was only an ordinary body. If he were careful with it—gave it proper rest and food, did not allow it to be injured—it would last him a few more weeks. If he drove it, though, as he had been driving it to reach Anyanwu, he would use it up much sooner. He held his hands before him, palms down, and was not surprised to see that they were shaking.

"Anyanwu, I must sleep. Wake me when the food is ready."

"Wait!"

The sharpness of her voice stopped him, made him look back.

"Answer," she said. "What happens when people will not follow you?"

Was that all? He ignored her, climbed onto one of the

couches, lay down on the mat that covered it, and closed his eyes. He thought he heard her come into the room and go out again before he drifted off to sleep, but he paid no attention. He had long ago discovered that people were much more cooperative if he made them answer questions like hers for themselves. Only the stupid actually needed to hear his answer, and this woman was not stupid.

When she woke him, the house was full of the odor of food and he got up alert and ravenous. He sat with her, washed his hands absently in the bowl of water she gave him, then used his fingers to scoop up a bit of pounded yam from his platter and dip it into the common pot of peppery soup. The food was good and filling, and for some time he concentrated on it, ignoring Anyanwu except to notice that she was also eating and did not seem inclined to talk. He recalled distantly that there had been some small religious ceremony between the washing of hands and the eating when he had last been with her people. An offering of food and palm wine to the gods. He asked about it once he had taken the edge off his hunger.

She glanced at him. "What gods do you respect?"

"None."

"And why not?"

"I help myself," he said.

She nodded. "In at least two ways, you do. I help myself too."

He smiled a little, but could not help wondering how hard it might be to tame even partially a wild seed woman who had been helping herself for three hundred years. It would not be hard to make her follow him. She had sons and she cared for them, thus she was vulnerable. But she might very well make him regret taking her—especially since she was too valuable to kill if he could possibly spare her.

"For my people," she said, "I respect the gods. I speak as the voice of a god. For myself... In my years, I have seen that people must be their own gods and make their own good fortune. The bad will come or not come anyway."

"You are very much out of place here."

She sighed. "Everything comes back to that. I am content here, Doro. I have already had ten husbands to tell me what to do. Why should I make you the eleventh? Because you will kill me if I refuse? Is that how men get wives in your homeland—by threatening murder? Well, perhaps you cannot kill me. Perhaps we should find out!"

He ignored her outburst, noticed instead that she had automatically assumed that he wanted her as his wife. That was a natural assumption for her to make, perhaps a correct assumption. He had been asking himself which of his people she should be mated with first, but now he knew he would take her himself—for a while, at least. He often kept the most powerful of his people with him for a few months, perhaps a year. If they were children, they learned to accept him as father. If they were men, they learned to obey him as master. If they were women, they accepted him best as lover or husband. Anyanwu was one of the handsomest women he had ever seen. He had intended to take her to bed this night, and many more nights until he got her to the seed village he was assembling in the British-ruled Colony of New York. But why should that be enough? The woman was a rare find. He spoke softly.

"Shall I try to kill you then, Anyanwu? Why? Would you kill me if you could?"

"Perhaps I can!"

"Here I am." He looked at her with eyes that ignored the male form she still wore. Eyes that spoke to the woman inside—or he hoped they did. It would be much more pleasant to have her come to him because she wanted to rather than because she was afraid.

She said nothing—as though his mildness confused her. He had intended it to.

"We would be right together, Anyanwu. Have you never wanted a husband who was worthy of you?"

"You think very much of yourself."

"And of you—or why would I be here?"

"I have had husbands who were great men," she said. "Titled men of proven courage even though they had no special ability such as yours. I have sons who are priests, wealthy sons, men of standing. Why should I want a husband who must prey on other men like a wild beast?"

He touched his chest. "This man came to prey on me. He attacked me with a machete."

That stopped her for a moment. She shuddered. "I have been cut that way—cut almost in half."

"What did you do?"

"I . . . I healed myself. I would not have thought I could heal so quickly."

"I mean what did you do to the man who cut you?"

"Men. Seven of them came to kill me."

"What did you do, Anyanwu?"

She seemed to shrink into herself at the memory. "I killed them," she whispered. "To warn others and because . . . because I was angry."

Doro sat watching her, seeing remembered pain in her eyes. He could not recall the last time he had felt pain at killing a man. Anger, perhaps, when a man of power and potential became arrogant and had to be destroyed—anger at the waste. But not pain.

"You see?" he said softly. "How did you kill them?"

"With my hands." She spread them before her, ordinary hands now, not even remarkably ugly as they had been when she was an old woman. "I was angry," she repeated. "I have been careful not to get too angry since then."

"But what did you do?"

"Why do you want to know all the shameful details!" she demanded. "I killed them. They are dead. They were my people and I killed them!"

"How can it be shameful to kill those who would have killed you?"

She said nothing.

"Surely those seven are not the only ones you've killed."

She sighed, stared into the fire. "I frighten them when I

can, kill only when they make me. Most often, they are already afraid and easy to drive away. I am making the ones here rich so that none of them have wanted me dead for years."

"Tell me how you killed the seven."

She got up and went outside. It was dark out now—deep, moonless darkness, but Doro did not doubt that Anyanwu could see with those eyes of hers. Where had she gone, though, and why?

She came back, sat down again, and handed him a rock. "Break it," she said tonelessly.

It was a rock, not hardened mud, and though he might have broken it with another rock or metal tool, he could make no impression on it with his hands. He returned it to her whole.

And she crushed it in one hand.

He had to have the woman. She was wild seed of the best kind. She would strengthen any line he bred her into, strengthen it immeasurably.

"Come with me, Anyanwu. You belong with me, with the people I'm gathering. We are people you can be part of—people you need not frighten or bribe into letting you live."

"I was born among these people," she said. "I belong with them." And she insisted, "You and I are not alike."

"We are more like each other than like other people. We need not hide from each other." He looked at her muscular young man's body. "Become a woman again, Anyanwu, and I will show you that we should be together."

She managed a wan smile. "I have borne forty-seven children to ten husbands," she said. "What do you think you can show me?"

"If you come with me, I think someday, I can show you children you will never have to bury." He paused, saw that he now had her full attention. "A mother should not have to watch her children grow old and die," he continued. "If you live, they should live. It is the fault of their fathers that they die. Let me give you children who will live!"

She put her hands to her face, and for a moment he thought she was crying. But her eyes were dry, when she looked at him. "Children from your stolen loins?" she whispered.

"Not these loins." He gestured toward his body. "This man was only a man. But I promise you, if you come with me, I will give you children of your own kind."

There was a long silence. She sat staring into the fire again, perhaps making up her mind. Finally, she looked at him, studied him with such intensity he began to feel uncomfortable. His discomfort amazed him. He was more accustomed to making other people uncomfortable. And he did not like her appraising stare—as though she were deciding whether or not to buy him. If he could win her alive, he would teach her manners someday!

It was not until she began to grow breasts that he knew for certain he had won. He got up then, and when the change was complete, he took her to the couch.

2

They arose before dawn the next day. Anyanwu gave Doro a machete and took one for herself. She seemed content as she put a few of her belongings into a long basket to be carried with her. Now that she had made her decision, she expressed no more doubts about leaving with him, though she was concerned for her people.

"You must let me guide you past the villages," she told him. She again wore the guise of a young man, and had twisted her cloth around her and between her legs in the way of a man. "There are villages all around me here so that no stranger can reach me without paying. You were fortunate to reach me without being stopped. Or perhaps my people were fortunate. I must see that they are fortunate again."

He nodded. As long as she kept him going in the right direction, she could lead as long as she wanted to. She had given him pounded yam from the night before to break his fast, and during the night, she had managed to exhaust his strong young body with lovemaking. "You are a good man," she had observed contentedly. "And it has been too long since I had this."

He was surprised to realize how much her small compliment pleased him—how much the woman herself pleased him. She was a worthwhile find in many ways. He watched her take a last look at her house, left swept and neat; at her compound, airy and pleasant in spite of its smallness. He wondered how many years this had been her home.

"My sons helped me build this place," she told him softly. "I told them I needed a place apart where I could be free to make my medicines. All but one of them came to help me. That one was my oldest living son, who said I must live in his compound. He was surprised when I ignored him. He is wealthy and arrogant and used to being listened to even when what he says is nonsense—as it often is. He did not understand anything about me, so I showed him a little of what I have shown you. Only a little. It closed his mouth."

"It would," laughed Doro.

"He is a very old man now. I think he is the only one of my sons who will not miss me. He will be glad to find me gone—like some others of my people, even though I have made them rich. Few of them living now are old enough to remember my great changes here—from woman to leopard to python. They have only their legends and their fear." She got two yams and put them into her basket, then got several more and threw them to her goats, who scrambled first to escape them, then to get them. "They have never eaten so well," she said laughing. Then she sobered, went to a small shelter where clay figurines representing gods sat.

"This is for my people to see," she told Doro. "This and the ones inside." She gestured toward her house.

"I did not see any inside."

Her eyes seemed to smile through her somber expression. "You almost sat on them."

Startled, he thought back. He usually tried not to outrage people's religious beliefs too quickly, though Anyanwu did not seem to have many religious beliefs. But to think he had come near sitting on religious objects without recognizing them . . .

"Do you mean those clay lumps in the corner?"

"Those," she said simply. "My mothers."

Symbols of ancestral spirits. He remembered now. He shook his head. "I am getting careless," he said in English.

"What are you saying?"

"That I am sorry. I've been away from your people too long."

"It does not matter. As I said, these things are for others to see. I must lie a little, even here."

"No more," he said.

"This town will think I am finally dead," she said staring at the figurines. "Perhaps they will make a shrine and give it my name. Other towns have done that. Then at night when they see shadows and branches blowing in the wind they can tell each other they have seen my spirit."

"A shrine with spirits will frighten them less than the living woman, I think," Doro said.

Not quite smiling, Anyanwu led him through the compound door, and they began the long trek over a maze of footpaths so narrow that they could walk only in a single file between the tall trees. Anyanwu carried her basket on her head and her machete sheathed at her side. Her bare feet and Doro's made almost no sound on the path—nothing to confuse Anyanwu's sensitive ears. Several times as they moved along at the pace she set—a swift walk—she turned aside and slipped silently into the bush. Doro followed with equal skill and always shortly afterward people passed by. There were women and children bearing water pots or firewood on their heads. There were men carrying hoes and machetes. It was as Anyanwu had said. They were in the middle of her town, surrounded by villages. No European would have recognized a town, however, since most of the time there were no dwellings in sight. But on his way to her, Doro had stumbled across the villages, across one large compound after another and either slipped past them or walked past boldly as though he had legitimate business. Fortunately, no one had challenged him. People often hesitated to challenge a man who seemed important and purposeful. They would not, how-ever, have hesitated to challenge strangers who hid them-selves, who appeared to be spying. As Doro followed Anyanwu now, he worried that he still might wind up wearing the body of one of her kinsmen—and having great trouble with her. He was relieved when she told him they had left her peo-ple's territory behind.

At first, Anyanwu was able to lead Doro along already cleared paths through territory she knew either because she had once lived in it or because her daughters lived in it now. Once, as they walked, she was telling him about a daughter who had married a handsome, strong, lazy young man, then run away to a much less imposing man who had some am-bition. He listened for a while, then asked: "How many of your children lived to adulthood, Anyanwu?"

"Every one," she said proudly. "They were all strong and well and had no forbidden things wrong with them."

Children with "forbidden" things wrong with them—twins, for instance, and children born feet first, children with almost any deformity, children born with teeth—these chil-dren were thrown away. Doro had gotten some of his best stock from earlier cultures who, for one reason or another, put infants out to die.

"You had forty-seven children," he said in disbelief, "and all of them lived and were perfect?"

"Perfect in their bodies, at least. They all survived."

"They are my people's children! Perhaps some of them and their descendants should come with us after all."

Anyanwu stopped so suddenly that he almost ran into her. "You will not trouble my children," she said quietly.

He stared down at her—she had still not bothered to make herself taller though she told him she could—and tried to swallow sudden anger. She spoke to him as though he were one of her children. She did not yet understand his power!

"I am here," she said in the same quiet voice. "You have me."

"Do I?"

"As much as any man could."

That stopped him. There was no challenge in her voice, but he realized at once she was not telling him she was all his—his property. She was saying only that he had whatever small part of herself she reserved for her men. She was not used to men who could demand more. Though she came from a culture in which wives literally belonged to their husbands, she had power and her power had made her independent, accustomed to being her own person. She did not yet realize that she had walked away from that independence when she walked away from her people with him.

"Let's go on," he said.

But she did not move. "You have something to tell me," she said.

He sighed. "Your children are safe, Anyanwu." For the moment.

She turned and led on. Doro followed, thinking that he had better get her with a new child as quickly as he could. Her independence would vanish without a struggle. She would do whatever he asked then to keep her child safe. She was too valuable to kill, and if he abducted any of her descendants, she would no doubt goad him into killing her. But once she was isolated in America with an infant to care for, she would learn submissiveness.

Paths became occasional luxuries as they moved into country Anyanwu did not know. More and more, they had to use their machetes to clear the way. Streams became a problem. They flowed swiftly through deep gorges that had to be crossed somehow. Where the streams interrupted footpaths, local people had placed log bridges. But where Doro and Anyanwu found neither paths nor bridges, they had to cut their own logs. Travel became slower and more dangerous. A fall would not have killed either of them directly, but

Doro knew that if he fell, he would not be able to stop him-self from taking over Anyanwu's body. She was too close to him. On his way north, he had crossed several rivers by sim-ply abandoning his body and taking over the body nearest to him on the far side. And since he was leading now, allowing his tracking sense to draw him to the crew aboard his ship, he could not send her ahead or leave her behind. He would not have wanted to anyway. They were in the country of peo-ple who waged war to get slaves to sell to the Europeans. These were people who would cut her to pieces if she began reshaping herself before them. Some of them even had Eu-ropean guns and powder.

Their slow progress was not a complete waste of time, though. It gave him a chance to learn more about Anyanwu—and there was more to learn. He discovered that he would not have to steal food while she was with him. Once the two yams were roasted and eaten, she found food everywhere. Each day as they traveled, she filled her basket with fruit, nuts, roots, whatever she could find that was edible. She threw stones with the speed and force of a sling and brought down birds and small animals. At day's end, there was always a hearty meal. If a plant was unfamiliar to her she tasted it and sensed within herself whether or not it was poison. She ate several things she said were poison, though none of them seemed to harm her. But she never gave him anything other than good food. He ate whatever she gave him, trusting her abilities. And when a small cut on his hand became infected, she gave him even more reason to trust her.

The infected hand had begun to swell by the time she noticed it, and it was beginning to make him sick. He was already deciding how he would get a new body without en-dangering her. Then, to his surprise, she offered to help him heal.

"You should have told me," she said. "You let yourself suffer needlessly."

He looked at her doubtfully. "Can you get the herbs you need out here?"

She met his eyes. "Sometimes the herbs were for my people—like the gods in my compound. If you will let me, I can help you without them."

"All right." He gave her his swollen, inflamed hand.

"There will be pain," she warned.

"All right," he repeated.

She bit his hand.

He bore it, holding himself rigid against his own deadly reaction to sudden pain. She had done well to warn him. This was the second time she had been nearer to death than she could imagine.

For a time after biting him, she did nothing. Her attention seemed to turn inward, and she did not answer when he spoke to her. Finally, she brought his hand to her mouth again and there was more pain and pressure, but no more biting. She spat three times, each time returning to his hand, then she seemed to caress the wound with her tongue. Her saliva burned like fire. After that she kept a watch on the hand, attending it twice more with that startling, burning pain. Almost at once, the swelling and sickness went away and the wound began to heal.

"There were things in your hand that should not have been there," she told him. "Living things too small to see. I have no name for them, but I can feel them and know them when I take them into my body. As soon as I know them, I can kill them within myself. I gave you a little of my body's weapon against them."

Tiny living things too small to see, but large enough to make him sick. If his wound had not begun to heal so quickly and cleanly, he would not have believed a word she said. As it was, though, his trust in her grew. She was a witch, surely. In any culture she would be feared. She would have to fight to keep her life. Even sensible people who did not believe in witches would turn against her. And Doro, breeder of witches that he was, realized all over again what a treasure she was. Nothing, no one, must prevent his keeping her.

It was not until he reached one of his contacts near the coast that someone decided to try.

Anyanwu never told Doro that she could jump all but the widest of the rivers they had to cross. She thought at first that he might guess because he had seen the strength of her hands. Her legs and thighs were just as powerful. But Doro was not used to thinking as she did about her abilities, not used to taking her strength or metamorphosing ability for granted. He never guessed, never asked what she could do.

She kept silent because she feared that he too could leap the gorges—though in doing so, he might leave his body behind. She did not want to see him kill for so small a reason. She had listened to the stories he told as they traveled, and it seemed to her that he killed too easily. Far too easily—unless the stories were lies. She did not think they were. She did not know whether he would take a life just to get across a river quickly, but she feared he might. This made her begin to think of escaping from him. It made her think longingly of her people, her compound, her home. . . .

Yet she made herself womanly for him at night. He never had to ask her to do this. She did it because she wanted to, because in spite of her doubts and fears, he pleased her very much. She went to him as she had gone to her first husband, a man for whom she had cared deeply, and to her surprise, Doro treated her much as her first husband had. He listened with respect to her opinions and spoke with respect and friendship as though to another man. Her first husband had taken much secret ridicule for treating her this way. Her second husband had been arrogant, contemptuous, and brutal, yet he had been considered a great man. She had run away from him as she now wished to run away from Doro. Doro could not have known what dissimilar men he brought alive in her memory.

He had still given her no proof of the power he claimed, no proof that her children would be in danger from other than an ordinary man if she managed to escape. Yet she continued to believe him. She could not bring herself to get up while he slept and vanish into the forest. For her children's sake she had to stay with him, at least until she had proof one way or the other.

She followed him almost grimly, wondering what it would be like finally to be married to a man she could neither escape nor outlive. The prospect made her cautious and gentle. Her earlier husbands would not have known her. She sought to make him value her and care for her. Thus she might have some leverage with him, some control over him later when she needed it. Much married as she was, she knew she would eventually need it.

They were in the lowlands now, passing through wetter country. There was more rain, more heat, many more mosquitoes. Doro got some disease and coughed and coughed. Anyanwu got a fever, but drove it out of herself as soon as she sensed it. There was enough misery to be had without sickness.

"When do we pass through this land!" she asked in disgust. It was raining now. They were on someone's pathway laboring through sucking ankle-deep mud.

"There is a river not far ahead of us," he told her. He stopped for a moment to cough. "I have an arrangement with people at a riverside town. They will take us the rest of the way by canoe."

"Strangers," she said with alarm. They had managed to avoid contact with most of the people whose lands they had crossed.

"You will be the stranger here," Doro told her. "But you need not worry. These people know me. I have given them gifts—dash, they call it—and promised them more if they rowed my people down the river."

"Do they know you in this body?" she asked, using the question as an excuse to touch the hard flat muscle of his shoulder. She liked to touch him.

"They know me," he said. "I am not the body I wear, Anyanwu. You will understand that when I change—soon, I think." He paused for another fit of coughing. "You will know me in another body as soon as you hear me speak."

"How?" She did not want to talk about his changing, his killing. She had tried to cure his sickness so that he would not change, but though she had eased his coughing, prevented him from growing sicker, she had not made him well. That meant she might soon be finding out more about his changing whether she wanted to or not. "How will I know you?" she asked.

"There are no words for me to tell you—as with your tiny living things. When you hear my voice, you will know me. That's all."

"Will it be the same voice?"

"No."

"Then how . . . ?"

"Anyanwu . . ." He glanced around at her. "I am telling you, you will know!"

Startled, she kept silent. She believed him. How was it she always believed him?

The village he took her to was a small place that seemed not much different from waterside communities she had known nearer home. Here some of the people stared at her and at Doro, but no one molested them. She heard speech here and there and sometimes it had a familiar sound to it. She thought she might understand a little if she could go closer to the speakers and listen. As it was, she understood nothing. She felt exposed, strangely helpless among people so alien. She walked closely behind Doro.

He led her to a large compound and into that compound as though it belonged to him. A tall, lean young man confronted him at once. The young man spoke to Doro and when Doro answered, the young man's eyes widened. He took a step backward.

Doro continued to speak in the strange language, and Anyanwu discovered that she could understand a few words—but not enough to follow the conversation. This language was at least more like her own than the new speech, the *English*,

Doro was teaching her. English was one of the languages spoken in his homeland, he had told her. She had to learn it. Now, though, she gathered what she could from the unspoken language of the two men, from their faces and voices. It was obvious that instead of the courteous greeting Doro had expected, he was getting an argument from the young man. Finally, Doro turned away in disgust. He spoke to Anyanwu.

"The man I dealt with before has died," he told her. "This fool is his son." He stopped to cough. "The son was present when his father and I bargained. He saw the gifts I brought. But now that his father has died, he feels no obligation to me."

"I think he fears you," Anyanwu said. The young man was blustering and arrogant; that she could see despite the different languages. He was trying hard to seem important. As he spoke, though, his eyes shifted and darted and looked at Doro only in brief glances. His hands shook.

"He knows he is doing a dangerous thing," Doro said. "But he is young. His father was a king. Now the son thinks he will use me to prove himself. He has chosen a poor target."

"Have you promised him more gifts?"

"Yes. But he sees only my empty hands. Move away from me, Anyanwu, I have no more patience."

She wanted to protest, but her mouth was suddenly dry. Frightened and silent, she stumbled backward away from him. She did not know what to expect, but she was certain the young man would be killed. How would he die? Exactly what would Doro do?

Doro stepped past the young man and toward a boy-child of about seven years who had been watching the men talk. Before the young man or the child could react, Doro collapsed.

His body fell almost on top of the boy, but the child jumped out of the way in time. Then he knelt on the ground and took Doro's machete. People were beginning to react as the boy stood up and leaned on the machete. The sounds of their questioning voices and their gathering around almost drowned out the child's voice when he spoke to the young man. Almost.

The child spoke calmly, quietly in his own language, but as Anyanwu heard him, she thought she would scream aloud. The child was Doro. There was no doubt of it. Doro's spirit had entered the child's body. And what had happened to the child's spirit? She looked at the body lying on the ground, then she went to it, turned it over. It was dead.

"What have you done?" she said to the child.

"This man knew what his arrogance could cost," Doro said. And his voice was high and childlike. There was no sound of the man Doro had been. Anyanwu did not understand what she was hearing, what she was recognizing in the boy's voice.

"Keep away from me," Doro told her. "Stay there with the body until I know how many others of his household this fool will sacrifice to his arrogance."

She wanted nothing more than to keep away from him. She wanted to run home and try to forget she had ever seen him. She lowered her head and closed her eyes, fighting panic. There was shouting around her, but she hardly heard it. Intent on her own fear, she paid no attention to anything else until someone knocked her down.

Then someone seized her roughly, and she realized she was to pay for the death of the child. She thrust her attacker away from her and leaped to her feet ready to fight.

"That is enough!" Doro shouted. And then more quietly, "Do not kill him!"

She saw that the person she had thrust away was the young man—and that she had pushed him harder than she thought. Now he was sprawled against the compound wall, half conscious.

Doro went to him and the man raised his hands as though to deflect a blow. Doro spoke to him in quiet, chilling tones that should never have issued from the mouth of a child. The man cringed, and Doro spoke again more sharply.

The man stood up, looked at the people of the household he had inherited from his father. They were clearly alarmed and confused. Most had not seen enough to know what was going on, and they seemed to be questioning each other. They stared at the new head of their household. There were several young children, women, some of whom must have been wives or sisters of the young man, men who were probably brothers and slaves. Everyone had come to see.

Perhaps the young man felt that he had shamed himself before his people. Perhaps he was thinking about how he had cringed and whimpered before a child. Or perhaps he was merely the fool Doro took him to be. Whatever his reasoning, he made a fatal error.

With shouted words that had to be curses, the man seized the machete from Doro's hand, raised it, and brought it slashing down through the neck of the unresisting child-body.

Anyanwu looked away, absolutely certain of what would happen. There had been ample time for the child to avoid the machete. The young man, perhaps still groggy from Anyanwu's blow, had not moved very quickly. But the child had stood still and awaited the blow with a shrug of adult weariness. Now she heard the young man speaking to the crowd, and she could hear Doro in his voice. Of course.

The people fled. Several of them ran out of the compound door or scrambled over the wall. Doro ignored them, went to Anyanwu.

"We will leave now," he said. "We will take a canoe and row ourselves."

"Why did you kill the child?" she whispered.

"To warn this young fool," he said hitting the chest of his lean, new body. "The boy was the son of a slave and no great loss to the household. I wanted to leave a man here who had authority and who knew me, but this man would not learn. Come, Anyanwu."

She followed him dumbly. He could turn from two casual murders and speak to her as though nothing had happened. He was clearly annoyed that he had had to kill the young man, but annoyance seemed to be all he felt.

Beyond the walls of the compound, armed men waited. Anyanwu slowed, allowed Doro to move well ahead of her as he approached them. She was certain there would be more killing. But Doro spoke to the men—said only a few words to them—and they drew back out of his path. Then Doro made a short speech to everyone, and the people drew even farther away from him. Finally, he led Anyanwu down to the river, where they stole a canoe and paddles.

"You must row," she told him as they put the craft into the water. "I will try to help you when we are beyond sight of this place."

"Have you never rowed a canoe?"

"Not perhaps three times as long as this new body of yours has been alive."

He nodded and paddled the craft alone.

"You should not have killed the child," she said sadly. "It was wrong no matter why you did it."

"Your own people kill children."

"Only the ones who must be killed—the abominations. And even with them . . . sometimes when the thing wrong with the child was small, I was able to stop the killing. I spoke with the voice of the god, and as long as I did not violate tradition too much, the people listened."

"Killing children is wasteful," he agreed. "Who knows what useful adults they might have grown into? But still, sometimes a child must be sacrificed."

She thought of her sons and their children, and knew positively that she had been right to get Doro away from them. Doro would not have hesitated to kill some of them to intimidate others. Her descendants were ordinarily well able to take care of themselves. But they could not have stopped Doro from killing them, from walking about obscenely clothed in their flesh. What could stop such a being—a spirit. He was a spirit, no matter what he said. He had no flesh of his own.

Not for the first time in her three hundred years, Anyanwu wished she had gods to pray to, gods who would help her. But she had only herself and the magic she could perform with her own body. What good was that against a being who could steal her body away from her? And what would he feel if he decided to "sacrifice" her? Annoyance? Regret? She looked at him and was surprised to see that he was smiling.

He took a deep breath and let it out with apparent pleasure. "You need not row for a while," he told her. "Rest. This body is strong and healthy. It is so good not to be coughing."

3

Doro was always in a good mood after changing bodies—especially when he changed more than once in quick succession or when he changed to one of the special bodies that he bred for his use. This time, his pleasurable feelings were still with him when he reached the coast. He noticed that Anyanwu had been very quiet, but she had her quiet times. And she had just seen a thing that was new to her. Doro knew people took time to get used to his changes. Only his children seemed to accept them naturally. He was willing to give Anyanwu all the time she needed.

There were slavers on the coast. An English factor lived there, an employee of the Royal African Company, and incidentally, Doro's man. Bernard Daly was his name. He had three black wives, several half-breed children, and apparently, strong resistance to the numerous local diseases. He also had only one hand. Years before, Doro had cut off the other.

Daly was supervising the branding of new slaves when

Doro and Anyanwu pulled their canoe onto the beach. There was a smell of cooking flesh in the air and the sound of a slave boy screaming.

"Doro, this is an evil place," Anyanwu whispered. She kept very close to him.

"No one will harm you," he said. He looked down at her. She always spent her days as a small, muscular man, but somehow, he could never think of her as masculine. He had asked her once why she insisted on going about as a man. "I have not seen you going about in women's bodies," she retorted. "People will think before they attack a man—even a small man. And they will not become as angry if a man gives them a beating."

He had laughed, but he knew she was right. She was somewhat safer as a man, although here, among African and European slavers, no one was truly safe. He himself might be forced out of his new body before he could reach Daly. But Anyanwu would not be touched. He would see to it.

"Why do we stop here?" she asked.

"I have a man here who might know what happened to my people—the people I came to get. This is the nearest seaport to them."

"Seaport . . ." She repeated the word as he had said it— in English. He did not know the word in her language for sea. He had described to her the wide, seemingly endless water that they had to cross, but in spite of his description, she stared at it in silent awe. The sound of the surf seemed to frighten her as it mixed with the screaming of slaves being branded. For the first time, she looked as though the many strange new things around her would overwhelm her. She looked as though she would turn and run back into the forest as slaves often tried to do. Completely out of character, she looked terrified.

He stopped, faced her, took her firmly by the shoulders. "Nothing will harm you, Anyanwu." He spoke with utter conviction. "Not these slavers, not the sea, not anything at all. I have not brought you all this way only to lose you. You know my power." He felt her shudder. "That power will not harm you either. I have accepted you as my wife. You have only to obey me."

She stared at him as he spoke, as though these eyes of hers could read his expression and discern truth. Ordinary people could not do that with him, but she was far from ordinary. She had had time enough in her long life to learn to read people well—as Doro himself had learned. Some of his people believed he could read their unspoken thoughts, so transparent were their lies to him. Half-truths, though, could be another matter.

Anyanwu seemed to relax, reassured. Then something off to one side caught her eye and she stiffened. "Is that one of your white men?" she whispered. He had told her about Europeans, explaining that in spite of their pale skins, they were neither albinos nor lepers. She had heard of such people but had not seen any until now.

Doro glanced at the approaching European, then spoke to Anyanwu. "Yes," he said, "but he is only a man. He can die as easily as a black man. Move away from me."

She obeyed quickly.

Doro did not intend to kill the white man if he could avoid it. He had killed enough of Daly's people back at their first meeting to put the Englishman out of business. Daly had proved tractable, however, and Doro had helped him to survive.

"Welcome," the white man said in English. "Have you more slaves to sell us?" Clearly, Doro's new body was no stranger here. Doro glanced at Anyanwu, saw how she was staring at the slaver. The man was bearded and dirty and thin as though wasted by disease—which was likely. This land swallowed white men. The slaver was a poor example of his kind, but Anyanwu did not know that. She was having a good look. Her curiosity now seemed stronger than her fear.

"Are you sure you know me?" Doro asked the man quietly. And his voice had the expected effect.

The man stopped, frowned in confusion and surprise. "Who are you?" he demanded. "Who . . . what do you want here?" He was not afraid. He did not know Doro. He merely assumed he had made a mistake. He stood peering up at the tall black man and projecting hostility.

"I'm a friend of Bernard Daly," Doro said. "I have business with him." Doro spoke in English as did the slaver and there was no doubt that the man understood him. Thus, when the slaver continued to stare, Doro started past him, walked toward the branding where he could see Daly talking with someone else.

But the slaver was not finished. He drew his sword. "You want to see the captain?" he said. Daly had not been master of a ship for fifteen years, but he still favored the title. The slaver grinned at Doro, showing a scattering of yellow teeth. "You'll see him soon enough!"

Doro glanced at the sword, annoyed. In a single movement almost too swift to follow, he raised his heavy machete and knocked the lighter weapon from the slaver's hand.

Then the machete was at the man's throat. "That could have been your hand," Doro said softly. "It could have been your head."

"My people would kill you where you stand."

"What good would that do you—in hell?"

Silence.

"Turn, and we'll go to see Daly."

The slaver obeyed hesitantly, muttering some obscenity about Doro's ancestry.

"Another word will cost you your head," Doro said.

Again, there was silence.

The three marched single file past the chained slaves, past the fire where the branding had stopped, past Daly's men who stared at them. They went to the tree-shaded, three-sided shelter where Daly sat on a wooden crate, drinking from an earthen jug. He lowered the jug, though, to stare at Doro and Anyanwu.

"I see business is good," Doro said.

Daly stood up. He was short and square and sunburned and unshaven. "Speak again," he growled. "Who are you?" He was a little hard of hearing, but Doro thought he had heard enough. Doro could see in him the strange combination of apprehension and anticipation that Doro had come to expect from his people. He knew when they greeted him this way that they were still his servants, loyal and tame.

"You know me," he said.

The slaver took a step back.

"I've left your man alive," Doro said. "Teach him manners."

"I will." He waved the confused, angry man away. The man glared at Doro and at the now lowered machete. Finally, he stalked away.

When he was gone, Doro asked Daly, "Has my crew been here?"

"More than once," the slaver said. "Just yesterday, your son Lale chose two men and three women. Strong young blacks they were—worth much more than I charged."

"I'll soon see," Doro said.

Suddenly Anyanwu screamed.

Doro glanced at her quickly to see that she was not being molested. Then he kept his eyes on Daly and on his men. "Woman, you will cause me to make a mistake!" he muttered.

"It is Okoye," she whispered. "The son of my youngest daughter. These men must have raided her village."

"Where is he?"

"There!" She gestured toward a young man who had just been branded. He lay on the ground dirty, winded, and bruised from his struggles to escape the hot iron.

"I will go to him," Anyanwu said softly, "though he will not know me."

"Go," Doro told her. Then he switched back to English. "I may have more business for you, Daly. That boy."

"But . . . that one is taken. A company ship—"

"A pity," Doro said. "The profit will not be yours then."

The man raised his stump to rub his hairy chin. "What are you offering?" It was his habit to supplement his meager salary by trading with interlopers—non-Company men—like Doro. Especially Doro. It was a dangerous business, but England was far away and he was not likely to be caught.

"One moment," Doro told him, then switched language. "Anyanwu, is the boy alone or are there other members of your family here?"

"He is alone. The others have been taken away."

"When?"

She spoke briefly with her grandson, then faced Doro again. "The last ones were sold to white men many days ago."

Doro sighed. That was that, then. The boy's relatives, strangers to him, were even more completely lost than the people of his seed village. He turned and made Daly an offer for the boy—an offer that caused the slaver to lick his lips. He would give up the boy without coercion and find some replacement for whoever had bought him. The blackened, cooked gouge on the boy's breast had become meaningless. "Unchain him," Doro ordered.

Daly gestured to one of his men, and that man removed the chains.

"I'll send one of my men back with the money," Doro promised.

Daly shook his head and stepped out of the shelter. "I'll walk with you," he said. "It isn't far. One of your people might shoot you if they see you looking that way with only two more blacks as companions."

Doro laughed and accepted the man's company. He wanted to talk to Daly about the seed village anyway. "Do you think I'll cheat you?" he asked. "After all this time?"

Daly smiled, glanced back at the boy who walked with Anyanwu. "You could cheat me," he said. "You could rob me whenever you choose, and yet you pay well. Why?"

"Perhaps because you are wise enough to accept what you cannot understand."

"You?"

"Me. What do you tell yourself I am?"

"I used to think you were the devil himself."

Doro laughed again. He had always permitted his people the freedom to say what they thought—as long as they stopped when he silenced them and obeyed when he commanded them. Daly had belonged to him long enough to know this. "Who are you, then?" he asked the slaver. "Job?"

"No." Daly shook his head sadly. "Job was a stronger man."

Doro stopped, turned, and looked at him. "You are content with your life," he said.

Daly looked away, refusing to meet whatever looked through the very ordinary eyes of the body Doro wore. But when Doro began to walk again, Daly followed. He would follow Doro to his ship, and if Doro himself offered payment for the young slave, Daly would refuse to take it. The boy would become a gift. Daly had never taken money from Doro's hand. And always, he had sought Doro's company.

"Why does the white animal follow?" asked Anyanwu's grandson loudly enough for Doro to hear. "What has he to do with us now?"

"My master must pay him for you," said Anyanwu. She had presented herself to the boy as a distant kinsman of his mother. "And also," she added, "I think this man serves him somehow."

"If the white man is a slave, why should he be paid?"

Doro answered this himself. "Because I choose to pay him, Okoye. A man may choose what he will do with his slaves."

"Do you send your slaves to kill our kinsmen and steal us away?"

"No," Doro said. "My people only buy and sell slaves." And only certain slaves at that if Daly was obeying him. He would know soon.

"Then they send others to prey on us. It is the same thing!"

"What I permit my people to do is my affair," Doro said.

"But they—!"

Doro stopped abruptly, turned to face the young man who was himself forced to come to an awkward stop. "What I permit them to do is my affair, Okoye. That is all."

Perhaps the boy's enslavement had taught him caution. He said nothing. Anyanwu stared at Doro, but she too kept silent.

"What were they saying?" Daly asked.

"They disapprove of your profession," Doro told him.

"Heathen savages," Daly muttered. "They're like animals. They're all cannibals."

"These aren't," Doro said, "though some of their neighbors are."

"All of them," Daly insisted. "Just give them the chance."

Doro smiled. "Well, no doubt the missionaries will reach them eventually and teach them to practice only symbolic cannibalism."

Daly jumped. He considered himself a pious man in spite of his work. "You shouldn't say such things," he whispered. "Not even you are beyond the reach of God."

"Spare me your mythology," Doro said, "and your righteous indignation." Daly had been Doro's man too long to be pampered in such matters. "At least we cannibals are honest about what we do," Doro continued. "We don't pretend as your slavers do to be acting for the benefit of our victims' souls. We don't tell ourselves we've caught them to teach them civilized religion."

Daly's eyes grew round. "But . . . I did not mean you were a . . . a . . . I did not mean . . ."

"Why not?" Doro looked down at him, enjoying his confusion. "I assure you, I'm the most efficient cannibal you will ever meet."

Daly said nothing. He wiped his brow and stared seaward. Doro followed his gaze and saw that there was a ship in sight now, lying at anchor in a little cove—Doro's own

ship, the *Silver Star*, small and hardy and more able than any
of his larger vessels to go where it was not legally welcome
and take on slave cargo the Royal African Company had reserved for itself. Doro could see some of his men a short distance away loading yams onto a longboat. He would be on
his way home soon.

Doro invited Daly out to the ship. There, he first settled Anyanwu and her grandson in his own cabin. Then he
ate and drank with Daly and questioned the slaver about
the seed village.

"Not a coastal people," Doro said. "An island tribe from
the grasslands beyond the forests. I showed you a few of
them years ago when we met."

"These blacks are all alike," Daly said. "It's hard to tell."
He took a swallow of brandy.

Doro reached across the small table and grasped Daly's
wrist just above the man's sole remaining hand. "If you can't
do better than that," he said, "you're no good to me."

Daly froze, terrified, arresting a sudden effort to jerk his
hand away. He sat still, perhaps remembering how his men
had died years before whether Doro touched them or not.
"It was a joke," he whispered hoarsely.

Doro said nothing, only looked at him.

"Your people have Arab blood," Daly said quickly. "I remember their looks and the words of their language that you
taught me and their vile tempers. Not an easy people to enslave and keep alive. None like them have gone through my
hands without being tested."

"Speak the words I taught you."

Daly spoke them—words in the seed people's own language asking them whether they were followers of Doro,
whether they were "Doro's seed"—and Doro released Daly's
wrist. The slaver had said the words perfectly and none of
Doro's seed villagers had failed to respond. They were, as
Daly had said, difficult people—bad-tempered, more suspicious than most of the strangers, more willing than most to

murder each other or attack their far-flung neighbors, more willing to satisfy their customs and their meat-hunger with human flesh. Doro had isolated them on their sparsely populated savanna for just that reason. Had they been any closer to the larger, stronger tribes around them, they would have been wiped out as a nuisance.

They were also a highly intuitive people who involuntarily saw into each other's thoughts and fought with each other over evil intentions rather than evil deeds. This without ever realizing that they were doing anything unusual. Doro had been their god since he had assembled them generations before and commanded them to marry only each other and the strangers he brought to them. They had obeyed him, throwing away clearly defective children born of their inbreeding, and strengthening the gifts that made them so valuable to him. If those same gifts made them abnormally quick to anger, vicious, and savagely intolerant of people unlike themselves, it did not matter. Doro had been very pleased with them, and they had long ago accepted the idea that pleasing him was the most important thing they could do.

"Your people are surely dead if they have been taken," Daly said. "The few that you brought here with you years ago made enemies wherever they went."

Doro had brought five of the villagers out to cross-breed them with certain others he had collected. They had insulted everyone with their arrogance and hostility, but they had also bred as Doro commanded them and gotten fine children—children with ever greater, more controllable sensitivity.

"Some of them are alive," Doro said. "I can feel their lives drawing me when I think of them. I'm going to have to track as many of them as I can before someone does kill them though."

"I'm sorry," Daly said. "I wish they had been brought to me. As bad as they are, I would have held them for you."

Doro nodded, sighed. "Yes, I know you would have."

And the last of the slaver's tension melted away. He

knew Doro did not blame him for the seed people's demise, knew he would not be punished. "What is the little Igbo you have brought aboard?" he asked curiously. There was room for curiosity now.

"Wild seed," Doro said. "Carrier of a bloodline I believed was lost—and, I think, of another that I did not know existed. I have some exploring to do in her homeland once she is safely away."

"She! But . . . that black is a man."

"Sometimes. But she was born a woman. She is a woman most of the time."

Daly shook his head, unbelieving. "The monstrosities you collect! I suppose now you will breed creatures who don't know whether to piss standing or squatting."

"They will know—if I can breed them. They will know, but it won't matter."

"Such things should be burned. They are against God!"

Doro laughed and said nothing. He knew as well as Daly how the slaver longed to be one of Doro's monstrosities. Daly was still alive because of that desire. Ten years before, he had confronted what he considered to be just another black savage leading five other less black but equally savage-looking men. All six men appeared to be young, healthy—fine potential slaves. Daly had sent his own black employees to capture them. He had lost thirteen men that day. He had seen them swept down as grain before a scythe. Then, terrified, confronted by Doro in the body of the last man killed, he had drawn his own sword. The move cost him his right hand. He never understood why it had not cost him his life. He did not know of Doro's habit of leaving properly disciplined men of authority scattered around the world ready to serve whenever Doro needed them. All Daly understood was that he had been spared—that Doro had cauterized his wound and cared for him until he recovered.

And by the time he recovered, he had realized that he was no longer a free man—that Doro was capable of taking the life he had spared at any time. Daly was able to accept this as others had accepted it before him. "Let me work for you," he had said. "Take me aboard one of your ships or even back to your homeland. I'm still strong. Even with one hand, I can work. I can handle blacks."

"I want you here," Doro had told him. "I've made arrangements with some of the local kings while you were recovering. They'll trade with you exclusively from now on."

Daly had stared at him in amazement. "Why would you do such a thing for me?"

"So that you can do a few things for me," Doro had answered.

And Daly had been back in business. Doro sent him black traders who sold him slaves and his company sent him white traders who bought them. "Someone else would set up a factory here if you left," Doro told him. "I can't stop the trade even where it might touch my people, but I can control it." So much for his control. Neither his support of Daly nor his spies left along the coast—people who should have reported to Daly—had been enough. Now they were useless. If they had been special stock, people with unusual abilities, Doro would have resettled them in America, where they could be useful. But they were only ordinary people bought by wealth or fear or belief that Doro was a god. He would forget them. He might forget Daly also once he had returned to Anyanwu's homeland and sought out as many of her descendants as he could find. At the moment, though, Daly could still be useful—and he could still be trusted; Doro knew that now. Perhaps the seed people had been taken to Bonny or New Calabar or some other slave port, but they had not passed near Daly. The most talented and deceptive of Doro's own children could not have lied to him successfully while he was on guard. Also, Daly had discovered he enjoyed being an arm of Doro's power.

"Now that your people are gone," Daly said, "why not take me to Virginia or New York where you have blacks working. I'm sick to death of this country."

"Stay here," Doro ordered. "You can still be useful. I'll be coming back."

Daly sighed. "I almost wish I was one of those strange beings you call your people," he admitted.

Doro smiled and had the ship's captain, John Woodley, pay for the boy, Okoye, and send Daly ashore.

"Slimy little bastard," Woodley muttered when Daly was gone.

Doro said nothing. Woodley, one of Doro's ordinary, ungifted sons, had always disliked Daly. This amused Doro since he considered the two men much alike. Woodley was the child of a casual liaison Doro had had forty-five years before with a London merchant's daughter. Doro had married the woman and provided for her when he learned she would bear his child, but he quickly left her a widow, well off, but alone except for her infant son. Doro had seen John Woodley twice as the boy grew toward adulthood. When on the second visit, Woodley expressed a desire to go to sea, Doro had him apprenticed to one of Doro's shipmasters. Woodley had worked his own way up. He could have become wealthy, could have been commanding a great ship instead of one of Doro's smallest. But he had chosen to stay near Doro. Like Daly, he enjoyed being an arm of Doro's power. And like Daly, he was envious of others who might outrank him in Doro's esteem.

"That little heathen would sail with you today if you'd let him," Woodley told Doro. "He's no better than one of his blacks. I don't see what good he is to you."

"He works for me," Doro said. "Just as you do."

"It's not the same!"

Doro shrugged and let the contradiction stand. Woodley knew better than Daly ever could just how much it was the same. He'd worked too closely with Doro's most gifted children to overestimate his own value. And he knew the living generations of Doro's sons and daughters would populate a city. He knew how easily both he and Daly could be replaced. After a moment he sighed as Daly had sighed. "I suppose the new blacks you brought aboard have some special talent," he said.

"That's right," Doro answered. "Something new."

"Godless animals!" Woodley muttered bitterly. He turned and walked away.

4

The ship frightened Anyanwu, but it frightened Okoye more. He had seen that the men aboard were mostly white men, and in his life, he had had no good experiences with white men. Also, fellow slaves had told him the whites were cannibals.

"We will be taken to their land and fattened and eaten," he told Anyanwu.

"No," Anyanwu assured him. "It is not their custom to eat men. And if it were, our master would not permit us to be eaten. He is a powerful man."

Okoye shuddered. "He is not a man."

Anyanwu stared at him. How had he discovered Doro's strangeness so quickly?

"It was he who bought me, then sold me to the whites. I remember him; he beat me. It is the same face, the same skin. But something different is living inside. Some spirit."

"Okoye." Anyanwu spoke very softly and waited until he turned from his terrified gazing into space and looked at her. "If Doro is a spirit," she said, "then he has done you a service. He has killed your enemy for you. Is that reason to fear him?"

"You fear him yourself. I have seen it in your eyes."

Anyanwu gave him a sad smile. "Not as much as I should, perhaps."

"He is a spirit!"

"You know I am your mother's kinsman, Okoye."

He stared at her for a time without answering. Finally he asked, "Have her people also been enslaved?"

"Not when I last saw them."

"Then how were you taken?"

"Do you remember your mother's mother?"

"She is the oracle. The god speaks through her."

"She is Anyanwu, your mother's mother," Anyanwu said. "She fed you pounded yam and healed the sickness that threatened to take your life. She told you stories of the tortoise, the monkey, the birds. . . . And sometimes when you looked at her in the shadows of the fire and the lamp, it seemed to you that she became these creatures. You were frightened at first. Then you were pleased. You asked for the stories and the changes. You wanted to change too."

"I was a child," Okoye said. "I was dreaming."

"You were awake."

"You cannot know!"

"I know."

"I never told anyone!"

"I never thought you would," Anyanwu said. "Even as a child, you seemed to know when to talk and when to keep quiet." She smiled, remembering the small, stoic boy who had refused to cry with the pain of his sickness, who had refused to smile when she told him the old fables her mother had told her. Only when she startled him with her changes did he begin to pay attention.

She spoke softly. "Do you remember, Okoye, your mother's mother had a mark here?" She drew with her finger the jagged old scar that she had once carried beneath her left eye. As she drew it, she aged and furrowed the flesh so that the scar appeared.

Okoye bolted toward the door.

Anyanwu caught him, held him easily in spite of his greater size and his desperate strength. "What am I that I was not before?" she asked when the violence had gone out of his struggles.

"You are a man!" he gasped. "Or a spirit."

"I am no spirit," she said. "And should it be so difficult for a woman who can become a tortoise or a monkey to become a man?"

He began to struggle again. He was a young man now, not a child. The easy childhood acceptance of the impossible was gone, and she dared not let him go. In his present state, he might jump into the water and drown.

"If you will be still, Okoye, I will become the old woman you remember."

Still he struggled.

"*Nwadiani*—daughter's child—do you remember that even the pain of sickness could not make you weep when your mother brought you to me, but you wept because you could not change as I could?"

He stopped his struggles, stood gasping in her grip.

"You are my daughter's son," she said. "I would not harm you." He was still now, so she released him. The bond between a man and his mother's kin was strong and gentle. But for the boy's own safety, she kept her body between his and the door.

"Shall I become as I was?" she asked.

"Yes," the boy whispered.

She became an old woman for him. The shape was familiar and easy to slip into. She had been an old woman for so long.

"It is you," Okoye said wonderingly.

She smiled. "You see? Why should you fear an old woman?"

To her surprise, he laughed. "You always had too many

teeth to be an old woman, and strange eyes. People said the god looked out of your eyes."

"What do you think?"

He stared at her with great curiosity, walked around her to look at her. "I cannot think at all. Why are you here? How did you become this Doro's slave?"

"I am not his slave."

"I cannot see how any man would hold you in slavery. What are you?"

"His wife."

The boy stared speechless at her long breasts.

"I am not this wrinkled woman, Okoye. I allowed myself to become her when my last husband, the father of your mother, died. I thought I had had enough husbands and enough children; I am older than you can imagine. I wanted to rest. When I had rested for many years as the people's oracle, Doro found me. In his way, he is as different as I am. He wanted me to be his wife."

"But he is not merely different. He is something other than a man!"

"And I am something other than a woman."

"You are not like him!"

"No, but I have accepted him as my husband. It was what I wanted—to have a man who was as different from other men as I am from other women." If this was not entirely true, Okoye did not need to know.

"Show me . . ." Okoye paused as though not certain of what he wanted to say. "Show me what you are."

Obligingly, she let her true shape flow back to her, became the young woman whose body had ceased to age when she was about twenty years old. At twenty, she had a violent, terrible sickness during which she had heard voices, felt pain in one part of her body after another, screamed and babbled in foreign dialects. Her young husband had feared she would die. She was *Anasi*, his first wife, and though she was in disfavor with his family because after five years of marriage, she had produced no children, he fought hard against losing her. He sought help for her, frantically paying borrowed money to the old man who was then the oracle, making sacrifices of valuable animals. No man ever cared more for her than he did. And it seemed that the medicine worked. Her body ceased its thrashing and struggling, and her senses returned, but she found herself vastly changed. She had a control over her body that was clearly beyond anything other people could manage. She could look inside herself and control or alter what she saw there. She could finally be worthy of her husband and of her own womanhood; she could become pregnant. She bore her husband ten strong children. In the centuries that followed, she never did more for any man.

When she realized the years had ceased to mark her body, she experimented and learned to age herself as her husband aged. She learned quickly that it was not good to be too different. Great differences caused envy, suspicion, fear, charges of witchcraft. But while her first husband lived, she never entirely gave up her beauty. And sometimes when he came to her at night, she allowed her body to return to the youthful shape that came so easily, so naturally—the true shape. In that way, her husband had a young senior wife for as long as he lived. And now Okoye had a mother's mother who appeared to be younger than he was.

"*Nneochie?*" the boy said doubtfully. "Mother's mother?"

"Still," Anyanwu said. "This is the way I look when I do nothing. And this is the way I look when I marry a new husband."

"But . . . you are old."

"The years do not touch me."

"Nor him . . . ? Your new husband?"

"Nor him."

Okoye shook his head. "I should not be here. I am only a man. What will you do with me?"

"You belong to Doro. He will say what is to be done with you—but you need not worry. He wants me as his wife. He will not harm you."

*   *   *

The water harmed him.

Soon after Anyanwu had revealed herself, he began to grow ill. He became dizzy. His head hurt him. He said he thought he would vomit if he did not leave the confinement of the small room.

Anyanwu took him out on deck where the air was fresh and cooler. But even there, the gentle rocking of the ship seemed to bother him—and began to bother her. She began to feel ill. She seized on the feeling at once, examining it. There was drowsiness, dizziness, and a sudden cold sweat. She closed her eyes, and while Okoye vomited into the water, she went over her body carefully. She discovered that there was a wrongness, a kind of imbalance deep within her ears. It was a tiny disturbance, but she knew her body well enough to notice the smallest change. For a moment, she observed this change with interest. Clearly, if she did nothing to correct it, her sickness would grow worse; she would join Okoye, vomiting over the rail. But no. She focused on her inner ears and remembered perfection there, remembered organs and fluids and pressures in balance, their wrongness righted. Remembering and correcting were one gesture; balance was restored. It had taken her much practice—and much pain—to learn such ease of control. Every change she made in her body had to be understood and visualized. If she was sick or injured, she could not simply wish to be well. She could be killed as easily as anyone else if her body was damaged in some way she could not understand quickly enough to repair. Thus, she had spent much of her long life learning the diseases, disorders, and injuries that she could suffer—learning them often by inflicting mild versions of them on herself, then slowly, painfully, by trial and error, coming to understand exactly what was wrong and how to impress healing. Thus, when her enemies came to kill her, she knew more about surviving than they did about killing.

And now she knew how to set right this new disturbance that could have caused her considerable misery. But her knowledge was of no help to Okoye—yet. She searched through her memory for some substance that would help him. Within her long memory was a catalogue of cures and poisons—often the same substances given in different quantities, with different preparation, or in different combinations. Many of them she could manufacture within her body as she had manufactured a healing balm for Doro's hand.

This time, though, before she thought of anything that might be useful, a white man came to her, bringing a small metal container full of some liquid. The man looked at Okoye, then nodded and put the container into Anyanwu's hands. He made signs to indicate that she should get Okoye to drink.

Anyanwu looked at the container, then sipped from it herself. She would not give anyone medicine she did not understand.

The liquid was startlingly strong stuff that first choked her, then slowly, pleasantly warmed her, pleased her. It was like palm wine, but much stronger. A little of it might make Okoye forget his misery. A little more might make him sleep. It was no cure, but it would not hurt him and it might help.

Anyanwu thanked the white man in her own language and saw that he was looking at her breasts. He was a beardless, yellow-haired young man—a physical type completely strange to Anyanwu. Another time, her curiosity would have driven her to learn more about him, try to communicate with him. She found herself wondering obscurely whether the hair between his legs was as yellow as that on his head. She laughed aloud at herself, and the young man, unknowing, watched her breasts jiggle.

Enough of that!

She took Okoye back into the cabin, and when the yellow-haired man followed, she stepped in front of him and gestured unmistakably for him to leave. He hesitated, and she decided that if he touched her uninvited, she would throw him into the sea. *Sea*, yes. That was the English word for water. If she said it, would he understand?

But the man left without coercion.

Anyanwu coaxed Okoye to swallow some of the liquid. It made him cough and choke at first, but he got it down. By the time Doro came to the cabin, Okoye was asleep.

Doro opened the door without warning and came in. He looked at her with obvious pleasure and said, "You are well, Anyanwu. I thought you would be."

"I am always well."

He laughed. "You will bring me luck on this voyage. Come and see whether my men have bought any more of your relatives."

She followed him deeper into the vessel through large rooms containing only a few people segregated by sex. The people lounged on mats or gathered in pairs or small groups to talk—those who had found others who spoke their language.

No one was chained as the slaves on shore had been. No one seemed to be hurt or frightened. Two women sat nursing their babies. Anyanwu heard many languages, including, finally, her own. She stopped at the mat of a young woman who had been singing softly to her.

"Who are you?" she asked the woman in surprise.

The woman jumped to her feet, took Anyanwu's hands. "You can speak," she said joyfully. "I thought I would never again hear words I could understand. I am Udenkwo."

The woman's own speech was somewhat strange to Anyanwu. She pronounced some of her words differently or used different words so that Anyanwu had to replay everything in her mind to be certain what had been said. "How did you get here, Udenkwo?" she asked. "Did these whites steal you from your home?" From the corner of her eye, she saw Doro turn to look at her indignantly. But he allowed Udenkwo to answer for herself.

"Not these," she said. "Strangers who spoke much as you do. They sold me to others. I was sold four times—finally to these." She looked around as though dazed, surprised. "No one has beaten me here or tied me."

"How were you taken?"

"I went to the river with friends to get water. We were all taken and our children with us. My son . . ."

"Where is he?"

"They took him from me. When I was sold for the second time, he was not sold with me." The woman's strange accent did nothing to mask her pain. She looked from Anyanwu to Doro. "What will be done with me now?"

This time Doro answered. "You will go to my country. You belong to me now."

"I am a freeborn woman! My father and my husband are great men!"

"That is past."

"Let me go back to my people!"

"My people will be your people. You will obey me as they obey."

Udenkwo sat still, but somehow seemed to shrink from him. "Will I be tied again? Will I be beaten?"

"Not if you obey."

"Will I be sold?"

"No."

She hesitated, examining him as though deciding whether or not to believe him. Finally, tentatively, she asked: "Will you buy my son?"

"I would," Doro said, "but who knows where he may have been taken—one boy. How old was he?"

"About five years old."

Doro shrugged. "I would not know how to find him."

Anyanwu had been looking at Udenkwo uncertainly. Now, as the woman seemed to sink into depression at the news that her son was forever lost to her, Anyanwu asked: "Udenkwo, who is your father and his father?"

The woman did not answer.

"Your father," Anyanwu repeated, "his people."

Listlessly, Udenkwo gave the name of her clan, then went on to name several of her male ancestors. Anyanwu listened until the names and their order began to sound familiar—

until one of them was the name of her eighth son, then her third husband.

Anyanwu stopped the recitation with a gesture. "I have known some of your people," she said. "You are safe here. You will be well treated." She began to move away. "I will see you again." She drew Doro with her and when they were beyond the woman's hearing, she asked: "Could you not look for her son?"

"No," Doro said. "I told her the truth. I would not know where to begin—or even whether the boy is still alive."

"She is one of my descendants."

"As you said, she will be well treated. I can offer no more than that." Doro glanced at her. "The land must be full of your descendants."

Anyanwu looked somber. "You are right. They are so numerous, so well scattered, and so far from me in their generations that they do not know me or each other. Sometimes they marry one another and I hear of it. It is abomination, but I cannot speak of it without focusing the wrong kind of attention on the young ones. They cannot defend themselves as I can."

"You are right to keep silent," Doro said. "Sometimes ways must be different for people as different as ourselves."

"We," she said thoughtfully. "Did you have children of . . . of a body born to your mother?"

He shook his head. "I died too young," he said. "I was thirteen years old."

"That is a sad thing, even for you."

"Yes." They were on deck now, and he stared out at the sea. "I have lived for more than thirty-seven hundred years and fathered thousands of children. I have become a woman and borne children. And still, I long to know that my body could have produced. Another being like myself? A companion?"

"Perhaps not," said Anyanwu. "You might have been like me, having one ordinary child after another."

Doro shrugged and changed the subject. "You must take

your daughter's son to meet that girl when he is feeling better. The girl's age is wrong, but she is still a little younger
than Okoye. Perhaps they will comfort each other."

"They are kinsmen!"

"They will not know that unless you tell them, and you
should be silent once more. They have only each other,
Anyanwu. If they wish, they can marry after the customs of
their new land."

"And how is that?"

"There is a ceremony. They pledge themselves to each
other before a"—he said an English word, then translated—
"a priest."

"They have no family but me, and the girl does not know
me."

"It does not matter."

"It will be a poor marriage."

"No. I will give them land and seed. Others will teach
them to live in their new country. It is a good place. People
need not stay poor there if they will work."

"Children of mine will work."

"Then all will be well."

He left her and she wandered around the deck looking
at the ship and the sea and the dark line of trees on shore.
The shore seemed very far away. She watched it with the beginnings of fear, of longing. Everything she knew was back
there deep within those trees through strange forests. She
was leaving all her people in a way that seemed far more permanent than simply walking away.

She turned away from the shore, frightened of the sudden emotion that threatened to overwhelm her. She looked
at the men, some black, some white, as they moved about
the deck doing work she did not understand. The yellow-
haired white man came to smile at her and stare at her breasts
until she wondered whether he had ever seen a woman before. He spoke to her slowly, very distinctly.

"Isaac," he said pointing to his chest. "Isaac." Then he

jabbed a finger toward her, but did not touch her. He raised his bushy pale eyebrows questioningly.

"Isaac?" she said stumbling over the word.

"Isaac." He slapped his chest. Then he pointed again. "You?"

"Anyanwu!" she said understanding. "Anyanwu." She smiled.

And he smiled and mispronounced her name and walked her around the deck naming things for her in English. The new language, so different from anything she had ever heard, had fascinated her since Doro began teaching it to her. Now she repeated the words very carefully and strove to remember them. The yellow-haired Isaac seemed delighted. When finally, someone called him away, he left her reluctantly.

The loneliness returned as soon as he was gone. There were people all around her, but she felt completely alone on this huge vessel at the edge of endless water. Loneliness. Why should she feel it so strongly now? She had been lonely since she realized she would not die like other people. They would always leave her—friends, husbands, children. . . . She could not remember the face of her mother or her father.

But now, the solitude seemed to close in on her as the waters of the sea would close over her head if she leaped into them.

She stared down into the constantly moving water, then away at the distant shore. The shore seemed even farther away now, though Doro had said the ship was not yet under way. Anyanwu felt that she had moved farther from her home, that already perhaps she was too far away ever to return.

She gripped the rail, eyes on the shore. What was she doing, she wondered. How could she leave her homeland, even for Doro? How could she live among these strangers? White skins, yellow hairs—what were they to her? Worse than strangers. Different ones, people who could be all around her working and shouting, and still leave her feeling alone.

She pulled herself up onto the rail.

"Anyanwu!"

She did not quite hesitate. It was as though a mosquito had whined past her ear. A tiny distraction.

"Anyanwu!"

She would leap into the sea. Its waters would take her home, or they would swallow her. Either way, she would find peace. Her loneliness hurt her like some sickness of the body, some pain that her special ability could not find and heal. The sea . . .

Hands grasped her, pulled her backward and down onto the deck. Hands kept her from the sea.

"Anyanwu!"

The yellow hair loomed above her. The white skin. What right had he to lay hands on her?

"Stop, Anyanwu!" he shouted.

She understood the English word "stop," but she ignored it. She brushed him aside and went back to the rail.

"Anyanwu!"

A new voice. New hands.

"Anyanwu, you are not alone here."

Perhaps no other words could have stopped her. Perhaps no other voice could have driven away her need to end the terrible solitude so quickly. Perhaps only her own language could have overwhelmed the call of the distant shore.

"Doro?"

She found herself in his arms, held fast. She realized that she had been on the verge of breaking those arms, if necessary, to get free, and she was appalled.

"Doro, something happened to me."

"I know."

Her fury was spent. She looked around dazedly. The yellow hair—what had happened to him? "Isaac?" she said fearfully. Had she thrown the young man into the sea?

There was a burst of foreign speech behind her, frightened and defensive in tone. Isaac. She turned and saw him alive and dry and was too relieved to wonder at his tone. He and Doro exchanged words in their English, then Doro spoke to her.

"He did not hurt you, Anyanwu?"

"No." She looked at the young man who was holding a red place on his right arm. "I think I have hurt him." She turned away in shame, appealed to Doro. "He helped me. I would not have hurt him, but . . . some spirit possessed me."

"Shall I apologize for you?" Doro seemed amused.

"Yes." She went over to Isaac, said his name softly, touched the injured arm. Not for the first time, she wished she could mute the pain of others as easily as she could mute her own. She heard Doro speak for her, saw the anger leave the young man's face. He smiled at her, showing bad teeth, but good humor. Apparently he forgave her.

"He says you are as strong as a man," Doro told her.

She smiled. "I can be as strong as many men, but he need not know that."

"He can know," Doro said. "He has strengths of his own. He is my son."

"Your . . ."

"The son of an American body." Doro smiled as though he had made a joke. "A mixed body, white and black and Indian. Indians are a brown people."

"But he is white."

"His mother was white. German and yellow-haired. He is more her son than mine—in appearance, at least."

Anyanwu shook her head, looking longingly at the distant coast.

"There is nothing for you to fear," Doro said softly. "You are not alone. Your children's children are here. I am here."

"How can you know what I feel?"

"I would have to be blind not to know, not to see."

"But . . ."

"Do you think you are the first woman I have taken from her people? I have been watching you since we left your village, knowing that this time would come for you. Our kind have a special need to be with either our kinsmen or others who are like us."

"You are not like me!"

He said nothing. He had answered this once, she remembered. Apparently, he did not intend to answer it again.

She looked at him—at the tall young body, well made and handsome. "Will I see, someday, what you are like when you are not hiding in another man's skin?"

For an instant, it seemed that a leopard looked at her through his eyes. A thing looked at her, and that thing feral and cold—a spirit thing that spoke softly.

"Pray to your gods that you never do, Anyanwu. Let me be a man. Be content with me as a man." He put his hand out to touch her and it amazed her that she did not flinch away, that she trembled, but stood where she was.

He drew her to him and to her surprise, she found comfort in his arms. The longing for home, for her people, which had threatened to possess her again receded—as though Doro, whatever he was, was enough.

When Doro had sent Anyanwu to look after her grandson, he turned to find his own son watching her go—watching the sway of her hips. "I just told her how easy she was to read," Doro said.

The boy glanced downward, knowing what was coming.

"You're fairly easy to read yourself," Doro continued.

"I can't help it," Isaac muttered. "You ought to put more clothes on her."

"I will, eventually. For now, just restrain yourself. She's one of the few people aboard who could probably kill you—just as you're one of the few who could kill her. And I'd rather not lose either of you."

"I wouldn't hurt her. I like her."

"Obviously."

"I mean . . ."

"I know, I know. She seems to like you too."

The boy hesitated, stared out at the blue water for a moment, then faced Doro almost defiantly. "Do you mean to keep her for yourself?"

Doro smiled inwardly. "For a while," he said. This was a

favorite son, a rare, rare young one whose talent and temperament had matured exactly as Doro had intended. Doro had controlled the breeding of Isaac's ancestors for millennia, occasionally producing near successes that could be used in breeding, and dangerous, destructive failures that had to be destroyed. Then, finally, true success. Isaac. A healthy, sane son no more rebellious than was wise for a son of Doro, but powerful enough to propel a ship safely through a hurricane.

Isaac stared off in the direction Anyanwu had gone. He shook his head slowly.

"I can't imagine how your ability and hers would combine," Doro said, watching him.

Isaac swung around in sudden hope.

"It seems to me the small, complex things she does within her body would require some of the same ability you use to move large objects outside your body."

Isaac frowned. "How can she tell what she's doing down inside herself?"

"Apparently, she's also a little like one of my Virginia families. They can tell what's going on in closed places or in places miles from them. I've been planning to get you together with a couple of them."

"I can see why. I'd be better myself if I could see that way. Wouldn't have run the *Mary Magdalene* onto those rocks last year."

"You did well enough—kept us afloat until we made port."

"If I got a child by Anyanwu, maybe he'd have that other kind of sight. I'd rather have her than your Virginians."

Doro laughed aloud. It pleased him to indulge Isaac, and Isaac knew it. Doro was surprised sometimes at how close he felt to the best of his children. And, damn his curiosity, he did want to know what sort of child Isaac and Anyanwu could produce. "You'll have the Virginians," he said. "You'll have Anyanwu too. I'll share her with you. Later."

"When?" Isaac did nothing to conceal his eagerness.

"Later, I said. This is a dangerous time for her. She's leaving behind everything she's ever known, and she has no clear idea what she's exchanging it for. If we force too much on her now, she could kill herself before she's been of any use to us."

5

Okoye stayed in Doro's cabin where Anyanwu could care for him until his sickness abated. Then Doro sent him below with the rest of the slaves. Once the ship was under way and beyond sight of the African coast, the slaves were permitted to roam where they pleased above or below deck. In fact, since they had little or no work to do, they had more freedom than the crew. Thus, there was no reason for Okoye to find the change restrictive. Doro watched him carefully at first to see that he was intelligent enough—or frightened enough—not to start trouble. But Anyanwu had introduced him to Udenkwo, and the young woman seemed to occupy much of his time from then on. Rebellion seemed not to occur to him at all.

"They may not please each other as much as they seem to," Anyanwu told Doro. "Who knows what is in their minds?"

Doro only smiled. What was in the young people's minds was apparent to everyone. Anyanwu was still bothered by their blood relationship. She was more a captive of her people's beliefs than she realized. She seemed to feel especially guilty about this union since she could have stopped it so easily. But it was clear even to her that Okoye and Udenkwo needed each other now as she needed Doro. Like her, they were feeling very vulnerable, very much alone.

Several days into the voyage, Doro brought Okoye on deck away from Udenkwo and told him that the ship's captain had the authority to perform a marriage ceremony.

"The white man, Woodley?" Okoye asked. "What has he to do with us?"

"In your new country, if you wish to marry, you must pledge yourselves before a priest or a man of authority like Woodley."

The boy shook his head doubtfully. "Everything is different here. I do not know. My father had chosen a wife for me, and I was pleased with her. Overtures had already been made to her family."

"You will never see her again." Doro spoke with utter conviction. He met the boy's angry glare calmly. "The world is not a gentle place, Okoye."

"Shall I marry because you say so?"

For a moment, Doro said nothing. Let the boy think about his stupid words for a moment. Finally, Doro said: "When I speak to be obeyed, young one, you will know, and you will obey."

Now it was Okoye who kept silent thoughtfully, and though he tried to conceal it, fearfully. "Must I marry?" he said at last.

"No."

"She had a husband."

Doro shrugged.

"What will you do with us in this homeland of yours?"

"Perhaps nothing. I will give you land and seed and some of my people will help you learn the ways of your new home. You will continue to learn English and perhaps Dutch. You will live. But in exchange for what I give, you will obey me whether I come to you tomorrow or forty years from now."

"What must I do?"

"I don't know yet. Perhaps I will give you a homeless child to care for or a series of children. Perhaps you will give shelter to adults who need it. Perhaps you will carry messages or deliver goods or hold property for me. Perhaps anything. Anything at all."

"Wrong things as well as right?"

"Yes."

"Perhaps I will not obey then. Even a slave must follow his own thoughts sometimes."

"That is your decision," Doro agreed.

"What will you do? Kill me?"

"Yes."

Okoye looked away, rubbed his breast where the branding iron had gouged. "I will obey," he whispered. He was silent for a moment, then spoke again wearily. "I wish to marry. But must the white man make the ceremony?"

"Shall I do it?"

"Yes." Okoye seemed relieved.

So it was. Doro had no legal authority. He simply ordered John Woodley to take credit for performing the ceremony. It was the ceremony Doro wanted the slaves to accept, not the ship's captain. As they had begun to accept unfamiliar foods and strange companions, they must accept new customs.

There was no palm wine as Okoye's family would have provided had Okoye taken a wife at home in his village, but Doro offered rum and there were the familiar yams and other foods, less familiar; there was a small feast. There were no relatives except Doro and Anyanwu, but by now the slaves and some members of the crew were familiar and welcome as guests. Doro told them in their own language what was happening and they gathered around with laughter and gestures and comments in their own languages and in fragmentary English. Sometimes their meaning was unmistakably clear, and Okoye and Udenkwo were caught between embarrassment and laughter. In the benign atmosphere of the ship, all the slaves were recovering from their invariably harsh homeland experiences. Some of them had been kidnapped from their villages. Some had been sold for witchcraft or for other crimes of which they were usually not guilty. Some had been born slaves. Some had been enslaved during war. All had been treated harshly at some time during their captivity. All had lived through pain—more pain than they cared to remember. All had left kinsmen behind—husbands, wives, parents, children . . . people they realized by now that they would not see again.

But there was kindness on the ship. There was enough food—too much, since the slaves were so few. There were no chains. There were blankets to warm them and the sea air on deck to cool them. There were no whips, no guns. No woman was raped. People wanted to go home, but like Okoye, they feared Doro too much to complain or revolt. Most of them could not have said why they feared him, but he was the one man they all knew—the one who could speak, at least in limited fashion, with all of them. And once he had spoken with them, they shied away from attacking him, from doing anything that might bring his anger down on them.

"What have you done to them to make them so afraid?" Anyanwu asked him on the night of the wedding.

"Nothing," Doro said honestly. "You have seen me with them. I've harmed no one." He could see that she was not satisfied with this, but that did not matter. "You do not know what this ship could be," he told her. And he began to describe to her a slave ship—people packed together so that they could hardly move and chained in place so that they had to lie in their own filth, beatings, the women routinely raped, torture . . . large numbers of slaves dying. All suffering.

"Waste!" Doro finished with disgust. "But those ships carry slaves for sale. My people are only for my own use."

Anyanwu stared at him in silence for a moment. "Shall I be glad that your slaves will not be wasted?" she asked. "Or shall I fear the uses you will find for them?"

He laughed at her seriousness and gave her a little brandy to drink in celebration of her grandchildren's wedding. He would put her off for as long as he could. She did not want answers to her questions. She could have answered them herself. Why did *she* fear him? To what use did *she* expect to be put? She understood. She was simply sparing herself. He would spare her too. She was his most valuable cargo, and he was inclined to treat her gently.

Okoye and Udenkwo had been married for only two days when the great storm hit. Anyanwu, sleeping beside Doro in his too-soft bed, was awakened by the drumming of rain and running feet above. The ship lurched and rolled sickeningly, and Anyanwu resigned herself to enduring another storm. Her first storm at sea had been brief and violent and terrifying, but at least experiencing it gave her some idea what to expect now. The crew would be on deck, shouting, struggling with the sails, rushing about in controlled confusion. The slaves would be sick and frightened in their quarters, and Doro would gather with Isaac and a few other members of the crew whose duties seemed to involve nothing more than standing together, watching the trouble, and waiting for it to end.

"What do you do when you gather with them?" she had asked him once, thinking that perhaps even he had gods he turned to in times of danger.

"Nothing," he told her.

"Then . . . why do you gather?"

"We might be needed," he answered. "The men I gather with are my sons. They have special abilities that could be useful."

He would tell her nothing more—would not speak of these newly acknowledged sons except in warning. "Leave them alone," he said. "Isaac is the best of them, safe and stable. The others are not safe—not even for you."

Now he went up to his sons again, throwing on the white man's clothing he had taken to wearing as he ran. Anyanwu followed him, depending on her strength and agility to keep her safe.

On deck, she found wind and rain more violent than she

had imagined. There were blue-white flares of lightning followed by absolute blackness. Great waves swept the deck and would surely have washed her overboard, but for her speed and strength. She held on, adjusting her eyes as quickly as she could. There was always a little light, even when ordinary vision perceived nothing. Finally, she could see—and she could hear above the wind and rain and waves. Fragments of desperate English reached her and she longed to understand. But if the words were meaningless, there was no mistaking the tone. These people thought they might die soon.

Someone slammed into her, knocking her down, then fell on her. She could see that it was only a crewman, battered by wind and waves. Most men had lashed themselves securely to whatever well-anchored objects they could find, and now, strove only to endure.

The wind picked up suddenly, and with it came a great mountain of water—a wave that rolled the ship over almost onto its side. Anyanwu caught the crewman's arm and, with her other hand, held onto the rail. If she had not, both she and the man would have been swept overboard. She dragged the man closer to her so that she could get an arm around him. Then for several seconds she simply held on. Back past the third of the great treelike masts, on what Isaac had called the poop deck, Doro stood with Isaac and three other men— the sons, waiting to see whether they could be useful. Surely it was time for them to do whatever they could.

She could distinguish Isaac easily from the others. He stood apart, his arms raised, his face turned down and to one side to escape some of the wind and rain, his clothing and yellow hair whipping about. For an instant, she thought he looked at her—or in her direction—but he could not have seen her through the darkness and rain. She watched him, fascinated. He had not tied himself to anything as the others had, yet he stood holding his strange pose while the ship rolled beneath him.

The wind blew harder. Waves swept high over the deck

and there were moments when Anyanwu found even her great strength strained, moments when it would have been so easy to let the half-drowned crewman go. But she had not saved the man's life only to throw it away. She could see that other crewmen were holding on with fingers and line. She saw no one washed overboard. But still, Isaac stood alone, not even holding on with his hands, and utterly indifferent to wind and waves.

The ship seemed to be moving faster. Anyanwu felt increased pressure from the wind, felt her body lashed so hard by the rain that she tried to curl away from it against the crewman's body. It seemed that the ship was sailing against the wind, moving like a spirit-thing, raising waves of its own. Terrified, Anyanwu could only hold on.

Then, gradually, the cloud cover broke, and there were stars. There was a full moon reflecting fragmented light off calm waters. The waves had become gentle and lapped harmlessly at the ship, and the wind became no more than a cold breeze against Anyanwu's wet, nearly naked body.

Anyanwu released the crewman and stood up. Around the ship, people were suddenly shouting, freeing themselves, rushing to Isaac. Anyanwu's crewman picked himself up slowly, looked at Isaac, then at Anyanwu. Dazed, he looked up at the clear sky, the moon. Then with a hoarse cry and no backward glance at Anyanwu, he rushed toward Isaac.

Anyanwu watched the cheering for a moment—knew it to be cheering now—then stumbled below, and back to her cabin. There, she found water everywhere. It sloshed on the floor and the bed was sodden. She stood in it staring helplessly until Doro came to her, saw the condition of the cabin, and took her away to another, somewhat drier one.

"Were you on deck?" he asked her.

She nodded.

"Then you saw."

She turned to stare at him, uncomprehending. "What did I see?"

"The very best of my sons," he said proudly. "Isaac doing

what he was born to do. He brought us through the storm—faster than any ship was ever intended to move."

"How?"

"How!" Doro mocked, laughing. "How do you change your shape, woman. How have you lived for three hundred years?"

She blinked, went to lie down on the bed. Finally, she looked around at the cabin he had brought her to. "Whose place is this?"

"The captain's," said Doro. "He'll have to make do with less for a while. You stay here. Rest."

"Are all your sons so powerful?"

He laughed again. "Your mind is leaping around tonight. But that's not surprising, I suppose. My other sons do other things. None of them manage their abilities as well as Isaac, though."

Anyanwu lay down wearily. She was not especially tired—her body was not tired. The strain she had endured was of a kind that should not have bothered her at all once it was over. It was her spirit that was weary. She needed time to sleep. Then she needed to go and find Isaac and look at him and see what she could see beyond the smiling, yellow-haired young man.

She closed her eyes and slept, not knowing whether Doro would lie down beside her or not. It was not until later, when she awoke alone that she realized he had not. Someone was pounding on her door.

She shook off sleep easily and got up to open the door. The moment she did, a very tall, thin crewman thrust a semiconscious Isaac through it into her arms.

She staggered for a moment, more from surprise than from the boy's weight. She had caught him reflexively. Now she felt the cold waxiness of his skin. He did not seem to know her, or even to see her. His eyes were half open and staring. Without her arms around him, he would have fallen.

She lifted him as though he was a child, laid him on the bed, and covered him with a blanket. Then she looked up

and saw that the thin crewman was still there. He was a
green-eyed man with a head that was too long and bones
that seemed about to break through his splotchy, unshaven
brown skin. He was a white man, but the sun had parched
him unevenly and he looked diseased. He was one of the
ugliest men Anyanwu had ever seen. And he was one of
those who had stood beside Doro during the storm—another
son. A much lesser son, if looks mattered. This was one of
the sons Doro had ordered her to avoid. Well, she would willingly avoid him if he would only leave. He had brought her
Isaac. Now, he should go away and let her give the boy what
care she could. In the back of her mind, she wondered over
and over what could be wrong with a boy who could speed
great ships through the water. What had happened? Why had
Doro not told her Isaac was sick?

Her thought of Doro repeated itself strangely as a kind
of echo within her mind. She could see Doro suddenly—or
an image of him. She saw him as a white man, yellow-haired
like Isaac, and green-eyed like the ugly crewman. She had
never seen Doro as white, had never heard him describe one
of his white bodies, but she knew absolutely that she was seeing him as he had appeared in one of them. She saw the
image giving Isaac to her—placing the half-conscious boy into
her arms. Then abruptly, wrenchingly, she saw herself engaged
in wild frantic sexual intercourse, first with Isaac, then with
this ugly green-eyed man whose name was Lale. Lale Sachs.

How did she know that?

What was happening!

The green-eyed man laughed, and somehow his grating
laughter echoed within her as had the thought of Doro. Somehow, this man was within her very thoughts!

She lunged at him and thrust him back through the door,
her push hard enough to move a much heavier man. He flew
backward out of control, and she slammed the door shut the
instant he was through it. Even so, the terrible link she had
with him was not broken. She felt pain as he fell and struck

his head—stunning pain that dropped her to her knees where she crouched dizzily holding her head.

Then the pain was gone. He was gone from her thoughts. But he was coming through the door again, shouting words that she knew were curses. He seized her by the throat, literally lifted her to her feet by her neck. He was no weak man, but his strength was nothing compared to her own. She struck him randomly, as she broke away, and heard him cry out with pain.

She looked at him, and for an instant, she saw him clearly, the too-long face twisted with pain and anger, its mouth open and gasping, its nose smashed flat and spurting blood. She had hurt him more than she intended, but she did not care. No one had the right to go tampering with the very thoughts in her mind. Then the bloody face was gone.

A thing stood before her—a being more terrible than any spirit she could imagine. A great, horned, scaly lizard-thing of vaguely human shape, but with a thick lashing tail and a scaly dog head with huge teeth set in jaws that could surely break a man's arm.

In terror, Anyanwu transformed herself.

It was painful to change so quickly. It was agonizing. She bore the pain with a whimper that came out as a snarl. She had become a leopard, lithe and strong, fast and razor-clawed. She sprang.

The spirit screamed, collapsed, and became a man again.

Anyanwu hesitated, stood on his chest staring down at him. He was unconscious. He was a vicious, deadly being. Best to kill him now before he could come to and control her thoughts again. It seemed wrong to kill a helpless man, but if this man came to, he might well kill her.

"Anyanwu!"

Doro. She closed her ears to him. With a snarl, she tore out the throat of the being under her feet. In one way, that was a mistake. She tasted blood.

The speed of her change had depleted her as nothing else could. She had to feed soon. Now! She slashed her victim's shirt out of the way and tore flesh from his breast. She fed desperately, mindlessly until something struck her hard across the face.

She spat in pain and anger, realized dimly that Doro had kicked her. Her muscles tensed. She could kill him. She could kill anyone who interfered with her now.

He stood inches from her, head back, as though offering her his throat. Which was exactly what he was doing, of course.

"Come," he challenged. "Kill again. It has been a long time since I was a woman."

She turned from him, hunger driven, and tore more flesh from the body of his son.

He lifted her bodily and threw her off the corpse. When she tried to return to it, he kicked her, beat her.

"Control yourself," he ordered. "Become a woman!"

She did not know how she made the change. She did not know what held her from tearing him to pieces. Fear? She would not have thought that even fear could hold her at such a time. Doro had not seen the carnage she wrought on her own people so long ago when they attacked her and forced her to change too quickly. She had almost forgotten that part of the killing herself—the shame! Her people did not eat human flesh—but she had eaten it then. She had terrorized them into forgiving her, they outlived all but the legend of what she had done—or her mother had done, or her grandmother. People died. Their children ceased to be certain of exactly what had happened. The story became interwoven with spirits and gods. But what would she do now? She could not terrorize Doro into forgetting the grisly corpse on the floor.

Human again, she lay on the floor, face down and averted from the corpse. She was surprised that Doro did not go on beating her, that he did not kill her. She had no doubt that he could.

He lifted her, ignoring the blood that covered much of her body, and placed her on the bed beside Isaac. She lay there, limp, not looking at him. Oh, but the meat was warm inside her. Sustenance. She needed more!

"Why is Isaac here?" asked Doro. There was nothing in his voice. Not even anger.

"The other one brought him. Lale Sachs. He said you sent Isaac to me. . . ." She stopped, confused. "No. He did not say it, he . . . he was in my thoughts, he . . .".

"I know."

She turned finally to look at him. He looked tired, haggard. He looked like a man in pain, and she wanted to touch him, comfort him. But her hands were covered with blood.

"What else did he tell you?"

She shook her head back and forth against the bed. "I do not know. He showed an image of me lying with Isaac, then lying with him. He made me see it—almost made me want it." She turned away again. "When I tried to send him away without . . . harming him, he did another thing. . . . Doro, I must have food!" This last was a cry of pain.

He heard. "Stay here," he said softly. "I'll bring you something."

He went away. When he was gone, it seemed that she could smell the meat on the floor. It beckoned to her. She moaned and turned her face down to the mattress. Beside her, Isaac made a small sound and moved closer to her. Surprised, she raised her head to look at him.

He was still semiconscious. His eyes were closed now, but she could see that they moved under the lids. And his lips moved, formed silent words. He had almost a black man's mouth, the lips fuller than those of the other whites she had seen. Stiff yellow hairs grew from his face, showing that he had not shaved for a while. He had a broad, square face not unattractive to Anyanwu, and the sun had burned him a good, even brown. She wondered what white women thought of him. She wondered how white women looked.

"Food, Anyanwu," Doro said softly.

She jumped, startled. She was becoming a deaf woman!

Doro had never been able to approach her unheard before. But that did not matter. Not now.

She seized the bread and meat from his hands. Both were hard and dry—the kind of food the crew ate all the time, but they were no challenge to her teeth and jaws. Doro gave her wine and she gulped it down. The fresh meat on the floor would have been better, but now that she was in control of herself, nothing would make her touch that again.

"Tell me all that happened," said Doro when she had eaten what he had given her.

She told him. She needed sleep now, but not as badly as she had needed food. And he deserved to know why his son had died.

She expected some comment or action from him when she finished, but he only shook his head and sighed. "Sleep now, Anyanwu. I will take Lale away, and Isaac."

"But . . ."

"Sleep. You are almost asleep now, almost talking in your sleep." He reached over her and lifted Isaac from the bed.

"What happened to him?" she whispered.

"He overextended himself just as you did. He will heal."

"He is cold . . . so cold."

"You would warm him if I left him here. You would warm him as Lale intended. Even your strength would not be enough to stop him once he began to awaken."

And before her slow, drowsy mind could question this, Doro and Isaac were gone. She never heard him come back for Lale, never knew whether he returned to sleep beside her that night, never cared.

Lale Sachs was dropped into the sea the next day. Anyanwu was present at the small ceremony Captain Woodley made. She had not wanted to be, but Doro commanded it. He told everyone what she had done, then made her appear before them. She thought he did it to shame her, and she was ashamed. But later, he explained.

"It was for your protection," he told her. "Everyone aboard

has been warned against molesting you. My sons have been doubly warned. Lale chose to ignore me. I cannot seem to breed stupidity out of some of my people. He thought it would be interesting to watch when Isaac came to as hungry for a woman as you were for food. He thought perhaps he would have you too when Isaac had finished."

"But how could he reach out and change the thoughts in my mind?"

"It was his special ability. I've had men who were better at it—good enough to control you absolutely, even control your changes. You would be no more than clay for such a man to mold. But Lale was the best of his generation to survive. His kind often don't survive long."

"I can understand that!" Anyanwu said.

"No, you can't," Doro told her. "But you will."

She turned away. They were on deck, so she stared out at the sea where several large fish were leaping into the air and arcing down again into the water. She had watched such creatures before, watched them longingly. She thought she could do what they did, thought she could become one of them. She could almost feel the sensation of wetness, of strength, of moving through the water as swiftly as a bird through the air. She longed to try, and she feared to try. Now, though, she did not think of trying. She thought only of the body of Lale Sachs, wrapped in cloth, its gaping wounds hidden. Would the leaping fish finish what she had begun? Consume the rest of the foolish, ugly, evil man?

She closed her eyes. "What shall we do now, Doro? What will you do with me?"

"What shall I do with you?" he mocked. He put his hands around her waist and pulled her against him.

Startled, she moved away. "I have killed your son."

"Do you think I blame you for that?"

She said nothing, only stared at him.

"I wanted him to live," Doro said. "His kind are so troublesome and so short-lived. . . . He has fathered only three children. I wanted more from him, but, Anyanwu, if you had not killed him, if he had succeeded in what he meant to do, I would have killed him myself."

She lowered her head, somehow not really surprised. "Could you have done it? Your son?"

"Anyone," he said.

She looked up at him, questioning, yet not wanting answers.

"I control powerful people," he said. "My people. The destruction they can cause if they disobey me is beyond your imagining. Any one of them, any group of them who refuse to obey is useless to me and dangerous to the rest of my people."

She moved uncomfortably, understanding what he was telling her. She remembered his voice when he spoke to her the night before. *"Come. Kill again. It has been a long time since I was a woman!"* He would have consumed her spirit as she had consumed his son's flesh. He would be wearing her body today.

She turned to look out at the leaping fish again, and when he drew her to his side this time, she did not move away. She was not afraid; she was relieved. Some part of her mind wondered how this could be, but she had no answer. People did not react rationally to Doro. When he did nothing, they feared him. When he threatened them, they believed him, but did not hate him or flee.

"Isaac is well," he told her.

"Is he? What did he do for his hunger?"

"Endured it until it went away."

To her surprise, his words sparked guilt in her. She had the foolish urge to find the young man and apologize for not keeping him with her. He would think she had lost her senses. "You should get him a wife," she told Doro.

Doro nodded absently. "Soon," he said.

There came a time when Doro said land was near—a time when the strange food was rotten and full of worms and the drinking water stank and the ship stank and the slaves

fought among themselves and the crewmen fished desperately
to vary their disgusting diet and the sun's heat intensified and
the wind did not blow. In the midst of all this discomfort,
there were events that Anyanwu would recall with pleasure
for the rest of her life. This was when she came to understand clearly just what Isaac's special ability was, and he came
to understand her own.

After Lale's death, she avoided the boy as best she could
in the confined space of the ship, thinking that he might not
be as indifferent to the death of a brother as Doro was to
the death of a son. But Isaac came to her.

He joined her at the rail one day as she stood watching
the leaping fish. He watched them himself for a moment,
then laughed. She glanced up at him questioningly, and he
pointed out to sea. When she looked there again, she saw
one of the great fish hanging high above the water, struggling
in midair.

It was as though the creature had been caught in some
invisible net. But there was no net. There was nothing.

She looked at Isaac in amazement. "You?" she asked in
her uncertain English. "You do this?"

Isaac only smiled. The fish, struggling wildly, drifted closer
to the ship. Several crewmen noticed it and began shouting
at Isaac. Anyanwu could not understand most of what they
said, but she knew they wanted the fish. Isaac made a gesture presenting it to Anyanwu, though it still hung over the
water. She looked around at the eager crewmen, then grinned.
She beckoned for the fish to be brought aboard.

Isaac dropped it at her feet.

Everyone ate well that night. Anyanwu ate better than
anyone, because for her, the flesh of the fish told her all she
needed to know about the creature's physical structure—all
she needed to know to take its shape and live as it did. Just
a small amount of raw flesh told her more than she had words
to say. Within each bite, the creature told her its story clearly
thousands of times. That night in their cabin, Doro caught
her experimentally turning one of her arms into a flipper.

"What are you doing!" he demanded, with what sounded like revulsion.

She laughed like a child and stood up to meet him, her arm flowing easily back to its human shape. "Tomorrow," she said, "you will tell Isaac how to help me, and I will swim with the fish! I will be a fish! I can do it now! I have wanted to for so long."

"How do you know you can?" Curiosity quickly drove any negative feelings from him, as usual. She told him of the message she had read within the flesh of the fish. "Messages as clear and fine as those in your books," she told him. Privately she thought her flesh-messages even more specific than the books he had introduced her to, read to her from. But the books were the only example she could think of that he might understand. "It seems that you could misunderstand your books," she said. "Other men made them. Other men can lie or make mistakes. But the flesh can only tell me what it is. It has no other story."

"But how do you read it?" he asked. *Read.* If he used that English word, he too saw the similarity.

"My body reads it—reads everything. Did you know that fish breathes air as we do? I thought it would breathe water like the ones we caught and dried at home."

"It was a dolphin," Doro murmured.

"But it was more like a land thing than a fish. Inside, it is much like a land animal. The changes I make will not be as great as I thought."

"Did you have to eat leopard flesh to learn to become a leopard?"

She shook her head. "No, I could see what the leopard was like. I could mold myself into what I saw. I was not a true leopard, though, until I killed one and ate a little of it. At first, I was a woman pretending to be a leopard—clay molded into leopard shape. Now when I change, I am a leopard."

"And now you will be a dolphin." He gazed at her. "You

cannot know how valuable you are to me. Shall I let you do this?"

That startled her. It had not occurred to her that he would disapprove. "It is a harmless thing," she said.

"A dangerous thing. What do you know of the sea?"

"Nothing. But tomorrow I will begin to learn. Have Isaac watch me; I will stay near the surface. If he sees that I'm in trouble, he can lift me out of the water and let me change back on deck."

"Why do you want to do this?"

She cast about for a reason she could put into words, a reason other than the wrenching longing she had felt when she watched the dolphins leaping and diving. It was like the days at home when she had watched eagles fly until she could no longer stand to only watch. She had killed an eagle and eaten and learned and flown as no human was ever meant to fly. She had flown away, escaping her town, her duties, her kinsmen. But after a while, she had flown back to her people. Where else could she go? Afterward, though, when the seasons with them grew long and the duties tiresome, when the kinsmen by themselves became a great tribe, she would escape again. She would fly. There was danger. Men hunted her and once had nearly killed her. She made an exception- ally large, handsome eagle. But fear never kept her out of the sky. Nor would it keep her out of the water.

"I want this," she told Doro. "I will do it without Isaac if you keep him from helping me."

Doro shook his head. "Were you this way with your other husbands—telling them what you would do in spite of their wishes?"

"Yes," she said seriously, and was very much relieved when he laughed aloud. Better to amuse him than to anger him.

The next day she stood by the rail, watching Doro and Isaac argue in English. It was Isaac who did most of the ar- guing. Doro said only a few words, and then later repeated them exactly. Anyanwu could find only one word in what Isaac said that was repeated. The word was "shark," and Isaac said it with vehemence. But he stopped when he saw how little attention Doro was paying to him. And Doro turned to face her.

"Isaac fears for you," he told her.

"Will he help?"

"Yes—though I told him he didn't have to."

"I thought you were speaking for me!"

"In this, I am only translating."

His attitude puzzled her. He was not angry, not even annoyed. He did not even seem to be as concerned for her as Isaac was, and yet he said he valued her. "What is a shark?" she asked.

"A fish," Doro said. "A large flesh eater, a killer at least as deadly in the sea as your leopards are on land."

"You did not say there were such things."

He looked at the water. "It is as dangerous down there as in your forests," he told her. "You need not go."

"You didn't try hard to stop me from going."

"No."

"Why?"

"I want to see whether you can do it or not."

He reminded her of one of her sons who, when he was very young, had thrown several fowls into the river to see whether they could swim.

"Stay near the dolphins if they let you," Doro said. "Dolphins know how to deal with sharks."

Anyanwu tore off her cloth and dived into the sea before her confidence deserted her entirely. There, she transformed herself as quickly as was comfortable. She became the dolphin whose flesh she had eaten.

And she was moving through the water alongside the ship, propelling her long, sleek body forward with easy beats of her tail. She was seeing differently, her eyes now on the sides of her head instead of in front. Her head had extended itself into a hard beak. She was breathing differently—or rather, she was not breathing at all until she felt the need and found herself surfacing in a slow forward roll that exposed her blowhole-nose briefly and allowed her to expel her breath and take new air into her lungs. She observed herself minutely, saw that her dolphin body used the air it breathed much more efficiently than an ordinary human body. The dolphin body knew tricks her own human body had taken time and pain to learn. How to expel and renew a much larger portion of the air in its lungs with each breath. How to leach more of the usable portion of that air from the rest, the waste, and use it to fuel the body. Other things. None of it was new to her, but she thought she would have learned it all much sooner and more easily with the help of a bit of dolphin flesh. Instead, she had had only men who attempted to drown her.

She reveled in the strength and speed of her new body, and in its keen hearing. In her human shape, she kept her hearing abnormally keen—kept all her senses keen. But dolphin hearing was superior to anything she had ever created in herself. As a dolphin, she could close her eyes and perceive an only slightly diminished world around her with her ears. She could make sounds and they would come back to her as echoes bearing with them the story of all that lay before her. She had never imagined such hearing.

Finally, she directed her attention from herself to the other dolphins. She had heard them too, chattering not far from her, keeping alongside the ship as she did. Strangely, their chatter sounded more human now—more like speech, like a foreign speech. She swam toward them slowly, uncertainly. How did they greet strangers? How would they greet one small, ignorant female? If they were speaking among themselves somehow, they would think her mute—or mad.

A dolphin swam to meet her, paralleled her, observing her out of one lively eye. This was a male, she realized, and she watched him with interest. After a moment, he swam closer and rubbed his body against hers. Dolphin skin, she discovered, was pleasantly sensitive. It was not scaly as was the skin of true fish which she had never imitated, but whose bodies she understood. The male brushed her again, chattering in a way she felt was questioning, then swam away. She turned, checking the position of the ship, and saw that by keeping up with the dolphins, she was also keeping up with it. She swam after the male.

There were advantages, she thought, to being a female animal. The males of some species fought each other, mindlessly possessive of territory or females. She could remember being bullied as a female animal, being pursued by persistent males, but only in her true woman-shape could she remember being seriously hurt by males—men. It was only accident that made her a female dolphin; she had eaten the flesh of a female. But it was a fortunate accident.

A very small dolphin, a baby, she assumed, came to make her acquaintance, and she swam slowly, allowing it to investigate her. Eventually, its mother called it away, and she was alone again. Alone, but surrounded by creatures like herself—creatures she was finding it harder to think of as animals. Swimming with them was like being with another people. A friendly people. No slavers with brands and chains here. No Doro with gentle, terrible threats to her children, to her.

As time passed, several dolphins approached to touch her, rub themselves against her, get acquainted. When the male who had touched her first returned, she was startled to realize that she recognized him. His touch was his touch—not quite like that of any of the others as they were not quite like each other.

Suddenly, he leaped high out of the water and arced back, landing some distance ahead of her. She wondered why she had not tried this herself and leaped a short distance. Her dolphin body was wonderfully agile. She seemed to fly through the air, plunging back smoothly and leaping again without strain or weariness. This was the best body she had ever shaped for herself. If only dolphin speech came as easily as dolphin movement. Some part of her mind wondered why it did not, wondered whether Doro was superior to her in this. Did he gain a new language, new knowledge when he took a new body—since he actually did possess the body, not merely duplicate it?

Her male dolphin came to touch her again and drove all thoughts of Doro from her mind. She understood that the dolphin's interest had become more than casual. He stayed close to her now, touching her, matching his movements with her own. She realized that she did not mind his attention. She had avoided animal matings in the past. She was a woman. Intercourse with an animal was abomination. She would feel unclean reverting to her human form with the seed of a male animal inside her.

But now . . . it was as though the dolphins were not animals.

She performed a kind of dance with the male, moving and touching, certain that no human ceremony had ever drawn her in so quickly. She felt both eager and restrained, both willing and hesitant. She would accept him, had already accepted him. He was surely no more strange than the ogbanje, Doro. Now seemed to be a time for strange matings.

She continued the dance, wishing she had a song to go with it. The male seemed to have a song. She wondered whether he would leave her after the mating, and thought he probably would. But his would not be the greatest leave-taking. He would not leave the group as she would, deserting everyone. But that was something to think about in the future. It did not matter. Only what was happening now mattered.

Then, suddenly, there was a man in the water. Startled, both Anyanwu and her male swam a short distance away, their dance interrupted. The group of dolphins shied away from the man, but he pursued them, sometimes in the water, sometimes above it. He did not swim or leap or dive, but somehow arrowed through water and air holding his body still, apparently not using his muscles.

Finally, Anyanwu separated herself from the school and approached the man. It was Isaac, she knew. He looked very different to her now—a clumsy thing, stiff and strange, but not remarkably ugly or frightening. He was a threat, though. He had had no reason to lose his taste for dolphin flesh, but she had. He might make another kill if she did not distract him. She turned and swam to him, approaching very slowly so that he would see her and understand that she meant no harm. She was certain that he could not distinguish her from any other dolphin. She swam in a small circle around where he hovered now, just above the water.

He spoke in low, strange tones, said her name several times before she recognized it. Then, without stopping to wonder how she did it, she brought herself upright on her tail for a moment and managed a kind of nod. She swam to him, and he lowered himself into the water. She swam past his side, near enough to be touched. He caught her dorsal fin and said something else. She listened closely.

"Doro wants you back at the ship."

That was that. She looked back at the dolphins regretfully, trying to pick out her male. She found him surprisingly nearby—dangerously nearby. It would have been so good to return to him, stay with him, just for a while. The mating would have been good. She wondered whether Doro had known or suspected what she was doing when he sent Isaac out to get her.

It did not matter. Isaac was here, and he had to be taken away before he noticed the other dolphins so temptingly near. She swam back toward the ship, allowing him to keep his hold on her fin. She did not mind towing him.

"I'll go up first," he said when they reached the ship. "Then I'll lift you."

He rose straight out of the water and drifted onto the ship. He could fly without wings as easily as he could direct the ship out of a storm. She wondered whether he could be sick and need a woman after this too. Then something touched her, gripped her firmly but not painfully, lifted her out of the water. It was not, as she had thought, like being lifted by a net or by the arms of men. There was no special feeling of pressure on any part of her body. It was like being held and supported by the air itself—softness that seemed to envelop her entire body, firmness that all her strength could not free her from.

But she did not use her strength, did not struggle. She had seen the futility of the dolphin's struggles the day before, and she had felt the speed of the great ship as it plunged through the storm, propelled by Isaac's power. No strength of her muscles could resist such power. Besides, she trusted the boy. He handled her more carefully than he had the other dolphin, gestured crewmen back out of his way before he set her down gently on deck. Then the crewmen, Doro, and Isaac watched, fascinated, as she began to grow legs. She had had to absorb her legs almost completely, leaving only the useless detached hip bones natural to her dolphin body—as though the dolphin itself were slowly developing legs—or losing them. Now, she began with this large change. And her flippers began to look more like arms. Her neck, her entire body, grew slender again and her tiny excellent dolphin ears enlarged to become less efficient human ears. Her nose migrated back to her face and she absorbed her beak, her tail, and her fin. There were internal changes that those watching could not be aware of. And her gray skin changed color and texture. That change caused her to begin thinking about what she might have to do to herself if someday she decided to vanish into this land of white people that she was approaching. She would have to do some experimenting later. It was always useful to be able to camouflage oneself to hide or to learn the things people either would not or could not deliberately teach her about themselves. This when she could speak English well, of course. She would have to work harder at the language.

When the transformation was complete, she stood up, and Doro handed her her cloth. Before the staring men, she wrapped it around her waist and tied it. It had been centuries since she had gone naked in the way of unmarried young girls. She felt ashamed now to be seen by so many men, but she understood that again, Doro wanted his people to see her power. If he could not breed stupidity out of them, he would frighten it out.

She looked around at them, allowing no hint of her shame to reach her expression. Why should they know what she felt? She read awe in their expressions, and two who were near her actually stepped back when she looked at them. Then Doro hugged her wet body to him and she was able to relax. Isaac laughed aloud, breaking the tension, and said something to Doro. Doro smiled.

In her language, he said: "What children you will give me!" She was caught by the intensity she could sense behind his words. It reminded her that his was more than an ordinary man's desire for children. She could not help thinking of her own children, strong and healthy, but as short-lived and powerless as the children of any other woman. Could she give Doro what he wanted—what she herself had wanted for so long—children who would not die?

"What children you will give me, husband," she whispered, but the words were more questioning than his had been.

And strangely, Doro also seemed to become uncertain. She looked at him and caught a troubled expression on his face. He was staring out at the dolphins who were leaping again, some of them just ahead of the ship. He shook his head slowly.

"What is it?" she asked.

He looked away from the dolphins, and for a moment, his expression was so intense, so feral that she wondered if he hated the animals, or envied her because she could join them.

"What is it?" she repeated.

He seemed to force himself to smile. "Nothing," he said. He pulled her head to his shoulder reassuringly, and stroked her glossy, newly grown skullcap of hair. Unreassured, she accepted the caress and wondered why he was lying.

6

Anyanwu had too much power.

In spite of Doro's fascination with her, his first inclination was to kill her. He was not in the habit of keeping alive people he could not control absolutely. But if he killed her and took over her body, he would get only one or two children from her before he had to take a new body. Her longevity would not help him keep her body alive. He did not acquire the use of his victims' special abilities with his transmigrations. He inhabited bodies. He consumed lives. That was all. Had he killed Lale, he would not have acquired the man's thought-transfer ability. He would only have been able to pass on that ability to children of Lale's body. And if he killed Anyanwu, he would not acquire her malleability, longevity, or healing. He would have only his own special ability lodged within her small, durable body until he began to hunger—hunger in a way Anyanwu and Isaac could never understand. He would hunger, and he would have to feed. Another life. A new body. Anyanwu would last him no longer than any other good kill.

Therefore, Anyanwu must live and bear her valuable young. But she had too much power. In her dolphin form, and before that, in her leopard form, Doro had discovered that his mind could not find her. Even when he could see her, his mind, his tracking sense, told him she was not there. It was as though she had died, as though he confronted a true animal—a creature beyond his reach. And if he could not reach her, he could not kill her and take her body while she was in animal form. In her human shape, she was as vulnerable to him as anyone else, but as an animal, she was beyond him as animals had always been beyond him. He longed now for one of the animal sensitives his controlled breeding occasionally produced. These were people whose abilities extended to touching animal minds, receiving sensation and emotion from them, people who suffered every time someone wrung a chicken's neck or gelded a horse or slaughtered a pig. They led short, unenviable lives. Sometimes Doro killed them before they could waste their valuable bodies in suicide. But now, he could have used a living one. Without one, his control of Anyanwu was dangerously limited.

And if Anyanwu ever discovered that limitation, she might run away from him whenever she chose. She might go the moment he demanded more of her than she was willing to give. Or she might go if she discovered that he meant to have both her and the children she had left behind in Africa. She believed her cooperation had bought their freedom—believed he would give up such potentially valuable people. If she found out the truth, she would surely run, and he would lose her. He had never before lost anyone in that way. He lost people to disease, accident, war, causes beyond his control. People were stolen from him or killed as had been his people of the savanna. This was bad enough. It was waste, and he intended to end much of it by bringing his people to less widely scattered communities in the Americas. But no individual had ever succeeded in escaping him. Individuals who ran from him were caught and most often killed. His own people knew better than to run from him.

But Anyanwu, wild seed that she was, did not know. Yet.

He would have to teach her, instruct her quickly and begin using her at once. He wanted as many children as he could get from her before it became necessary to kill her. Wild seed always had to be destroyed eventually. It could never conform as children born among his people conformed. But like no other wild seed, Anyanwu would learn to fear him and bend herself to his will. He would use her for breeding and healing. He would use her children, present and future, to create more acceptable long-lived types. The troublesome shape-changing ability could probably be bred out of her line if it appeared. The fact that it had not appeared so far told him he might be able to extinguish it entirely. But then, none of her special abilities had appeared among her children. They had inherited nothing more than potential—good blood that might produce special abilities after a few generations of inbreeding. Perhaps he would fail with them. Perhaps he would discover that Anyanwu could not be duplicated, or that there could be no longevity without shape-changing. Perhaps. But any finding, positive or negative, was generations away.

Meanwhile, Anyanwu must never learn of his limitation, must never know it was possible for her to escape him, avoid him, live free of him even as an animal. This meant he must not restrict her transformations any more strenuously than he restricted his children in the use of their abilities. She would not be permitted to show what she could do among ordinary people or harm his people except in self-defense. That was all. She would fear him, obey him, consider him almost omnipotent, but she would notice nothing in his attitude that might start her wondering. There would be nothing for her to notice.

Thus, as the journey neared its end, he allowed Anyanwu and Isaac to indulge in wild, impossible play, using their abilities freely, behaving like the witch-children they were. They went into the water together several times when there was enough wind and Isaac was not needed to propel the ship.

The boy was not fighting a storm now. He was able to handle the ship without overextending himself, able to expend energy cavorting in the water with a dolphin-shaped Anyanwu. Then Anyanwu took to the air as a great bird, and Isaac followed, doing acrobatics that Doro would never have permitted over land. Here, there was no one to shoot the boy out of the sky, no mob to chase him down and try to burn him as a witch. He had to restrain himself so much on land that Doro placed no restraints on him now.

Doro worried about Anyanwu when she ventured under water alone—worried that he would lose her to sharks or other predators. But when she was finally attacked by a shark, it was near the surface. She suffered only a single wound which she sealed at once. Then she managed to ram her beak hard into the shark's gills. She must also have managed to take an undolphinlike bite out of the shark, since she immediately shifted to the sleek, deadly shark form. As it happened, the change was unnecessary. The shark was crippled, perhaps dying. But the change had been made, and made too quickly. Anyanwu had to feed. With strength and speed she tore the true shark to pieces and gorged herself on it. When she became a woman again, Doro could find no sign of the wound she had suffered. He found her drowsy and content, not at all the shaking, tormented creature who had killed Lale. This time, her drive to feed had been quickly satisfied. Apparently, that was important.

She adopted the dolphins, refusing to let Isaac bring any more aboard to be killed. "They are like people," she insisted in her fast-improving English. "They are not fish!" She swore she would have nothing more to do with Isaac if he killed another of them.

And Isaac, who loved dolphin flesh, brought no more dolphins aboard. Doro listened to the boy's muttered complaints, smiled, and said nothing. Isaac listened to the crewmen's complaints, shrugged, and gave them other fish. He continued to spend his spare time with Anyanwu, teaching her English, flying or swimming with her, merely being with her whenever he could. Doro neither encouraged nor discouraged this, though he did approve. He had been thinking a great deal about Isaac and Anyanwu—how well they got along in spite of their communication problems, in spite of their potentially dangerous abilities, in spite of their racial differences. Isaac would marry Anyanwu if Doro ordered it. The boy might even like the idea. And once Anyanwu accepted the marriage, Doro's hold on her would be secure. The children would come—desirable, potentially multi-talented children—and Doro could travel as he pleased to look after his other peoples. When he returned to his New York village of Wheatley, Anyanwu would still be there. Her children would hold her if her husband did not. She could become an animal or alter herself enough to travel freely among whites or Indians, but several children would surely slow her down. And she would not abandon them. She was too much a mother for that. She would stay—and if Doro found another man he wished to breed her with he could come to her wearing that man's body. It would be a simple matter.

What would not be simple would be giving Anyanwu her first hard lesson in obedience. She would not want to go to Isaac. Among her people, a woman could divorce her husband by running away from him and seeing that the bride-wealth he had given for her was returned. Or her husband could divorce her by driving her away. If her husband was impotent, he could, with her consent, give her to another man so that she could bear children in her husband's name. If her husband died, she could marry his successor, usually his oldest son as long as this was not also her own son. But there was no provision for what Doro planned to do—give her to his son while he, Doro, was still alive. She considered Doro her husband now. No ceremony had taken place, but none was necessary. She was not a young girl passing from the hands of her father to those of her first husband. It was enough that she and Doro had chosen each other. She would think it wrong to go to Isaac. But her thinking would change as had the thinking of other powerful, self-

willed people whom Doro had recruited. She would learn ι
right and wrong were what he said they were.

At the place Doro had called "New York Harbor," everyone except the crew was to change ships, move to a pair of
smaller "river sloops" to travel up the "Hudson River" to
Doro's village of "Wheatley."

With less experience at absorbing change and learning
new dialects if not new languages, Anyanwu thought she
would have been utterly confused. She would have been
frightened into huddling together with the slaves and looking around with suspicion and dread. Instead, she stood on
deck with Doro, waiting calmly for the transfer to the new
ships. Isaac and several others had gone ashore to make
arrangements.

"When will we change?" she had asked Doro in English.
She often tried to speak English now.

"That depends on how soon Isaac can hire the sloops,"
he said. Which meant he did not know. That was good.
Anyanwu hoped the wait would be long. Even she needed
time to absorb the many differences of this new world. From
where she stood she could see a few other large, square-rigged
ships lying at anchor in the harbor. And there were smaller
boats either moving under billowing, usually triangular sails
or tied up at the long piers Doro had pointed out to her. But
ships and boats seemed familiar to her now. She was eager
to see how these new people lived on land. She had asked
to go ashore with Isaac, but Doro had refused. He had chosen to keep her with him. She stared ashore longingly at the
rows and rows of buildings, most two, three, even four stories high, and side against side as though like ants in a hill,
the people could not bear to be far apart. In much of her
own country, one could stand in the middle of a town and
see little more than forest. The villages of the towns were
well-organized, often long-established, but they were more a
part of the land they occupied, less of an intrusion upon it.

"Where does one compound end and another begin?" she asked, staring at the straight rows of pointed roofs.

"Some of those buildings are used for storage and other things," Doro said. "Of the others, consider each one a separate compound. Each one houses a family."

She looked around, startled. "Where are the farms to feed so many?"

"Beyond the city. We will see farms on our way upriver. Also, many of the houses have their own gardens. And look there." He pointed to a place where the great concentration of buildings tapered off and ended. "That is farmland."

"It seems empty."

"It is sown with barley now, I think. And perhaps a few oats."

These English names were familiar to her because he and Isaac had told her about them. Barley for making the beer that the crew drank so much of, oats for feeding the horses the people of this country rode, wheat for bread, maize for bread and for eating in other ways, tobacco for smoking, fruits and vegetables, nuts and herbs. Some of these things were only foreign versions of foods already known to her, but many were as new to her as the anthill city.

"Doro, let me go to see these things," she pleaded. "Let me walk on land again. I have almost forgotten how it feels to stand on a surface that does not move."

Doro rested one arm comfortably around her. He liked to touch her before others more than any man she had ever known, but it did not seem that any of his people were amused or contemptuous of his behavior. Even the slaves seemed to accept whatever he did as the proper thing for him to do. And Anyanwu enjoyed his touches even now when she thought they were more imprisoning than caressing. "I will take you to see the city another time," he said. "When you know more of the ways of its people, when you can dress as they do and behave as one of them. And when I get myself a white body. I am not interested in trying to prove to one suspicious white man after another that I own myself."

"Are all black men slaves, then?"

"Most are. It is the responsibility of blacks to prove that they are free—if they are. A black without proof is taken to be a slave."

She frowned. "How is Isaac seen?"

"As a white man. He knows what he is but he was raised white. This is not an easy place to be black. Soon it will not be an easy place to be Indian."

She was silent for a moment, then asked fearfully, "Must I become white?"

"Do you want to?" He looked down at her.

"No! I thought with you I could be myself."

He seemed pleased. "With me, and with my people, you can. Wheatley is a long way upriver from here. Only my people live there, and they do not enslave each other."

"All belonging, as they do, to you," she said.

He shrugged.

"Are blacks there as well as whites?"

"Yes."

"I will live there then. I could not live in a place where being myself would mean being thought a slave."

"Nonsense," Doro said. "You are a powerful woman. You could live in any place I chose."

She looked at him quickly to see whether he was laughing at her—speaking of her power and at the same time reminding her of his own power to control her. But he was watching the approach of a small, fast-moving boat. As the boat came alongside, its one passenger and his several bundles rose straight up and drifted onto the ship. Isaac, of course. Anyanwu realized suddenly that the boy had used neither oars nor sails to propel the boat.

"You're among strangers!" Doro told him sharply, and the boy dropped, startled, to the deck.

"No one saw me," he said. "But look, speaking of being among strangers . . ." He unrolled one of the bundles that had drifted aboard with him, and Anyanwu saw that it was a long, full, bright blue petticoat of the kind given to slave women when they grew cold as the ship traveled north. Anyanwu could protect herself from the cold without such coverings though she had cut a petticoat apart to make new cloths from it. She disliked the idea of covering her body so completely, smothering herself, she called it. She thought the slave women looked foolish so covered.

"You've come to civilization," Isaac was telling her. "You've got to learn to wear clothes now, do as the people here do."

"What is civilization?" she asked.

Isaac glanced at Doro uncomfortably, and Doro smiled. "Never mind," Isaac said after a moment. "Just get dressed. Let's see how you look with clothes on."

Anyanwu touched the petticoat. The material felt smooth and cool beneath her fingers—not like the drab, coarse cloth of the slave women's petticoats. And the color pleased her— a brilliant blue that went well with her dark skin.

"Silk," Isaac said. "The best."

"Who did you steal it from?" Doro asked.

Isaac blushed dark beneath his tan and glared at his father.

"Did you steal it, Isaac?" Anyanwu demanded, alarmed.

"I left money," he said defensively. "I found someone your size, and I left twice the money these things are worth."

Anyanwu glanced at Doro uncertainly, then stepped away from him as she saw how he was looking at Isaac.

"If you're ever caught and pulled down in the middle of a stunt like that," Doro said, "I'll let them burn you."

Isaac licked his lips, put the petticoat into Anyanwu's arms. "Fair enough," he said softly. "If they can."

Doro shook his head, said something harshly in a language other than English. Isaac jumped. He glanced at Anyanwu as though to see whether she had understood. She stared back at him blankly, and he managed a weak smile of what she supposed to be relief at her ignorance. Doro gathered Isaac's bundles and spoke in English to Anyanwu. "Come on. Let's get you dressed."

"It would be easier to become an animal and wear nothing," she muttered, and was startled when he pushed her toward the hatchway.

In their cabin, Doro seemed to relax and let go of his anger. He carefully unwrapped the other bundles. A second petticoat, a woman's waistcoat, a cap, underclothing, stockings, shoes, some simple gold jewelry . . .

"Another woman's things," Anyanwu said, lapsing into her own language.

"Your things now," Doro said. "Isaac was telling the truth. He paid for them."

"Even though he did not ask first whether the woman wished to sell them."

"Even so. He took a foolish, unnecessary risk. He could have been shot out of the air or trapped, jailed, and eventually executed for witchcraft."

"He could have gotten away."

"Perhaps. But he would probably have had to kill a few people. And for what?" Doro held up the petticoat.

"You care about such things?" she asked. "Even though you kill so easily?"

"I care about my people," he said. "Every witch-scare one person's foolishness creates can hurt many. We are all witches in the eyes of ordinary people, and I am the only witch they cannot eventually kill. Also, I care about my son. I would not want Isaac making a marked man of himself—marked in his own eyes as well as the eyes of others. I know him. He is like you. He would kill, then suffer over it, wallowing in shame."

She smiled, laid one hand on his arm. "It is only his youth making him foolish. He is good. He gives me hope for our children."

"He is not a child," Doro said. "He is twenty-five years old. Think of him as a man."

She shrugged. "To me, he is a boy. And to you, both he and I are children. I have seen you watching us like an all-knowing father."

Doro smiled, denying nothing. "Take off your cloth," he said. "Get dressed."

She stripped, eyeing the new clothing with distaste.

"Accustom your body to these things," he told her as he began helping her dress. "I have been a woman often enough to know how uncomfortable women's clothing can be, but at least this is Dutch, and not as confining as the English."

"What is Dutch?"

"A people, like the English. They speak a different language."

"White people?"

"Oh yes. Just a different nationality—a different tribe. If I had to be a woman, though, I think I'd rather pass as Dutch than as English. I would here, anyway."

She looked at his tall, straight black man's body. "It is hard to think of you ever being a woman."

He shrugged. "It would be hard for me to imagine you as a man if I hadn't seen you that way."

"But . . ." She shook her head. "You would make a bad woman, however you looked. I would not want to see you as a woman."

"You will, though, sooner or later. Let me show you how to fasten that."

It became almost possible to forget that he was not a woman now. He dressed her carefully in the stifling layers of clothing, stepped back to give her a quick critical glance, then commented that Isaac had a good eye. The clothing fit almost perfectly. Anyanwu suspected that Isaac had used more than his eyes to learn the dimensions of her body. The boy had lifted her, even tossed her into the air many times without his hand coming near her. But who knew what he could measure and remember with his strange ability? She felt her face go hot. Who knew, indeed. She decided not to allow the boy to use his ability on her so freely any longer.

Doro cut off some of her hair and combed the rest with a wooden comb clearly purchased somewhere near her own country. She had seen Doro's smaller white man's comb made of bone. She found herself giggling like the young girl she appeared to be at the thought of Doro combing her hair.

"Can you braid it for me?" she asked him. "Surely you should be able to do that, too."

"Of course I can," he said. He took her face between his hands, looked at her, tilted her head to see her from a slightly different angle. "But I will not," he decided. "You look better with it loose and combed this way. I used to live with an island tribe who wore their hair this way." He hesitated. "What do you do with your hair when you change? Does it change, too?"

"No, I take it into myself. Other creatures have other kinds of hair. I feed on my hair, nails, any other parts of my body that I cannot use. Then later, I re-create them. You have seen me growing hair."

"I did not know whether you were growing it or it was . . . somehow the same hair." He handed her his small mirror. "Here, look at yourself."

She took it eagerly, lovingly. Since the first time he had shown it to her, she had wanted such a glass of her own. He had promised to buy her one.

Now she saw that he had cut and combed her hair into a softly rounded black cloud around her head. "It would be better braided," she said. "A woman of the age I seem to be would braid her hair."

"Another time." He glanced at two small bits of gold jewelry. "Either Isaac has not looked at your ears, or he thinks it would be no trouble for you to create small holes to attach these earrings. Can you?"

She looked at the earrings, at the pins meant to fasten them to her ears. Already she wore a necklace of gold and small jewels. It was the only thing she had on that she liked. Now she liked the earrings as well. "Touch where the holes should be," she said.

He clasped each of her earlobes in the proper places—then jerked his hands away in surprise.

"What is the matter?" she asked, surprised herself.

"Nothing. I . . . I suppose it's just that I've never touched you before while you were changing. The texture of your flesh is . . . different."

"Is not the texture of clay different when it is pliable and when it has set?"

". . . yes."

She laughed. "Touch me now. The strangeness is gone."

He obeyed hesitantly and seemed to find what he felt more familiar this time. "It was not unpleasant before," he said. "Only unexpected."

"But not truly unfamiliar," she said. She looked off to one side, not meeting his eyes, smiling.

"But it is. I've never . . ." He stopped and began to interpret the look on her face. "What are you saying, woman? What have you been doing?"

She laughed again. "Only giving you pleasure. You have told me how well I please you." She lifted her head. "Once I married a man who had seven wives. When he had married me, though, he did not go as often to the others."

Slowly, his expression of disbelief dissolved into amusement. He stepped closer to her with the earrings and began to attach them through the small new holes in her earlobes. "Someday," he murmured, vaguely preoccupied, "we will both change. I will become a woman and find out whether you make an especially talented man."

"*No!*" She jerked away from him, then cried out in pain and surprise when her sudden movement caused him to hurt her ear. She doused the pain quickly and repaired the slight injury. "We will *not* do such a thing!"

He gave her a smile of gentle condescension, picked up the earring from where it had fallen, and put it on her ear.

"Doro, we will not do it!"

"All right," he said agreeably. "It was only a suggestion. You might enjoy it."

"No!"

He shrugged.

"It would be a vile thing," she whispered. "Surely an abomination."

"All right," he repeated.

She looked to see whether he was still smiling, and he was. For an instant, she wondered herself what such a switch might be like. She knew she could become an adequate man, but could this strange being ever be truly womanly? What if . . . ? No!

"I will show Isaac the clothing," she said coldly.

He nodded. "Go." And the smile never left his face.

There was, in Isaac's eyes when Anyanwu stepped before him in the strange clothing, a look that warned her of another kind of abomination. The boy was open and easy to accept as a young stepson. Anyanwu was aware, however, that he would have preferred another relationship. In a less confined environment, she would have avoided him. On the ship, she had done the easy thing, the pleasurable thing, and accepted his company. Doro often had no time for her, and the slaves, who knew her power now, were afraid of her. All of them, even Okoye and Udenkwo, treated her with great formality and respect, and they avoided her as best they could. Doro's other sons were forbidden to her and it would not have been proper for her to spend time with other members of the crew. She had few wifely duties aboard. She did not cook or clean. She had no baby to tend. There were no markets to go to—she missed the crowding and the companionship of the markets very much. During several of her marriages, she had been a great trader. The produce of her garden and the pottery and tools she created were always very fine. Her goats and fowls were always fat.

Now there was nothing. Not even sickness to heal or gods to call upon. Both the slaves and the crew seemed remarkably healthy. She had seen no diseases but what Doro called seasickness among the slaves, and that was nothing. In her boredom, Anyanwu accepted Isaac's companionship. But now she could see that it was time to stop. It was wrong to torment the boy. She was pleased, though, to realize that he saw beauty in her even now, smothered as she was in so much cloth. She had feared that to eyes other than Doro's she would look ridiculous.

"Thank you for these things," she said softly in English.

"They make you even more beautiful," he told her.

"I am like a prisoner. All bound."

"You'll get used to it. Now you can be a real lady."

Anyanwu turned that over in her mind. "Real lady?" she said, frowning. "What was I before?"

Isaac's face went red. "I mean you look like a New York lady."

His embarrassment told her that he had said something wrong, something insulting. She had thought she was misunderstanding his English. Now she realized she had understood all too well.

"Tell me what I was before, Isaac," she insisted. "And tell me the word you used before: Civilization. What is civilization?"

He sighed, met her eyes after a moment of gazing past her at the main mast. "Before, you were Anyanwu," he said, "mother of I-don't-know-how-many children, priestess to your people, respected and valued woman of your town. But to the people here, you would be a savage, almost an animal if they saw you wearing only your cloth. Civilization is the way one's own people live. Savagery is the way foreigners live." He smiled tentatively. "You're already a chameleon, Anyanwu. You understand what I'm saying."

"Yes." She did not return his smile. "But in a land where most of the people are white, and of the few blacks, most are slaves, can only a few pieces of cloth make me a 'real lady.'"

"In Wheatley I can!" he said quickly. "I'm white and black and Indian, and I live there without trouble."

"But you look like a 'real man.'"

He winced. "I'm not like you," he said. "I can't help the way I look."

"No," she admitted.

"And it doesn't matter anyway. Wheatley is Doro's 'American' village. He dumps all the people he can't find places for in his pure families on us. Mix and stir. No one can afford to worry about what anyone else looks like. They don't know who Doro might mate them with—or what their own children might look like."

Anyanwu allowed herself to be diverted. "Do people even marry as he says?" she asked. "Does no one resist him?"

Isaac gave her a long, solemn look. "Wild seed resists sometimes," he said softly. "But he always wins. Always."

She said nothing. She did not need to be reminded of how dangerous and how demanding Doro could be. Reminders awakened her fear of him, her fear of a future with him. Reminders made her want to forget the welfare of her children whose freedom she had bought with her servitude. Forget and run!

"People run away sometimes," Isaac said, as though reading her thoughts. "But he always catches them and usually wears their bodies back to their home towns so that their people can see and be warned. The only sure way to escape him and cheat him out of the satisfaction of wearing your body, I guess, is my mother's way." He paused. "She hanged herself."

Anyanwu stared at him. He had said the words with no particular feeling—as though he cared no more for his mother than he had for his brother Lale. And he had told her he could not remember a time when he and Lale had not hated each other.

"Your mother died because of Doro?" she asked, watching him carefully.

He shrugged. "I don't know, really. I was only four. But I don't think so. She was like Lale—able to send and receive thoughts. But she was better at it than he was, especially better at receiving. From Wheatley, sometimes she could hear people in New York City over a hundred and fifty miles away." He glanced at Anyanwu. "A long way. A damned long way for that kind of thing. She could hear anything. But sometimes she couldn't shut things out. I remember I was afraid of her. She used to crouch in a corner and hold her head or scratch her face bloody and scream and scream and scream." He shuddered. "That's all I remember of her. That's the only image that comes when I think of her."

Anyanwu laid a hand on his arm in sympathy for both mother and son. How could he have come from such a family and remained sane himself, she wondered. What was Doro doing to his people, to his own children, in his attempt to make them more as the children of his own lost body might have been. For each one like Isaac, how many were there like Lale and his mother?

"Isaac, has there been nothing good in your life?" she asked softly.

He blinked. "There's been a lot. Doro, the foster parents he found me when I was little, the travel, this." He rose several inches above the deck. "It's been good. I used to worry that I'd be crazy like my mother or mad-dog vicious like Lale, but Doro always said I wouldn't."

"How could he know?"

"He used a different body to father me. He wanted a different ability in me, and sometimes he knows exactly which families to breed together to get what he wants. I'm glad he knew for me."

She nodded. "I would not want to know you if you were like Lale."

He looked down at her in that intense disturbing way he had developed over the voyage, and she took her hand away from his arm. No son should look at his father's wife that way. How stupid of Doro not to find a good girl for him. He should marry and begin fathering yellow-haired sons. He should be working his own farm. What good was sailing back and forth across the sea, taking slaves, and becoming wealthy when he had no children?

In spite of slight faltering winds, the trip upriver to Wheatley took only five days. The Dutch sloop captains and their

Dutch-speaking, black-slave crews peered at the sagging sails, then at each other, clearly frightened. Doro complimented them in pretended ignorance on the fine time they were making. Then in English, he warned Isaac, "Don't frighten them too badly, boy. Home isn't that far away."

Isaac grinned at him and continued to propel the sloops along at exactly the same speed.

Cliffs, hills, mountains, farmland and forests, creeks and landings, other sloops and smaller craft, fishermen, Indians . . . Doro and Isaac, having little to do as passengers on other men's vessels, entertained Anyanwu by identifying and pronouncing in English whatever caught her interest. She had an excellent memory, and by the time they reached Wheatley, she was even exchanging a few words with the Afro-Dutch crew. She was beautiful and they taught her eagerly until Doro or Isaac or their duties took her from them.

Finally, they reached "Gilpin" as the captains and crews called the village of Wheatley. Gilpin was the name given to the settlement sixty years before by its first European settlers, a small group of families led by Pieter Willem Gilpin. But the English settlers whom Doro had begun bringing in well before the 1664 British takeover had renamed the village Wheatley; wheat being its main crop, and Wheatley being the name of the English family whose leadership Doro had supported. The Wheatleys had been Doro's people for generations. They had vague, not-too-troublesome, mind-reading abilities that complemented their good business sense. With a little help from Doro, old Jonathan Wheatley now owned slightly less land than the Van Rensselaers. Doro's people had room to spread and grow. Without the grassland village, they would not grow as quickly as Doro had hoped, but there would be others, odd ones, witches. Dutch, German, English, various African and Indian peoples. All were either good breeding stock or, like the Wheatleys, served other useful purposes. In all its diversity, Wheatley pleased Doro more than any of his other New World settlements. In America, Wheatley was his home.

Now, welcomed with quiet pleasure by his people, he dispersed the new slaves to several separate households. Some were fortunate enough to go to houses where their native languages were spoken. Others had no fellow tribesmen in or around the village and they had to be content with a more alien household. Relatives were kept together. Doro explained to each individual or group exactly what was happening. All knew they would be able to see each other again. Friendships begun during the voyage did not have to end now. They were apprehensive, uncertain, reluctant to leave what had become a surprisingly tight-knit group, but they obeyed Doro. Lale had chosen them well—had hand-picked every one of them, searching out small strangenesses, buddings, beginnings of talents like his own. He had gone through every group of new slaves brought out of the forest to Bernard Daly while Doro was away—gone through picking and choosing and doubtless terrifying people more than was necessary. No doubt he had missed several who could have been useful. Lale's ability had been limited and his erratic temperament had often gotten in his way. But he had not included anyone who did not deserve to be included. Only Doro himself could have done a better job. And now, until some of his other potentially strong young thought readers matured, Doro would have to do the job himself. He did not seek people out as Lale did, deliberately, painstakingly. He found them almost as effortlessly as he had found Anyanwu—though not from as great a distance. He became aware of them as easily as a wolf became aware of a rabbit when the wind was right—and in the beginning he had gone after them for exactly the same reason wolves went after rabbits. In the beginning, he had bred them for exactly the same reason people bred rabbits. These strange ones, his witches, were good kills. They offered him the most satisfying durable food and shelter. He still preyed on them. Soon he would take one from Wheatley. The people of Wheatley expected it, accepted it, treated it as a kind of religious sacrifice. All his towns and villages fed him willingly now. And the breeding projects he carried on among them entertained him as nothing else could. He had brought them so far—from tiny, blind, latent talents to Lale, to Isaac, and even, in a roundabout way, to Anyanwu. He was building a people for himself, and he was feeding well. If he was sometimes lonely as his people lived out their brief lives, he was at least not bored. Short-lived people, people who could die, did not know what enemies loneliness and boredom could be.

There was a large, low yellow-brick farmhouse at the edge of town for Doro—an ex-Dutch farmhouse that was more comfortable than handsome. Jonathan Wheatley's manor house was much finer, as was his mansion in New York City, but Doro was content with his farmhouse. In a good year, he might visit it twice.

An English couple lived in Doro's house, caring for it and serving Doro when he was at home. They were a farmer, Robert Cutler, and his wife, youngest of the nine Wheatley daughters, Sarah. These were sturdy, resilient people who had raised Isaac through his worst years. The boy had been difficult and dangerous during his adolescent years as his abilities matured. Doro had been surprised that the couple survived. Lale's foster parents had not—but then, Lale had been actively malevolent. Isaac had done harm only by accident. Also, neither of Lale's foster parents had been Wheatleys. Sarah's work with Isaac had proved again the worth of her kind—people with too little ability to be good breeding stock or food. It occurred to Doro that if his breeding projects were successful, there might come a time—in the far future—when he had to make certain such people continued to exist. Able people, but not so powerful that their ability might turn on them and cripple or kill them.

For now, though, it was his witches who had to be protected—even protected from him. Anyanwu, for instance. He would tell her tonight that she was to marry Isaac. In telling her, he would have to treat her not as ordinary recalcitrant wild seed, but as one of his daughters—difficult, but worth taking time with. Worth molding and coercing with more gentleness and patience than he would bother to use on less valuable people. He would talk to her after one of Sarah's good meals when they were alone in his room, warm and comfortable before a fire. He would do all he could to make her obey and live.

He thought about her, worried about her stubbornness as he walked toward home where she waited. He had just placed Okoye and Udenkwo in a home with a middle-aged pair of their countrymen—people from whom the young couple could learn a great deal. He walked slowly, answering the greetings of people who recognized his current body and worrying about the pride of one small forest peasant. People sat outside, men and women, Dutch fashion, gossiping on the stoops. The women's hands were busy with sewing or knitting while the men smoked pipes. Isaac got up from a bench where he had been sitting with an older woman and fell into step with Doro.

"Anneke is near her transition," the boy said worriedly. "Mrs. Waemans says she's been having a lot of trouble."

"That's to be expected," Doro answered. Anneke Strycker was one of his daughters—a potentially good daughter. With luck, she would replace Lale when her transition was complete and her abilities mature. She lived now with her foster mother, Margaret Waemans, a big, physically powerful, mentally stable widow of fifty. No doubt, the woman needed all her resources to handle the young girl now.

Isaac cleared his throat. "Mrs. Waemans is afraid she'll . . . do something to herself. She's been talking about dying."

Doro nodded. Power came the way a child came—with agony. People in transition were open to every thought, every emotion, every pleasure, every pain from the minds of others. Their heads were filled with a continuous screaming jumble of mental "noise." There was no peace, little sleep, many nightmares—everyone's nightmares. Some of Doro's best people—too many of them—stopped at this stage. They could pass their potential on to their children if they lived long enough to have any, but they could not benefit from it them-

selves. They could never control it. They became hosts for
Doro, or they became breeders. Doro brought them mates
from distant unrelated settlements because that kind of cross-
breeding most often produced children like Lale. Only great
care and fantastic good luck produced a child like Isaac. Doro
glanced at the boy fondly. "I'll see Anneke first thing tomorrow," he told him.

"Good," Isaac said with relief. "That will help. Mrs. Waemans says she calls for you sometimes when the nightmares
come." He hesitated. "How bad will it get for her?"

"As bad as it was for you and for Lale."

"My God!" Isaac said. "She's only a girl. She'll die."

"She has as much of a chance as you and Lale did."

Isaac glared at Doro in sudden anger. "You don't care
what happens to her, do you? If she does die, there will always be someone else."

Doro turned to look at him, and after a moment, Isaac
looked away.

"Be a child out here if you like," Doro told him. "But act
your age when we go in. I'm going to settle things between
you and Anyanwu tonight."

"Settle . . . you're finally going to give her to me?"

"Think of it another way. I want you to marry her."

The boy's eyes widened. He stopped walking, leaned
against a tall maple tree. "You . . . you've made up your mind,
I suppose. I mean . . . you're sure that's what you want."

"Of course." Doro stopped beside him.

"Have you told her?"

"Not yet. I'll tell her after dinner."

"Doro, she's wild seed. She might refuse."

"I know."

"You might not be able to change her mind."

Doro shrugged. Worried as he was, it did not occur to
him to share his concern with Isaac. Anyanwu would obey
him or she wouldn't. He longed to be able to control her
with some refinement of Lale's power, but he could not—nor
could Isaac.

"If you can't reach her," Isaac said, "if she just won't understand, let me try. Before you . . . do anything else, let me try."

"All right."

"And . . . don't make her hate me."

"I don't think I could. She might come to hate me for a while, but not you."

"Don't hurt her."

"Not if I can help it." Doro smiled a little, pleased by the boy's concern. "You like the idea," he observed. "You want to marry her."

"Yes. But I never thought you'd let me."

"She'll be happier with a husband who does more than visit her once or twice a year."

"You're going to leave me here to be a farmer?"

"Farm if you want to—or open a store or go back to smithing. No one could handle that better than you. Do whatever you like, but I am going to leave you here, at least for a while. She'll need someone to help her fit in here when I'm gone."

"God," Isaac said. "Married." He shook his head, then began to smile.

"Come on." Doro started toward the house.

"No."

Doro looked back at him.

"I can't see her until you tell her . . . now that I know. I can't. I'll eat with Anneke. She could use the company anyway."

"Sarah won't think much of that."

"I know." Isaac glared homeward guiltily. "Apologize for me, will you?"

Doro nodded, turned, and went in to Sarah Cutler's linen-clothed, heavily laden table.

Anyanwu watched carefully as the white woman placed first a clean cloth, then dishes and utensils on the long, narrow table at which the household was to eat. Anyanwu was glad that some of the food and the white people's ways of eating it were familiar to her from the ship. She could sit down and have a meal without seeming utterly ignorant. She could not have cooked the meal, but that would come, too, in time. She would learn. For now, she merely observed and allowed the interesting smells to intensify her hunger. Hunger was familiar and good. It kept her from staring too much at the white woman, kept her from concentrating on her own nervousness and uncertainty in the new surroundings, kept her attention on the soup, thick with meat and vegetables, and the roast deer flesh—venison, the white woman had called it—and a huge fowl—a turkey. Anyanwu repeated the words to herself, reassured that they had become part of her vocabulary. New words, new ways, new foods, new clothing . . . She was glad of the cumbersome clothing, though, finally. It made her look more like the other women, black and white, whom she had seen in the village, and that was important. She had lived in enough different towns through her various marriages to know the necessity of learning to behave as others did. What was common in one place could be ridiculous in another and abomination in a third. Ignorance could be costly.

"How shall I call you?" she asked the white woman. Doro had said the woman's name once, very quickly, in introduction, then hurried off on business of his own. Anyanwu remembered the name—Sarahcutler—but was not certain she could say it correctly without hearing it again.

"Sarah Cutler," the woman said very distinctly. "Mrs. Cutler."

Anyanwu frowned, confused. Which was right? "Mrs. Cutler?"

"Yes. You say it well."

"I am trying to learn." Anyanwu shrugged. "I must learn."

"How do you say your name?"

"Anyanwu." She said it very slowly, but still the woman asked:

"Is that all one name?"

"Only one. I have had others, but Anyanwu is best. I come back to it."

"Are the others shorter?"

"Mbgafo. That is the name my mother gave me. And once I was called Atagbusi, and honored by that name. I have been called—"

"Never mind." The woman sighed, and Anyanwu smiled to herself. She had had to give five of her former names to Isaac before he shrugged and decided Anyanwu was a good name after all.

"Can I help to do these things?" she asked. Sarah Cutler was beginning to put food on the table now.

"No," the woman said. "Just watch now. You'll be doing this soon enough." She glanced at Anyanwu curiously. She did not stare, but allowed herself these quick curious glances. Anyanwu thought they each probably had an equal number of questions about the other.

Sarah Cutler asked: "Why did Doro call you 'Sun Woman'?"

Doro had taken to doing that affectionately when he spoke to her in English, though Isaac complained that it made her sound like an Indian.

"Your word for my name is 'Sun,'" she answered. "Doro said he would find an English name for me, but I did not want one. Now he makes English of my name."

The white woman shook her head and laughed. "You're more fortunate than you know. With him taking such an interest in you, I'm surprised you're not already Jane or Alice or some such."

Anyanwu shrugged. "He has not changed his own name. Why should he change mine?"

The woman gave her what seemed to be a look of pity.

"What is Cutler?" Anyanwu asked.

"What it means?"

"Yes."

"A cutler is a knifemaker. I suppose my husband had ancestors who were knifemakers. Here, taste this." She gave

Anyanwu a bit of something sweet and oily, fruit-filled, and delicious.

"It is very good!" Anyanwu said. The sweet was unlike anything she had tasted before. She did not know what to say about it except the words of courtesy Doro had taught her. "Thank you. What is this called?"

The woman smiled, pleased. "It's a kind of cake I haven't made before—special for Isaac and Doro's homecoming."

"You said . . ." Anyanwu thought for a moment. "You said your husband's people were knifemakers. Cutler is his name?"

"Yes. Here, a woman takes the name of her husband after marriage. I was Sarah Wheatley before I married."

"Then Sarah is the name you keep for yourself."

"Yes."

"Shall I call you Sarah—your own name?"

The woman glanced at her sidelong. "Shall I call you . . . Mbgafo?" She mispronounced it horribly.

"If you like. But there are very many Mbgafos. That name only tells the day of my birth."

"Like . . . Monday or Tuesday?"

"Yes. You have seven. We have only four: Eke, Oye, Afo, Nkwo. People are often named for the day they were born."

"Your country must be overflowing with people of the same name."

Anyanwu nodded. "But many have other names as well."

"I suppose Anyanwu really is better."

"Yes." Anyanwu smiled. "Sarah is good too. A woman should have something of her own."

Doro came in then, and Anyanwu noted how the woman brightened. She had not been sad or grim before, but now, years seemed to drop from her. She only smiled at him and said dinner was ready, but there was a warmth in her voice that had not been there before in spite of all her friendliness. At some time, this woman had been wife or lover to Doro. Probably lover. There was still much fondness between them, though the woman was no longer young. Where was her husband, Anyanwu wondered. How was it that a woman here could cook for a man neither her kinsman nor in-law while her husband probably sat with others in front of one of the houses and blew smoke out of his mouth?

Then the husband came in, bringing two grown sons and a daughter, along with the very young, shy wife of one of the sons. The girl was slender and olive-skinned, black-haired and dark-eyed, and even to Anyanwu's eyes, very beautiful. When Doro spoke to her courteously, her answer was a mere moving of the lips. She would not look at him at all except once when his back was turned. But the look she gave him then spoke as loudly as had Sarah Cutler's sudden brightening. Anyanwu blinked and began to wonder what kind of man she had. The women aboard the ship had not found Doro so desirable. They had been terrified of him. But these women of his people . . . Was he like a cock among them, going from one hen to another? They were not, after all, his kinsmen or his friends. They were people who had pledged loyalty to him or people he had bought as slaves. In a sense, they were more his property than his people. The men laughed and talked with him, but none presumed as much as Isaac had. All were respectful. And if their wives or sisters or daughters looked at Doro, they did not notice. Anyanwu strongly suspected that if Doro looked back, if he did more than look, they would make an effort not to notice that either. Or perhaps they would be honored. Who knew what strange ways they practiced?

But now, Doro gave his attention to Anyanwu. She was shy in this company—men and women together eating strange food and talking in a language she felt she spoke poorly and understood imperfectly. Doro kept making her talk, speaking to her of trivial things.

"Do you miss the yams? There are none quite like yours here."

"It does not matter." Her voice was like the young girl's— no more than a moving of the lips. She felt ashamed to speak before all these strangers—yet she had always spoken before strangers, and spoken well. One had to speak well and firmly when people came for medicine and healing. What faith could they have in someone who whispered or bowed her head?

Determinedly, she raised her head and ceased concentrating so intently on her soup. She did miss the yams. Even the strange soup made her long for an accompanying mound of pounded yam. But that did not matter. She looked around, meeting the eyes first of Sarah Cutler, then of one of Sarah's sons and finding only friendliness and curiosity in both. The young man, thin and brown-haired, seemed to be about Isaac's age. Thoughts of Isaac made Anyanwu look around.

"Where is Isaac?" she asked Doro. "You said this was his home."

"He's with a friend," Doro told her. "He'll be in later."

"He'd better!" Sarah said. "His first night back and he can't come home to supper."

"He had reason," Doro told her. And she said nothing more.

But Anyanwu found other things to say. And she no longer whispered. She paid some attention to spooning up the soup as the others did and to eating the other meats and breads and sweets correctly with her fingers. People here ate more carefully than had the men aboard the ship; thus, she ate more carefully. She spoke to the shy young girl and discovered that the girl was an Indian—a Mohawk. Doro had matched her with Blake Cutler because both had just a little of the sensitivity Doro valued. Both seemed pleased with the match. Anyanwu thought she would have been happier with her own match with Doro had her people been nearby. It would be good for the children of their marriage to know her world as well as Doro's—to be aware of a place where blackness was not a mark of slavery. She resolved to make her homeland live for them whether Doro permitted her to show it to them or not. She resolved not to let them forget who they were.

Then she found herself wondering whether the Mohawk girl would have preferred to forget who she was as the conversation turned to talk of war with Indians. The white people at the table were eager to tell Doro how, earlier in the year, "Praying Indians" and a group of whites called French had stolen through the gates of a town west of Wheatley— a town with the unpronounceable name of Schenectady— and butchered some of the people there and carried off others. There was much discussion of this, much fear expressed until Doro promised to leave Isaac in the village, and leave one of his daughters, Anneke, who would soon be very powerful. This seemed to calm everyone somewhat. Anyanwu felt that she had only half understood the dispute between so many foreign people, but she did ask whether Wheatley had ever been attacked.

Doro smiled unpleasantly. "Twice by Indians," he said. "I happened to be here both times. We've had peace since that second attack thirty years ago."

"That's time enough for them to forget anything," Sarah said. "Anyway, this is a new war. French and Praying Indians!" She shook her head in disgust.

"Papists!" her husband muttered. "Bastards!"

"My people could tell them what powerful spirits live here," whispered the Mohawk girl, smiling.

Doro looked at her as though not certain whether she were serious, but she ducked her head.

Anyanwu touched Doro's hand. "You see?" she said. "I told you you were a spirit!"

Everyone laughed, and Anyanwu felt more comfortable among them. She would find out another time exactly what Papists and Praying Indians were and what their quarrel was with the English. She had had enough new things for one day. She relaxed and enjoyed her meal.

She enjoyed it too much. After much eating and drinking, after everyone had gathered around the tall, blue-tiled parlor hearth for talking and smoking and knitting, she began to feel pain in her stomach. By the time the gathering broke up, she was controlling herself very closely lest she vomit up all the food she had eaten and humiliate herself before all these people. When Doro showed her her room with its fireplace and its deep soft down mattresses covering a great bed, she undressed and lay down at once. There she discovered that her body had reacted badly to one specific food—a rich sweet that she knew no name for, but that she had loved. This on top of the huge amount of meat she had eaten had finally been too much for her stomach. Now, though, she controlled her digestion, soothed the sickness from her body. The food did not have to be brought up. Only gotten used to. She analyzed slowly, so intent on her inner awareness that she appeared to be asleep. If someone had spoken to her, she would not have heard. Her eyes were closed. This was why she had waited, had not healed herself downstairs in the presence of others. Here, though, it did not matter what she did. Only Doro was present—across the large room sitting at a great wooden desk much finer than the one he had had on the ship. He was writing, and she knew from experience that he would be making marks unlike those in any of his books. "It's a very old language," he had told her once. "So old that no one living can read it."

"No one but you," she had said.

And he had nodded and smiled. "The people I learned it from stole me away into slavery when I was only a boy. Now they're all dead. Their descendants have forgotten the old wisdom, the old writing, the old gods. Only I remember."

She had not known whether she heard bitterness or satisfaction in his voice then. He was very strange when he talked about his youth. He made Anyanwu want to touch him and tell him that he was not alone in outliving so many things. But he also roused her fear of him, reminded her of his deadly difference. Thus, she said nothing.

Now, as she lay still, analyzing, learning not only which food had made her ill, but which ingredient in that food, she was comfortably aware of Doro nearby. If he had left the room in complete silence, she would have known, would have missed him. The room would have become colder.

It was milk that had sickened her. Animal milk! These people cooked many things with animal milk! She covered her mouth with her hand. Did Doro know? But of course he did. How could he not? These were his people!

Again it required all her control to prevent herself from vomiting—this time from sheer revulsion.

"Anyanwu?"

She realized that Doro was standing over her between the long cloths that could be closed to conceal the bed. And she realized that this was not the first time he had said her name. Still, it surprised her that she had heard him without his shouting or touching her. He had only spoken quietly.

She opened her eyes, looked up at him. He was beautiful standing there with the light of candles behind him. He had stripped to the cloth he still wore sometimes when they were alone together. But she noticed this with only part of her mind. Her main thoughts were still of the loathsome thing she had been tricked into doing—the consumption of animal milk.

"Why didn't you tell me!" she demanded.

"What?" He frowned, confused. "Tell you what?"

"That these people were feeding me animal milk!"

He burst into laughter.

She drew back as though he had hit her. "Is it a joke then? Are the others laughing too now that I cannot hear?"

"Anyanwu . . ." He managed to stop his laughter. "I'm sorry," he told her. "I was thinking of something else or I wouldn't have laughed. But, Anyanwu, we all ate the same food."

"But why was some of it cooked with—"

"Listen. I know the custom among your people not to drink animal milk. I should have warned you—would have, if I had been thinking. No one else who ate with us knew the milk would offend you. I assure you, they're not laughing."

She hesitated. He was sincere; she was certain of that. It was a mistake then. But still . . . "These people cook with animal milk all the time?"

"All the time," Doro said. "And they drink milk. It's their custom. They keep some cattle especially for milking."

"Abomination!" Anyanwu said with disgust.

"Not to them," Doro told her. "And you will not insult them by telling them they are committing abomination."

She looked at him. He did not seem to give many orders, but she had no doubt that this was one. She said nothing.

"You can become an animal whenever you wish," he said. "You know there's nothing evil about animal milk."

"It is for animals!" she said. "I am not an animal now! I did not just eat a meal with animals!"

He sighed. "You know you must change to suit the customs here. You have not lived three hundred years without learning to accept new customs."

"I will not have any more milk!"

"You need not. But let others have theirs in peace."

She turned away from him. She had never in her long life lived among people who violated this prohibition.

"Anyanwu!"

"I will obey," she muttered, then faced him defiantly. "When will I have my own house? My own cooking fire?"

"When you've learned what to do with them. What kind of meal could you cook now with foods you've never seen before? Sarah Cutler will teach you what you need to know. Tell her milk makes you sick and she'll leave it out of what she teaches you." His voice softened a little, and he sat down beside her on the bed. "It did make you sick, didn't it?"

"It did. Even my flesh knows abomination."

"It didn't make anyone else sick."

She only glared at him.

He reached under the blanket, rubbed her stomach gently. Her body was almost buried in the too-soft feather mattress. "Have you healed yourself?" he asked.

"Yes. But with so much food, it took me a long time to learn what was making me sick."

"Do you have to know?"

"Of course. How can I know what to do for healing until

I know what healing is needed and why? I think I knew all
the diseases and poisons of my people. I must learn the ones
here."

"Does it hurt you—the learning?"

"Oh yes. But only at first. Once I learn it, it does not
hurt again." Her voice became bantering. "No, give me your
hand again. You can touch me even though I am well."

He smiled and there was no more tension between them.
His touches became more intimate.

"That is good," she whispered. "I healed myself just in
time. Now lie down here and show me why all those women
were looking at you."

He laughed quietly, untied his cloth, and joined her in
the too-soft bed.

"We must talk tonight," he said later when both were sa-
tiated and lying side by side.

"Do you still have strength for talking, husband?" she said
drowsily. "I thought you would go to sleep and not awaken
until sunrise."

"No." There was no humor in his voice now. She had
laid her head on his shoulder because he had shown her in
the past that he wanted her near him, touching him until he
fell asleep. Now, though, she lifted her head and looked at
him.

"You've come to your new home, Anyanwu."

"I know that." She did not like the flat strangeness of his
tone. This was the voice he used to frighten people—the
voice that reminded her to think of him as something other
than a man.

"You are home, but I will be leaving again in a few weeks."

"But—"

"I will be leaving. I have other people who need me to
rid them of enemies or who need to see me to know they
still belong to me. I have a fragmented people to hunt and
reassemble. I have women in three different towns who could

bear powerful children if I give them the right mates. And more. Much more."

She sighed and burrowed deeper into the mattress. He was going to leave her here among strangers. He had made up his mind. "When you come back," she said resignedly, "there will be a son for you here."

"Are you pregnant now?"

"I can be now. Your seed still lives inside me."

"No!"

She jumped, startled at his vehemence.

"This is not the body I want to beget your first children here," he said.

She made herself shrug, speak casually. "All right. I'll wait until you have . . . become another man."

"You need not. I have another plan for you."

The hairs at the back of her neck began to prickle and itch. "What plan?"

"I want you to marry," he said. "You'll do it in the way of the people here with a license and a wedding."

"It makes no difference. I will follow your custom."

"Yes. But not with me."

She stared at him, speechless. He lay on his back staring at one of the great beams that held up the ceiling.

"You'll marry Isaac," he said. "I want children from the two of you. And I want you to have a husband who does more than visit you now and then. Living here, you could go for a year, two years, without seeing me. I don't want you to be that alone."

"Isaac?" she whispered. "Your son?"

"My son. He's a good man. He wants you, and I want you with him."

"He's a boy! He's . . ."

"What man is not a boy to you, except me? Isaac is more a man than you think."

"But . . . he's your son! How can I have the son when his father, my husband, still lives? That is abomination!"

"Not if I command it."

"You cannot! It is abomination!"

"You have left your village, Anyanwu, and your town and your land and your people. You are here where I rule. Here, there is only one abomination: disobedience. You will obey."

"I will not! Wrong is wrong! Some things change from place to place, but not this. If your people wish to debase themselves by drinking the milk of animals, I will turn my head. Their shame is their own. But now you want me to shame myself, make myself even worse than they. How can you ask it of me, Doro? The land itself will be offended! Your crops will wither and die!"

He made a sound of disgust. "That's foolishness! I thought I had found a woman too wise to believe such nonsense."

"You have found a woman who will not soil herself! How is it here? Do sons lie with their mothers also? Do sisters and brothers lie down together?"

"Woman, if I command it, they lie down together gladly."

Anyanwu moved away from him so that no part of her body touched his. He had spoken of this before. Of incest, of mating her own children together with doglike disregard for kinship. And in revulsion, she had led him quickly from her land. She had saved her children, but now . . . who would save her?

"I want children of your body and his," Doro repeated. He stopped, raised himself to his elbow so that he leaned over her. "Sun Woman, would I tell you to do something that would hurt my people? The land is different here. *It is my land!* Most of the people here exist because I caused their ancestors to marry in ways your people would not accept. Yet everyone lives well here. No angry god punishes them. Their crops grow and their harvests are rich every year."

"And some of them hear so much of the thoughts of others that they cannot think their own thoughts. Some of them hang themselves."

"Some of your own people hang themselves."

"Not for such terrible reasons."

"Nevertheless, they die. Anyanwu, obey me. Life can be

very good for you here. And you will not find a better husband than my son."

She closed her eyes, dismissed his pleading as she had his commands. She strove to dismiss her budding fear also, but she could not. She knew that when both commanding and pleading failed, he would begin to threaten.

Within her body, she killed his seed. She disconnected the two small tubes through which her own seed traveled to her womb. She had done this many times when she thought she had given a man enough children. Now she did it to avoid giving any children at all, to avoid being used. When it was done, she sat up and looked down at him. "You have been telling me lies from the day we met," she said softly.

He shook his head against the pillow. "I have not lied to you."

" 'Let me give you children who will live,' you said. 'I promise that if you come with me, I will give you children of your own kind,' you said. And now, you send me away to another man. You give me nothing at all."

"You will bear my children as well as Isaac's."

She cried out as though with pain, and climbed out of his bed. "Get me another room!" she hissed. "I will not lie there with you. I would rather sleep on the bare floor. I would rather sleep on the ground!"

He lay still, as though he had not heard her. "Sleep wherever you wish," he said after a while.

She stared at him, her body shaking with fear and anger. "What is it you would make of me, Doro? Your dog? I cared for you. It has been lifetimes since I cared as much for a man."

He said nothing.

She stepped nearer to the bed, looked down into his expressionless face, pleading herself now. She did not think it was possible to move him by pleading once he had made up his mind, but so much was at stake. She had to try.

"I came here to be a wife to you," she said. "But there were always others to cook for you, others to serve you in

nearly all the ways of a wife. And if there had not been others, I know so little of this place that I would have performed
my duties poorly. You knew it would be this way for me, but
still you wanted me—and I wanted you enough to begin again
like a child, completely ignorant." She sighed and looked
around the room, feeling as though she were hunting for the
words that would reach him. There was only the alien furniture: the desk, the bed, the great wooden cabinet beside
the door—a *kas*, it was called, a Dutch thing for storing clothing. There were two chairs and several mats—rugs—of heavy,
colorful cloth. It was all as alien as Doro himself. It gave her
a feeling of hopelessness—as though she had come to this
strange place only to die. She stared into the fire in the fireplace—the only familiar thing in the room—and spoke softly:

"Husband, it may be a good thing that you're going away.
A year is not so long, or two years. Not to us. I have been
alone before for many times that long. When you come back,
I will know how to be a wife to you here. I will give you
strong sons." She turned her eyes back to him, saw that he
was watching her. "Do not cast me aside before I show you
what a good wife I can be."

He sat up, put his feet on the floor. "You don't understand," he said softly. He pulled her down to sit beside him
on the bed. "Haven't I told you what I'm building? Over the
years, I've taken people with so little power they were almost
ordinary, and bred them together again and again until in
their descendants, small abilities grew large, and a man like
Isaac could be born."

"And a man like Lale."

"Lale wasn't as bad as he seemed. He handled what ability he had very well. And I've created others of his kind who
had more ability and a better temperament."

"Did you create him, then? From what? Mounds of clay?"

"Anyanwu!"

"Isaac tells me the whites believe their god made the first
people of clay. You talk as though you think you were that
god!"

He drew a deep breath, looked at her sadly. "What I am or think I am need not concern you at all. I've told you what you must do—no, be quiet. Hear me."

She closed her mouth, swallowed a new protest.

"I said you didn't understand," he continued. "Now I think you're deliberately misunderstanding. Do you truly believe I mean to cast you aside because you've been a poor wife?"

She looked away. No, of course she did not believe that. She had only hoped to reach him, make him stop his impossible demands. No, he was not casting her aside for any reason at all. He was merely breeding her as one bred cattle and goats. He had said it: "I want children of your body and his." What she wanted meant nothing. Did one ask a cow or a nanny goat whether it wished to be bred?

"I am giving you the very best of my sons," he told her. "I expect you to be a good wife to him. I would never send you to him if I thought you couldn't."

She shook her head slowly. "It is you who have not understood me." She gazed at him—at his very ordinary eyes, at his long, handsome face. Until now, she had managed to avoid a confrontation like this by giving in a little, obeying. Now she could not obey.

"You are my husband," she said quietly, "or I have no husband. If I need another man, I will find one. My father and all my other husbands are long dead. You gave no gifts for me. You can send me away, but you cannot tell me where I must go."

"Of course I can." His quiet calm matched her own, but in him it was clearly resignation. "You know you must obey, Anyanwu. Must I take your body and get the children I want from it myself?"

"You cannot." Within herself, she altered her reproductive organs further, made herself literally no longer a woman, but not quite a man—just to be certain. "You may be able to push my spirit from my body," she said. "I think you can, though I have never felt your power. But my body will give you no satisfaction. It would take too long for you to learn to repair all the things I have done to it—if you can learn. It will not conceive a child now. It will not live much longer itself without me to keep watch on it."

She could not have missed the anger in his voice when he spoke again. "You know I will collect your children if I cannot have you."

She turned her back on him, not wanting him to see her fear and pain, not wanting her own eyes to see him. He was a loathsome thing.

He came to stand behind her, put his hands on her shoulders. She struck them away violently. "Kill me!" she hissed. "Kill me now, but never touch me that way again!"

"And your children?" he said unmoved.

"No child of mine would commit the abominations you want," she whispered.

"Now who's lying?" he said. "You know your children don't have your strength. I'll get what I want from them, and their children will be as much mine as the people here."

She said nothing. He was right, of course. Even her own strength was mere bravado, a façade covering utter terror. It was only her anger that kept her neck straight. And what good was anger or defiance? He would consume her very spirit; there would be no next life for her. Then he would use and pervert her children. She felt near to weeping.

"You'll get over your anger," he said. "Life will be rich and good for you here. You'll be surprised to see how easily you blend with these people."

"I will not marry your son, Doro! No matter what threats you make, no matter what promises, I will not marry your son!"

He sighed, tied his cloth around him, and started for the door. "Stay here," he told her. "Put something on and wait."

"For what!" she demanded bitterly.

"For Isaac," he answered.

And when she turned to face him, mouth open to curse

both him and his son, he stepped close to her and struck her across the face with all his strength.

There was an instant before the blow landed when she could have caught his arm and broken the bones within it like dry sticks. There was an instant before the blow landed when she could have torn out his throat.

But she absorbed the blow, moved with it, made no sound. It had been a long time since she had wanted so powerfully to kill a man.

"I see you know how to be quiet," he said. "I see you're not as willing to die as you thought. Good. My son asked for a chance to talk to you if you refused to obey. Wait here."

"What can he say to me that you have not said?" she demanded harshly.

Doro paused at the door to give her a look of contempt. His blow had had less power to hurt her than that look.

When the door closed behind him, she went to the bed and sat down to stare, unseeing, into the fire. By the time Isaac knocked on the door, her face was wet with tears she did not remember shedding.

She made him wait until she had wrapped a cloth around herself and dried her face. Then with leaden, hopeless weariness, she opened the door and let the boy in.

He looked as depleted as she felt. The yellow hair hung limp into his eyes and the eyes themselves were red. His sun-browned hair looked as pale as Anyanwu had ever seen it. He seemed not only tired, but sick.

He stood gazing at her, saying nothing, making her want to go to him as though to Okoye, and try to give him comfort. Instead, she sat down in one of the room's chairs so that he could not sit close to her.

Obligingly, he sat opposite her in the other chair. "Did he threaten you?" he asked softly.

"Of course. That is all he knows how to do."

"And promise you a good life if you obey?"

". . . yes."

"He'll keep his word, you know. Either way."

"I have seen how he keeps his word."

There was a long, uncomfortable silence. Finally, Isaac whispered, "Don't make him do it, Anyanwu. Don't throw away your life!"

"Do you think I want to die?" she said. "My life has been good, and very long. It could be even longer and better. The world is a much wider place than I thought; there is so much for me to see and know. But I will not be his dog! Let him commit his abominations with other people!"

"With your children?"

"Do you threaten me too, Isaac?"

"No!" he cried. "You know better, Anyanwu."

She turned her face away from him. If only he would go away. She did not want to say things to hurt him. He spoke softly:

"When he told me I would marry you, I was surprised and a little afraid. You've been married many times, and I not even once. I know Okoye is your grandson—one of your younger grandsons—and he's at least my age. I didn't see how I could measure up against all your experience. But I wanted to try! You don't know how I wanted to try."

"Will you be bred, Isaac? Does it mean nothing to you?"

"Don't you know I wanted you long before he decided we should marry?"

"I knew." She glanced at him. "But wrong is wrong!"

"It isn't wrong here. It . . ." He shrugged. "People from outside always have trouble understanding us. Not very many things are forbidden here. Most of us don't believe in gods and spirits and devils who must be pleased or feared. We have Doro, and he's enough. He tells us what to do, and if it isn't what other people do, it doesn't matter—because we won't last long if we don't do it, no matter what outsiders think of us."

He got up, went to stand beside the fireplace. The low flame seemed to comfort him too. "Doro's ways aren't strange to me," he said. "I've lived with them all my life. I've shared women with him. My first woman . . ." He hesitated, glanced at her as though to see how she was receiving such talk, whether she was offended. She was almost indifferent. She had made up her mind. Nothing the boy said would change it.

"My first woman," he continued, "was one he sent to me. The women here are glad to go to him. They didn't mind coming to me either when they saw how he favored me."

"Go to them then," Anyanwu said quietly.

"I would," he said, matching her tone. "But I don't want to. I'd rather stay with you—for the rest of my life."

She wanted to run out of the room. "Leave me alone, Isaac!"

He shook his head slowly. "If I leave this room tonight, you'll die tonight. Don't ask me to hurry your death."

She said nothing.

"Besides, I want you to have the night to think." He frowned at her. "How can you sacrifice your children?"

"Which children, Isaac? The ones I have had or the ones he will make me have with you and with him?"

He blinked. "Oh."

"I cannot kill him—or even understand what there is to kill. I have bitten him when he was in another body, and he seemed no more than flesh, no more than a man."

"You never touched him," Isaac said. "Lale did once—he reached out in that way of his to change Doro's thoughts. He almost died. I think he would have died if Doro hadn't struggled hard not to kill him. Doro wears flesh, but he isn't flesh himself—nor spirit, he says."

"I cannot understand that," she said. "But it does not matter. I cannot save my children from him. I cannot save myself. But I will not give him more people to defile."

He turned from the fire, went back to his chair and pulled it close to her. "You could save generations unborn if you wished, Anyanwu. You could have a good life for yourself, and you could stop him from killing so many others."

"How can I stop him?" she said in disgust. "Can one stop a leopard from doing what it was born to do?"

"He's not a leopard! He's not any sort of mindless animal!"

She could not help hearing the anger in his voice. She sighed. "He is your father."

"Oh God," muttered Isaac. "How can I make you see . . . I wasn't resenting an insult to my father, Anyanwu, I was saying that in his own way, he can be a reasonable being. You're right about his killing; he can't help doing it. When he needs a new body, he takes one whether he wants to or not. But most of the time, he transfers because he wants to, not because he has to, and there are a few people—four or five—who can influence him enough sometimes to stop him from killing, save a few of his victims. I'm one of them. You could be another."

"You do not mean stop him," she said wearily. "You mean"—she hunted through her memory for the right word—"you mean delay him."

"I mean what I said! There are people he listens to, people he values beyond their worth as breeders or servants. People who can give him . . . just a little of the companionship he needs. They're among the few people in the world that he can still love—or at least care for. Although compared to what the rest of us feel when we love or hate or envy or whatever, I don't think he feels very much. I don't think he can. I'm afraid the time will come when he won't feel anything. If it does—there's no end to the harm he could do. I'm glad I won't have to live to see it. You, though, you could live to see it—or live to prevent it. You could stay with him, keep him at least as human as he is now. I'll grow old; I'll die like all the others, but you won't—or, you needn't. You are treasure to him. I don't think he's really understood that yet."

"He knows."

"He knows, of course, but he doesn't . . . doesn't feel it yet. It's not yet real to him. Don't you see? He's lived for more than thirty-seven hundred years. When Christ, the Son of God of most white people in these colonies, was born, Doro was already impossibly old. Everyone has always been temporary for him—wives, children, friends, even tribes and nations, gods and devils. Everything dies but him. And maybe you, Sun Woman, and maybe you. Make him know you're not like everyone else—make him feel it. Prove it to him, even if for a while, you have to do some things you don't like. Reach out to him; keep reaching. Make him know he's not alone anymore!"

There was a long period of silence. Only the log in the fireplace slipped, then spat and crackled as new wood began to burn. Anyanwu covered her face, shook her head slowly. "I wish I knew you to be a liar," she whispered. "I am afraid and angry and desperate, yet you heap burdens on me."

He said nothing.

"What is forbidden here, Isaac? What is so evil that a man could be taken out and killed?"

"Murder," Isaac said. "Theft sometimes, some other things. And of course, defying Doro."

"If a man killed someone and Doro said he must not be punished, what would happen?"

Isaac frowned. "If the man had to be kept alive—maybe for breeding, Doro would probably take him. Or if it was too soon, if he was being saved for a girl still too young, Doro would send him away from the colony. He wouldn't ask us to tolerate him here."

"And when the man was no longer needed, he would die?"

"Yes."

Anyanwu took a deep breath. "Perhaps you try to keep some decency then. Perhaps he has not made animals of you yet."

"Submit to him now, Anyanwu, and later, you can keep him from ever making animals of us."

Submit to him. The words brought a vile taste to her mouth, but she looked at Isaac's haggard face, and his obvi-

ous misery and his fear for her calmed her somehow. She
spoke softly. "When I hear you speak of him, I think you love
him more than he loves you."

"What does that matter?"

"It does not matter. You are a man to whom it need not
matter. I thought he could be a good husband. On the ship,
I worried that I could not be the wife he needed. I wanted
to please him. Now I can only think that he will never let
me go."

"Never?" Isaac repeated with gentle irony. "That's a long
time, even for you and him."

She turned away. Another time she might have been
amused to hear Isaac counseling patience. He was not a patient young man. But now, for her sake, he was desperate.

"You'll get freedom, Anyanwu," he said, "but first you'll
have to reach him. He's like a tortoise encased in a shell that
gets thicker every year. It will take a long time for you to
reach the man inside, but you have a long time, and there
is a man inside who must be reached. He was born as we
were. He's warped because he can't die, but he's still a man."
Isaac paused for breath. "Take the time, Anyanwu. Break the
shell; go in. He might turn out to be what you need, just as
I think you're what he needs."

She shook her head. She knew now how the slaves had
felt as they lay chained on the bench, the slaver's hot iron
burning into their flesh. In her pride, she had denied that
she was a slave. She could no longer deny it. Doro's mark
had been on her from the day they met. She could break free
of him only by dying and sacrificing her children and leaving him loose upon the world to become even more of an
animal. So much of what Isaac said seemed to be right. Or
was it her cowardice, her fear of Doro's terrible way of killing
that made his words seem so reasonable? How could she
know? Whatever she did would result in evil.

Isaac got up, came to her, took her hands, and drew her
to her feet. "I don't know what kind of husband I could be

to . . . to someone like you," he said. "But if wanting to please you counts for anything . . ."

Wearily, hopelessly, she allowed him to draw her closer. Had she been an ordinary woman, he could have crushed the breath from her. After a moment, she said, "If Doro had done this differently, Isaac, if he had told me when we met that he wanted a wife for his son and not for himself, I would not have shamed you by refusing you."

"I'm not ashamed," he whispered. "Just as long as you're not going to make him kill you . . ."

"If I had the courage of your mother, I would kill myself."

He stared at her in alarm.

"No, I will live," she said reassuringly. "I have not the courage to die. I had never thought before that I was a coward, but I am. Living has become too precious a habit."

"You're no more a coward than the rest of us," he said.

"The rest of you, at least, are not doing evil in your own eyes."

"Anyanwu . . ."

"No." She rested her head against him. "I have decided. I will not tell any more brave lies, even to myself." She looked up at his young face, his boy face. "We will marry. You are a good man, Isaac. I am the wrong wife for you, but perhaps, somehow, in this place, among these people, it will not matter."

He lifted her with the strength of his arms alone and carried her to the great soft bed, there to make the children who would prolong her slavery.

BOOK II

Lot's Children

1741

7

Doro had come to Wheatley to see to the welfare of one of his daughters. He had a feeling something was wrong with her, and as usual, he allowed such feelings to guide him.

As he rode into town from the landing, he could hear a loud dispute in progress—something about one man's cow ruining another's garden.

Doro approached the disputants slowly, watching them. They stood before Isaac, who sat on a bench in front of the house he and Anyanwu had built over fifty years before. Isaac, slender and youthful-looking in spite of his age and his thick gray hair, had no official authority to settle disputes. He had been a farmer, then a merchant—never a magistrate. But even when he was younger, people brought their disagreements to him. He was one of Doro's favorite sons. That made him powerful and influential. Also, he was known for his honesty and fairness. People liked him as they could not quite like Doro. They could worship Doro as a god, they could give him their love, their fear, their respect, but most found him too intimidating to like. One of the reasons Doro came back to a son like Isaac, old and past most of his usefulness, was that Isaac was a friend as well as a son. Isaac was one of the few people who could enjoy Doro's company without fear or falseness. And Isaac was an old man, soon to die. They all died so quickly. . . .

Doro reached the house and sat slouched for a moment on his black mare—a handsome animal who had come with his latest less-than-handsome body. The two men arguing over the cow had calmed down by now. Isaac had a way of calming unreasonable people. Another man could say and do exactly what Isaac said and did and be knocked down for his trouble. But people listened to Isaac.

"Pelham," Isaac was saying to the older of the two men—a gaunt, large-boned farmer whom Doro remembered as poor breeding stock. "Pelham, if you need help repairing that fence, I'll send one of my sons over."

"My boy can handle it," Pelham answered. "Anything to do with wood, he can handle."

Pelham's son, Doro recalled, had just about enough sense not to wet himself. He was a huge, powerful man with the mind of a child—a timid, gentle child, fortunately. Doro was glad to hear that he could handle something.

Isaac looked up, noticed for the first time the small sharp-featured stranger Doro was just then, and did what he had always done. With none of the talents of his brother Lale to warn him, Isaac inevitably recognized Doro. "Well," he said, "it's about time you got back to us." Then he turned toward the house and called, "Peter, come out here."

He stood up sprly and took the reins of Doro's horse, handing them to his son Peter as the boy came out of the house.

"Someday, I'm going to get you to tell me how you always know me," Doro said. "It can't be anything you see."

Isaac laughed. "I'd tell you if I understood it myself. You're you, that's all."

Now that Doro had spoken, Pelham and the other man

recognized him and spoke together in a confused babble of welcome.

Doro held up his hand. "I'm here to see my children," he said.

The welcomes subsided. The two men shook his hand, wished him a good evening, and hurried off to spread the news of his return. In his few words, he had told them that his visit was unofficial. He had not come to take a new body, and thus would not hold court to settle serious grievances or offer needed financial or other aid in the way that had become customary in Wheatley and some of his other settlements. This visit, he was only a man come to see his children—of whom there were forty-two here, ranging from infants to Isaac. It was rare for him to come to town for no other purpose than to see them, but when he did, other people left him alone. If anyone was in desperate need, they approached one of his children.

"Come on in," Isaac said. "Have some beer, some food." He did not have an old man's voice, high and cracking. His voice had become deeper and fuller—it contributed to his authority. But all Doro could hear in it now was honest pleasure.

"No food yet," Doro said. "Where's Anyanwu?"

"Helping with the Sloane baby. Mrs. Sloane let it get sick and almost die before she asked for help. Anyanwu says it has pneumonia." Isaac poured two tankards of beer.

"Is it going to be all right?"

"Anyanwu says so—although she was ready to strangle the Sloanes. Even they've been here long enough to know better than to let a child suffer that way with her only a few doors away." Isaac paused. "They're afraid of her blackness and her power. They think she's a witch, and the mold-medicine she made some poison."

Doro frowned, took a swallow of beer. The Sloanes were his newest wild seed—a couple who had found each other before Doro found them. They were dangerous, unstable, painfully sensitive people who heard the thoughts of others in intermittent bursts. When one received a burst of pain, anger, fear, any intense emotion, it was immediately transmitted to the other, and both suffered. None of this was deliberate or controlled. It simply happened. Helplessly, the Sloanes did a great deal of fighting and drinking and crying and praying for it to stop happening, but it would not. Not ever. That was why Doro had brought them to Wheatley. They were amazingly good breeding stock to be wild seed. He suspected that in one way or another, they were each descended from his people. Certainly, they were enough like his people to make excellent prey. And as soon as they had produced a few more children, Doro intended to take them both. It would be almost a kindness.

But for now, they would go on being abysmal parents, neglecting and abusing their children not out of cruelty, but because they hurt too badly themselves to notice their children's pain. In fact, they were likely to notice that pain only as a new addition to their own. Thus, sometimes their kind murdered children. Doro had not believed the Sloanes were dangerous in that way. Now, he was less certain.

"Isaac . . . ?"

Isaac looked at him, understood the unspoken question. "I assume you mean to keep the parents alive for a while."

"Yes."

"Then you'd better find another home for the child—and for every other child they have. Anyanwu says they should never have had any."

"Which means, of course, that they should have as many as possible."

"From your point of view, yes. Good useful people. I've already begun talking to them about giving up the child."

"Good. And?"

"They're worried about what people might think. I got the impression they'd be glad to get rid of the child if not for that—and one other thing."

"What?"

Isaac looked away. "They're worried about who'll care for

them when they're old. I told them you'd talk to them about that."

Doro smiled thinly. Isaac refused to lie to the people he thought Doro had selected as prey. Most often, he refused to tell them anything at all. Sometimes such people guessed what was being kept from them, and they ran. Doro took pleasure in hunting them down. Lann Sloane, Doro thought, would be especially good game. The man had a kind of animal awareness about him.

"Anyanwu would say you have on your leopard face now," Isaac commented.

Doro shrugged. He knew what Anyanwu would say, and that she meant it when she compared him to one kind of animal or another. Once she had said such things out of fear or anger. Now she said them out of grim hatred. She had made herself the nearest thing he had to an enemy. She obeyed. She was civil. But she could hold a grudge as no one Doro had ever known. She was alive because of Isaac. Doro had no doubt that if he had tried to give her to any of his other sons, she would have refused and died. He had asked her what Isaac said to change her mind, and when she refused to tell him, he had asked Isaac. To his surprise, Isaac refused to tell him, too. His son refused him very little, angered him very rarely. But this time . . .

"You've given her to me," Isaac had said. "Now she and I have to have things of our own." His face and his voice told Doro he would not say any more. Doro had left Wheatley the next day, confident that Isaac would take care of the details—marry the woman, build himself a house, help her learn to live in the settlement, decide on work for himself, start the children coming. Even at twenty-five, Isaac had been very capable. And Doro had not trusted himself to stay near either Isaac or Anyanwu. The depth of his own anger amazed him. Normally, people had only to annoy him to die for their error. He had to think to remember how long it had been since he had felt real anger and left those who caused it alive. But his son and this tiresome little forest peasant who was, fortunately for her, the best wild seed he had ever found, had lived. There was no forgiveness in Anyanwu, though. If she had learned to love her husband, she had not learned to forgive her husband's father. Now and then, Doro tried to penetrate her polite, aloof hostility, tried to break her, bring her back to what she was when he took her from her people. He was not accustomed to people resisting him, not accustomed to their hating him. The woman was a puzzle he had not yet solved—which was why now, after she had given him eight children, given Isaac five children, she was still alive. She would come to him again, without the coldness. She would make herself young without being told to do so, and she would come to him. Then, satisfied, he would kill her.

He licked his lips thinking about it, and Isaac coughed. Doro looked at his son with the old fondness and amended his thought. Anyanwu would live until Isaac died. She was keeping Isaac healthy, perhaps keeping him alive. She was doing it for herself, of course. Isaac had captured her long ago as he captured everyone, and she did not want to lose him any sooner than she had to. But her reasons did not matter. Inadvertently, she was doing Doro a service. He did not want to lose Isaac any sooner than he had to either. He shook his head, spoke to divert himself from the thought of his son's dying.

"I was down in the city on business," he said. "Then about a week ago when I was supposed to leave for England, I found myself thinking about Nweke." This was Anyanwu's youngest daughter. Doro claimed her as his daughter too, though Anyanwu disputed this. Doro had worn the body that fathered the girl, but he had not worn it at the time of the fathering. He had taken it afterward.

"Nweke's all right," Isaac said. "As all right as she can be, I suppose. Her transition is coming soon and she has her bad days, but Anyanwu seems to be able to comfort her."

"You haven't noticed her having any special trouble in the past few days?"

Isaac thought for a moment. "No, not that I recall. I

haven't seen too much of her. She's been helping to sew for a friend who's getting married—the Van Ness girl, you know."

Doro nodded.

"And I've been helping with the Boyden house. I guess you could say I've been building the Boyden house. I have to use what I've got now and then, no matter how Anyanwu nags me to slow down. Otherwise, I find myself walking a foot or so off the ground or throwing things. The ability doesn't seem to weaken with age."

"So I've noticed. Do you still enjoy it?"

"You couldn't know how much," Isaac said, smiling. He looked away, remembered pleasure flickering across his face, causing him to look years younger than he was. "Do you know we still fly sometimes—Anyanwu and I? You should see her as a bird of her own design. Color you wouldn't believe."

"I'm afraid I'll see you as a corpse if you go on doing such things. Firearms are improving slowly. Flying is a stupid risk."

"It's what I do," Isaac said quietly. "You know better than to ask me to give it up entirely."

Doro sighed. "I suppose I do."

"Anyway, Anyanwu always goes along with me—and she always flies slightly lower."

Anyanwu the protector, Doro thought with bitterness that surprised him. Anyanwu the defender of anyone who needed her. Doro wondered what she would do if he told her he needed her. Laugh? Very likely. She would be right, of course. Over the years it had become almost as difficult for him to get a lie past her as it was for her to lie successfully to him. The only reason she did not know of his colony of her African descendants in South Carolina was that he had never given her reason to ask. Even Isaac did not know.

"Does it bother you?" he asked Isaac. "Having her protecting you that way?"

"It did, at first," Isaac said. "I would outdistance her. I'm faster than any bird if I want to be. I would leave her behind and ignore her. But she was always there, laboring to catch up, hampered by winds that didn't bother me at all.

She never gave up. After a while, I began expecting her to be there. Now, I think I'd be more bothered if she didn't come along."

"Has she been shot?"

Isaac hesitated. "That's what the bright colors are for, I guess," he said finally. "To distract attention from me. Yes, she's been shot a couple of times. She falls a few yards, flops about to give me time to get away. Then she recovers and follows."

Doro looked up at the portrait of Anyanwu on the wall opposite the high, shallow fireplace. The style of the house was English here, Dutch there, Igbo somewhere else. Anyanwu had made earthen pots, variations of those she had once sold in the marketplaces of her homeland, and stout handsome baskets. People bought them from her and placed them around their houses as she had. Her work was both decorative and utilitarian, and here in her house with its Dutch fireplace and kas, its English settle and thronelike wainscot chairs, it evoked memories of a land she would not see again. Anyanwu had never sanded the floor as Dutch women did. Dirt was for sweeping out, she said contemptuously, not for scattering on the floor. She was more house proud than most English women Doro knew, but Dutch women shook their heads and gossiped about her "slovenly" housekeeping and pretended to pity Isaac. In fact, in the easy atmosphere of Wheatley, nearly every woman pitied Isaac so much that had he wished, he could have spread his valuable seed everywhere. Only Doro drew female attention more strongly—and only Doro took advantage of it. But then, Doro did not have to worry about outraged husbands—or an outraged wife.

The portrait of Anyanwu was extraordinary. Clearly, the Dutch artist had been captured by her beauty. He had draped her in a brilliant blue that set off her dark skin beautifully as blue always had. Even her hair had been hidden in blue cloth. She was holding a child—her first son by Isaac. The child, too, only a few months old, was partly covered by the blue. He looked out of the painting, large-eyed and handsomer than any infant should have been. Did Anyanwu deliberately conceive only handsome children? Every one of them was beautiful, even though Doro had fathered some with hideous bodies.

The portrait was a black madonna and child right down to Anyanwu's too-clear, innocent-seeming eyes. Strangers were moved to comment on the likeness. Some were appreciative, looking at the still handsome Anyanwu—she kept herself looking well for Isaac even as she aged herself along with him. Others were deeply offended, believing that someone actually had tried to portray the Virgin and Child as "black savages." Race prejudice was growing in the colonies— even in this formerly Dutch colony where things had once been so casual. Earlier in the year, there had been mass executions at New York City. Someone had been setting fires and the whites decided it must be the blacks. On little or no evidence, thirty-one blacks were killed—thirteen of them burned at the stake. Doro was beginning to worry about this upriver town. Of all his English colonial settlements, only in this one did his blacks not have the protection of powerful white owners. How soon before whites from elsewhere began to see them as fair game?

Doro shook his head. The woman in the portrait seemed to look down at him as he looked up. He should have had too much on his mind to think about her or about her daughter Ruth, called Nweke. He should not have allowed himself to be drawn back to Wheatley. It was good to see Isaac . . . but that woman!

"She was the right wife for me after all," Isaac was saying. "I remember her telling me she wasn't once before we married, but that was one of the few times I've known her to be wrong."

"I want to see her," Doro said abruptly. "And I want to see Nweke. I think the girl's a lot closer to her change than you realize."

"You think that's why you were pulled back here?"

Doro did not like the word "pulled," but he nodded without comment.

Isaac stood up. "Nweke first, while you're still in a fairly good mood." He went out of the house without waiting for Doro to answer. He loved Doro and he loved Anyanwu and it bothered him that the two got along so badly together.

"I don't see how you can be such a fool with her," he told Doro once—to Doro's surprise. "The woman is not temporary. She can be everything you need if you let her—mate, companion, business partner, her abilities complement yours so well. Yet all you do is humiliate her."

"I've never hurt her," Doro had told him. "Never hurt one of her children. You show me one other wild-seed woman I've allowed to live as long as she has after childbearing." He had not touched her children because from the first, she promised him that if any one of them was harmed, she would bear no more. No matter what he did to her, she would bear no more. Her sincerity was unmistakable; thus he refrained from preying on her least successful children, refrained from breeding her daughters to her sons—or bedding those daughters himself. She did not know what care he had taken to keep her content. She did not know, but Isaac should have.

"You treat her a little better than the others because she's a little more useful," Isaac had said. "But you still humiliate her."

"If she chooses to be humiliated by what I have her do, she's creating her own problem."

Isaac had looked at him steadily, almost angrily, for several seconds. "I know about Nweke's father," he had said. He had said it without fear. Over the years, he had come to learn that he was one of the few people who did not have to be afraid.

Doro had gone away from him feeling ashamed. He had not thought it was still possible for him to feel shame, but Anyanwu's presence seemed to be slowly awakening several long dormant emotions in him. How many women had he sent Isaac to without feeling a thing. Isaac had done as he was told and come home. Home from Pennsylvania, home from Maryland, home from Georgia, home from Spanish Florida . . . Isaac didn't mind either. He didn't like being away from Anyanwu and the children for long periods, but he didn't mind the women. And they certainly didn't mind him. He didn't mind that Doro had begotten eight of Anyanwu's children. Or seven. Only Anyanwu minded that. Only she felt humiliated. But Nweke's father was, perhaps, another matter.

The girl, eighteen years old, small and dark like her mother, came through the door, Isaac's arm around her shoulders. She was red-eyed as though she had been crying or as though she hadn't been sleeping. Probably both. This was a bad time for her.

"Is it you?" she whispered, seeing the sharp-featured stranger.

"Of course," Doro said, smiling.

His voice, the knowledge that he was indeed Doro, triggered tears. She went to him crying softly, looking for comfort in his arms. He held her and looked over her shoulder at Isaac.

"Whatever you've got to say to me, I deserve it," Isaac said. "I didn't notice and I should have. After all these years, I surely should have."

Doro said nothing, motioned Isaac back out the door.

Isaac obeyed silently, probably feeling more guilt than he should have. This was no ordinary girl. None of her brothers or sisters had reached Doro miles away with their desperation as their transitions neared. What had he felt about her? Anxiety, worry, more. Some indefinable feeling not only that she was near transition, but that she was on the verge of becoming something he had not known before. Something new. It was as though from New York City he had sensed another Anyanwu—new, different, attracting him, pulling him. He had never followed a feeling more willingly.

The girl moved in his arms and he took her to the high-backed settle near the fireplace. The narrow bench was nearly as uncomfortable as the wainscot chairs. Not for the first time, Doro wondered why Isaac and Anyanwu did not buy or have made some comfortable modern furniture. Surely they could afford it.

"What am I going to do?" the girl whispered. She had put her head against his shoulder, but even that close, Doro could hardly hear her. "It hurts so much."

"Endure it," he said simply. "It will end."

"*When!*" From a whisper to almost a scream. Then back to a whisper. "When?"

"Soon." He held her away from him a little so that he could see the small face, swollen and weary. The girl's coloring was gray rather than its usual rich dark brown. "You haven't been sleeping?"

"A little. Sometimes. The nightmares . . . only they aren't nightmares, are they?"

"You know what they are."

She shrank against the back of the bench. "You know David Whitten, two houses over?"

Doro nodded. The Whitten boy was twenty. Fairly good breeding stock. His family would be worth more in generations to come. They had a sensitivity that puzzled Doro. He did not know quite what they were becoming, but the feeling he got from them was good. They were a pleasant mystery that careful inbreeding would solve.

"Almost every night," Nweke said, "David . . . he goes to his sister's bed."

Startled, Doro laughed aloud. "Does he?"

"Just like married people. Why is that funny? They could get into trouble—brother and sister. They could . . ."

"They'll be all right."

She looked at him closely. "Did you know about it?"

"No." Doro was still smiling. "How old is the girl? Around sixteen?"

"Seventeen." Nweke hesitated. "She likes it."

"So do you," Doro observed.

Nweke twisted away, embarrassed. There was no coyness

to her; her embarrassment was real. "I didn't want to know about it. I didn't try to know!"

"Do you imagine I'm criticizing you for knowing? Me?"

She blinked, licked her lips. "Not you, I guess. Were you going to . . . to put them together anyway?"

"Yes."

"Here?"

"No. I was going to move them down to Pennsylvania. I see now that I'd better prepare a place for them quickly."

"They were almost a relief," Nweke said. "It was so easy to get caught up in what they were doing that sometimes I didn't have to feel other things. Last night, though . . . last night there were some Indians. They caught a white man. He had done something—killed one of their women or something. I was in his thoughts and they were all blurred at first. They tortured him. It took him so long . . . so long to die." Her hands were clinched tight around each other, her eyes wide with remembering. "They tore out his fingernails, then they cut him and burned him and the women bit him—bit pieces away like wolves at their kill. Then . . ." She stopped, choked. "Oh, God!"

"You were with him the whole time?" Doro asked.

"The whole time—through . . . everything." She was crying silently, not sobbing, only staring straight ahead as tears ran down her face and her nails dug themselves into her palms. "I don't understand how I can be alive after all that," she whispered.

"None of it happened to you," Doro said.

"All of it happened to me, every bit of it!"

Doro took her hands and unclinched the long, slender fingers. There were bloody marks on her palms where the nails had punctured. Doro ran a finger across the hard, neatly cut nails. "All ten," he said, "right where they should be. *None of it happened to you.*"

"You don't understand."

"I've been through transition, girl. In fact, I may have

been the first person ever to go through it—back more years than you can imagine. I understand, all right."

"Then you've forgotten! Maybe what happens doesn't leave marks on your body, but it leaves marks. It's real. Oh God, it's so real!" She began sobbing now. "If someone whips a slave or a criminal, I feel it, and it's as real to me as to the person under the lash!"

"But no matter how many times others die," Doro said, "you won't die."

"Why not? People die in transition. You died!"

He grinned. "Not entirely." Then he sobered. "Listen, the one thing you don't have to worry about is becoming what I am. You're going to be something special, all right, but nothing like me."

She looked at him timidly. "I would like to be like you."

Only the youngest of his children said such things. He pushed her head back to his shoulder. "No," he said, "that wouldn't be safe. I know what you're supposed to be. It wouldn't be a good idea for you to surprise me."

She understood and said nothing. Like most of his people, she did not try to move away from him when he warned or threatened. "What will I be?" she asked.

"I hope, someone who will be able to do for others what your mother can do for herself. A healer. The next step in healers. But even if you inherit talent from only one of your parents, you'll be formidable, and nothing like me. Your father, before I took him, could not only read thoughts but could see into closed places—mentally 'see.'"

"You're my father," she said against him. "I don't want to hear about anyone else."

"Hear it!" he said harshly. "When your transition is over, you'll see it in Isaac's mind and Anyanwu's. You should know from Anneke that a mind reader can't delude herself for long." Anneke Strycker Croon. She was the one who should have been having this talk with Nweke. She had been his best mind reader in a half-dozen generations—beautifully controlled. Once her transition was ended, she never entered another person's mind unless she wanted to. Her only flaw was that she was barren. Anyanwu tried to help her. Doro brought her one male body after another, all in vain. Thus, finally, Anneke had half adopted Nweke. The young girl and the old woman had found a similarity in each other that pleased Doro. It was rare for someone with Anneke's ability to take any pleasure at all in children. Doro saw the friendship as a good omen for Nweke's immature talents. But now, Anneke was three years dead, and Nweke was alone. No doubt her next words came at least partially out of her loneliness.

"Do you love us?" she asked.

"All of you?" Doro asked, knowing very well that she did not mean everyone—all his people.

"The ones of us who change," she said, not looking at him. "The different ones."

"You're all different. It's only a matter of degree."

She seemed to force herself to meet his eyes. "You're laughing at me. We endure so much pain . . . because of you, and you're laughing."

"Not at your pain, girl." He took a deep breath and stilled his amusement. "Not at your pain."

"You don't love us."

"No." He felt her start against him. "Not all of you."

"Me?" she whispered timidly, finally. "Do you love me?"

The favorite question of his daughters—only his daughters. His sons hoped he loved them, but they did not ask. Perhaps they did not dare to. Ah, but this girl . . .

When she was healthy, her eyes were like her mother's— clear whites and browns, baby's eyes. She had finer bones than Anyanwu—slenderer wrists and ankles, more prominent cheekbones. She was the daughter of one of Isaac's older sons—a son he had had by a wild-seed Indian woman who read thoughts and saw into distant closed places. The Indians were rich in untrapped wild seed that they tended to tolerate or even revere rather than destroy. Eventually, they would learn to be civilized and to understand as the whites understood that the hearing of voices, the seeing of visions, the moving of inanimate objects when no hand touched them, all the strange feelings, sensitivities, and abilities were evil or dangerous, or at the very least, imaginary. Then they too would weed out or grind down their different ones, thus freezing themselves in time, depriving their kind of any senses but those already familiar, depriving their children and their children's children of any weapons with which to confront Doro's people. And surely, in some future time, the day of confrontation would come. This girl, as rare and valuable for her father's blood as for her mother's, might well live to see that day. If ever he was to breed a long-lived descendant from Anyanwu, it would be this girl. He felt utterly certain of her. Over the years, he had taught himself not to assume that any new breed would be successful until transition ended and he saw the success before him. But the feelings that came to him from this girl were too powerful to doubt. He had no more certain urge than the urge that directed him toward the very best prey. Now it spoke to him as it had never spoken before, even for Isaac or Anyanwu. The girl's talent teased and enticed him. He would not kill her, of course. He did not kill the best of his children. But he would have what he could of her now. And she would have what she wanted of him.

"I came back because of you," he said, smiling. "Not because of any of the others, but because I could feel how near you were to your change. I wanted to see for myself that you were all right."

That was apparently enough for her. She caught him in a joyful stranglehold and kissed him not at all as a daughter should kiss her father.

"I do like it," she said shyly. "What David and Melanie do. Sometimes I try to know when they're doing it. I try to share it. But I can't. It comes to me of itself or not at all." And she echoed her stepfather—her grandfather. "I have to have something of my own!" Her voice had taken on a fierceness, as though Doro owed her what she was demanding.

"Why tell me?" he said, playing with her. "I'm not even handsome right now. Why not choose one of the town boys?"

She clutched at his arms, her hard little nails now digging into his flesh. "You're laughing again!" she hissed. "Am I so ridiculous? Please . . . ?"

To his disgust, Doro found himself thinking about Anyanwu. He had always resisted the advances of her daughters before. It had become a habit. Nweke was the last child Doro had coerced Anyanwu into bearing, but Doro had gone on respecting Anyanwu's superstitions—not that Anyanwu appreciated the kindness. Well, Anyanwu was about to lose her place with him to this young daughter. Whatever he had been reaching for, trying to bribe from the mother, the daughter would supply. The daughter was not wild seed with years of freedom to make her stubborn. The daughter had been his from the moment of her conception—his property as surely as though his brand were burned into her flesh. She even thought of herself as his property. His children, young and old, male and female, most often made the matter of ownership very simple for him. They accepted his authority and seemed to need his assurance that strange as they were, they still belonged to someone.

"Doro?" the girl said softly.

She had a red kerchief tied over her hair. He pushed it back to reveal her thick dark hair, straighter than her mother's but not as straight as her father's. She had combed it back and pinned it in a large knot. Only a single heavy curl hung free to her smooth brown shoulder. He resisted the impulse to remove the pins, let the other curls free. He and the girl would not have much time together. He did not want her wasting what they had pinning up her hair. Nor did he want her appearance to announce at once to Anyanwu what had happened. Anyanwu would find out—probably very quickly— but she would not find out through any apparent brazenness on the part of her daughter. She would find out in such a way as to cause her to blame Doro. Her daughter still needed her too badly to alienate her. No one in any of Doro's set-

tlements was as good at helping people through transition as
Anyanwu. Her body could absorb the physical punishment of
restraining a violent, usually very strong young person. She
did not hurt her charges or allow them to hurt themselves.
They did not frighten or disgust her. She was their companion, their sister, their mother, their lover through their agony.
If they could survive their own mental upheaval, they would
come through to find that she had taken good care of their
physical bodies. Nweke would need that looking after—whatever she needed right now.

He lifted the girl, carried her to an alcove bed in one of
the children's bedrooms. He did not know whether it was her
bed, did not care. He undressed her, brushing away her hands
when she tried to help, laughing softly when she commented
that he seemed to know pretty well how to get a woman out
of her clothes. She did not know much about undressing a
man, but she fumbled and tried to help him.

And she was as lovely as he had expected. A virgin of
course. Even in Wheatley, young girls usually saved themselves for husbands, or for Doro. She was ready for him. She
had some pain, but it didn't seem to matter to her.

"Better than with David and Melanie," she whispered
once, and held onto him as though fearing he might leave
her.

Nweke and Doro were in the kitchen popping corn and
drinking beer when Isaac and Anyanwu came in. The bed
had been remade and Nweke had been properly dressed and
cautioned against even the appearance of brazenness. "Let
her be angry at me," Doro had said, "not at you. Say nothing."

"I don't know how to think about her now," Nweke said.
"My sisters whispered that we could never have you because
of her. Sometimes I hated her. I thought she kept you for
herself."

"Did she?"

". . . no." She glanced at him uncertainly. "I think she

tried to protect us from you. She thought we needed it."
Nweke shuddered. "What will she feel for me now?"

Doro did not know, and he did not intend to leave until
he found out. Until he could see that any anger Anyanwu
felt would do her daughter no harm.

"Maybe she won't find out," the girl said hopefully.

That was when Doro took her into the kitchen to investigate the stew Anyanwu had left simmering and the bread
untended in its bake kettle, hot and tender, unburned in the
coals. They set the table, then Nweke suggested beer and
popcorn. Doro agreed, humoring her, hoping she would relax
and not worry about facing her mother. She seemed peace-
ful and content when Isaac and Anyanwu came in, yet she
avoided her mother's eyes. She stared down into her beer.

Doro saw Anyanwu frown, saw her go to Nweke and take
the small chin in her fingers and raise it so that she could
see Nweke's frightened eyes.

"Are you well?" she asked Nweke in her own language.
She spoke perfect English now, along with Dutch and a few
words of some Indian and foreign African dialects, but at
home with her children, she often spoke as though she had
never left home. She would not adopt a European name or
call her children by their European names—though she had
condescended to give them European names at Doro's insistence. Her children could speak and understand as well as
she could. Even Isaac, after all the years, could understand
and speak fairly well. No doubt, he heard as clearly as Doro
and Nweke the wariness and tension in Anyanwu's soft question.

Nweke did not answer. Frightened, she glanced at Doro.
Anyanwu followed the glance and her infant-clear, bright eyes
took on a look of incongruous ferocity. She said nothing. She
only stared with growing comprehension. Doro met her gaze
levelly until she turned back to look at her daughter.

"Nweke, little one, are you well?" she whispered urgently.

Something happened within Nweke. She took Anyanwu's
hands between her own, held them for a moment, smiling.

Finally she laughed aloud—delighted child's laughter with no hint of falseness or gloating. "I'm well," she said. "I didn't know how well until this moment. It has been so long since there were no voices, nothing pulling at me or hurting me." Relief made her forget her fear. She met Anyanwu's eyes, her own eyes full of the wonder of her newfound peace.

Anyanwu closed her eyes for a moment, drew a long, shuddering breath.

"She's all right," Isaac said from where he sat at the table. "That's enough."

Anyanwu looked at him. Doro could not read what passed between them, but after a moment, Isaac repeated, "That's enough."

And it seemed to be. At that moment, the twenty-two-year-old son Peter, incongruously called Chukwuka—God is Supreme—arrived, and dinner was served.

Doro ate slowly, recalling how he had laughed at the boy's Igbo name. He had asked Anyanwu where she had found her sudden devotion to God—any god. Chukwuka was a common enough name in her homeland, but it was not a name he would have expected from a woman who claimed she helped herself. Predictably, Anyanwu had been silent and unamused at his question. It took him a surprisingly long time to begin to wonder whether the name was supposed to be a charm—her pathetic attempt to protect the boy from him. Where had Anyanwu found her sudden devotion to God? Where else but in her fear of Doro? Doro smiled to himself.

Then he stopped smiling as Nweke's brief peace ended. The girl screamed—a long, ragged, terrible sound that reminded Doro of cloth tearing. Then she dropped the dish of corn she had been bringing to the table and collapsed to the floor unconscious.

8

Nweke lay twitching, still unconscious in the middle of Isaac and Anyanwu's bed. Anyanwu said it was easier to care for her here in a bed merely enclosed within curtains than in one of the alcove beds. Oblivious to Doro's presence, Anyanwu had stripped Nweke to her shift and removed the pins from her hair. The girl looked even smaller than she was now, looked lost in the deep, soft feather mattress. She looked like a child. Doro felt a moment of unease, even fear for her. He remembered her laughter minutes earlier and wondered whether he would hear it again.

"This is transition," Anyanwu said to him, neutral-voiced.

He glanced at her. She stood beside the bed looking weary and concerned. Her earlier hostility had been set aside—and only set aside. Doro knew her too well to think it had been forgotten.

"Are you sure?" he asked. "She's passed out before, hasn't she?"

"Oh yes. But this is transition. I know it."

He thought she was probably right. He sensed the girl

very strongly now. If his body had been a lesser one or one he had given long use, he would not have dared to stay so near her.

"Will you stay?" Anyanwu asked, as though hearing his thoughts.

"For a while."

"Why? You have never stayed before when my children changed."

"This one is special."

"So I have seen." She gave him another of her venomous looks. "Why, Doro?"

He did not pretend to misunderstand. "Do you know what she has been receiving? What thoughts she has been picking up?"

"She told me about the man last night—the torture."

"Not that. She's been picking up people making love—picking it up often."

"And you thought that was not enough for an unmarried girl!"

"She's eighteen years old. It wasn't enough."

Nweke made a small sound as though she were having a bad dream. No doubt she was. The worst of dreams. And she would not be permitted to wake fully until it was over.

"You have not molested my children before," she said.

"I wondered whether you had noticed."

"Is that it?" She turned to face him. "Were you punishing me for my . . . my ingratitude?"

". . . no." His eyes looked past her for a moment though he did not move. "I'm not interested in punishing you any longer."

She turned a little too quickly and sat down beside the bed. She sat on a chair Isaac had made for her—a taller-than-normal chair so that in spite of her small size and the height of the bed, she could see and reach Nweke easily. Eventually she would move onto the bed with the girl. People in transition needed close physical contact to give them some hold on reality.

But for now, Anyanwu's move to the chair was to conceal emotion. Fear, Doro wondered, or shame or anger or hatred. . . . His last serious attempt to punish her had involved Nweke's father. That attempt had stood between them all Nweke's life. Of all the things she considered that he had done to her, that was the worst. Yet it was a struggle she had come very near winning. Perhaps she had won. Perhaps that was why the incident could still make him uneasy.

Doro shook his head, turned his attention to the girl. "Do you think she'll come through all right?" he asked.

"I have never had any of them die in my care."

He ignored the sarcasm in her voice. "What do you feel, Anyanwu? How can you help them so well when you cannot reach their minds in even the shadowy way that I can?"

"I bit her a little. She is strong and healthy. There is nothing, no feeling of death about her." He had opened his mouth, but she held up a hand to stop him. "If I could tell you more clearly, I would. Perhaps I will find a way—on the day you find a way to tell me how you move from body to body."

"Touché," he said, and shrugged. He took a chair from beside the fireplace and brought it to the foot of the bed. There, he waited. When Nweke came to, shaking and crying wildly, he spoke to her, but she did not seem to hear him. Anyanwu went onto the bed silent, grim-faced, and held the girl until her tears had slowed, until she had stopped shaking.

"You are in transition," Doro heard Anyanwu whisper. "Stay with us until tomorrow and you will have the powers of a goddess." That was all she had time to say. Nweke's body stiffened. She made retching sounds and Anyanwu drew back from her slightly. But instead of vomiting, she went limp again, her consciousness gone to join someone else's.

Eventually, she seemed to come to again, but her open eyes were glazed and she made the kind of gibbering sounds Doro had heard in madhouses—especially in the madhouses to which his people had been consigned when their transitions caught them outside their settlements. Nweke's face was like something out of a madhouse, too—twisted and unrecognizable, covered with sweat, eyes, nose, and mouth streaming. Wearily, sadly, Doro got up to leave.

There had been a time when he had to watch transitions—when no one else could be trusted not to run away or murder his writhing charge or perform some dangerous, stupid ritual of exorcism. But that was long ago. He was not only building a people now; they were building themselves. It was no longer necessary for him to do everything, see everything.

He looked back once as he reached the door and saw that Anyanwu was watching him.

"It is easier to doom a child to this than to stay and watch it happen, isn't it?" she said.

"I watched it happen to your ancestors!" he said angrily. "And I'll watch it happen to your descendants when even you are dust!" He turned and left her.

When Doro had gone, Anyanwu clambered off the featherbed and went to the washstand. There she poured water from the pitcher to the basin and wet a towel. Nweke was having a difficult time already, poor girl. That meant a long, terrible night. There was no duty Anyanwu hated more than this—especially with her own children. But no one else could handle it as well as she could.

She bathed the girl's face, thinking, praying: *Oh, Nweke, little one, stay until tomorrow. The pain will go away tomorrow.*

Nweke quieted as though she could hear the desperate thoughts. Perhaps she could. Her face was gray and still now. Anyanwu caressed it, seeing traces of the girl's father in it as she always did. There was a man damned from the day of his birth—all because of Doro. He was fine breeding stock, oh yes. He was a forest animal unable to endure the company of other people, unable to get any peace from their thoughts. He had not been as Nweke was now, receiving only large emotions, great stress. He received everything. And also, he saw visions of things far from him, beyond the range of even her eyes, of things closed away from any eyes. In a city, even in a small town, he would have gone mad. And his vulnerability was not a passing thing, not a transition from powerlessness to godlike power. It was a condition he had had to endure to the day of his death. He had loved Doro pathetically because Doro was the only person whose thoughts could not entangle him. His mind would not reach into Doro's. Doro said this was a matter of self-preservation; the mind that reached into his became his. It was consumed, extinguished, and Doro took over the body it had animated. Doro said even people like this man—Thomas, his name was—even people whose mind-reading ability seemed completely out of control somehow never reached into Doro's thoughts. People with control could force themselves to try— as they could force their hands into fire—but they could not make the attempt without first feeling the "heat" and knowing they were doing a dangerous thing.

Thomas could not force his "hands" into anything at all. He lived alone in a filthy cabin well hidden within a dark, awesome Virginia woods. When Doro brought her to him, he cursed her. He told her she should not mind the way he lived, since she was from Africa where people swung through the trees and went naked like animals. He asked Doro what wrong he had done to be given a nigger woman. But it was not his wrong that had won him Anyanwu. It was hers.

Now and then, Doro courted her in his own way. He arrived with a new body—sometimes an appealing one. He paid attention to her, treated her as something more than only a breeding animal. Then, courting done, he took her from Isaac's bed to his own and kept her there until he was certain she was pregnant. Still, Isaac urged her to use these times to tie Doro to her and strengthen whatever influence she had with him. But Anyanwu never learned to forgive Doro's unnecessary killings, his casual abuse when he was not courting her, his open contempt for any belief of hers that did not concur with his, the blows for which she could not retaliate

and from which she could not flee, the acts she must perform for him no matter what her beliefs. She had lain with
him as a man while he wore the body of a woman. She had
not been able to become erect naturally. He was a beautiful
woman, but he repelled her. Nothing he did gave her pleasure. Nothing.

No . . .

She sighed and stared down at her daughter's still face.
No, her children gave her pleasure. She loved them, but she
also feared for them. Who knew what Doro might decide to
do to them? What would he do to this one?

She lay down close to Nweke, so that the girl would not
awaken alone. Perhaps even now, some part of Nweke's spirit
knew that Anyanwu was nearby. Anyanwu had seen that people in transition thrashed around less if she lay close to them
and sometimes held them. If her nearness, her touch, gave
them any peace, she was willing to stay close. Her thoughts
returned to Thomas.

Doro had been angry with her. He never seemed to get
truly angry with anyone else—but then, his other people loved
him. He could not tell her that he was angry because she did
not love him. Even he could not utter such foolishness. Certainly, he did not love her. He did not love anyone except
perhaps Isaac and a very few of his other children. Yet he
wanted Anyanwu to be like his many other women and treat
him like a god in human form, competing for his attention
no matter how repugnant his latest body nor even whether
he might be looking for a new body. They knew he took
women almost as readily as he took men. Especially, he took
women who had already given him what he wanted of them—
usually several children. They served him and never thought
they might be his next victims. Someone else. Not them.
More than once, Anyanwu wondered how much time she
might have left. Had Doro merely been waiting for her to
help this last daughter through transition? If so, he might be
in for a surprise. Once Nweke had power and could care for
herself, Anyanwu did not plan to stay in Wheatley. She had

had enough of Doro and everything to do with him; and no person was better fitted to escape him than she was.

If only Thomas had been able to escape . . .

But Thomas had not had power—only potential, unrealized, unrealizable. He had had a long sparse beard when Doro took her to him, and long black hair clotted together with the grease and dirt of years of neglect. His clothing might have stood alone, starched as it was with layers of dirt and sweat, but it was too ragged to stand. In some places, it seemed to be held together by the dirt. There were sores on his body, ignored and filthy—as though he were rotting away while still alive. He was a young man, but his teeth were almost gone. His breath, his entire body, stank unbelievably.

And he did not care. He did not care about anything—beyond his next drink. He looked, except for the sparse beard, like an Indian, but he thought of himself as a white man. And he thought of Anyanwu as a nigger.

Doro had known what he was doing when in exasperation, he had said to her, "You think I ask too much of you? You think I abuse you? I'm going to show you how fortunate you've been!"

And he gave her to Thomas. And he stayed to see that she did not run away or kill the grotesque ruin of a man instead of sharing his vermin-infested bed.

But Anyanwu had never killed anyone except in self-defense. It was not her business to kill. She was a healer.

At first, Thomas cursed her and reviled her blackness. She ignored this. "Doro has put us together," she told him calmly. "If I were green, it would make no difference."

"Shut your mouth!" he said. "You're a black bitch brought here for breeding and nothing more. I don't have to listen to your yapping!"

She had not struck back. After the first moments, she had not even been angry. Nor had she been pitying or repelled. She knew Doro expected her to be repelled, but that proved nothing more than that he could know her for decades without really knowing her at all. This was a man sick in a dozen ways—the remnants of a man. Healer that she was, creator of medicines and poisons, binder of broken bones, comforter—could she take the remnants here and build them into a man again?

Doro looked at people, healthy or ill, and wondered what kind of young they could produce. Anyanwu looked at the sick—especially those with problems she had not seen before—and wondered whether she could defeat their disease.

Helplessly, Thomas caught her thoughts. "Stay away from me!" he muttered alarmed. "You heathen! Go rattle your bones at someone else!"

Heathen, yes. He was a god-fearing man himself. Anyanwu went to his god and said, "Find a town and buy us food. That man won't sire any children as he is now, living mostly on beer and cider and rum—which he probably steals."

Doro stared at her as though he could not think of anything to say. He was wearing a big burly body and had been using it to chop wood while Anyanwu and Thomas got acquainted.

"There's food enough here," he protested finally. "There are deer and bear and game birds and fish. Thomas grows a few things. He has what he needs."

"If he has it, he is not eating it!"

"Then he'll starve. But not before he gets you with a child."

In anger that night, Anyanwu took her leopard form for the first time in years. She hunted deer, stalking them as she had at home so long ago, moving with the old stealth, using her eyes and her ears even more efficiently than a true leopard might. The result was as it had been at home. Deer were deer. She brought down a sleek doe, then took her human form again, threw her prize across her shoulders, and carried it to Thomas' cabin. By morning, when the two men awoke, the doe had been skinned, cleaned, and butchered. The cabin was filled with the smell of roasting venison.

Doro ate heartily and went out. He didn't ask where the fresh meat had come from or thank Anyanwu for it. He simply accepted it. Thomas was less trusting. He drank a little rum, sniffed at the meat Anyanwu gave him, nibbled at a little of it.

"Where'd this come from?" he demanded.

"I hunted last night," Anyanwu said. "You have nothing here."

"Hunted with what? My musket? Who allowed you to . . ."

"I did not hunt with your musket! It's there, you see?" She gestured toward where the gun, the cleanest thing in the cabin, hung from a peg by the door. "I don't hunt with guns," she added.

He got up and checked the musket anyway. When he was satisfied, he came to stand over her, reeking and forcing her to breathe very shallowly. "What did you hunt with, then?" he demanded. He wasn't a big man, but sometimes, like now, he spoke in a deep rumbling voice. "What did you use?" he repeated. "Your nails and teeth?"

"Yes," Anyanwu said softly.

He stared at her for a moment, his eyes suddenly wide. "A cat!" he whispered. "From woman to cat to woman again. But how . . . ?" Doro had explained that since this man had never completed transition, he had no control over his ability. He could not deliberately look into Anyanwu's thoughts, but he could not refrain from looking into them either. Anyanwu was near him and her thoughts, unlike Doro's, were open and unprotected.

"I was a cat," she said simply. "I can be anything. Shall I show you?"

"No!"

"It's like what you do," she reassured him. "You can see what I'm thinking. I can change my shape. Why not eat the meat? It is very good." She would wash him, she decided. This day, she would wash him and start on the sores. The stink was unendurable.

He snatched up his portion of food and threw it into the fire. "Witch food!" he muttered, and turned his jug up to his mouth.

Anyanwu stifled an impulse to throw the rum into the fire. Instead, she stood up and took it from his hands as he lowered it. He did not try to keep it from her. She set it aside and faced him.

"We are all witches," she said. "All Doro's people. Why would he notice us if we were ordinary?" She shrugged. "He wants a child from us because it will not be ordinary."

He said nothing. Only stared at her with unmistakable suspicion and dislike.

"I have seen what you can do," she continued. "You keep speaking my thoughts, knowing what you should not know. I will show you what I can do."

"I don't want to—"

"Seeing it will make it more real to you. It isn't a hard thing to watch. I don't become ugly. Most of the changes happen inside me." She was undressing as she spoke. It was not necessary. She could shrug out of the clothing as she changed, shed it as a snake sheds its skin, but she wanted to move very slowly for this man. She did not expect her nudity to excite him. He had seen her unclothed the night before and he had turned away and gone to sleep—leaving her to go hunting. She suspected that he was impotent. She had made her body slender and young for him, hoping to get his seed in her and escape quickly, but last night had convinced her that she had more work to do here than she had thought. And if the man was impotent, all that she did might not be enough. What would Doro do then?

She changed very slowly, took the leopard form, all the while keeping her body between Thomas and the door. Between Thomas and the gun. That was wise because when she had finished, when she stretched her small powerful cat-body and spread her claws, leaving marks in the packed earth floor, he dived for his gun.

Claws sheathed, Anyanwu batted him aside. He screamed and shrank back from her. By his manner, arm thrown up to protect his throat, eyes wide, he seemed to expect her to leap upon him. He was waiting to die. Instead, she approached him slowly, her body relaxed. Purring, she rubbed her head against his knee. She looked up at him, saw that the protective arm had come down from the throat. She rubbed her fur against his leg and went on purring. Finally, almost unwillingly, his hand touched her head, caressed tentatively. When she had him scratching her neck—which did not itch—and muttering to himself, "My God!" she broke away, went over and picked up a piece of venison and brought it back to him.

"I don't want that!" he said.

She began to growl low in her throat. He took a step back but that put him against the rough log wall. When Anyanwu followed, there was nowhere for him to go. She tried to put the meat into his hand, but he snatched the hand away. Finally, around the meat, she gave a loud, coughing roar.

Thomas sank to the floor terrified, staring at her. She dropped the meat into his lap and roared again.

He picked it up and ate—for the first time in how long, she wondered. If he wanted to kill himself, why was he doing it in this slow terrible way, letting himself rot alive? Oh, this day she would wash him and begin his healing. If he truly wanted to die, let him hang himself and be done with it.

When he had finished the venison, she became a woman again and calmly put on her clothing as he watched.

"I could see it," he whispered after a long silence. "I could see your body changing inside. Everything changing . . ." He shook his head uncomprehending, then asked: "Could you turn white?"

The question startled her. Was he really so concerned about her color? Usually Doro's people were not. Most of them had backgrounds too thoroughly mixed for them to sneer at anyone. Anyanwu did not know this man's ancestry but she was certain he was not as white as he seemed to think. The Indian appearance was too strong.

"I have never made myself white," she said. "In Wheatley, everyone knows me. Who would I deceive—and why should I try?"

"I don't believe you," he said. "If you could become white, you would!"

"Why?"

He stared at her hostilely.

"I'm content," she said finally. "If I have to be white some day to survive, I will be white. If I have to be a leopard to hunt and kill, I will be a leopard. If I have to travel quickly across land, I'll become a large bird. If I have to cross the sea, I'll become a fish." She smiled a little. "A dolphin, perhaps."

"Will you become white for me?" he asked. His hostility had died as she spoke. He seemed to believe her. Perhaps he was hearing her thoughts. If so, he was not hearing them clearly enough.

"I think you will have to endure it somehow that I am black," she said with hostility of her own. "This is the way I look. No one has ever told me I was ugly!"

He sighed. "No, you're not. Not by some distance. It's just that . . ." He stopped, wet his lips. "It's just that I thought you could make yourself look like my wife . . . just a little."

"You have a wife?"

He rubbed at a scabbed-over sore on his arm. Anyanwu could see it through a hole in his sleeve and it did not look as though it was healing properly. The flesh around the scab was very red and swollen.

"I had a wife," he said. "Big, handsome girl with hair yellow as gold. I thought it would be all right if we didn't live in a town or have neighbors too nearby. She wasn't one of Doro's people, but he let me have her. He gave me enough money to buy some land, get a start in tobacco. I thought things would be fine."

"Did she know you could hear her thoughts?"

He gave her a look of contempt. "Would she have married me if she had? Would anyone?"

"One of Doro's people, perhaps. One who could also hear thoughts."

"You don't know what you're talking about," he said bitterly.

His tone made her think, made her remember that some of the most terrible of Doro's people were like Thomas. They weren't as sensitive, perhaps. Living in towns didn't seem to bother them. But they drank too much and fought and abused or neglected their children and occasionally murdered each other before Doro could get around to taking them. Thomas was probably right to marry a more ordinary woman.

"Why did your wife leave?" she asked.

"Why do you think! I couldn't keep out of her thoughts any more than I can keep out of yours. I tried not to let her know, but sometimes things came to me so clearly . . . I'd answer, thinking she had spoken aloud and she hadn't and she didn't understand and . . ."

"And she was afraid."

"God, yes. After a while, she was terrified. She went home to her parents and wouldn't even see me when I went after her. I guess I don't blame her. After that there were only . . . women like you that Doro brings me."

"We're not such bad women. I'm not."

"You can't wait to get away from me!"

"What would you feel for a woman who was covered with filth and sores?"

He blinked, looked at himself. "And I guess you're used to better!"

"Of course I am! Let me help you and you will be better. You could not have been this way for your wife."

"You're not her!"

"No. She could not help you. I can."

"I didn't ask for your—"

"Listen! She ran away from you because you are Doro's. You are a witch and she was afraid and disgusted. I am not afraid or disgusted."

"You'd have no right to be," he muttered sullenly. "You're

more witch than I'll ever be. I still don't believe what I saw you do."

"If my thoughts are reaching you even some of the time, you should believe what I do and what I say. I have not been telling you lies. I am a healer. I have lived for over three hundred and fifty years. I have seen leprosy and huge growths that bring agony and babies born with great holes where their faces should be and other things. You are far from being the worst thing I have seen."

He stared at her, frowned intently as though reaching for a thought that eluded him. It occurred to her that he was trying to hear her thoughts. Finally, though, he seemed to give up. He shrugged and sighed. "Could you help any of those others?"

"Sometimes I could help. Sometimes I can dissolve away dangerous growths or open blind eyes or heal sores that will not heal themselves. . . ."

"You can't take away the voices or the visions, can you?"

"The thoughts you hear from other people?"

"Yes, and what I 'see.' Sometimes I can't tell reality from vision."

She shook her head sadly. "I wish I could. I have seen others tormented as you are. I'm better than what your people call a doctor. Much better. But I am not as good as I long to be. I think I am flawed like you."

"All Doro's children are flawed—godlings with feet of clay."

Anyanwu understood the reference. She had read the sacred book of her new land, the Bible, in the hope of improving her understanding of the people around her. In Wheatley, Isaac told people she was becoming a Christian. Some of them did not realize he was joking.

"I was not born to Doro," she told Thomas. "I am what he calls wild seed. But it makes no difference. I am flawed anyway."

He glanced at her, then down at the floor. "Well, I'm not

as flawed as you think." He spoke very softly. "I'm not impotent."

"Good. If you were and Doro found out . . . he might decide you could not be useful to him any longer."

It was as though she had said something startling. He jumped, peered at her in a way that made her draw back in alarm, then demanded: "What's the matter with you! How can you care what happens to me? How can you let Doro breed you like a goddamn cow—and to me! You're not like the others."

"You said I was a dog. A black bitch."

Even through the dirt, she could see him redden. "I'm sorry," he said after several seconds.

"Good. I almost hit you when you said it—and I am very strong."

"I don't doubt it."

"I care what Doro does to me. He knows I care. I tell him."

"People don't, normally."

"Yes. That's why I'm here. Things are not right to me merely because he says they are. He is not my god. He brought me to you as punishment for my sacrilege." She smiled. "But he does not understand that I would rather lie with you than with him."

Thomas said nothing for so long that she reached out and touched his hand, concerned.

He looked at her, smiled without showing his bad teeth. She had not seen him smile before. "Be careful," he said. "Doro should never find out how thoroughly you hate him."

"He has known for years."

"And you're still alive? You must be very valuable."

"I must be," she agreed bitterly.

He sighed. "I should hate him myself. I don't somehow. I can't. But . . . I think I'm glad you do. I never met anyone who did before." He hesitated again, raised his night-black eyes to hers. "Just be careful."

She nodded, thinking that he reminded her of Isaac. Isaac

too was always cautioning her. Then Thomas got up and went to the door.

"Where are you going?" she asked.

"To the stream out back to wash." The smile again, tentatively. "Do you really think you can take care of these sores? I've had some of them for a long time."

"I can heal them. They will come back, though, if you don't stay clean and stop drinking so much. Eat food!"

"I don't know whether you're here to conceive a child or turn me into one," he muttered, and closed the door behind him.

Anyanwu went out and fashioned a crude broom of twigs. She swept the mounds of litter out of the cabin, then washed what could be washed. She did not know what to do about the vermin. The fleas alone were terrible. Left to herself, she would have burned the cabin and built another. But Thomas would not be likely to go along with that.

She cleaned and cleaned and cleaned and the terrible little cabin still did not suit her. There were no clean blankets, there was no clean clothing for Thomas. Eventually, he came in wearing the same filthy rags over skin scrubbed pale and nearly raw. He seemed acutely embarrassed when Anyanwu began stripping the rags from him.

"Don't be foolish," she told him. "When I start on those sores, you won't have time for shame—or for any other thing."

He became erect. Scrawny and sick as his body was, he was, as he had said, not impotent.

"All right," murmured Anyanwu with gentle amusement. "Have your pleasure now and your pain later."

His clumsy fingers had begun fumbling with her clothing, but they stopped suddenly. "*No!*" he said as though the pain had to come first after all. "No." He turned his back to her.

"But . . . why?" Anyanwu laid a hand on his shoulder. "You want to, and it's all right. Why else am I here?"

He spoke through his teeth as though every word was

hurting him. "Are you still so eager to get away from me? Can't you stay a little while?"

"Ah." She rubbed the shoulder, feeling the bones sharply through their thin covering of flesh. "The women take your seed and leave you as quickly as possible."

He said nothing.

She stepped closer to him. He was smaller than Isaac, smaller than most of the male bodies Doro brought her. It was strange to be able to meet a man's eyes without looking up. "It will be that way for me too," she said. "I have a husband. I have children. And also . . . Doro knows how quickly I can conceive. I am always deliberately quick with him. I must take your seed and leave you. But I will not leave you today."

He stared at her for a moment, the black eyes intent as though again he was trying to control his ability, hear her thoughts now when he wanted to hear them. She found herself hoping her child—his child—would have those eyes. They were the only things about him that had never needed cleaning or healing to show their beauty. That was surprising considering how much he drank.

He seized her suddenly, as though it had just occurred to him that he could, and held her tightly for long moments before leading her to his splintery shelf bed.

Doro came in hours later, bringing flour, sugar, coffee, corn meal, salt, eggs, butter, dry peas, fresh fruit and vegetables, blankets, cloth that could be sewn into clothing, and, incidentally, a new body. He had bought or stolen someone's small crudely made wagon to carry his things.

"Thank you," Anyanwu told him gravely, wanting him to see that her gratitude was real. It was rare these days for him to do what she asked. She wondered why he had bothered this time. Certainly he had not planned to the day before.

Then she saw him looking at Thomas. The bath had made the most visible difference in Thomas' appearance, and Anyanwu had shaved him, cut off much of his hair, and combed the rest. But there were other more subtle changes. Thomas was smiling, was helping to carry the supplies into the cabin instead of standing aside apathetically, instead of muttering at Anyanwu when she passed him, her arms full.

"Now," he said, happily oblivious to Doro's eyes on him. "Now we'll see how well you can cook, Sun Woman."

That stupid name, she thought desperately. Why had he called her that? He must have read it in her thoughts. She had not told him it was Doro's name for her.

Doro smiled. "I never thought you could do this so well," he said to her. "I would have brought you my sick ones before."

"I am a healer," she said. His smile terrified her for Thomas' sake. It was a smile full of teeth and utterly without humor. "I have conceived," she said, though she had not meant to tell him that for days—perhaps weeks. Suddenly, though, she wanted him away from Thomas. She knew Doro. Over the years, she had come to know him very well. He had given her to a man he hoped would repel her, make her know how well off she had been. Instead, she had immediately begun helping the man, healing him so that eventually he would not repel anyone. Clearly, she had not been punished.

"Already," Doro said in mock surprise. "Shall we leave then?"

"Yes."

He glanced toward the cabin where Thomas was.

Anyanwu came around the wagon and caught Doro's arms. He was wearing the body of a round-faced very young-looking white man. "Why did you bring the supplies?" she demanded.

"You wanted them," he said reasonably.

"For him. So he could heal."

"And now you want to leave him before that healing is finished."

Thomas came out of the cabin and saw them standing together. "Is something wrong?" he asked. Anyanwu realized later that it was probably her expression or her thoughts that alerted him. If only he could have read Doro's thoughts.

"Anyanwu wants to go home," said Doro blandly.

Thomas stared at her with disbelief and pain. "Anyanwu . . . ?"

She did not know what to do—what would make Doro feel that he had extracted enough pain, punished her enough. What would stop him now that he had decided to kill?

She looked at Doro. "I will leave with you today," she whispered. "Please, I will leave with you now."

"Not quite yet," Doro said.

She shook her head, pleaded desperately: "Doro, what do you want of me? Tell me and I will give it."

Thomas had come closer to them, looking at Anyanwu, his expression caught between anger and pain. Anyanwu wanted to shout at him to stay away.

"I want you to remember," Doro said to her. "You've come to think I couldn't touch you. That kind of thinking is foolish and dangerous."

She was in the midst of a healing. She had endured abuse from Thomas. She had endured part of a night beside his filthy body. Finally, she had been able to reach him and begin to heal. It was not only the sores on his body she was reaching for. Never had Doro taken a patient from her in the midst of healing, never! Somehow, she had not thought he would do such a thing. It was as though he had threatened one of her children. And, of course, he was threatening her children. He was threatening everything dear to her. He was not finished with her, apparently, and thus would not kill her. But since she had made it clear that she did not love him, that she obeyed him only because he had power, he felt some need to remind her of that power. If he could not do it by giving her to an evil man because that man obstinately ceased to be evil, then he would take that man from her now while her interest in him was strongest. And also, perhaps Doro had realized the thing she had told Thomas—that she would rather share Thomas' bed than Doro's. For a man accustomed to adoration, that realization must have been a heavy blow. But what could she do?

"Doro," she pleaded, "it's enough. I understand. I have been wrong. I will remember and behave better toward you."

She was clinging to both his arms now, and lowering her head before the smooth young face. Inside, she screamed with rage and fear and loathing. Outside, her face was as smooth as his.

But out of stubbornness or hunger or a desire to hurt her, he would not stop. He turned toward Thomas. And by now, Thomas understood.

Thomas backed away, his disbelief again clear in his expression. "Why?" he said. "What have I done?"

"Nothing!" shouted Anyanwu suddenly, and her hands on Doro's arms locked suddenly in a grip Doro would not break in any normal way. "You've done nothing, Thomas, but serve him all your life. Now he thinks nothing of throwing away your life in the hope of hurting me. Run!"

For an instant, Thomas stood frozen.

"Run!" screamed Anyanwu. Doro had actually begun struggling against her—no doubt a reflex of anger. He knew he could not break her grip or overcome her by physical strength alone. And he would not use his other weapon. He was not finished with her yet. There was a potentially valuable child in her womb.

Thomas ran off toward the woods.

"I'll kill her," shouted Doro. "Your life or hers."

Thomas stopped, looked back.

"He's lying," Anyanwu said almost gleefully. Man or devil, he could not get a lie past her. Not any longer. "Run, Thomas. He is telling lies!"

Doro tried to hit her, but she tripped him, and as he fell, she changed her grip on his arms so that he would not move again except in pain. Very much pain.

"I would have submitted," she hissed into his ear. "I would have done anything!"

"Let me go," he said, "or you won't live, even to submit. It's truth now, Anyanwu. Get up."

There was death frighteningly close to the surface in his voice. This was the way he sounded when he truly meant to kill—his voice went flat and strange and Anyanwu felt that the thing he was, the spirit, the feral hungry demon, the twisted ogbanje was ready to leap out of his young man's body and into hers. She had pushed him too far.

Then Thomas was there. "Let him go, Anyanwu," he said. She jerked her head up to stare at him. She had risked everything to give him a chance to escape—at least a chance—and he had come back.

He tried to pull her off Doro. "Let him go, I said. He'd go through you and take me two seconds later. There's nobody else out here to confuse him."

Anyanwu looked around and realized that he was right. When Doro transferred, he took the person nearest to him. That was why he sometimes touched people. In a crowd, the contact assured his taking the one person he had chosen. If he decided to transfer, though, and the person nearest to him was a hundred miles away, he would take that person. Distance meant nothing. If he was willing to go through Anyanwu, he could reach Thomas.

"I've got nothing," Thomas was saying. "This cabin is my future—staying here, getting older, drunker, crazier. I'm nothing to die for, Sun Woman, even if your dying could save me."

With far less strength than Doro had in his current body, he pulled her to her feet, freeing Doro. Then he pushed her behind him so that he stood nearest to Doro.

Doro stood up slowly, watching them as though daring them to run—or encouraging them to panic and run hopelessly. Nothing human looked out of his eyes.

Seeing him, Anyanwu thought she would die anyway. Both she and Thomas would die.

"I was loyal," Thomas said to him as though to a reasonable man.

Doro's eyes focused on him.

"I gave you loyalty," Thomas repeated. "I never dis-obeyed." He shook his head slowly from side to side. "I loved you—even though I knew this day might come." He held out a remarkably steady right hand. "Let her go home to her hus-band and children," he said.

Without a word, Doro grasped the hand. At his touch, the smooth young body he had worn collapsed and Thomas' body, thin and full of sores, stood a little straighter. Anyanwu stared at him wide-eyed, terrified in spite of herself. In an instant, the eyes of a friend had become demon's eyes. Would she be killed now? Doro had promised nothing. Had not even given his worshiper a word of kindness.

"Bury that," Doro said to her from Thomas' mouth. He gestured toward his own former body.

She began to cry. Shame and relief made her turn away from him. He was going to let her live. Thomas had bought her life.

Thomas' hand caught her by the shoulder and shoved her toward the body. She hated her tears. Why was she so weak? Thomas had been strong. He had lived no more than thirty-five years, yet he had found the strength to face Doro and save her. She had lived many times thirty-five years and she wept and cowered. This was what Doro had made of her—and he could not understand why she hated him.

He came to stand over her and somehow she kept her-self from cringing away. He seemed taller in Thomas' body than Thomas had.

"I have nothing to dig with," she whispered. She had not intended to whisper.

"Use your hands!" he said.

She found a shovel in the cabin, and an adz that she could swing to break up the earth—probably the same tool Thomas had used to dress the timbers of his cabin. As she dug the grave, Doro stood watching her. He never moved to help, never spoke, never looked away. By the time she had finished a suitable hole—rough and oblong rather than rectangular, but large and deep enough—she was trembling. The gravedigging had tired her more than it should have. It was hard work and she had done it too quickly. A man half again her size would not have finished so soon—or perhaps he would have, with Doro watching over him.

What was Doro thinking? Did he mean to kill her after all? Would he bury Thomas' body with the earlier nameless one and walk away clothed in her flesh?

She went to the young man's body, straightened it, and wrapped it in some of the linen Doro had brought. Then, somehow, she struggled it into the grave. She was tempted to ask Doro to help, but one look at his face changed her mind. He would not help. He would curse her. She shuddered. She had not seen him make a kill since their trip from her homeland. He did kill, of course, often. But he was private about it. He arrived in Wheatley wearing one body and left wearing another, but he did not make the change in public. Also, he usually left as soon as he had changed. If he meant to stay in town for a while, he stayed wearing the body of a stranger. He did not let his people forget what he was, but his reminders were discreet and surprisingly gentle. If they had not been, Anyanwu thought as she filled in the grave, if Doro flaunted his power before others as he was flaunting it now before her, even his most faithful worshipers would have fled from him. His way of killing would terrify anyone. She looked at him and saw Thomas' thin face recently shaved by her own hand, recently taught a small, thin-lipped smile. She looked away, trembling.

Somehow, she finished filling in the grave. She tried to think of a white man's prayer to say for the nameless corpse, and for Thomas. But with Doro watching, her mind refused to work. She stood empty and weary and frightened over the grave.

"Now you'll do something about these sores," Doro said. "I mean to keep this body for a while."

Thus she would live—for a while. He was telling her she

188 ⟶ OCTAVIA E. BUTLER

would live. She met his eyes. "I have already begun with them. Do they hurt?"

"Not much."

"I put medicine into them."

"Will they heal?"

"Yes, if you keep very clean and eat well and . . . don't drink the way he did."

Doro laughed. "Tend these things again," he said. "I want them healed as soon as possible."

"But there is medicine in them now. It has not had time to work." She did not want to touch him, even in healing. She had not minded touching Thomas, had quickly come to like the man in spite of his wretchedness. Without his un-controlled ability hurting him, he would have been a good man. In the end, he was a good man. She would willingly bury his body when Doro left it, but she did not want to touch it while Doro wore it. Perhaps Doro knew that.

"I said tend the sores!" he ordered. "What will I have to do next to teach you to obey?"

She took him into the cabin, stripped him, and went over the sick, scrawny body again. When she finished, he made her undress and lie with him. She did not weep because she thought that would please him. But afterward, for the first time in centuries, she was uncontrollably sick.

9

Nweke had begun to scream. Doro listened calmly, accepting the fact that the girl's fate was temporarily out of his hands. There was nothing for him to do except wait and remind himself of what Anyanwu had said. She had never lost anyone to transition. She would not be likely to tarnish that record with the death of one of her own children.

And Nweke was strong. All Anyanwu's children were strong. That was important. Doro's personal experience with transition had taught him the danger of weakness. He let his thoughts go back to the time of his own transition and away from worry over Nweke. He could remember his transition very clearly. There were long years following it that he could not remember, but his childhood and the transition that ended that childhood were still clear to him.

He had been a sickly, stunted boy, the last of his mother's twelve children and the only one to survive—just right for the name Anyanwu sometimes called him: Ogbanje. People said his brothers and sisters had been robust healthy-looking babies, and they had died. He had been scrawny and tiny and strange, and only his parents seemed to think it right that he had lived. People whispered about him. They said he was something other than a child—some spirit. They whispered that he was not the son of his mother's husband. His mother shielded him as best she could while he was very young, and his father—if the man was his father—claimed him and was pleased to have a son. He was a poor man and had little else.

His parents were all he could recall that had been good about his youth. Both had loved and valued him extravagantly after eleven dead babies. Other people avoided him when they could. His were a tall, stately people—Nubians, they came to be called much later. It soon became clear to them that Doro would never be tall or stately. Eventually, it also became clear that he was possessed. He heard voices. He fell to the ground writing with fits. Several people, fearful that he might loose his devils on them, wanted to kill him, but somehow, his parents protected him. Even then, he had not known how. But there was little, perhaps nothing, they would not have done to save him.

He was thirteen when the full agony of transition hit him. He knew now that that was too young. He had never known one of his witches to live when transition came that early. He had not lived himself. But unlike anyone he had managed to breed so far, he had not quite died either. His body had died, and for the first time, he had transferred to the living human body nearest to him. This was the body of his mother in whose lap his head had rested.

He found himself looking down at himself—at his own body—and he did not understand. He screamed. Terrified, he tried to run away. His father stopped him, held him, demanded to know what had happened. He could not answer. He looked down, saw his woman's breasts, his woman's body, and he panicked. Without knowing how or what he did, he transferred again—this time to his father.

In his once quiet Nile River village, he killed and killed

and killed. Finally, his people's enemies inadvertently rescued them. Raiding Egyptians captured him as they attacked the village. By then, he was wearing the body of a young girl— one of his cousins. Perhaps he killed some of the Egyptians too. He hoped so. His people had lived without the interference of Egypt for nearly two centuries while Egypt wallowed in feudal chaos. But now Egypt was back, wanting land, mineral wealth, slaves. Doro hoped he had killed many of them. He would never know. His memory stopped with the arrival of the Egyptians. There was a gap of what he later calculated to be about fifty years before he came to himself again and discovered that he had been thrown into an Egyptian prison, discovered that he now possessed the body of some middle-aged stranger, discovered that he was both more and less than a man, discovered that he could have and do absolutely anything.

It had taken him years to decide even approximately how long he had been out of his mind. It took more time to learn exactly where his village had been and that it was no longer there. He never found any of his kinsmen, anyone from his village. He was utterly alone.

Eventually, he began to realize that some of his kills gave him more pleasure than others. Some bodies sustained him longer. Observing his own reactions, he learned that age, race, sex, physical appearance, and except in extreme cases, health, did not affect his enjoyment of victims. He could and did take anyone. But what gave the greatest pleasure was something he came to think of as witchcraft or a potential for witchcraft. He was seeking out his spiritual kin—people possessed or mad or just a little strange. They heard voices, saw visions, other things. He did none of those things any longer— not since his transition ended. But he fed on those who did. He learned to sense them effortlessly—like following an aroma of food. Then he learned to gather reserves of them, breed them, see that they were protected and cared for. They, in turn, learned to worship him. After a single generation, they were his. He had not understood this, but he had accepted it. A few of them seemed to sense him as clearly as he sensed them. Their witch-power warned them but never seemed to make them flee sensibly. Instead, they came to him, competed for his attention, loved him as a god, parent, mate, friend.

He learned to prefer their company to that of more normal people. He chose his companions from among them and restricted his killing to the others. Slowly, he created the Isaacs, the Annekes, the best of his children. These he loved as they loved him. They accepted him as ordinary people could not, enjoyed him, felt little or no fear of him. In one way, it was as though he repeated his own history with each generation. His best children loved him without qualification as his parents had. The others, like the other people of his village, viewed him through their various superstitions—though at least this time the superstitions were favorable. And this time, it was not his loved ones who fed his hunger. He plucked the others from their various settlements like ripe, sweet fruit and kept his special ones safe from all but sickness, old age, war, and sometimes, the dangerous effects of their own abilities. Occasionally, this last forced him to kill one of his special ones. One of them, drunk with his own power, displayed his abilities, drew attention to himself, and endangered his people. One of them refused to obey. One of them simply went mad. It happened.

These were the kills he should have enjoyed most. Certainly, on a sensory level, they were the most pleasurable. But in Doro's mind, these killings were too much like what he had done accidentally to his parents. He never kept these bodies long. He consciously avoided mirrors until he could change again. At these times more than any others, he felt again utterly alone, forever alone, longing to die and be finished. What was he, he wondered, that he could have anything at all but an end?

People like Isaac and soon Nweke did not know how safe they were from him. People like Anyanwu—good, stable wild seed—did not know how safe they could be—though for

Anyanwu herself, it was too late. Years too late, in spite of Isaac's occasional pleas for her. Doro did not want the woman any longer—did not want her condemning stare, her silent, palpable hatred, her long-lived, grudge-holding presence. As soon as she was of no more use to Isaac, she would die.

Isaac paced around the kitchen, restless and frightened, unable to shut out the sound of Nweke's screams. It was difficult for him not to go to her. He knew there was nothing he could do, no help he could give. People in transition did not respond well to him. Anyanwu could hold them and pet them and become their mother whether she actually was or not. And in their pain, they clung to her. If Isaac tried to comfort them, they struggled against him. He had never understood that. They always seemed to like him well enough before and after transition.

Nweke loved him. She had grown up calling him father, knowing he was not her father, and never caring. She was not Doro's daughter either, but Isaac loved her too much to tell her that. He longed to be with her now to still the screaming and take away the pain. He sat down heavily and stared toward the bedroom.

"She'll be all right," Doro said from the table, where he was eating a sweet cake Isaac had found for him.

"How can even you know that?" Isaac challenged.

"Her blood is good. She'll be fine."

"My blood is good too, but I nearly died."

"You're here," Doro said reasonably.

Isaac rubbed a hand across his forehead. "I don't think I would feel this nervous if she were giving birth. She's such a little thing—so like Anyanwu."

"Even smaller," Doro said. He looked at Isaac, smiled as though at some secret joke.

"She's to be your next Anyanwu, isn't she?" Isaac asked.

"Yes." Doro's expression did not change. The smile remained in place.

"She's not enough," Isaac said. "She's a beautiful, lively

young girl. After tonight, she'll be a powerful young girl. But you've said she'd keep some of the mind-listening ability."

"I believe she will."

"It kills." Isaac stared at the bedroom door, imagining the favored young stepdaughter turning vicious and bitter like his long-dead half-brother Lale, like his mother who had hanged herself. "That ability kills," he repeated sadly. "It may not kill quickly, but it kills." Poor Nweke. Even transition would not mean an end to her pain. Should he wish her life or death? And what should he wish for her mother?

"I've had people as good at mental communication as you are at moving things," Doro said. "Anneke, for instance."

"Do you think she'll be like Anneke?"

"She'll complete her transition. She'll have some control."

"Is she related to Anneke?"

"No." Doro's tone indicated that he did not wish to discuss Nweke's ancestry. Isaac changed his approach.

"Anyanwu has perfect control over what she does," he said.

"Yes, within the limits of her ability. But she's wild seed. I'm tired of the effort it takes to control her."

"Are you?" Nweke had stopped screaming. The room was suddenly still and silent except for Isaac's two words.

Doro swallowed the last of his sweet. "You have something to say?"

"That it would be stupid to kill her. That it would be a waste."

Doro looked at him—a look Isaac had come to recognize, a look that gave him permission to say what Doro would not hear from others. Over the years, Isaac's usefulness and loyalty had won him the right to say what he felt and be heard—though not necessarily heeded.

"I won't take her from you," Doro said quietly.

Isaac nodded. "If you did, I wouldn't last long." He rubbed his chest. "There's something wrong with my heart. She makes a medicine for it."

"With your heart!"

"She takes care of it. She says she doesn't like being a widow."

"I . . . thought she might be helping you a little."

"She was helping me 'a little' twenty years ago. How many children have I gotten for you in the past twenty years?"

Doro said nothing. He watched Isaac without expression.

"She's helped both of us," Isaac said.

"What do you want?" Doro asked.

"Her life." Isaac paused, but Doro said nothing. "Let her live. She'll marry again after a while. She always has. Then you'll have more of her children. She's a breed unto herself, after all. Something even you've never seen before."

"I had another healer once."

"Did she live to be three hundred? Did she bear dozens of children? Was she able to change her shape at will?"

"He. And no to all three questions. No."

"Then keep her. If she annoys you, ignore her for a while. Ignore her for twenty years or thirty. What difference would it make to you—or to her? When you go back to her, she'll have changed in one way or another. But, Doro, don't kill her. Don't make the mistake of killing her."

"I don't want or need her any longer."

"You're wrong. You do. Because left alone, she won't die or allow herself to be killed. She isn't temporary. You haven't accepted that yet. When you do, and when you take the trouble to win her back, you'll never be alone again."

"You don't know what you're talking about!"

Isaac stood up, went to the table to look down on Doro. "If I don't know the two of you and your needs, who does? She's exactly right for you—not so powerful that you would have to worry about her, yet powerful enough to take care of herself and of others on her own. You might not see each other for years at a time, but as long as both of you are alive, neither of you will be alone."

Doro had begun to watch Isaac with greater interest, causing Isaac to wonder whether he had really been too set in his ways to see the woman's value.

"You said you knew about Nweke's father," Doro said.

Isaac nodded. "Anyanwu told me. She was so angry and frustrated—I think she had to tell someone."

"How do you feel about it?"

"What difference does that make?" Isaac demanded. "Why bring it up now?"

"Answer."

"All right." Isaac shrugged. "I said I knew you—and her—so I wasn't surprised at what you'd done. You're both stubborn, vengeful people at times. She's kept you angry and frustrated for years. You tried to get even. You do that now and then, and it only fuels her anger. The only person I pity is the man, Thomas."

Doro lifted an eyebrow. "He ran. He sided with her. He had outlived his usefulness."

Isaac heard the implied threat and faced Doro with annoyance. "Do you really think you have to do that?" he asked quietly. "I'm your son, not wild seed, not sick, not stranded halfway through transition. I could never hate you or run from you no matter what you did, and I'm one of the few of your children who could have made a successful escape. Did you think I didn't know that? I'm here because I want to be." Deliberately, Isaac extended his hand to Doro. Doro stared at him for a moment, then gave a long sigh and clasped the large, calloused hand in his own briefly, harmlessly.

For a time, they sat together in relaxed silence, Doro getting up once to put another log on the fire. Isaac let his thoughts go back to Anyanwu, and it occurred to him that what he had said of him might also be true of her. She might be another of the very few people who could escape Doro—the way she could change her form and travel anywhere . . . Perhaps that was one of the things that bothered Doro about her. Though it shouldn't have.

Doro should have let her go wherever she chose, do whatever she chose. He should only see her now and then when he was feeling lonely, when people died and left him, as everyone but her had to leave him. She was a healer in more ways than Doro seemed to understand. Nweke's father had probably understood. And now, in her pain, no doubt Nweke understood. Ironically, Anyanwu herself often seemed not to understand. She thought the sick came to her only for her medicines and her knowledge. Within herself, she had something she did not know she had.

"Nweke will be a better healer than Anyanwu could ever be," Doro said as though responding to Isaac's thoughts. "I don't think her mind reading will cripple her."

"Let Nweke become whatever she can," Isaac said wearily. "If she's as good as you think she'll be, then you'll have two very valuable women. You'd be a damned fool to waste either of them."

Nweke began screaming again—hoarse, terrible sounds.

"Oh God," Isaac whispered.

"Her voice will soon be gone at that rate," Doro said. Then, offhandedly, "Do you have any more of those cakes?"

Isaac knew him too well to be surprised. He got up to get the plate of fruit-filled Dutch *olijkoecks* that Anyanwu had made earlier. It was rare for another person's pain to disturb Doro. If the girl seemed to be dying, he would be concerned that good seed was about to be lost. But if she were merely in agony, it did not matter. Isaac forced his thoughts back to Anyanwu.

"Doro?" He spoke so softly that the girl's screams almost drowned his single word. But Doro looked up. He held Isaac's gaze, not questioningly or challengingly, not with any reassurance or compassion. He only looked back. Isaac had seen cats stare at people that way. Cats. That was apt. More and more often, nothing human looked out of Doro's eyes. When Anyanwu was angry, she said Doro was only a man pretending to be a god. But she knew better. No man could frighten her—and Doro, whatever he had failed to accomplish with her, had taught her to fear him. He had taught Isaac to fear for him.

"What will you lose," Isaac said, "if you leave Anyanwu her life?"

"I'm tired of her. That's all. That's enough. I'm just tired of her." He sounded tired—good, honest, human weariness, annoyance, and frustration.

"Then let her go. Send her away and let her make her own life."

Doro frowned, looked as harassed as Isaac had ever seen him. Surely that was a good sign. "Think about it," he said. "Finally to have someone who isn't temporary—and wild seed that she is, you'll have lifetimes to tame her. Surely she can feel loneliness too. She should be a challenge to you, not an annoyance."

He said nothing more. It was not good to try to get promises from Doro. Isaac had learned that long ago. It was best to push him almost to agreement, then leave him alone. Sometimes that worked. Sometimes Isaac did it well enough to save lives. And sometimes he failed.

They sat together, Doro slowly eating olijkoecks and Isaac listening to the sounds of pain from the bedroom—until those sounds ceased, Nweke's voice all but gone. The hours passed. Isaac made coffee.

"You should sleep," Doro told him. "Take one of the children's beds. It will be over when you wake."

Isaac shook his head wearily. "How could I sleep not knowing?"

"All right, then, don't sleep, but at least lie down. You look terrible." Doro took Isaac by the shoulder and steered him into one of the bedrooms. The room was dark and cold, but Doro made a fire and lit a single candle.

"Shall I wait with you here?" he asked.

"Yes," Isaac said gratefully. Doro brought a chair.

The screaming began again, and for a moment it confused Isaac. The girl's voice had become only a hoarse whisper long ago, and except for an occasional jarring or creaking of the bed and the harsh, ragged breathing of the two women, the house had been silent. Now there was screaming.

Isaac sat up suddenly and put his feet on the floor.

"What's the matter?" Doro asked.

Isaac barely heard him. Suddenly he was up and running toward the other bedroom. Doro tried to stop him but Isaac brushed the restraining hands away. "Can't you hear?" he shouted. "It's not Nweke. It's Anyanwu!"

It seemed to Doro that Nweke's transition was ending. The time was right—early morning, a few hours before dawn. The girl had survived the usual ten to twelve hours of agony. For some time now, she had been silent, not screaming, or groaning or even moving around enough to shake the bed. That was not to say, though, that she could not move. Actually, the final hours of transition were the most dangerous. They were the hours in which people lost control of their bodies, not only feeling what others felt, but moving as others moved. This was the time when someone like Anyanwu, physically strong, unafraid, and comforting, was essential. Anyanwu herself was perfect because she could not be hurt— or at least, not in any permanent way.

Doro's people had told him this was the time they suffered most, too. This was the time when the madness of absorbing everyone else's feelings seemed endless—when, in desperation, they would do anything to stop the pain. Yet this was also the time when they began to feel there was a way just beyond their reach—a way of controlling the madness, shutting themselves away from it. A way of finding peace.

But instead of peace for Nweke, there was more screaming, and there was Isaac springing up like a boy, running for the door, shouting that the screams were not Nweke's, but Anyanwu's.

And Isaac was right. What had happened? Had Anyanwu been unable to keep the girl alive in spite of her healing ability? Or was it something else, some other trouble with transition? What could make the formidable Anyanwu scream that way?

"Oh my God," Isaac cried from within the bedroom. "What have you done? My God!"

Doro ran into the room, stood near the door staring. Anyanwu lay on the floor, bleeding from her nose and mouth. Her eyes were closed and she made no sound now at all. She seemed only barely alive.

On the bed, Nweke sat up, her body half concealed by the feather mattress. She was staring down at Anyanwu. Isaac had stopped for a moment beside Anyanwu. He shook her as though to rouse her and her head lolled over bonelessly.

He looked up and saw Nweke's face over a bulge of feather-filled cloth. Before Doro could guess what he meant to do Isaac seized the girl, slapped her hard across the face.

"Stop what you're doing!" he shouted. "Stop it! She's your mother!"

Nweke put a hand to her face, her expression startled, uncomprehending. Doro realized that before Isaac's blow, her face had held no expression at all. She had looked at Anyanwu, fallen and bleeding, with no more interest than she might have expressed in a stone. She had looked, but she had almost certainly not seen—did not see now. Perhaps she felt the pain of Isaac's blow. Perhaps she heard him shouting—though Doro doubted that she was able to distinguish words. All that reached her was pain, noise, confusion. And she had had enough of all three.

Her small, pretty, empty face contorted, and Isaac screamed. It had happened before. Doro had seen it happen. Some people's bodies survived transition well enough, but their minds did not. They gained power and control of that power, but they lost all that would have made that power meaningful or useful. Why had Doro been so slow to understand? What if the damage to Isaac could not be repaired? What if both Isaac and Nweke were lost?

Doro stepped over Anyanwu and around Isaac, who was now writhing on the floor, and to the girl.

He seized her, slapped her as Isaac had done. *"That's enough!"* he said, not shouting at all. If his voice reached her, she would live. If it did not, she would die. Gods, let it reach her. Let her have her chance to come back to her senses—if she had any left.

She drew back from Doro like a cornered animal. Whatever she had done to hurt Isaac and perhaps kill Anyanwu, she did nothing to Doro. His voice had reached her—after a fashion.

She half leaped and half fell from the bed to get away from him and somehow she landed on Isaac. Anyanwu was farther away, as though she had been trying to escape when Nweke struck her down. Also, Anyanwu was unconscious. She would probably never have known it if the girl had landed on her. But Isaac knew, and he reacted instantly to this new pain.

He gripped Nweke, threw her upward away from his pain-racked body—threw her upward with all the power he had used so many times to propel great ships out of storms. He did not know what he was doing any more than she did. He never saw her hit the ceiling, never saw her body flatten into it, distorted, crushed, never saw her head slam into one of the great beams and break and send down a grisly rain of blood and bits of bone and brain.

Her body fell toward Doro, rag-limp and ruined. Somehow he caught it, kept it from landing on Isaac again. The girl was lost. She would have been lost with such wounds had she been twice the healer Doro had hoped for. He put her body on the bed hastily and bent to see whether Isaac was also lost. Later, he would feel this. Later, perhaps he would leave Wheatley—leave it for several years.

Isaac's face was pale—a gray, ugly color. He was still now, very still though not quite unconscious. Doro could hear him panting, trying to catch his breath. Trouble with his heart, he had said. Could Nweke have aggravated that somehow? Why not? Who was more suited to causing illness than one born to cure it?

Desperately, Doro turned to Anyanwu. The moment his attention was focused on her, he knew she was still alive. He could sense it. She felt like prey, not like a useless corpse. Doro took her hand, then released it because it felt limp and dead. He touched her face, leaned down close to her ear. "Can you hear me, Anyanwu?"

She gave no sign.

"Anyanwu, Isaac needs you. He'll die without your help."

Her eyes opened. She stared up at him for a second, perhaps reading his desperation on his face. "Am I on a rug?" she whispered finally.

He frowned wondering whether she too had gone out of her mind. But she was Isaac's only hope. "Yes," he said.

"Then use it to pull me close to him. As close as you can. Don't touch me otherwise." She took a deep breath. "Please don't touch me."

He moved back from her and drew her toward Isaac with the rug.

"She went mad," Anyanwu whispered. "Her mind broke somehow."

"I know," Doro said.

"Then she tried to break everything inside me. Like being cut and torn from the inside. Heart, lungs, veins, stomach, bladder . . . She was like me, like Isaac, like . . . maybe like Thomas too—reaching into minds, seeing into my body. She must have been able to see."

Yes. Nweke had been all Doro had hoped for and more. But she was dead. "Help Isaac, Anyanwu!"

"Go get me food," she said. "Is there some stew left?"

"Can you reach Isaac?"

"Yes. Go!"

Trying to trust her, Doro left the room.

Somehow, Anyanwu healed herself enough so that moving would not start her bleeding inside again. There was so much damage, and it had all been done so quickly, so savagely. When she changed her shape, she transformed organs that already existed and formed any necessary new organs while sustained by old ones. She was still partly human in most changes long after she had ceased to look human. But Nweke had all but destroyed organ after organ. If the girl had gone to work on her brain, Anyanwu knew she would have died before she could heal herself. Even now, there were massive repairs to be made and massive illnesses to be avoided. Even not touching her brain at all, Nweke had nearly killed her.

How could she make herself fit now to help Isaac? But she had to. She had known in the first year of their marriage that she had been wrong about him. He had been the best possible husband. With his power and hers, they had built this house. People came to watch them and watch *for* them so that no strangers happened by to see the witchcraft. Her strength had fascinated Isaac, but it had never disturbed him. His power she trusted absolutely. She had seen him carry great logs from the forest and strip them of bark. She had seen him kill wolves without touching them. In a fight once, she had seen him kill a man—a fool who had drunk too much and chosen to take offense at Isaac's quiet, easy refusal to be insulted. The fool had a gun and Isaac did not. Isaac never went armed. There was no need. The man died as the wolves had died—instantly, his head broken and bloodied as though he had been bludgeoned. Afterward, Isaac himself was sickened by the killing.

Anyanwu had seen these things, but none of them had made her fear her husband as she had feared Doro. Sometimes Isaac tossed her about and she screamed or laughed or swore at him—whichever seemed right for the occasion—but she never feared him. And she never held him in contempt. "He has more sense than men two and three times his age," she had told Doro when Isaac was young and she and Doro were on slightly better terms. In some ways, Isaac had more sense than Doro. And Isaac understood even better than she did that he would have to share her, at least with Doro. And she would have to share him with the women Doro gave to him. She was used to sharing a man, but she had had no experience in being shared. She did not like it. She grew to hate the sound of Doro's voice identifying him, warning her that she must give him another child. Isaac accepted each of her children as though they were his own. He accepted her without bitterness or anger when she came to him from Doro's bed. And somehow, he helped her to endure even when Doro strove to break and reshape her when her increasingly silent obedience ceased to be enough for him. Strangely, though she could not forgive Doro any longer even for small things, she felt no resentment when Isaac forgave him. The bond between Isaac and Doro was at least as firm as that between an ordinary father and a son of his body. If Isaac had not loved Doro, and if that love had not been returned strongly in Doro's own way, Doro would have seemed totally inhuman.

She did not want to think what her life would be like without Isaac—how she would endure Doro without Isaac. Not since her first husband had she allowed herself to become so dependent on anyone, husband or child. Other people were temporary. They died—except for Doro. Why, *why* could it not be Isaac who lived and lived, and Doro who died?

She kissed Isaac. She had given him many such kisses as he grew old. They were of more than love. Within her body, she synthesized medicine for him. She had studied him very carefully, had aged herself, her own organs to study the effects of age. It had been dangerous work. A miscalculation could have killed her before she understood it enough to counter it. She listened closely as Isaac described the pain he felt—the fearful tightening, the squeezing within his chest, the dizziness, the too-rapid beating of his heart, the way the pain spread from his chest to his left shoulder and arm.

The fist time he felt the pain—twenty years before—he had thought he was dying. The first time she managed to induce such pain in her body, she too had feared she was dying. It was terrible, but she lived as Isaac had lived, and she came to understand how old age and too much good, rich food could combine to steal away the youthful flexibility in his blood vessels—especially, if her simulations had led her aright, the blood vessels that nourished his heart.

What needed doing, then? How could aging, fat-narrowed blood vessels be restored? She could restore her own, of course. Since the pain had not killed her, and since she understood what she had done to produce the disorder, she could simply, carefully replace the damaged vessels, then dissolve away the useless hardened tissue, become the physiologically young woman she had been since the time of her transition. But transition had not frozen Isaac in youth. It had paid him other wages, good wages, but was useless in prolonging his life. If only she could give him some of her power . . .

That was pointless dreaming. If she could not heal the damage age and bad habits had caused, she could at least try to prevent further damage. He must not eat so much any longer, must not eat some foods at all. He must not smoke or work so hard—not with his muscles nor with his witchpower. Both took a physical toll. He would save no more ships from storms. Lighter tasks were all right as long as they did not bring on pain, but she told Doro very firmly that unless he wanted to kill Isaac, he would have to find a younger man for his heavy lifting and towing.

That done, Anyanwu spent long painful hours trying to discover or create a medicine that would ease Isaac's pain when it did come. In the end, she so tired and weakened herself that even Isaac begged her to stop. She did not stop. She poisoned herself several times trying plant and animal substances she had not used before, noting minutely her every reaction. She rechecked familiar substances, found that as simple a thing as garlic had some ability to help, but not enough. She worked on, gained knowledge that helped others later. For Isaac, she at last, almost accidentally created a potentially dangerous medicine that would open wide the healthy blood vessels he had left, thus relieving the pressure on his undernourished heart and easing the pain. When his pain came again, she gave him the medicine. The pain vanished and he was amazed. He took her into New York City and made her choose the finest cloth. Then he took her to a dressmaker—a black freedwoman who stared at her with open curiosity. Anyanwu began telling the woman what she wanted, but when she paused for breath, the dressmaker spoke up.

"You are the Onitsha woman," she said in Anyanwu's native language. And she smiled at Anyanwu's surprise. "Are you well?"

Anyanwu found herself greeting a countrywoman, perhaps a kinswoman. This was another gift Isaac was giving her. A new friend. He was good, Isaac. He could not die now and leave her.

But this time, the medicine that had always worked seemed to be failing. Isaac gave no sign that his pain was ending.

He lay ashen, sweating and gasping for breath. When she lifted her head from him, he opened his eyes. She did not know what to do. She wanted to look away from him, but could not. In her experimenting, she had found conditions of the heart that could kill very easily—and that could grow out of the problem he already had. She had almost killed herself learning about them. She had been so careful in her efforts to keep Isaac alive, and now, somehow, poor Nweke had undone all her work.

"Nweke?" Isaac whispered as though he had heard her thought.

"I don't know," Anyanwu said. She looked around, saw how the feather mattress billowed. "She is asleep."

"Good," he gasped. "I thought I had hurt her. I dreamed . . ."

He was dying! Nweke had killed him. In her madness, she had killed him and he was worried that he might have hurt her! Anyanwu shook her head, thought desperately. What could she do? With all her vast knowledge, there must be something . . .

He managed to touch her hand. "You have lost other husbands," he said.

She began to cry.

"Anyanwu, I'm old. My life has been long and full—by ordinary standards, at least." His face twisted with pain. It was as though the pain knifed through Anyanwu's own chest.

"Lie by me," he said. "Lie here beside me."

She obeyed still weeping silently.

"You cannot know how I've loved you," he said.

Somehow, she controlled her voice. "With you it has been as though I never had another husband."

"You must live," he said. "You must make your peace with Doro."

The thought sickened her. She said nothing.

With an effort, he spoke in her language. "He will be your husband now. Bow your head, Anyanwu. Live!"

He said nothing more. There were only long moments of pain before he slipped into unconsciousness, then to death.

10

nyanwu had gotten shakily to her feet when Doro arrived with a tray of food. She was standing beside the bed staring at the ruin of Nweke's body. She did not seem to hear Doro when he put the tray down on a small table near her. He opened his mouth to ask her why she was not caring for Isaac, but the moment he thought of Isaac, his awareness told him Isaac was dead.

His awareness had never failed him. In past years, he had prevented a number of people from being buried alive by the certainty of his ability. Yet now he knelt beside Isaac and felt at the neck for a pulse. Of course, there was none.

Anyanwu turned and stared at him bleakly. She was young. In restoring her nearly destroyed body, she had returned to her true form. She looked like a girl mourning her grandfather and sister rather than a woman mourning her husband and daughter.

"He did not know," she whispered. "He thought it was only a dream that he had hurt her."

Doro glanced upward where Nweke's body had left bloody

smears on the ceiling. Anyanwu followed his gaze, then looked down again quickly. "He was out of his mind with pain," Doro said. "Then, by accident, she hurt him again. It was too much."

"One terrible accident after another." She shook her head dazed. "Everything is gone."

Surprisingly, she went to the food, took the tray out to the kitchen where she sat down and began to eat. He followed and watched her wonderingly. The damage Nweke had done her must have been even greater than he had thought if she could eat this way, tearing at the food like a starving woman while the bodies of those she loved most lay cooling in the next room.

After a while, she said, "Doro, they should have funerals."

She was eating a sweet cake from the plate Isaac had put on the table for Doro. Doro felt hungry too, but could not bring himself to touch food. Especially, not those cakes. He realized that it was not food he hungered for.

He had only recently taken the body he was wearing. It was a good, strong body taken from his settlement in the colony of Pennsylvania. Ordinarily, it would have lasted him several months. He could have used it to sire Nweke's first child. That would have been a fine match. There was stability and solid strength in his Pennsylvania settlers. Good stock. But stress, physical or emotional, took its toll, made him hunger when he should not have, made him long for the comfort of another change. He did not *have* to change. His present body would sustain him for a while longer. But he would feel hungry and uncomfortable until he changed. But he had no pressing reason to bear the discomfort. Nweke was dead; Isaac was dead. He looked at Anyanwu.

"We must give them a funeral," she repeated.

Doro nodded. Let her have the ritual. She had been good to Isaac. Then afterward . . .

"He said we should make our peace," she said.

"What?"

"Isaac. It was the last thing he said—that we should have peace between us."

Doro shrugged. "We'll have peace."

She said nothing more. Arrangements were made for the funeral, the numerous married children notified. It did not matter whether they were Isaac's children or Doro's, they had grown up accepting Isaac as their father. And there were several foster children—those Anyanwu had taken in because their parents were unfit or dead. And there was everyone else. Everyone in town had known Isaac and liked him. Everyone would come now to show their respect.

But on the day of the funeral, Anyanwu was nowhere to be found. To Doro's tracking sense, it was as though she had ceased to exist.

She flew as a large bird for a while. Then, far out at sea, she drifted down wearily to the water and took the long-remembered dolphin form. She had come down near where she saw a school of dolphins leaping through the water. They would accept her, surely, and she would become one of them. She would cause herself to grow until she was as large as most of them. She would learn to live in their world. It could be no more alien to her than the world she had just left. And perhaps when she learned their ways of communication, she would find them too honorable or too innocent to tell lies and plot murder over the still warm corpses of their children.

Briefly, she wondered how long she could endure being away from kinsmen, from friends, from any human beings. How long would she have to hide in the sea before Doro stopped hunting her—or before he found her. She remembered her sudden panic when Doro took her from her people. She remembered the loneliness that Doro and Isaac and her two now-dead grandchildren had eased. How would she stand it alone among the dolphins? How was it that she wanted to live so badly that even a life under the sea seemed precious?

Doro had reshaped her. She had submitted and submitted and submitted to keep him from killing her even though she had long ago ceased to believe what Isaac had told her— that her longevity made her the right mate for Doro. That she could somehow prevent him from becoming an animal. He was already an animal. But she had formed the habit of submission. In her love for Isaac and for her children, and in her fear of death—especially of the kind of death Doro would inflict—she had given in to him again and again. Habits were difficult to break. The habit of living, the habit of fear . . . even the habit of love.

Well. Her children were men and women now, able to care for themselves. She would miss them. No feeling was better than that of being surrounded by her own. Her children and grandchildren and great-grandchildren. She could never have been content moving constantly as Doro moved. It was her way to settle and make a tribe around her and stay within that tribe for as long as she could.

Would it be possible, she wondered, to make a tribe of dolphins? Would Doro give her the time she needed to try? She had committed what was considered a great sin among his people: She had run away from him. It would not matter that she had done so to save her life—that she could see he meant to kill her. After all her submission, he still meant to kill her. He believed it was his right to slaughter among his people as he chose. A great many of his people also believed this, and they did not run when he came for them. They were frightened, but he was their god. Running from him was useless. He invariably caught the runner and killed him or, very rarely, brought him home alive and chastened as proof to others that there was no escape. Also, to many, running was heretical. They believed that since he was their god, it was his right to do whatever he chose with them. "Jobs" she called them in her thoughts. Like the Job of the Bible, they had made the best of their situation. They could not escape Doro, so they found virtue in submitting to him.

Anyanwu found virtue in nothing that had to do with

212 ⟋ OCTAVIA E. BUTLER

him. He had never been her god, and if she had to run for a century, never stopping long enough to build the tribes that brought her so much comfort, she would do it. He would not have her life. The people of Wheatley would see that he was not all-powerful. He would never show himself to them wearing her flesh. Perhaps others would notice his failure and see that he was no god. Perhaps they would run too—and how many could Doro chase? Surely some would escape and be able to live their lives in peace with only ordinary human fears. The powerful ones like Isaac could escape. Perhaps even a few of her children . . .

She put away from her the memory that Isaac had never wanted to escape. Isaac was Isaac, set apart from other people and not to be judged. He had been the best of all her husbands, and she could not even attend his funeral rites. Thinking of him, longing for him, she wished she had kept her bird form longer, wished she had found some solitary place, some rocky island perhaps where she could mourn her husband and her daughter without fearing for her own life. Where she could think and remember and be alone. She needed time alone before she could be a fit companion for other creatures.

But the dolphins had reached her. Several approached, chattering incomprehensibly, and for a moment, she thought they might attack her. But they only came to rub themselves against her and become acquainted. She swam with them and none of them molested her. She fed with them, snatching passing fish as hungrily as she had eaten the finest foods of Wheatley and of her homeland. She was a dolphin. If Doro had not found her an adequate mate, he would find her an adequate adversary. He would not enslave her again. And she would never be his prey.

BOOK III

Canaan

1840

11

The old man had lived in Avoyelles Parish in the state of Louisiana for years, his neighbors told Doro. He had married daughters, but no sons. His wife was long dead and he lived alone on his plantation with his slaves—a number of whom were reputed to be his children. He kept to himself. He had never cared much for socializing, even when his wife was alive—nor had she.

Warrick, the old man's name was, Edward Warrick. Within the past century, he was the third human Doro had found himself drawn toward with the feeling that he was near Anyanwu.

Anyanwu.

He had not even said her name aloud for years. There was no one alive in the state of New York who had known her. Her children were dead. The grandchildren who had been born before she fled had also died. Wars had taken some of them. The War of Independence. The stupid 1812 War. The first had killed many of his people and sent others fleeing to Canada because they were too insular and apolitical for anyone's taste. British soldiers considered them rebels and colonists considered them Tories. Many lost all their possessions as they fled to Canada, where Doro found them months later. Now Doro had a Canadian settlement as well as a reconstructed Wheatley in New York. Now, also, he had settlements in Brazil, in Mexico, in Kentucky, and elsewhere, scattered over the two large, empty continents. Most of his best people were now in the New World where there was room for them to grow and increase their power—where there was room for their strangeness.

None of that was compensation for the near destruction of Wheatley, though, just as there could be no compensation for the loss in 1812 of several of his best people in Maryland. These Marylanders were the descendants of the people he had lost when he found Anyanwu. He had reassembled them painstakingly and got them breeding again. They had begun to show promise. Then suddenly the most promising ones were dead. He had had to bring in new blood to rebuild them for a third time—people as much like them as possible. That caused trouble because the people who proved to be most like them in ability were white. There was resentment and hatred on both sides and Doro had had to kill publicly a pair of the worst troublemakers to terrify the others back into their habit of obedience. More valuable breeders wasted. Trouble to settle with the surrounding whites who did not know quite what they had in their midst . . .

So much time wasted. There were years when he almost forgot Anyanwu. He would have killed her had he stumbled across her, of course. Occasionally, he had forgiven people who ran from him, people who were bright enough, strong enough to keep ahead of him for several days and give him a good hunt. But he forgave them only because once caught, they submitted. Not that they begged for their lives. Most did not. They simply ceased to struggle against him. They finally came to understand and acknowledge his power. They had first given him good entertainment, then, fully aware, they gave him themselves. When pardoned, they gave him a kind of loyalty, even friendship, equal to what he received from the best of his children. As with his children, after all, he had given them their lives.

There had been times when he thought he might spare Anyanwu. There had even been moments when, to his amazement and disgust, he simply missed her, wished to see her again. Most often, however, he thought of her when he bred together her African and American descendants. He was striving to create a more stable, controlled Nweke, and he had had some success—people who could perceive and to some degree control the inner workings not only of their own bodies, but the bodies of others. But their abilities were not dependable. They brought agony as often as they brought relief. They killed as often as they healed. They could perform what ordinary doctors saw as miracles—or, as easily, as accidentally, what the most brutal slaveholder would see as atrocities. Also, they did not live long. Sometimes they made lethal mistakes within their own bodies and could not correct them in time. Sometimes relatives of their dead patients killed them. Sometimes they committed suicide. The better ones committed suicide—often after an especially ghastly failure. They needed Anyanwu's control. Even now, if he could, Doro would have liked to breed her with some of them—let her give birth to superior human children for a change instead of the animal young she must have borne over her years of freedom. But it was too late for that. She was spoiled. She had known too much freedom. Like most wild seed, she had been spoiled long before he met her.

Now, finally, he went to complete the unfinished business of killing her and gathering up any new human descendants.

He located her home—her plantation—by tracking her while she was in human form. It was not easy. She kept changing even though she did not seem to travel far. For days, he would have nothing to track. Then she turned human again and he could sense that she had not moved geographically. He closed in, constantly fearing that she would take bird or fish form and vanish for more years. But she stayed, drawing him across country to Mississippi, to Louisiana, to the parish of Avoyelles, then through pine woods and wide fields of cotton.

When he reached the house that his senses told him concealed Anyanwu, he sat still on his horse for several minutes, staring at it from a distance. It was a large white frame house with tall, unnecessary columns and a porch with upper and lower galleries—a solid, permanent-looking place. He could see slave cabins extending out away from the house, almost hidden by trees. And there was a barn, a kitchen, and other buildings that Doro could not identify from a distance. He could see blacks moving around the grounds—children playing, a man chopping wood, a woman gathering something in the kitchen garden, another woman sweating over a steaming caldron of dirty clothes which she occasionally lifted on her stick. A boy with arms no longer than his forearms should have been was bending low here and there collecting trash with tiny hands. Doro looked long at this last slave. Was his deformity a result of some breeding project of Anyanwu's?

Without quite knowing why he did it, Doro rode on. He had planned to take Anyanwu as soon as he found her—take her while she was off guard, still human and vulnerable. Instead, he went away, found lodging for the night at the cabin of one of Anyanwu's poorer neighbors. That neighbor was a man, his wife, their four younger children, and several thousand fleas. Doro spent a miserable, sleepless night, but over both supper and breakfast, he found the family a good source of information about its wealthy neighbor. It was from this man and woman that Doro learned of the married daughters, the bastard slave children, Mr. Warrick's unneighborly behavior—a great sin in the eyes of these people. And there was the dead wife, the frequent trips Warrick made to who knew where, and most strangely, that the Warrick property was haunted by what the local Acadians called a *loup-garou*— a werewolf. The creature appeared to be only a large black dog, but the man in the family, born and raised within a few miles of where he now lived, swore the same dog had been roaming that property since he was a boy. It had been known to disarm grown men, then stand over their rifles growling and daring them to take back what was theirs. Rumor had it that the dog had been shot several times—shot point-blank—but never felled. Never. Bullets passed through it as though through smoke.

That was enough for Doro. For how many years had Anyanwu spent much of her time either away from home or in the form of a large dog? How long had it taken her to realize that he could not find her while she was an animal? Most important, what would happen now if she had spotted him somehow, if she took animal form and escaped? He should have killed her at once! Perhaps he could use hostages again—let his senses seek out those of her slaves who would make good prey. Perhaps he could force her back by threatening them. They would almost certainly be the best of her children.

The next morning Doro headed his black gelding up the pathway to Anyanwu's mansion. As he reached it an adolescent boy came to take his horse. It was the boy with the deformed arms.

"Is your master at home?" Doro asked.

"Yes, sir," said the boy softly.

Doro laid a hand on the boy's shoulder. "Leave the horse here. He'll be all right. Take me to your master." He had not expected to make such a quick decision, but the boy was perfect for what he wanted. Despite his deformity, he was highly desirable prey. No doubt Anyanwu treasured him—a beloved son.

The boy looked at Doro, unafraid, then started toward the house. Doro kept a grip on his shoulder, though he did not doubt that the boy could have gotten away easily. Doro was wearing the body of a short, slight Frenchman while the boy was well-muscled, powerful-looking in spite of his own short stature. All Anyanwu's children tended to be short.

"What happened to your arms?" Doro asked.

The boy glanced at him, then at the foreshortened arms. "Accident, massa," he said softly. "I tried to bring horses out of the stable fire. 'Fore I could get 'em out, de beam fell on me." Doro did not like his slave patois. It sounded false.

"But . . ." Doro frowned at the tiny child's arms on the young man's body. No accident could cause such a deformity. "I mean were you born with your arms that way?"

"No, sir. I was born with two good arms—long as yours."

"Then why do you have deformed arms now!" Doro demanded exasperated.

" 'Cause of de beam, massa. Old arms broken up and burnt. Had to grow new ones. Couple more weeks and dese be long enough."

Doro jerked the boy around to face him, and the boy smiled. For a moment, Doro wondered whether he was demented—as warped of mind as he was of body. But the eyes were intelligent—even mocking now. It seemed that the boy was perfectly intelligent, and laughing at him.

"Do you always tell people you can do such things—grow new arms?"

The boy shook his head, straightened so that he met Doro's eyes levelly. There was nothing of the slave in his gaze. When he spoke again, he ceased to make even his minimal effort to sound like a slave.

"I've never told any outsider before," he said. "But I'm told that if I let you know what I can do and that I'm the only one who can do it, I'll stand a better chance of living out the day."

There was no point in asking who had told him. Somehow, Anyanwu had spotted him. "How old are you?" he asked the boy.

"Nineteen."

"How old were you at transition?"

"Seventeen."

"What can you do?"

"Heal myself. I'm slower at it than she is, though, and I can't change my shape."

"Why not?"

"I don't know. I suppose because my father couldn't."

"What could he do?"

"I never knew him. He died. But she says he could hear what people were thinking."

"Can you?"

"Sometimes."

Doro shook his head. Anyanwu had come almost as near to success as he had—and with far less raw material. "Take me to her!" he said.

"She's here," the boy said.

Startled, Doro looked around, searching for Anyanwu, knowing she must be in animal form since he had not sensed her. She stood perhaps ten paces behind him near a yellow pine sapling. She was a large, sharp-faced black dog, standing statue-still, watching him. He spoke to her impatiently.

"I can't very well talk to you while you're like that!"

She began to change. She took her time about it, but he did not complain. He had waited too long for a few minutes to matter.

Finally, human, female, and unself-consciously naked, she walked past him onto the porch. In that moment, he meant to kill her. If she had taken any other form, become anyone other than her true self, she would have died. But she was now as she had been over a hundred and fifty years—a century and a half—before. She was the same woman he had shared a clay couch with thousands of miles away, lifetimes ago. He raised his hand toward her. She did not see it. He could have taken her then and there without further trouble. But he lowered the hand before it touched her smooth, dark shoulder. He stared at her, angry with himself, frowning.

"Come into the house, Doro," she said.

Her voice was the same, soft and young. He followed her in feeling oddly confused, suspended in time, with only the watchful, protective young son to jar him to reality.

He looked at the son, ragged and shoeless and dusty. The

boy should have seemed out of place inside the handsomely furnished home, but somehow, he did not.

"Come into the parlor," he said, catching Doro's arm in his child-sized hands. "Let her put her clothes on. She'll be back."

Doro did not doubt that she would. Apparently, the boy understood his role as hostage.

Doro sat down in an upholstered armchair and the boy sat opposite him on a sofa. Between them was a small wooden table and a fireplace of carved black stone. There was a large oriental rug on the floor and several other chairs and tables scattered around the room. A maid in a plain clean blue dress and white apron brought brandy and looked at the boy as though daring him to have any. He smiled and did not.

The maid would have been good prey too. A daughter? "What can she do?" Doro asked when she was gone.

"Nothing but have babies," the boy said.

"Did she had a transition?"

"No. She won't either. Not as old as she is."

A latent then. One who could pass her heritage on to her children, but could not use it herself. She should be bred to a near relative. Doro wondered whether Anyanwu had overcome her squeamishness enough to do this. Was that where this boy who was growing arms had come from? Inbreeding? Was his father, perhaps, one of Anyanwu's older sons?

"What do you know about me?" he asked the boy.

"That you're no more what you appear to be than she is." The boy shrugged. "She talked about you sometimes—how you took her from Africa, how she was your slave in New York back when they had slaves in New York."

"She was never my slave."

"She thinks she was. She doesn't think she will be again though."

In her bedroom, Anyanwu dressed quickly and casually as a man. She kept her body womanly—she wanted to be herself when she faced Doro—but after the easy unclothed freedom of the dog body, she could not have stood the layers of tight clothing women were expected to wear. The male clothing accented her womanliness anyway. No one had ever seen her this way and mistaken her for a man or boy.

Abruptly, she threw her shirt to the floor and stood, head in hands, before her dressing table. Doro would break Stephen into pieces if she ran now. He would probably not kill him, but he would make him a slave. There were people here in Louisiana and in the other Southern states who bred people as Doro did. They gave a man one woman after another and when the children came, the man had no authority over what was done to them, no responsibility to them or to their mothers. Authority and responsibility were the prerogatives of the masters. Doro would do that to her son, make him no more than a breeding animal. She thought of the sons and daughters she had left behind in Doro's hands. It was not likely that any of them were alive now, but she had no doubt of the way Doro had used them while they did live. She could not have helped them. It was all she had been able to do to get Doro to give his word not to harm them during her marriage to Isaac. Beyond that, she could have stayed with them and died, but she could not have helped them. And growing up as they had in Wheatley, they would not have wanted her help. Doro seduced people. He made them want to please him, made them strive for his approval. He terrified them into submission only when he could not seduce them.

And when he could not terrify them . . .

What could she do? She could not run again and leave him Stephen and the others. But she was no more able to help them by staying than she had been able to help her children in Wheatley. She could not even help herself. What would he do to her when she went downstairs? She had run away from him, and he murdered runaways. Had he allowed her to dress herself merely so that he would not have the inconvenience of taking over a naked body?

What could she do?

Doro and Stephen were talking like old friends when Anyanwu walked into the parlor. To her surprise, Doro stood up. He had always seemed lazily unconcerned with such courtesies before. She sat with Stephen on the sofa, noticing automatically that the boy's arms seemed to be forming well. He had been so good, so controlled on that terrible day when he lost them.

"Go back to your work now," she told him softly.

He looked at her, surprised.

"Go," she repeated. "I'm here now."

Clearly, that was what was concerning him. She had told him a great deal about Doro. He did not want to leave her, but finally, he obeyed.

"Good boy," Doro commented, sipping brandy.

"Yes," she agreed.

He shook his head. "What shall I do with him, Anyanwu? What shall I do with you?"

She said nothing. When had it ever mattered what she said to him? He did as he pleased.

"You've had more success than I have," he said. "Your son seems controlled—very sure of himself."

"I taught him to lift his head," she said.

"I meant his ability."

"Yes."

"Who was his father?"

She hesitated. He would ask, of course. He would inquire after the ancestry of her children as though after the bloodline of a horse. "His father was brought illegally from Africa," she said. "He was a good man, but . . . much like Thomas. He could see and hear and feel too much."

"And he survived a crossing on a slave ship?"

"Only part of him survived. He was mad most of the time, but he was docile. He was like a child. The slavers pretended that it was because he had not yet learned English that he seemed strange. They showed me how strong his muscles were—I had the form of a white man, you see."

"I know."

"They showed me his teeth and his hands and his penis and they said what a good breeder he would be. They would have pleased you, Doro. They thought very much as you do."

"I doubt it," he said amiably. He was being surprisingly amiable. He was at his first stage—seeking to seduce her as he had when he took her from her people. No doubt by his own reasoning he was being extremely generous. She had run from him, done what no one else could do, kept out of his hands for more than a lifetime; yet instead of killing her at once, he seemed to be beginning again with her—giving her a chance to accept him as though nothing had happened. That meant he wanted her alive, if she would submit.

Her own sense of relief at this realization startled her. She had come down the stairs to him expecting to die, ready to die, and here he was courting her again. And here she was responding. . . .

No. Not again. No more Wheatleys.

What then?

"So you bought a slave you knew was insane because he had a sensitivity you liked," Doro said. "You couldn't imagine how many times I've done things like that myself."

"I bought him in New Orleans because as he walked past me in chains on his way to the slave pens, he called to me. He said, 'Anyanwu! Does that white skin cover your eyes too?'"

"He spoke English?"

"No. He was one of my people. Not a descendant, I think; he was too different. In the moment he spoke to me, he was sane and hearing my thoughts. Slaves were passing in front of me all chained, and I was thinking, 'I have to take more sunken gold from the sea, then see the banker about buying the land that adjoins mine. I have to buy some books—medical books, especially to see what doctors are doing now. . . .' I was not seeing the slaves in front of me. I would not have thought I could be oblivious to such a thing. I had been white for too long. I needed someone to say what he said to me."

"So you brought him home and bore him a son."

"I would have borne him many sons. It seemed that his spirit was healing from what they had done to him on the ship. At the end, he was sane nearly all the time. He was a good husband then. But he died."

"Of what sickness?"

"None that I could find. He saw his son and said in praise, '*Ifeyinwa!*—what is like a child.' I made that Stephen's other name, Ifeyinwa. Then Mgbada died. I am a bad healer sometimes. I am no healer at all sometimes."

"No doubt the man lived much longer and better than he would have without you."

"He was a young man," she said. "If I were the healer I long to be, he would still be alive."

"What kind of healer is the boy?"

"Less than I am in some ways. Slower. But he has some of his father's sensitivity. Didn't you wonder how he knew you?"

"I thought you had seen me and warned him."

"I told him about you. Perhaps he knew your voice from hearing it in my thoughts. I don't ask him what he hears. But no, I did not see you before you arrived—not to know you, anyway." Did he really think she would have stayed to meet him, kept her children here so that he could threaten them? Did he think she had grown stupid with the years? "He can touch people sometimes and know what is wrong with them," she continued. "When he says a thing is wrong, it is. But sometimes he misses things—things I wouldn't miss."

"He's young," Doro said.

She shrugged.

"Will he ever grow old, Anyanwu?"

"I don't know." She hesitated, spoke her hope in a whisper. "Perhaps I have finally borne a son I will not have to bury." She looked up, saw that Doro was watching her intently. There was a kind of hunger in his expression—hunger that he masked quickly.

"Can he control his thought reading?" he asked, neutral-voiced.

"In that, he is his father's opposite. Mgbada could not control what he heard—like Thomas. That was why his people sold him into slavery. He was a sorcerer to them. But Stephen must make an effort to hear other people's thoughts. It has not happened by accident since his transition. But sometimes when he tries, nothing happens. He says it is like never knowing when he will be struck deaf."

"That is a tolerable defect," Doro said. "He might be frustrated sometimes, but he will never go mad with the weight of other people's thoughts pressing in on him."

"I have told him that."

There was a long silence. Something was coming, and it had to do with Stephen, Anyanwu knew. She wanted to ask what it was, but then Doro would tell her and she would have to find some way to defy him. When she did . . . when she did, she would fail, and he would kill her.

"He is to me what Isaac was to you," she whispered. Would he hear that as what it was—a plea for mercy?

He stared at her as though she had said something incomprehensible, as though he was trying to understand. Finally, he smiled a small, uncharacteristically tentative smile. "Did you ever think, Anyanwu, how long a hundred years is to an ordinary person—or a hundred and fifty years?"

She shrugged. Nonsense. He was talking nonsense while she waited to hear what he meant to do to her son!

"How do the years seem to you?" he asked. "Like days? Like months? What do you feel when good companions are suddenly old and gray and addled?"

Again, she shrugged. "People grow old. They die."

"All of them," he agreed. "All but you and I."

"You die constantly," she said.

He got up and went to sit beside her on the sofa. Somehow, she kept still, subdued her impulse to get up, move away from him. "I have never died," he said.

She stared past him at one of the candlesticks on the mantel. "Yes," she said. "I should have said you kill constantly."

He was silenced. She faced him, looked into eyes that were large and wide-set and brown. He had the eyes of a larger man—or his current body did. They gave him a false expression of gentleness.

"Did you come here to kill?" she asked. "Am I to die? Are my children to become mares and studs? Is that why you could not leave me alone!"

"Why do you want to be alone?" he asked.

She closed her eyes. "Doro, tell me what is to happen."

"Perhaps nothing. Perhaps eventually, I will bring your son a wife."

"One wife?" she said, disbelieving.

"One wife here, as with you and Isaac. I never brought women to Wheatley for him."

That was so. From time to time, he took Isaac away with him, but he never brought women to Isaac. Anyanwu knew that the husband she had loved most had sired dozens of children with other women. "Don't you care about them?" she had asked once, trying to understand. She cared about each one of her children, raised each one she bore and loved it.

"I never see them," he had answered. "They are his children. I sire them in his name. He sees that they and their mothers are well cared for."

"So he says!" She had been bitter that day, angry at Doro for making her pregnant when her most recent child by Isaac was less than a year old, angry at him for afterward killing a tall, handsome girl whom Anyanwu had known and liked. The girl, understanding what was to happen to her, had still somehow treated him as a lover. It was obscene.

"Have you ever known him to neglect the needs of the children he claims?" Isaac had asked. "Have you ever seen his people left landless or hungry? He takes care of his own."

She had gone away from Isaac to fly for hours as a bird and look down at the great, empty land below and wonder if there was nowhere in all the forests and rivers and mountains and lakes, nowhere in that endless land for her to escape and find peace and cleanness.

"Stephen is nineteen years old," she said. "He is a man. Your children and mine grow up very quickly, I think. He has been a man since his transition. But he's still young. You'll make him an animal if you use him as you used Isaac."

"Isaac was fifteen when I gave him his first woman," Doro said.

"Then he had been yours for fifteen years. For you, Stephen will be as much wild seed as I was."

Doro nodded agreeably. "It is better for me to get them before they reach their transitions—if they're going to have transitions. What will you give me then, Anyanwu?"

She turned to look at him in surprise. Was he offering to bargain with her? He had never bargained before. He had told her what he wanted and let her know what he would do to her or to her children if she did not obey.

Was he bargaining now, then, or was he playing with her? What could she lose by assuming that he was serious? "Bring Stephen the woman," she said. "One woman. When he is older, perhaps there can be others."

"Do you imagine there are none now?"

"Of course not. But he chooses his own. I don't tell him to breed. I don't send him women."

"Do women seem to like him?"

She surprised herself by smiling a little. "Some do. Not enough to suit him, of course. There is a widow paying a lot of attention to him now. She knows what she is doing. Left alone, he will find a good wife here when he is tired of wandering around."

"Perhaps I shouldn't let him get tired of it."

"I tell you, you will make an animal of him if you don't!" she said. "Haven't you seen the men slaves in this country who are used for breeding? They are never permitted to learn what it means to be a man. They are not permitted to care for their children. Among my people, children are wealth, they are better than money, better than anything. But to these

men, warped and twisted by their masters, children are almost nothing. They are to boast of to other men. One thinks
he is greater than another because he has more children.
Both exaggerate the number of women who have borne them
children, neither is doing anything a father should for his
children, and the master who is indifferently selling off his
own brown children is laughing and saying, 'You see? Niggers
are just like animals!' Slavery down here opens one's eyes,
Doro. How could I want such a life for my son?"

There was silence. He got up, wandered around the large
room examining the vases, lamps, the portrait of a slender
white woman with dark hair and solemn expression. "Was
this your wife?" he asked.

She wanted to shake him. She wanted to use her strength,
make him tell her what he meant to do. "Yes," she whispered.

"How did you like it—being a man, having a wife?"

"Doro . . . !"

"How did you like it?" He would not be rushed. He was
enjoying himself.

"She was a good woman. We pleased each other."

"Did she know what you were?"

"Yes. She was not ordinary herself. She saw ghosts."

"Anyanwu!" he said with disgust and disappointment.

She ignored his tone, stared up at the picture. "She was
only sixteen when I married her. If I hadn't married her, I
think she would have been put in an asylum eventually. People spoke about her in the way you just said my name."

"I don't blame them."

"You should. Most people believe in a life that goes on
after their bodies die. There are always tales of ghosts. Even
people who think they are too sophisticated to be frightened
are not immune. Talk to five people and at least three will
have seen what they believe was a ghost, or they will know
another person who has seen. But Denice really did see. She
was very sensitive; she could see when no one else could—
and since no one else could, people said she was mad. I think
she had had a kind of transition."

"And it gave her a private view into the hereafter."

Anyanwu shook her head. "You should be less skeptical. You are a kind of ghost yourself, after all. What is there of you that can be touched?"

"I've heard that before."

"Of course." She paused. "Doro, I will talk to you about Denice. I will talk to you about anyone, anything. But first, please, tell me what you plan for my son."

"I'm thinking about it. I'm thinking about you and your potential value to me." He looked again at the portrait. "You were right, you know. I came here to finish old business— kill you and take your children to one of my settlements. No one has ever done what you did to me."

"I ran from you and lived. Other people have done that."

"Only because I chose to let them live. They had their freedom for only a few days before I caught them. You know that."

"Yes," she said reluctantly.

"Now, a century after I lost you, I find you young and well—greeting me as though we had just seen each other yesterday. I find you in competition with me, raising witches of your own."

"There is no competition."

"Then why have you surrounded yourself with the kinds of people I seek out? Why do you have children by them?"

"They need me . . . those people." She swallowed, thinking of some of the things done to her people before she found them. "They need someone who can help them, and I can help. You don't want to help them, you want to use them. But I can help."

"Why should you?"

"I'm a healer, Doro."

"That's no answer. You chose to be a healer. What you really are is what's called in this part of the country loup-garou—a werewolf."

"I see you've been talking to my neighbors."

"I have. They're right, you know."

"The legends say werewolves kill. I have never killed except to save myself. I am a healer."

"Most . . . healers don't have children by their patients."

"Most healers do as they please. My patients are more like me than any other people. Why shouldn't I find mates among them?"

Doro smiled. "There is always an answer, isn't there? But it doesn't matter. Tell me about Denice and her ghosts."

She drew a deep breath and let it out slowly, calming herself. "Denice saw what people left behind. She went into houses and saw the people who had preceded her there. If someone had suffered or died there, she saw that very clearly. It terrified her. She would go into a house and see a child running, clothing afire, and there would be no child. But two, ten, twenty years before, a child would have burned to death there. She saw people stealing things days or years before. She saw slaves beaten and tortured, slave women raped, people shaking with ague or covered with smallpox. She did not feel things as people do in transition. She only saw them. But she could not tell whether what she was seeing was actually happening as she saw it or whether it was history. She was slowly going mad. Then her parents gave a party and I was invited because I seemed young and rich and handsome—perhaps a good prospect for a family with five daughters. I remember, I was standing with Denice's father telling lies about my origins, and Denice brushed past. She touched me, you see. She could see people's past lives when she touched them just as she could see the past of wood and brick. She saw something of what I am even in that brief touch, and she fainted. I didn't know what had happened until she came to me days later. I was the only person she had ever found to be stranger than herself. She knew all that I was before we married."

"Why did she marry you?"

"Because I believed her when she told me what she could do. Because I was not afraid or ridiculing. And because after a while, we started to want each other."

"Even though she knew you were a woman and black?"

"Even so." Anyanwu stared up at the solemn young woman, remembering that lovely, fearful courting. They had been as fearful of marrying as they had been of losing each other. "She thought at first that there could be no children, and that saddened her because she had always wanted children. Then she realized that I could give her girls. It took her a long time to understand all that I could do. But she thought the children would be black and people would say she had been with a slave. White men leave brown children all about, but a white woman who does this becomes almost an animal in the eyes of other whites."

"White women must be protected," Doro said, "whether they want to be or not."

"As property is protected." Anyanwu shook her head. "Preserved for the use of owners alone. Denice said she felt like property—like a slave plotting escape. I told her I could give her children who were not related to me at all if she wished. Her fear made me angry even though I knew the situation was not her fault. I told her my Warrick shape was not a copy of anyone. I had molded myself freely to create it, but if she wished, I could take the exact shape of one of the white men I had treated in Wheatley. Then as with the dolphins, I could have young who inherited nothing at all from me. Even male young. She did not understand that."

"Neither do I," Doro said. "This is something new."

"Only for me. You do it all the time—fathering or giving birth to children who are no blood kin to you. They are the children of the bodies you wear, even though you call them your own."

"But . . . you only wear one body."

"And you have not understood how completely that one body can change. I cannot leave it as you can, but I can make it over. I can make it over so completely in the image of someone else that I am no longer truly related to my parents. It makes me wonder what I am—that I can do this and still know myself, still return to my true shape."

"You could not do this before in Wheatley."

"I have always done it. Each time I learned a new animal shape, I did it. But I did not understand it very well until I began running from you. Until I began to hide. I bore dolphin young—and they were dolphins. Not human at all. They were the young of the dolphin Isaac caught and fed to us so long ago. My body was a copy of hers down to the smallest living part. There are no words for me to tell you how deep and complete such a change is."

"So you could become another person so completely that the children you gave Denice were not really yours."

"I could have. But when she understood, she did not want that. She said she would rather have no children at all. But that sacrifice was not necessary. I could give her girl children of my own body. Girl children who would have her coloring. It was hard work arranging all that. There are so many tiny things within even one cell of a human body. I could have given her a monstrosity if I had been careless."

"I made you study these things by driving you away?"

"You did. You made me learn very much. Much of the time, I had nothing to do but study myself, try things I had not thought of before."

"If you duplicated another man's shape then, you could father sons."

"The other man's sons."

Slowly, Doro drew his mouth into a smile. "That's the answer then, Anyanwu. You'll take your son's place. You'll take the place of a great many people."

"You mean . . . for me to go here and there getting children and then forgetting about them?"

"Either you go or I'll bring women to you here."

She got up wearily, without even outrage to make her stiff and hostile. "You are a complete fool," she told him quietly, and she walked into the hall, through the house, and out the back door. From there, through the trees she could see the bayou with its slow water. Nearer were the dependencies and the slave cabins that were not inhabited by slaves.

She owned no slaves. She had bought some of the people who worked for her and recruited the others among freedmen, but those she bought, she freed. They always stayed to work for her, feeling more comfortable with her and with each other than they had ever been elsewhere. That always surprised the new ones. They were not used to being comfortable with other people. They were misfits, malcontents, troublemakers—though they did not make trouble for Anyanwu. They treated her as mother, older sister, teacher, and, when she invited it, lover. Somehow, even this last intimacy did nothing to diminish her authority. They knew her power. She was who she was, no matter what role she chose.

And yet, she did not threaten them, did not slaughter among them as Doro did among his people. The worse she did was occasionally fire someone. Firing meant eviction. It meant leaving the safety and comfort of the plantation and becoming a misfit again in the world outside. It meant exile.

Few of them knew how difficult it was for Anyanwu to turn one of them out—or worse, turn a family out. Few of them knew how their presence comforted her. She was not Doro, breeding people as though they were cattle, though perhaps her gathering of all these special ones, these slightly strange ones would accomplish the same purpose as his breeding. She was herself, gathering family. No doubt some of these people were of her family, her descendants. They felt like her children. Perhaps, there had been intermarriage, her descendants drawn together by a comforting but indefinable similarity and not knowing of their common origins. And there were other people probably not related to her, who had rudimentary sensitivity that could become true thought reading in a few generations. Mgbada had told her this—that she was gathering people who were like his grandparents. He had told her she was breeding witches.

An old woman came up to her—a white woman, withered and gray, Luisa, who did what sewing she could for her keep. She was one of five white people on the place. There could have been many more whites, fitting in very comfortably, but the race-conscious culture made that dangerous. The four younger whites tried to lessen the danger by telling people they were octoroons. Luisa was a Creole—a French-Spanish mixture—and too old to care who knew it.

"Is there trouble?" Luisa asked.

Anyanwu nodded.

"Stephen said he was here—Doro, the one you told me about."

"Go and tell the others not to come in from the fields until I call them in myself."

Luisa stared hard at her. "What if he calls—with your mouth?"

"Then they must decide whether to run or not. They know about him. If they want to run now, they can. Later, if the black dog is seen in the woods again, they can come back." If Doro killed her, he would not be able to use her healing or metamorphosing abilities. She had learned that from her stay in Wheatley. He could possess someone's body and use it to have children, but he could use only the body. When he possessed Thomas so long ago, he had not gained Thomas' thought-reading ability. She had never known him to use any extra ability from a body he possessed.

The old woman took Anyanwu by the shoulders and hugged her. "What will you do?" she asked.

"I don't know."

"I have never seen him and I hate him."

"Go," Anyanwu told her.

Luisa hurried across the grass. She moved well for her age. Like Anyanwu's children, she had lived a long, healthy life. Cholera, malaria, yellow fever, typhus, and other diseases swept across the land and left Anyanwu's people almost untouched. If they caught a disease, they survived it and recovered quickly. If they hurt themselves, Anyanwu was there to care for them.

As Luisa disappeared into the trees, Doro came out of the house. "I could go after her," he said. "I know you sent her to warn your field hands."

Anyanwu turned to face him angrily. "You are many times as old as I am. You must have some inborn defect to keep you from getting wisdom to go with your years."

"Will you eventually condescend to tell me what wisdom you have gotten?" There was an edge to his voice finally. She was beginning to irritate him and end the seductive phase. That was good. How stupid of him to think she could be seduced again. It was possible, however, that she might seduce him.

"You were pleased to see me again, weren't you?" she said. "I think you were surprised to realize how pleased you were."

"Say what you have to say, Anyanwu!"

She shrugged. "Isaac was right."

Silence. She knew Isaac had spoken to him several times. Isaac had wanted them together so badly—the two people he loved best. Did that mean anything at all to Doro? It had not years before, but now . . . Doro had been glad to see her. He had marveled over the fact that she seemed unchanged— as though he was only now beginning to realize that she was only slightly more likely to die than he was, and not likely at all to grow decrepit with age. As though her immortality had been emotionally unreal to him until now, a fact that he had accepted with only half his mind.

"Doro, I will go on living unless you kill me. There is no reason for me to die unless you kill me."

"Do you think you can take over work I've spent millennia at?"

"Do you think I want to?" she countered. "I was telling the truth. These people need me, and I need them. I never set out to build a settlement like one of yours. Why should I? I don't need new bodies as you do. All I need is my own kind around me. My family or people who feel like my family. To you, most of my people here wouldn't even be good breeding stock, I think."

"Forty years ago, that old woman would have."

"Does that make it competition for me to give her a home now?"

"You have others. Your maid . . ."

"My daughter!"

"I thought so."

"She is unmarried. Bring her a man. If she likes him, let her marry him and bear interesting children. If she doesn't like him, then find her someone else. But she needs only one husband, Doro, as my son needs only one wife."

"Is that what your own way of life tells them? Or shall I believe you sleep alone because your husbands are dead?"

"If my children show any signs of growing as old as I am, they may do as they please."

"They will anyway."

"But without you to guide them, Doro. Without you to make them animals. What would my son be in your hands? Another Thomas? You are going everywhere tending ten different settlements, twenty, and not giving enough of yourself to any of them. I am staying here looking after my family and offering to let your children marry mine. And if the offspring are strange and hard to handle, I will handle them. I will take care of them. They need not live alone in the woods and drink too much and neglect their bodies until they are nearly dead."

To her surprise, he hugged her very much as Luisa had, and he laughed. He took her arm and walked her over to the slave quarters, still laughing. He quieted though as he pushed open a random door and peered into one of the neat, sturdy cabins. There was a large brick fireplace with a bake kettle down amid the nearly dead coals. Someone's supper bread. There was a large bed in one corner and a trundle bed beneath. There were a table and four chairs all of which looked homemade, but adequate. There was a cradle that also looked homemade—and much used. There were a wood box and a water bucket with its gourd dipper. There were bunches of herbs and ears of corn hung from the ceiling to dry and cooking utensils over and alongside the fireplace. Overall, the cabin gave the impression of being a plain but comfortable place to live.

"Is it enough?" Anyanwu asked.

"I have several people, black and white, who don't live this well."

"I don't."

He tried to draw her into the cabin toward the chairs or the bed—she did not know which—but she held back.

"This is someone else's home," she said. "We can go back into the house if you like."

"No. Later, perhaps." He put an arm around her waist. "You must feed me again and find us another earthen couch to lie on."

And hear you threaten my children again, she thought.

As though in answer, he said: "And I must tell you why I laughed. It isn't because your offer doesn't please me, Anyanwu; it does. But you have no idea what kinds of creatures you are volunteering to care for."

Didn't she? Hadn't she seen them in Wheatley?

"I'm going to bring you some of your own descendants," Doro said. "I think they will surprise you. I've done a great deal of work with them since Nweke. I think you won't be wanting to care for them or their children for long."

"Why? What new thing is wrong with them?"

"Perhaps nothing. Perhaps your influence is just what they need. On the other hand, perhaps they will disrupt the family you've made for yourself here as nothing else could. Will you still have them?"

"Doro, how can I know? You haven't told me anything."

Her hair was loose and short and rounded as it had been when he first styled it for her. Now he put his hands on either side of it, pressing it to her head. "Sun Woman, either you will accept my people in this way that you have defined or you will come with me, taking mates when and where I command, or you will give me your children. One way or another, you will serve me. What is your choice?"

Yes, she thought bitterly. *Now the threats.* "Bring me my grandchildren," she said. "Even though they have never seen me, they will remember me. Their bodies will remember me down to the smallest structures of their flesh. You cannot know how well people's bodies remember their ancestors."

"You will teach me," he said. "You seem to have learned a great deal since I saw you last. I've been breeding people nearly all my life and I still don't know why some things work and others don't, or why a thing will work only some of the time even with the same couple. You will teach me."

"You will not harm my people?" she asked, watching him carefully.

"What do they know about me?"

"Everything. I thought if you ever found us, there wouldn't be time for me to explain the danger."

"Tell them to obey me."

She winced as though in pain and looked away. "You cannot always take everything," she said. "Or just take my life. What is the good of living on and on and having nothing?"

There was silence for a moment. "Did they obey Denice?" he asked finally. "Or Mgbada?"

"Sometimes. They are a very independent people."

"But they obey you."

"Yes."

"Then tell them to obey me. If you don't, I'll have to tell them myself—in whichever way they understand."

"Don't hurt them!"

He shrugged. "If they obey me, I won't."

He was making a new Wheatley. He had settlements everywhere, families everywhere. She had only one, and he was taking it. He had taken her from one people and driven her from another, and now, he was casually reaching out to strip her of a third. And she was wrong. She could live on and on and have nothing. She would. He would see to it.

12

.

A nyanwu had never watched a group like her own break apart. She did not know whether there had ever before been a group like her own. Certainly, once Doro began to spend time at the plantation, exercising his authority as he chose while Anyanwu stood by and said nothing, the character of the group began to change. When he brought Joseph Toler as husband for one of Anyanwu's daughters, the young man changed the group more by refusing to do work of any kind. His foster parents had pampered him, allowed him to spend his time drinking and gambling and bedding young women. But he was a beautiful young man—honey-colored with curly black hair, tall and slender. Anyanwu's daughter Margaret Nneka was fascinated by him. She accepted him very quickly. Few other people on the plantation accepted him at all. He was not doing his share of the work, yet he could not be fired and sent away. He could, however, make a great deal of trouble. He had been on the plantation for only a few weeks when he went too far and lost a fistfight with Anyanwu's son Stephen.

Anyanwu was alone when Stephen came to tell her what had happened. She had just come from treating a four-year-old who had wandered down to the bayou and surprised a water moccasin. She had been able to manufacture within her own body a medicine to counter the poison easily, since one of the first things she had done on settling in Louisiana was allow herself to be bitten by such a snake. By now, countering the poison was almost second nature to her. She did like to have a meal afterward, though; thus Stephen, bruised and disheveled, found her in the dining room eating.

"You've got to get rid of that lazy, worthless bastard," he said.

Anyanwu sighed. There was no need to ask who the boy meant. "What has he done?"

"Tried to rape Helen."

Anyanwu dropped the piece of cornbread she had been about to bite. Helen was her youngest daughter—eleven years old. "He what!"

"I caught them in the Duran cabin. He was tearing her clothes off."

"Is she all right?"

"Yes. She's in her room."

Anyanwu stood up. "I'll see her in a little while, then. Where is he?"

"Lying in front of the Duran cabin."

She went out, not knowing whether she was going to give the young man another beating or help him if Stephen had hurt him seriously. But what kind of animal was he to try to rape a child? How could Anyanwu possibly tolerate him here after this? Doro would have to take him away, breeding be damned.

The young man was not beautiful when Anyanwu found him. He was half again as large as Stephen and strong in spite of his indolence, but Stephen had inherited much of Anyanwu's strength. And he knew how to administer a good beating, even with his tender, newly finished arms and hands.

The young man's face was a lumpy mass of bruised tissue. His nose was broken and bleeding. The flesh around his eyes was grotesquely swollen. The left ear was torn nearly off. He would lose it and look like one of the slaves marked and sold South for running away.

His body was so bruised beneath his shirt that Anyanwu was certain he had broken ribs. And he was lacking several of his front teeth. He would never be beautiful again. He began to come to as Anyanwu was probing at his ribs. He grunted, cursed, coughed, and with the cough, twisted in agony.

"Be still," Anyanwu said. "Breathe shallowly, and try not to cough anymore."

The young man whimpered.

"Be thankful Stephen caught you," she said. "If it had been me, you would take no more interest in women, I promise you. Not for the rest of your life."

In spite of his pain, the young man cringed away from her, clutching himself protectively.

"What can there be in you worth inflicting on descendants?" she asked in disgust. She made him stand up, ignoring his weakness, his moans of pain. "Now get into the house!" she said. "Or go lie in the barn with the other animals."

He made it into the house, did not pass out until he reached the stairs. Anyanwu carried him up to a small, hot attic bedroom, washed him, bandaged his ribs, and left him there with water, bread, and a little fruit. She could have given him something to ease his pain, but she did not.

The little girl, Helen, lay asleep on her bed still wearing her torn dress. Her face was swollen on one side as though from a heavy blow, and the sight of it made Anyanwu want to give the young man another beating. Instead, she woke the child gently.

In spite of her gentleness, Helen awoke with a start and cried out.

"You are safe," Anyanwu told her. "I'm here."

The child clung to her, not weeping, only holding tightly, holding with all her strength.

"Are you hurt?" Anyanwu asked. "Did he hurt you?"

The girl did not respond.

"Obiageli, are you hurt?"

The girl lay down again slowly and looked up at her. "He came into my thoughts," she said. "I could feel him come in."

". . . into your thoughts?"

"I could feel it. I knew it was him. He wanted me to go to Tina Duran's house."

"He made you go?"

"I don't know." Finally, the child began to cry. She pulled her pillow around her swollen face and wept into it. Anyanwu rubbed her shoulders and her neck and let her cry. She did not think the girl was crying because she had nearly been raped.

"Obiageli," she whispered. Before the girl's birth, a child-less white woman named Helen Matthews had asked Anyanwu to give a child her name. Anyanwu had never liked the name Helen, but the white woman had been a good friend—one of those who had overcome her own upbringing and her neighbors' noisy mouths and come to live on the plantation. She had never been able to have children, had been past the age of bearing when she met Anyanwu. Thus, Anyanwu's youngest daughter was named Helen. And Helen was the daughter Anyanwu most often called by her second name, Obiageli. Somehow, she had lost that custom with the others.

"Obiageli, tell me all that he did."

After a while, the girl sniffed, turned over, and wiped her face. She lay still, staring up at the ceiling, one small frown between her eyes.

"I was getting water," she said. "I wanted to help Rita." This was the os rouge cook—a woman of black and Indian ancestry and Spanish appearance. "She needed water, so I was at the well. He came to talk to me. He said I was pretty. He said he liked little girls. He said he had liked me for a long time."

"I should have thrown him into the pigsty," muttered Anyanwu. "Let his body wallow in shit so that it could be fit for his mind."

"I tried to go take the water to Rita," the girl continued. "But he told me to come with him. I went. I didn't like to go, but I could feel him in my thoughts. Then I was away from myself—someplace else watching myself walk with him. I tried to turn back, but I couldn't. My legs were walking without me." She stopped, looked at Anyanwu. "I never knew if Stephen was looking into my thoughts."

"But Stephen can only look," Anyanwu said. "He can't make you do anything."

"He wouldn't anyway."

"No."

Eyes downcast, the girl continued. "We went into Tina's cabin and he was closing the door when I found I could move my legs again. I ran out the door before he could get it shut. Then he took back my legs and I screamed and fell. I thought he would make me walk back, but he came out and grabbed me and dragged me back. I think that was when Stephen saw us." She looked up. "Did Stephen kill him?"

"No." Anyanwu shuddered, not wanting to think of what Doro might have done to Stephen if Stephen had killed the worthless Joseph. If there had to be killing, she must do it. Probably no one on the plantation disliked killing more than she did, but she had to protect her people from both Doro's malicious strangers and Doro himself. Still, she hoped Joseph would behave himself until Doro returned and took him away.

"Stephen should have killed him," Helen said softly. "Now maybe he'll make my legs move again. Or maybe he'll do something worse." She shook her head, her child's face hard and old.

Anyanwu took her hand, remembering—remembering Lale, her Isaac's unlikely, unworthy brother. In all her time with Doro, she had not met another of his people as determinedly vicious as Lale. Until now, perhaps. Why had Doro given her such a man? And why had he not at least warned her?

"What will you do with him?" the girl asked.

"Have Doro take him away."

"Will Doro do that—just because you say so?"

Anyanwu winced. *Just because you say so* . . . How long had things been going on on the plantation just because she said so? People had been content with what she said. If they had problems they could not solve, they came to her. If they quarreled and could not settle matters themselves, they came to her. She had never invited them to come to her with their troubles, but she had never turned them away either. They had made her their final authority. Now her eleven-year-old daughter wanted to know if a thing would happen just because she said so. Her eleven-year-old! It had taken time, patience, and at least some wisdom to build the people's confidence in her. It took only a few weeks of Doro's presence to erode that confidence so badly that even her children doubted her.

"Will Doro take him away?" the girl persisted.

"Yes," Anyanwu said quietly. "I will see to it."

That night, Stephen walked in his sleep for the first time in his life. He walked out onto the upper gallery of the porch and fell or jumped off.

There was no disturbance; Stephen did not cry out. At dawn, old Luisa found him sprawled on the ground, his neck so twisted that Luisa was not surprised to find his body cold.

The old woman climbed the stairs herself to wake Anyanwu and take her to an upstairs sitting room away from the young daughter who was sleeping with her. The daughter, Helen, slept on, content, moving over a little into the warm place Anyanwu had left.

In the sitting room, Luisa stood hesitant, silent before Anyanwu, longing for a way to ease the terrible news. Anyanwu did not know how she was loved, Luisa thought. She gathered people to her and cared for them and helped them care for each other. Luisa had a sensitivity that had made closeness with other people a torture to her for most of her life. Somehow, she had endured a childhood and adolescence on a true plantation, where the ordinary accepted cruelties of slaveholder to slave drove her away into a marriage that she should not have made. People thought she was merely kind and womanishly unrealistic to be in such sympathy with slaves. They did not understand that far too much of the time, she literally felt what the slaves felt, shared fragments of their meager pleasure and far too many fragments of their pain. She had had none of Stephen's control, had never completed the agonizing change that she knew had come to the young man two years before. The man-thing called Doro had told her this was because her ancestry was wrong. He said she was descended from his people. It was his fault then that she had lived her life knowing of her husband's contempt and her children's indifference. It was his fault that she had been sixty years old before she found people whose presence she could endure without pain—people she could love and be loved by. She was "grandmother" to all the children here. Some of them actually lived in her cabin because their parents could not or would not care for them. Luisa thought some parents were too sensitive to any negative or rebellious feelings in their children. Anyanwu thought it was more than that—that some people did not want any children around them, rebellious or not. She said some of Doro's people were that way. Anyanwu took in stray children herself—as well as stray adults. Her son had shown signs of becoming much like her. Now, that son was dead.

"What is it?" Anyanwu asked her. "What has happened?"

"An accident," Luisa said, longing to spare her.

"Is it Joseph?"

"Joseph!" That son of a whore Doro had brought to marry one of Anyanwu's daughters. "Would I care if it were Joseph?"

"Who then? Tell me, Luisa."

The old woman took a deep breath. "Your son," she said. "Stephen is dead."

There was a long, terrible silence. Anyanwu sat frozen, stunned. Luisa wished she would wail with a mother's grief so that Luisa could comfort her. But Anyanwu never wailed.

"How could he die?" Anyanwu whispered. "He was nineteen. He was a healer. How could he die?"

"I don't know. He . . . fell."

"From where?"

"Upstairs. From the gallery."

"But how? Why?"

"How can I know, Anyanwu? It happened last night. It . . . must have. I only found him a few moments ago."

"Show me!"

She would have gone down in her gown, but Luisa seized a cloak from her bedroom and wrapped her in it. She noticed as she left with Anyanwu that the little girl was moving restlessly in her sleep, moaning softly. A nightmare?

Outside, others had discovered Stephen's body. Two children stood back, staring at him wide-eyed, and a woman knelt beside him wailing as Anyanwu would not.

The woman was Iye, a tall, handsome, solemn woman of utterly confused ancestry—French and African, Spanish and Indian. The mixture blended all too well in her. Luisa knew her to have thirty-six years, but she could have passed easily for a woman of twenty-six or even younger. The children were her son and daughter and the one in her belly would be Stephen's son or daughter. She had married a husband who loved wine better than he could love any woman, and wine had finally killed him. Anyanwu had found her destitute with her two babies, selling herself to get food for them, and considering very seriously whether she should take her husband's rusty knife and cut their throats and then her own.

Anyanwu had given her a home and hope. Stephen, when he was old enough, had given her something more. Luisa could remember Anyanwu shaking her head over the match, saying, "She is like a bitch in heat around him! You would never know from her behavior that she could be his mother."

And Luisa had laughed. "You should hear yourself,

Anyanwu. Better yet, you should see yourself when you find a man that you want."

"I am not like that!" Anyanwu had been indignant.

"Of course not. You are very much better—and very much older."

And Anyanwu, being Anyanwu, had gone from angry silence to easy laughter. "No doubt he will be a better husband someday for having known her," she said.

"Or perhaps he will surprise you and marry her," Luisa countered. "Despite their ages, there is more than the ordinary pull between them. She is like him. She has some of what he has, some of the power. She cannot use it, but it is there. I can feel it in her sometimes—especially in those times when she is hottest after him."

Anyanwu had ignored this, preferring to believe that eventually her son would make a suitable marriage. Even now, Luisa did not know whether Anyanwu knew of the child coming. There was nothing showing yet, but Iye had told Luisa. She would not have told Anyanwu.

Now, Anyanwu went to the body, bent to touch the cold flesh of the throat. Iye saw her and started to move away, but Anyanwu caught her hand. "We both mourn," she said softly.

Iye hid her face and continued to weep. It was her youngest child, a boy of eight years, whose scream stopped both her crying and Anyanwu's more silent grief.

At the boy's cry, everyone looked at him, then upward at the gallery where he was looking. There, Helen was slowly climbing over the railing.

Instantly, Anyanwu moved. Luisa had never seen a human being move that quickly. When Helen jumped, Anyanwu was in position beneath her. Anyanwu caught her in careful, cushioning fashion, so that even though the girl had dived off the railing head first, her head did not strike the ground. Neither her head nor her neck were injured. She was almost as large as Anyanwu, but Anyanwu was clearly not troubled by her size or weight. By the time Luisa realized what was happening, it was over. Anyanwu was calming her weeping daughter.

"Why did she do it?" Luisa asked. "What is happening?"

Anyanwu shook her head, clearly frightened, bewildered.

"It was Joseph," Helen said at last. "He moved my legs again. I thought it was only a dream until . . ." She looked up at the gallery, then at her mother who still held her. She began to cry again.

"Obiageli," Anyanwu said. "Stay here with Luisa. Stay here. I'm going up to see him."

But the child clung to Anyanwu and screamed when Luisa tried to pry her loose. Anyanwu could have pried her loose easily, but she chose to spend a few moments more comforting her. When Helen was calmer, it was Iye, not Luisa, who took her.

"Keep her with you," Anyanwu said. "Don't let her go into the house. Don't let anyone in."

"What will you do?" Iye asked.

Anyanwu did not answer. Her body had already begun to change. She threw off her cloak and her gown. By the time she was naked, her body was clearly no longer human. She was changing very quickly, becoming a great cat this time instead of the familiar large dog. A great spotted cat.

When the change was complete, she went to the door, and Luisa opened it for her. Luisa started to follow her in. There would be at least one other door that needed opening, after all. But the cat turned and uttered a loud coughing cry. It barred Luisa's path until she turned and went outside again.

"My God," whispered Iye as Luisa returned. "I'm never afraid of her until she does something like that right in front of me."

Luisa ignored her, went to Stephen and straightened his neck and body, then covered him with Anyanwu's discarded cloak.

"What's she going to do?" Iye asked.

"Kill Joseph," Helen said gently.

"Kill?" Iye stared uncomprehending into the small solemn face.

"Yes," the child said. "And she ought to kill Doro too before he brings us somebody worse."

In leopard form, Anyanwu padded down the hall and up the main stairs, then up the narrower stairs to the attic. She was hungry. She had changed a little too quickly, and she knew she would have to eat soon. She would control herself, though; she would eat none of Joseph's disgusting flesh. Better to eat stinking meat crawling with maggots! How could even Doro have brought her human vermin like Joseph?

His door was shut, but Anyanwu opened it with a single blow of her paw. There was a hoarse sound of surprise from inside. Then, as she bounded into the room, something plucked at her forelegs, and she went sliding on chin and chest to jam her face against his washstand. It hurt, but she could ignore the pain. What she could not ignore was the fear. She had hoped to surprise him, catch him before he could use his ability. She had even hoped that he could not stop her while she was in a nonhuman form. Now, she gave her tearing, coughing roar of anger and of fear that she might fail.

For an instant, her legs were free. Perhaps she had frightened him into losing control. It did not matter. She leaped, claws extended, as though to the back of a running deer.

Joseph screamed and threw his arms up to shield his throat. At the same moment, he controlled her legs again. He was inhumanly quick in his desperation. Anyanwu knew that because she was inhumanly quick all the time.

Sensation left her legs, and she almost toppled off him. She seized a hold with her teeth, sinking them into one of his arms, tearing away flesh, meaning to get at the throat.

Feeling returned to her legs, but suddenly she could not breathe. Her throat felt closed, blocked somehow.

Instantly, she located the blockage, opened a place beneath it—a hole in her throat through which to breathe. And she got his throat between her teeth.

Utterly desperate, he jammed his fingers in the newly-made breathing hole.

At another time with other prey, she might have collapsed at the sudden, raw agony. But now the image of her dead son was before her, and her daughter nearly dead in the same way. What if he had merely closed their throats as he had just closed hers? She might never have known for sure. He might have gotten away with it.

She ripped his throat out.

He was dying when she gave way to her own pain. He was too far gone to hurt her any more. He died with soft bubbling noises and much bleeding as she lay across him reviving herself, mending herself. She was hungry. Great God, she was hungry. The smell of blood filled her nostrils as she restored her normal breathing ability, and the smell and the flesh beneath her tormented her.

She got up quickly and loped down the narrow stairs, down the main stairs. There, she hesitated. She wanted food before she changed again. She was sick with hunger now. She would be mad with it if she had to change to order food.

Luisa came into the house, saw her, and stopped. The old woman was not afraid of her. There was none of that teasing fear smell to make her change swiftly before she lost her head.

"Is he dead?" the old woman asked.

Anyanwu lowered her cat head in what she hoped would be taken for a nod.

"Good riddance," Luisa said. "Are you hungry?"

Two more quick nods.

"Go into the dining room. I'll bring food." She went through the house and out toward the kitchen. She was a good, steady, sensible friend. She did more than sewing for her keep. Anyanwu would have kept her if she had done nothing at all. But she was old. Over seventy. Soon some frailty that Anyanwu could not make a medicine for would take her life and another friend would be gone. People were temporary. So temporary.

Disobeying orders, Iye and Helen came in through the front door and saw Anyanwu, still bloody from her kill, and not yet gone to the dining room. If not for the presence of the child, Anyanwu would have roared her anger and dis-comfort at Iye. She did not like having her children see her at such a time. She loped away down the hall to the dining room.

Iye stayed where she was, but allowed Helen to follow Anyanwu. Anyanwu, struggling with fear smell, blood smell, hunger, and anger, did not notice the child until they were both in the dining room. There, wearily, Anyanwu lay down on a rug before the cold fireplace. Fearlessly, the child came to sit on the rug beside her.

Anyanwu looked up, knowing that her face was smeared with blood and wishing she had cleaned herself before she came downstairs. Cleaned herself and left her daughter in the care of someone more reliable.

Helen stroked her, fingered her spots, caressed her as though she were a large house cat. Like most children born on the plantation, she had seen Anyanwu change her shape many times. She was as accepting of the leopard now as she had been of the black dog and the white man named War-rick who had to put in an occasional appearance for the sake of the neighbors. Somehow, under the child's hands, Anyanwu began to relax. After a while, she began to purr.

"Agu," the little girl said softly. This was one of the few words of Anyanwu's language Helen knew. It meant simply, "leopard." "Agu," she repeated. "Be this way for Doro. He wouldn't dare hurt us while you're this way."

13

oro returned a month after Joseph Toler's grisly corpse had been buried in the weed patch that had once been a slaves' graveyard, and Stephen Ifeyinwa Mgbada had been buried in ground that had once been set aside for the master and his family. Joseph would be very lonely in his slave plot. No one else had been buried as a slave since Anyanwu bought the plantation.

Doro arrived knowing through his special senses that both Joseph and Stephen were dead. He arrived with replacements—two boy children no older than Helen. He arrived unannounced and walked through the front door as though he owned the house.

Anyanwu, unaware of his presence, was in the library writing out a list of supplies needed for the plantation. So much was purchased now instead of homemade. Soap, ordinary cloth, candles—even some medicines purchased ready-made could be trusted, though sometimes not for the purposes their makers intended. And of course, new tools were needed. Two mules had died and three others were old and would soon need replacing. Field hands needed shoes, hats. . . . It was cheaper to have people working in the fields bringing in large harvests than it was to have them making things that could be bought cheaply elsewhere. That was especially important here, where there were no slaves, where people were paid for their work and supplied with decent housing and good food. It cost more to keep people decently. If Anyanwu had not been a good manager, she would have had to return to the sea much more often for the wearisome task of finding and robbing sunken vessels, then carrying away gold and precious stones—usually within her own body.

She was adding a long column of figures when Doro entered with the two little boys. She turned at the sound of his footsteps and saw a pale, lean, angular man with lank, black hair and two fingers missing from the hand he used to lower himself into the armchair near her desk.

"It's me," he said wearily. "Order us a meal, would you? We haven't had a decent one for some time."

How courteous of him to ask her to give the order, she thought bitterly. Just then, one of her daughters came to the door, stopped, and looked at Doro with alarm. Anyanwu was in her youthful female shape, after all. But Edward Warrick was known to have a handsome, educated black mistress.

"We'll be having supper early," Anyanwu told the girl. "Have Rita get whatever she can ready as quickly as possible."

The girl vanished obediently, playing her role as a maid, not knowing the white stranger was only Doro.

Anyanwu stared at Doro's latest body, wanting to scream at him, order him out of her house. It was because of him that her son was dead. He had let the snake loose among her children. And what had he brought with him this time? Young snakes? God, she longed to be rid of him!

"Did they kill each other?" Doro asked her, and the two little boys looked at him wide-eyed. If they were not young snakes, he would teach them to crawl. Clearly, he did not care what was said before them.

She ignored Doro. "Are you hungry now?" she asked the boys.

One nodded, a little shy. "I am!" the other said quickly.

"Come with me then," she said. "Rita will give you bread and peach preserve." She noticed that they did not look to Doro for permission to leave. They jumped up, followed her, and ran out to the kitchen when she pointed it out to them. Rita would not be pleased. It was enough, surely, to ask her to rush supper. But she would feed the children and perhaps send them to Luisa until Anyanwu called for them. Sighing, Anyanwu went back to Doro.

"You were always one to overprotect children," he commented.

"I only allow them to be children for as long as they will," she said. "They will grow up and learn of sorrow and evil quickly enough."

"Tell me about Stephen and Joseph."

She went to her desk, sat down, and wondered whether she could discuss this calmly with him. She had wept and cursed him so many times. But neither weeping nor cursing would move him.

"Why did you bring me a man without telling me what he could do?" she asked quietly.

"What did he do?"

Anyanwu told him, told him everything, and ended with the same falsely calm question. "Why did you bring me a man without telling me what he could do?"

"Call Margaret," Doro said, ignoring her question. Margaret was the daughter who had married Joseph.

"Why?"

"Because when I brought Joseph here, he couldn't do anything. Not anything. He was just good breeding stock with the potential to father useful children. He must have had a transition in spite of his age, and he must have had it here."

"I would have known. I'm called here whenever anyone is sick. And there were no signs that he was approaching transition."

"Get Margaret. Let's talk to her."

Anyanwu did not want to call the girl. Margaret had suffered more than anyone over the killings, had lost both the beautiful, worthless husband she had loved, and the younger brother she had adored. She had not even a child to console her. Joseph had not managed to make her pregnant. In the month since his and Stephen's death, the girl had become gaunt and solemn. She had always been a lively girl who talked too much and laughed and kept people around her amused. Now, she hardly spoke at all. She was literally sick with grief. Recently, Helen had taken to sleeping with her and following her around during the day, helping her with her work or merely keeping her company. Anyanwu had watched this warily at first, thinking that Margaret might resent Helen as the cause of Joseph's trouble—Margaret was not in the most rational of moods—but this was clearly not the case. "She's getting better," Helen told Anyanwu confidentially. "She was by herself too much before." The little girl possessed an interesting combination of ruthlessness, kindness, and keen perception. Anyanwu hoped desperately Doro would never notice her. But the older girl was painfully vulnerable. And now, Doro meant to tear open wounds that had only just begun to heal.

"Let her alone for a while, Doro. This has hurt her more than it's hurt anyone else."

"Call her, Anyanwu, or I will."

Loathing him, Anyanwu went to find Margaret. The girl did not work in the fields as some of Anyanwu's children did, thus she was nearby. She was in the washhouse sweating and ironing a dress. Helen was with her, sprinkling and rolling other clothing.

"Leave that for a while," Anyanwu told Margaret. "Come in with me."

"What is it?" Margaret asked. She put one iron down to heat and, without thinking, picked up another.

"Doro," Anyanwu said softly.

Margaret froze, holding the heavy iron motionless and

upright in the air. Anyanwu took it from her hand and put it down on the bricks of the hearth far from the fire. She moved the other two irons away from where they were heating.

"Don't try to iron anything," she told Helen. "I have enough of a bill for cloth now."

Helen said nothing, only watched as Anyanwu led Margaret away.

Outside the washhouse, Margaret began to tremble. "What does he want with me? Why can't he leave us alone?"

"He will never leave us alone," Anyanwu said flatly.

Margaret blinked, looked at Anyanwu. "What shall I do?"

"Answer his questions—all of them, even if they are personal and offensive. Answer and tell him the truth."

"He scares me."

"Good. There is very much to fear. Answer him and obey him. Leave any criticizing or disagreeing with him to me."

There was silence until just before they reached the house. Then Margaret said, "We're your weakness, aren't we? You could outrun him for a hundred more years if not for us."

"I've never been content without my own around me," Anyanwu said. She met the girl's light brown eyes. "Why do you think I have all these children? I could have husbands and wives and lovers into the next century and never have a child. Why should I have so many except that I want them and love them? If they were burdens too heavy for me, they would not be here. You would not be here."

"But . . . he uses us to make you obey. I know he does."

"He does. That's his way." She touched the smooth, red-brown skin of the girl's face. "Nneka, none of this should concern you. Go and tell him what he wants to hear, then forget about him. I have endured him before. I will survive."

"You'll survive until the world ends," said the girl solemnly. "You and him." She shook her head.

They went into the house together and to the library where they found Doro sitting at Anyanwu's desk looking through her records.

"For God's sake!" Anyanwu said with disgust.

He looked up. "You're a better businesswoman than I thought with your views against slavery," he said.

To her amazement, the praise reached her. She was not pleased that he had gone snooping through her things, but she was abruptly less annoyed. She went to the desk and stood over him silently until he smiled, got up, and took his armchair again. Margaret took another chair and sat waiting.

"Did you tell her?" Doro asked Anyanwu.

Anyanwu shook her head.

He faced Margaret. "We think Joseph may have undergone transition while he was here. Did he show any signs of it?"

Margaret had been watching Doro's new face, but as he said the word *transition*, she looked away, studied the pattern of the oriental rug.

"Tell me about it," said Doro quietly.

"How could he have?" demanded Anyanwu. "There was no sign!"

"He knew what was happening," Margaret whispered. "I knew too because I saw it happen to . . . to Stephen. It took much longer with Stephen though. For Joe it came almost all at once. He was feeling bad for a week, maybe a little more, but nobody noticed except me. He made me promise not to tell anyone. Then one night when he'd been here for about a month, he went through the worst of it. I thought he would die, but he begged me not to leave him alone or tell anyone."

"Why?" Anyanwu demanded. "I could have helped you with him. You're not strong. He must have hurt you."

Margaret nodded. "He did. But . . . he was afraid of you. He thought you would tell Doro."

"It wouldn't have made much sense for her not to," Doro said.

Margaret continued to stare at the rug.

"Finish," Doro ordered.

She wet her lips. "He was afraid. He said you killed his brother when his brother's transition ended."

There was silence. Anyanwu looked from Margaret to Doro. "Did you do it?" she asked frowning.

"Yes. I thought that might be the trouble."

"But his brother! Why, Doro!"

"His brother went mad during transition. He was . . . like a lesser version of Nweke. In his pain and confusion he killed the man who was helping him. I reached him before he could accidentally kill himself, and I took him. I got five children by his body before I had to give it up."

"Couldn't you have helped him?" Anyanwu asked. "Wouldn't he have come back to his senses if you had given him time?"

"He attacked me, Anyanwu. Salvageable people don't do that."

"But . . ."

"He was mad. He would have attacked anyone who approached him. He would have wiped out his family if I hadn't been there." Doro leaned back and wet his lips, and Anyanwu remembered what he had done to his own family so long ago. He had told her that terrible story. "I'm not a healer," he said softly. "I save life in the only way I can."

"I had not thought you bothered to save it at all," Anyanwu said bitterly.

He looked at her. "Your son is dead," he said. "I'm sorry. He would have been a fine man. I would never have brought Joseph here if I had known they would be dangerous to each other."

He seemed utterly sincere. She could not recall the last time she had heard him apologize for anything. She stared at him, confused.

"Joe didn't say anything about his brother going crazy," Margaret said.

"Joseph didn't live with his family," Doro said. "He couldn't get along with them, so I found foster parents for him."

"Oh . . ." Margaret looked away, seeming to understand, to accept. No more than half the children on the plantation lived with their parents.

"Margaret?"

She looked up at him, then quickly looked down again. He was being remarkably gentle with her, but she was still afraid.

"Are you pregnant?" he asked.

"I wish I were," she whispered. She was beginning to cry.

"All right," Doro said. "All right, that's all."

She got up quickly and left the room. When she was gone, Anyanwu said, "Doro, Joseph was too old for a transition! Everything you taught me says he was too old."

"He was twenty-four. I haven't seen anyone change at that age before, but . . ." He hesitated, changed direction. "You never asked about his ancestry, Anyanwu."

"I never wanted to know."

"You do know. He's your descendant, of course."

She made herself shrug. "You said you would bring my grandchildren."

"He was the grandchild of your grandchildren. Both his parents trace their descent back to you."

"Why do you tell me that now? I don't want to know any more about it. He's dead!"

"He's Isaac's descendant too," Doro continued relentlessly. "People of Isaac's line are sometimes a little late going into transition, though Joseph is about as late as I've seen. The two children I've brought to you are sons of his brother's body."

"No!" Anyanwu stared at him. "Take them away! I want no more of that kind near me!"

"You have them. Teach them and guide them as you do your own children. I told you your descendants would not be easy to care for. You chose to care for them anyway."

She said nothing. He made it sound as though her choice had been free, as though he had not coerced her into choosing.

"If I had found you earlier, I would have brought them to you when they were even younger," he said. "Since I didn't, you'll have to do what you can with them now. Teach them responsibility, pride, honor. Teach them whatever you taught Stephen. But don't be foolish enough to teach them you believe they'll grow up to be criminals. They'll be powerful men someday and they're liable to fulfill your expectations—either way."

Still she said nothing. What was there for her to say—or do? He would be obeyed, or he would make her life and her children's lives not worth living—if he did not kill them outright.

"You have five to ten years before the boys' transitions," he said. "They will have transitions; I'm as sure as I can be of that. Their ancestry is just right."

"Are they mine, or will you interfere with them?"

"Until their transitions, they're yours."

"And then?"

"I'll breed them, of course."

Of course. "Let them marry and stay here. If they fit here, they'll want to stay. How can they become responsible men if their only future is to be bred?"

Doro laughed aloud, opening his mouth wide to show the empty spaces of several missing teeth. "Do you hear yourself, woman? First you want no part of them, now you don't want to let go of them even when they're grown."

She waited silently until he stopped laughing, then asked: "Do you think I'm willing to throw away any child, Doro? If there is a chance for those boys to grow up better than Joseph, why shouldn't I try to give them that chance? If, when they grow up, they can be men instead of dogs who know nothing except how to climb onto one female after another, why shouldn't I try to help?"

He sobered. "I knew you would help—and not grudgingly. Don't you think I know you by now, Anyanwu?"

Oh, he knew her—knew how to use her. "Will you do it then? Let them marry and stay here if they fit?"

"Yes."

She looked down, examining the rug pattern that had held so much of Margaret's attention. "Will you take them away if they don't fit, can't fit, like Joseph?"

"Yes," he repeated. "Their seed is too valuable to be wasted."

He thought of nothing else. Nothing!

"Shall I stay with you for a while, Anyanwu?"

She stared at him in surprise, and he looked back neutral-faced, waiting for an answer. Was he asking a real question, then? "Will you go if I ask you to?"

"Yes."

Yes. He was saying that so often now, being so gentle and cooperative—for him. He had come courting again.

"Go," she said as gently as she could. "Your presence is disruptive here, Doro. You frighten my people." Now. Let him keep his word.

He shrugged, nodded. "Tomorrow morning," he said.

And the next morning, he was gone.

Perhaps an hour after his departure, Helen and Luisa came hand in hand to Anyanwu to tell her that Margaret had hanged herself from a beam in the washhouse.

For a time after Margaret's death, Anyanwu felt a sickness that she could not dispel. Grief. Two children lost so close together. Somehow, she never got used to losing children—especially young children, children it seemed had been with her for only a few moments. How many had she buried now?

At the funeral, the two little boys Doro had brought saw her crying and came to take her hands and stand with her solemnly. They seemed to be adopting her as mother and Luisa as grandmother. They were fitting in surprisingly well, but Anyanwu found herself wondering how long they would last.

"Go to the sea," Luisa told her when she would not eat,

when she became more and more listless. "The sea cleanses you. I have seen it. Go and be a fish for a while."

"I'm all right," Anyanwu said automatically.

Luisa swept that aside with a sound of disgust. "You are not all right! You are acting like the child you appear to be! Get away from here for a while. Give yourself a rest and us a rest from you."

The words startled Anyanwu out of her listlessness. "A rest from me?"

"Those of us who can feel your pain as you feel it need a rest from you."

Anyanwu blinked. Her mind had been elsewhere. Of course the people who took comfort in her desire to protect them and keep them together, people who took pleasure in her pleasure, would also suffer pain when she suffered.

"I'll go," she told Luisa.

The old woman smiled. "It will be good for you."

Anyanwu sent for one of her white daughters to bring her husband and children for a visit. They were not needed or wanted to run the plantation, and they knew it. That was why Anyanwu trusted them to take her place for a while. They could fit in without taking over. They had their own strangeness. The woman, Leah, was like Denice, her mother, taking impressions from houses and pieces of furniture, from rocks, trees, and human flesh, seeing ghosts of things that had happened in the past. Anyanwu warned her to keep out of the washhouse. The front of the main house where Stephen had died was hard enough on her. She learned quickly where she should not step, what she should not touch if she did not want to see her brother climbing the railing, diving off head-first.

The husband, Kane, was sensitive enough to see occasionally into Leah's thoughts and know that she was not insane—or at least no more insane than he. He was a quadroon whose white father had educated him, cared for him, and unfortunately, died without freeing him—leaving him in the hands of his father's wife. He had run away, escaped just ahead of the slave dealer and left Texas for Louisiana, where he calmly used all his father had taught him to pass as a well-bred young white man. He had said nothing about his background until he began to understand how strange his wife's family was. He still did not fully understand, but he loved Leah. He could be himself with her without alarming her in any way. He was comfortable with her. To keep that comfort, he accepted without understanding. He could come now and then to live on a plantation that would run itself without his supervision and enjoy the company of Anyanwu's strange collection of misfits. He felt right at home.

"What's this about your going to sea?" he asked Anyanwu. He got along well with her as long as she kept her Warrick identity. Otherwise, she made him nervous. He could not accept the idea that his wife's father could become a woman—in fact, had been born a woman. For him, Anyanwu wore the thin, elderly Warrick guise.

"I need to go away from here for a while," she said.

"Where will you go this time?"

"To find the nearest school of dolphins." She smiled at him. The thought of going to sea again had made her able to smile. During her years of hiding, she had not only spent a great deal of time as a large dog or a bird, but she had left home often to swim free as a dolphin. She had done it first to confuse and evade Doro, then to get wealth and buy land, and finally because she enjoyed it. The freedom of the sea eased worry, gave her time to think through confusion, took away boredom. She wondered what Doro did when he was bored. Kill?

"You'll fly to open water won't you?" Kane asked.

"Fly and run. Sometimes it's safer to run."

"Christ!" he muttered. "I thought I'd gotten over envying you."

She was eating as he spoke. Eating what would probably be her last cooked meal for some time. Rice and stew, baked yams, cornbread, strong coffee, wine, and fruit. Her children complained that she ate like a poor woman, but she ignored them. She was content. Now she looked up at Kane through her blue white-man's-eyes.

"If you're not afraid," she said, "when I come back, I'll try to share the experience with you."

He shook his head. "I don't have the control. Stephen used to be able to share things with me . . . both of us working together, but me alone . . ." He shrugged.

There was an uncomfortable silence, then Anyanwu pushed back from the table. "I'm leaving now," she said abruptly. She went upstairs to her bedroom where she undressed, opened her door to the upper gallery of the porch, took her bird shape, and flew away.

More than a month passed before she flew back, eagle-shaped but larger than any eagle, refreshed by the sea and the air, and ravenous because in her eagerness to see home again, she had not stopped often enough to hunt.

She circled first to see that there were no visitors—strangers to be startled, and perhaps to shoot her. She had been shot three times this trip. That was enough.

When she had satisfied herself that it was safe, she came down into the grassy open space three quarters enclosed by the house, its dependencies, and her people's cabins. Two little children saw her and ran into the kitchen. Seconds later, they were back, each tugging at one of Rita's hands.

Rita walked over to Anyanwu, looked at her, and said with no doubt at all in her voice, "I suppose you're hungry."

Anyanwu flapped her wings.

Rita laughed. "You make a fine, handsome bird. I wonder how you would look on the dining-room table."

Rita had always had a strange sense of humor. Anyanwu flapped her wings again impatiently, and Rita went back to the kitchen and brought her two rabbits, skinned, cleaned, ready for cooking. Anyanwu held them with her feet and tore into them, glad Rita had not gotten around to cooking them. As she ate, a black man came out of the house, Helen at his side. The man was a stranger. Some local freedman, perhaps, or even a runaway. Anyanwu always did what she could for runaways, either feeding and clothing them and sending them on their way better equipped to survive or, on those rare occasions when one seemed to fit into the house, buying him.

This was a compact, handsome little black man not much bigger than Anyanwu was in her true form. She raised her head and looked at him with interest. If this one had a mind to match his body, she might buy him even if he did not fit. It had been too long since she had had a husband. Occasional lovers ceased to satisfy her after a while.

She went back to tearing at the rabbits unself-consciously, as her daughter and the stranger watched. When she finished, she wiped her beak on the grass, gave the attractive stranger a final glance, and flew heavily around to the upper gallery outside her room. There, comfortably full, she dozed for a while, giving her body a chance to digest the meal. It was good to be able to take her time, do things at a pace her body found comfortable.

Eventually, she became herself, small and black, young and female. Kane would not like it, but that did not matter. The stranger would like it very much.

She put on one of her best dresses and a few pieces of good jewelry, brushed her glossy new crown of hair, and went downstairs.

Supper had just been finished without her. Her people never waited for her when they knew she was in one or another of her animal forms. They knew her leisurely habits. Now, several of her adult children, Kane and Leah, and the black stranger sat eating nuts and raisins, drinking wine, and talking quietly. They made room for her, breaking their conversation for greeting and welcome. One of her sons got her a glass and filled it with her favorite Madeira. She had taken only a single pleasant sip from it when the stranger said, "The sea has done you good. You were right to go."

Her shoulders drooped slightly, though she managed not to change expression. It was only Doro.

He caught her eye and smiled, and she knew he had seen

her disappointment, had no doubt planned her disappointment. She contrived to ignore him, looked around the table to see exactly who was present. "Where is Luisa?" she asked. The old woman often took supper with the family, feeding her foster children first, then coming in, as she said, to re-learn adult conversation.

But now, at the mention of Luisa's name, everyone fell silent. The son next to her, Julien, who had poured her wine, said softly, "She died, Mama."

Anyanwu turned to look at him, yellow-brown and plain except for his eyes, utterly clear like her own. Years before when a woman he wanted desperately would have nothing to do with him, he had gone to Luisa for comfort. Luisa had told Anyanwu and Anyanwu had been amazed to find that she felt no resentment toward the old woman, no anger at Julien for taking his pain to a stranger. With her sensitivity, Luisa had ceased to be a stranger the day she arrived on the plantation.

"How did she die?" Anyanwu whispered finally.

"In her sleep," Julien said. "She went to bed one night, and the next morning, the children couldn't wake her up."

"That was two weeks ago," Leah said. "We got the priest to come out because we knew she'd want it. We gave her a fine funeral." Leah hesitated. "She . . . she didn't have any pain. I lay down on her bed to see, and I saw her go out just as easy . . ."

Anyanwu got up and left the table. She had gone away to find some respite from loved ones who died and died, and others whose rapid aging reminded her that they too were temporary. Leah, only thirty-five, had far too much gray mixed with her straight black hair.

Anyanwu went into the library, closed the door—closed doors were respected in her house—and sat at her desk, head down. Luisa had been seventy . . . seventy-eight years old. It was time for her to die. How stupid to grieve over an old woman who had lived what, for her kind, was a long life.

Anyanwu sat up and shook her head. She had been watching friends and relatives grow old and die for as long as she could remember. Why was it biting so deeply into her now, hurting her as though it were a new thing? Stephen, Margaret, Luisa . . . There would be others. There would always be others, suddenly here, then suddenly gone. Only she would remain.

As though to contradict her thought, Doro opened the door and came in.

She glared at him angrily. Everyone else in her house respected her closed doors—but then, Doro respected nothing at all.

"What do you want?" she asked him.

"Nothing." He pulled a chair over to the side of her desk and sat down.

"What, no more children for me to raise?" she said bitterly. "No more unsuitable mates for my children? Nothing?"

"I brought a pregnant woman and her two children, and I brought an account at a New Orleans bank to help pay their way. I didn't come to you to talk about them, though."

Anyanwu turned away from him not caring why he had come. She wished he would leave.

"It goes on, you know," he said. "The dying."

"It doesn't hurt you."

"It does. When my children die—the best of my children."

"What do you do?"

"Endure it. What is there to do but endure it? Someday, we'll have others who won't die."

"Are you still dreaming that dream?"

"What could I do, Anyanwu, if I gave it up?"

She said nothing. She had no answer. "I used to believe in it too," she said. "When you took me from my people, I believed it. For fifty years, I made myself believe it. Perhaps . . . perhaps sometimes I still believe it."

"You never behaved as though you believed it."

"I did! I let you do all the things you did to me and to

others, and I stayed with you until I could see you had de-cided to kill me."

He drew a deep breath. "That decision was a mistake," he said. "I made it out of habit as though you were just an-other not entirely controllable, wild-seed woman who had had her quota of children. Centuries-old habit said it was time to dispose of you."

"And what of your habit now?" she asked.

"It's broken now as far as you're concerned." He looked at her, looked past her. "I want you alive for as long as you can live. You cannot know how I have fought with myself over this."

She did not care how he had fought.

"I tried hard to make myself kill you," he said. "It would have been easier than trying to change you."

She shrugged.

He stood up and took her arms to raise her to her feet. She stood passively, knowing that if she let him have his way, they would wind up on the sofa together. He wanted her. He did not care that she had just suffered the loss of a friend, that she wanted to be alone.

"Do you like this body?" he asked. "It's my gift to you."

She wondered who had died so that he could give such a "gift."

"Anyanwu!" He shook her once, gently, and she looked at him. She did not have to look up. "You're still the little forest peasant, trying to climb the ship's railings and swim back to Africa," he said. "You still want what you can't have. The old woman is dead."

Again, she only shrugged.

"They'll all die, except me," he continued. "Because of me, you were not alone on the ship. Because of me, you will never be alone."

He took her to the sofa, finally, undressed her, made love to her. She found that she did not mind particularly. The lovemaking relaxed her, and when it was over, she escaped easily into sleep.

Not much time had passed when he woke her. The sunlight and the long shadows told her it was still evening. She wondered why he had not left her. He had what he wanted, and intentionally or not, he had given her peace. Now if only he would go away.

Anyanwu looked at him seated beside her half dressed, still shirtless. They were not crowded together on the large sofa as they would have been had he been wearing one of his usual large bodies. Again, she wondered about the original owner of his beautiful, unlikely, new body, but she asked no questions. She did not want to learn that it had been one of her descendants.

He caressed her silently for a moment and she thought he meant to resume the lovemaking. She sighed and decided that it did not matter. So little seemed to matter now.

"I'm going to try something with you," he said. "I've wanted to do it for years. Before you ran away, I assumed I would do it someday. Now . . . now everything is changed, but I mean to have some of this anyway."

"Some of what?" she asked wearily. "What are you talking about?"

"I can't explain," he said. "But . . . Look at me, Anyanwu. Look!"

She turned onto her side, faced him.

"I won't hurt you," he said. "Hear and see whatever it is that helps you know I'm being honest with you. I won't hurt you. You'll be in danger only if you disobey me. This body of mine is strong and young and new to me. My control is excellent. Obey me, and you will be safe."

She lay flat again. "Tell me what you want, Doro. What shall I do for you now?"

To her surprise, he smiled and kissed her. "Just lie still and trust me. Believe that I mean you no harm."

She did believe, though at the moment, she barely cared. How ironic that now he was beginning to care, beginning to see her as more than only another of his breeding animals. She nodded and felt his hands grip her.

Abruptly, she was in darkness, falling through darkness toward distant light, falling. She felt herself twisting, writhing, grasping for some support. She screamed in reflexive terror, and could not hear her own voice. Instantly, the darkness around her vanished.

She was on the sofa again, with Doro gasping beside her. There were bloody nail marks on his chest and he was massaging his throat as though it hurt. She was concerned in spite of herself. "Doro, have I hurt your throat?"

He took a deep ragged breath. "Not much. I was ready for you—or I thought I was."

"What did you do? It was like the kind of dream children wake screaming from."

"Alter your hands," he said.

"What?"

"Obey me. Make claws of your hands."

With a shrug, she formed powerful leopard claws.

"Good," Doro said. "I didn't even weaken you. My control is as steady as I thought. Now change back." He fingered his throat lightly. "I wouldn't want you going at me with those."

Again, she obeyed. She was behaving like one of his daughters, doing things she did not understand unquestioningly because he commanded it. That thought roused her to question.

"Doro, what are we doing?"

"Do you see," he said, "that the . . . the thing you felt has not harmed you in any way?"

"But what was it?"

"Wait, Anyanwu. Trust me. I'll explain all I can later, I promise you. For now, relax. I'm going to do it again."

"No!"

"It won't hurt you. It will be as though you were in midair under Isaac's control. He would never have hurt you, I won't either." He had begun stroking and caressing her again, trying to calm her—and succeeding. She had not really been hurt, after all. "Be still," he whispered. "Let me have this, Anyanwu."

"It will . . . please you somehow—as though we were making love?"

"Even more."

"All right." She wondered what she was saying all right to. It had nothing to do with Isaac's tossing her into the air and catching her with that gentle sure ability of his. This was nightmare stuff—helpless, endless falling. But it was not real. She had not fallen. She was not injured. Finally, Doro wanted something of her that would not hurt anyone. Perhaps if she gave it to him—and survived—she would gain leverage with him, be better able to protect her people from him. Let them live their brief lives in peace.

"Don't fight me this time," he said. "I'm no match for you in physical strength. You know that. Now that you know what to expect, you can be still and let it happen. Trust me."

She lay watching him, quiescent, waiting. "All right," she repeated. He moved closer to her, put his arm around her so that her head was pillowed on it.

"I like contact," he said, explaining nothing. "It's never as good without contact."

She glanced at him, then made herself comfortable with her body and his touching along their length.

"Now," he said softly.

There was the darkness again, the feeling of falling. But after a moment it seemed more like drifting slowly. Only drifting. She was not afraid. She felt warm and at ease and not alone. Yet it seemed that she was alone. There was a light far ahead of her, but nothing else, no one else.

She was drifting toward the light, watching it grow as she moved nearer. It was a distant star at first, faint and flickering. Eventually, it was the morning star, bright, dominating her otherwise empty sky.

Gradually, the light became a sun, filling her sky with brightness that should have blinded her. But she was not blinded, not uncomfortable in any way. She could feel Doro near her though she was no longer aware of his body or even her own body lying on the sofa. This was another kind of awareness, a kind she had no words to describe. It was good, pleasurable. He was with her. If he had not been, she would have been utterly alone. What had he said before the love-making, before the relaxed, easy sleep? That because of him, she would never be alone. The words had not comforted her then, but they comforted her now.

The sun's light enveloped her, and there was no darkness anywhere. In a sense now, she was blind. There was nothing to see except blazing light. But still, there was no discomfort. And there was Doro with her, touching her as no one had touched her before. It was as though he touched her spirit, enfolding it within himself, spreading the sensation of his touch through every part of her. She became aware slowly of his hunger for her—literal hunger—but instead of frightening her, it awakened a strange sympathy in her. She felt not only his hunger, but his restraint and his loneliness. The loneliness formed a kinship between them. He had been alone for so long. So impossibly long. Her own loneliness, her own long life seemed insignificant. She was like a child beside him. But child or not, he needed her. He needed her as he had never needed anyone else. She reached out to touch him, hold him, ease his long, long solitude. Or she seemed to reach.

She did not know what he did nor what she actually did but it was startlingly good. It was a blending that went on and on, a joining that it seemed to Anyanwu she controlled. Not until she rested, pleasantly weary, did she begin to realize she was losing herself. It seemed that his restraint had not held. The joining they had enjoyed was not enough for him. He was absorbing her, consuming her, making her part of his own substance. He was the great light, the fire that had en-globed her. Now he was killing her, little by little, digesting her little by little.

In spite of all his talk he was betraying her. In spite of all the joy they had just given each other, he could not forgo the kill. In spite of the new higher value he had tried to place on her, breeding and killing were still all that had meaning to him.

Well then, so be it. So be it; she was tired.

14

With meticulous care, Doro disentangled himself from Anyanwu. It was much easier than he had thought it would be—stopping in the middle of what could have been an intensely satisfying kill. But he had never intended to kill. He had gone further with her, though, than he did with the most powerful of his children. With them, he forced the potentially deadly contact to enable him to understand the limits of their power, understand whether that power could ever in any way threaten him. He did it soon after their transitions so that he found them physically depleted, emotionally weary, and too ignorant of their newly matured abilities to even begin to understand how to fight him—if they could fight him. Very rarely, he found someone who could, and that person died. He wanted allies, not rivals.

But he had not been testing Anyanwu. He knew she could not threaten him, knew he could kill her as long as she was in human form. He had never doubted it. She did not have the kinds of thought-reading and thought-controlling abilities

that he considered potentially dangerous. He destroyed anyone who showed the potential, the strength to someday read
or control his thoughts. Anyanwu had almost absolute control
of every cell of her malleable body, but her mind was as open
and defenseless as the mind of any ordinary person—which
meant she would eventually have trouble with the people he
was bringing her. They would marry into her large "family" and
cause dissension. He had warned her of that. Eventually, she
would have children and grandchildren here who were more
like Joseph and Lale than like the congenial, weakly sensitive
people she had collected around her. But that was another
matter. He could think about it later. Now, all that was important was that she revive whole and well. Nothing must happen to her. No amount of anger or stupidity on her part or his
must induce him to think again of killing her. She was too
valuable in too many ways.

She awoke slowly, opening her eyes, looking around to
find the library in darkness except for the fire he had made
in the fireplace and a single lamp on the table at her head.
He lay close beside her, warming himself by her warmth. He
wanted her close to him.

"Doro?" she whispered.

He kissed her cheek and relaxed. She was all right. She
had been so completely passive in her grief. He had been certain he could do this to her and not harm her. He had been
certain that this once she would not resist and make him
hurt or kill her.

"I was dying," she said.

"No you weren't."

"I was dying. You were—"

He put his hand over her mouth, then let her move it
away when he saw that she would be still. "I had to know
you that way at least once," he said. "I had to touch you that
way."

"Why?" she asked.

"Because it's the closest I'll ever come to you."

She did not respond to that for a long while. Eventually,

though, she moved her head to rest it on his chest. He could not remember when she had done that last on her own. He folded his arms over her, remembering that other more complete enfolding. How had he ever had the control to stop, he wondered.

"Is it that way, that easy for all the others?" she asked.

He hesitated, not wanting to lie to her, not wanting to talk about his kills at all. "Fear makes it worse for them," he said. "And they're always afraid. Also . . . I have no reason to be gentle with them."

"Do you hurt them? Is there pain?"

"No. I feel what they feel so I know. They don't feel pain any more than you did."

"It was . . . good," she said with wonder. "Until I thought you would kill me, it was so good."

He could only hold her and press his face into her hair.

"We should go upstairs," she said.

"Soon."

"What shall I do?" she asked. "I have fought you all these years. My reasons for fighting you still exist. What shall I do?"

"What Isaac wanted. What you want. Join with me. What's the good of fighting me? Especially now."

"Now . . ." She was still, perhaps, savoring their brief contact. He hoped she was. He was. He wondered what she would say if he told her no one had ever before enjoyed such contact with him. No one in nearly four thousand years. His people found contact with him terrifying. Thought readers and controllers who survived such contact quickly learned that they could not read or control him without sacrificing their lives. They learned to pay attention to the vague wariness they felt of him as soon as their transitions ended. Occasionally, he found a man or woman he cared for, enjoyed repeated contact with. These endured what he did since they could not prevent it, though their grim, long-suffering attitudes made him feel like a rapist. But Anyanwu had participated, had enjoyed, had even taken the initiative for a while, greatly intensifying his pleasure. He looked at her with wonder and delight. She looked back solemnly.

"Nothing is solved," she said, "except that now, I must fight myself as well as you."

"You're talking foolishness," he said.

She turned and kissed him. "Let it be foolishness for now," she said. "Let it be foolishness for this moment." She looked down at him in the dim light. "You don't want to go upstairs, do you?"

"No."

"We'll stay here then. My children will whisper about me."

"Do you care?"

"Now you are talking foolishness," she said, laughing. "Do I care! Whose house is this? I do as I please!" She covered them both with the wide skirt of her dress, blew out the lamp, and settled to sleep in his arms.

Anyanwu's children did whisper about her—and about Doro. They were careless—deliberately so, Doro thought—and he heard them. But after a while, they stopped. Perhaps Anyanwu spoke to them. For once, Doro did not care. He knew he was no longer fearsome to them; he was only another of Anyanwu's lovers. How long had it been since he was only someone's lover? He could not remember. He went away now and then to take care of his businesses, put in an appearance at one of his nearer settlements.

"Bring this body back to me as long as you can," Anyanwu would tell him. "There cannot be two as perfect as this."

He would laugh and promise her nothing. Who knew what punishment he might have to inflict, what madman he might have to subdue, what stupid, stubborn politician, businessman, planter, or other fool he might have to remove? Also, wearing a black body in country where blacks were under constant obligation to prove they had rights to even limited freedom was a hindrance. He traveled with one of his older white sons, Frank Winston, whose fine old Virginia family had belonged to Doro since Doro brought it from England 135 years before. The man could be as distinguished and aristocratic or as timid and naive as he chose to be, as Doro ordered him to be. He had no inborn strangeness great enough to qualify him as good breeding stock. He was simply the best actor, the best liar Doro knew. People believed what he told them even when he grew expansive and outrageous, when he said Doro was an African prince mistakenly enslaved, but now freed to return to his homeland and take the word of God back to his heathen people.

Though caught by surprise, Doro played his role with such a confusing mixture of arrogance and humility that slaveholders were first caught between bewilderment and anger, then convinced. Doro was like no nigger they had ever seen.

Later, Doro warned Frank to stick to more conventional lies—though he thought the man was probably laughing too hard to hear him.

He felt more at ease than he had for years—even at ease enough to laugh at himself—and his son enjoyed traveling with him. It was worth the inconvenience to keep Anyanwu happy. He knew that a kind of honeymoon phase of their relationship would end when he had to give up the body that pleased her so. She would not turn away from him again, he was certain, but their relationship would change. They would become occasional mates as they had been in Wheatley, but with better feelings. She would welcome him now, in whichever body he wore. She would have her men, and if she chose, her women—husbands, wives, lovers. He could not begrudge her these. There would be years, multiples of years, when he would not see her at all. A woman like her could not be alone. But there would always be room for him when he came back to her, and he would always go back to her. Because of her, he was no longer alone. Because of her, life was suddenly better than it had been for him in centuries, in millennia. It was as though she was the first of the race he was trying to create—except that he had not created her, had not been able to re-create her. In that way, she was only a promise unfulfilled. But someday . . .

Doro's woman Susan had her child a month after Iye bore Stephen's child. Both were boys, sturdy and healthy, promising to grow into handsome children. Iye accepted her son with love and gratitude that amazed Anyanwu. Anyanwu had delivered the child and all Iye could think of through her pain was that Stephen's child must live and be well. It had not been an easy birth, but the woman clearly did not care. The child was all right.

But Iye could not feed it. She had no milk. Anyanwu produced milk easily and during the day visited Iye's cabin regularly to nurse the child. At night, she kept the child with her.

"I'm glad you could do this," Iye told her. "I think it would be too hard for me to share him with anyone else." Anyanwu's prejudices against the woman were fast dissolving.

As were her prejudices against Doro—though this frightened and disturbed her. She could not look at him now with the loathing she had once felt, yet he continued to do loathsome things. He simply no longer did them to her. As she had predicted, she was at war with herself. But she showed him no signs of that war. For the time he wore the beautiful little body that had been his gift to her, it pleased her to please him. For that short time, she could refuse to think about what he did when he left her. She could treat him as the very special lover he appeared to be.

"What are you going to do now?" Doro asked her when he came home from a short trip to find her nursing the baby. "Push me away?"

They were alone in her upstairs sitting room so she gave him a look of mock annoyance. "Shall I do that? Yes, I think so. Go away."

He smiled, not believing her any more than she wished to be believed. He watched the nursing child.

"You will be father to one like this in seven months more," she said.

"You're pregnant now?"

"Yes. I wanted a child by this body of yours. I was afraid you would be getting rid of it soon."

"I will be," he admitted. "I'll have to. But eventually you'll have two children to nurse. Won't that be hard on you?"

"I can do it. Do you think I can't?"

"No." He smiled again. "If only I had more like you and Iye. That Susan . . ."

"I've found a home for her child," Anyanwu said. "It won't be fostered with the older ones, but it will have loving parents. And Susan is big and strong. She's a fine field hand."

"I didn't bring her here to be a field hand. I thought living with your people might help her—calm her and make her a little more useful."

"It has." She reached over and took his hand. "Here, if people fit in, I let them do whatever work they prefer. That helps to calm them. Susan prefers field work to anything indoors. She is willing to have as many more children as you want, but caring for them is beyond her. She seems especially sensitive to their thoughts. Their thoughts hurt her somehow. She is a good woman otherwise, Doro."

Doro shook his head as though dismissing Susan from his thoughts. He stared at the nursing child for a few seconds more, then met Anyanwu's eyes. "Give me some of the milk," he said softly.

She drew back in surprise. He had never asked such a thing, and this was certainly not the first child he had seen her nursing. But there were many new things between them now. "I had a man who used to do that," she said.

"Did you mind?"

"No."

He looked at her, waiting.

"Come here," she said softly.

*   *   *

The day after Anyanwu gave him milk, Doro awoke trembling, and he knew the comfortable time in the compact little body he had taken as a gift to her was over. It had not been a particularly powerful body. It had little of the inborn strangeness he valued. Anyanwu's child by it might be beautiful, but chances were, it would be very ordinary.

Now the body was used up. If he held onto it for much longer, he would become dangerous to those around him. Some simple excitement or pain that he would hardly notice normally might force transmigration. Someone whose life was important to him might die.

He looked over at Anyanwu, still asleep beside him, and sighed. What had she said that night months before? That nothing had really changed. They had finally accepted each other. They would keep each other from loneliness now. But beyond that, she was right. Nothing had changed. She would not want him near her for a while after he had changed. She would still refuse to understand that whether he killed out of need, accident, or choice, he had to kill. There was no way for him to avoid it. An ordinary human might be able to starve himself to death, but Doro could not. Better, then, to make a controlled kill than to just let himself go until he did not know who he would take. How many lifetimes would pass before Anyanwu understood that?

She awoke beside him. "Are you getting up?" she asked.

"Yes. But there is no reason for you to. It's not even dawn."

"Are you going away? You've just come back."

He kissed her. "Perhaps I'll come back again in a few days." To see how she reacted. To be certain that nothing had changed—or perhaps in the hope that they were both wrong, that she had grown a little.

"Stay a little longer," she whispered.

She knew.

"I can't," he said.

She was silent for a moment, then she sighed. "You were

asleep when I fed the child," she said. "But there is still milk for you if you want it."

At once, he lowered his head to her breast. Probably, there would not be any more of this either. Not for a long while. Her milk was rich and good and as sweet as this time with her had been. Now, for a while, they would begin the old tug of war again. She stroked his head and he sighed.

Afterward, he went out and took Susan. She was the kind of kill he needed now—very sensitive. As sweet and good to his mind as Anyanwu's milk had been to his former body.

He woke Frank and together they hauled his former body to the old slave graveyard. He did not want one of Anyanwu's people to find it and go running to Anyanwu. She would know what had happened without that. If it were possible, he wanted to make this time easy for her.

By the time he and Frank left, a hoe gang of field hands was trooping out toward the cotton fields.

"Are you going to be wearing that body long?" Frank asked him, looking at Susan's tall, stocky profile.

"No, I've already got what I need from it," Doro said. "It's a good body though. It could last a year, maybe two."

"But it wouldn't do Anyanwu much good."

"It might if it were anyone but Susan. Anyanwu's had wives, after all. But she knew Susan, liked her. Except in emergencies, I don't ask people to overcome feelings like that."

"You and Anyanwu," Frank muttered. "Changing sex, changing color, breeding like—"

"Shut your mouth," Doro said in annoyance, "or I'll tell you a few things you don't want to hear about your own family."

Startled, Frank fell silent. He was sensitive about his ancestry, his old Virginia family. For some foolish reason, it was important to him. Doro caught himself as he was about to destroy completely any illusions the man still had about his blue blood—or for that matter, his pure white skin. But there was no reason for Doro to do such a thing. No reason except that one of the best times he could remember was ending and he was not certain what would come next.

Two weeks later, when he went back to Anyanwu, home to Anyanwu, he was alone. He had sent Frank home to his family and put on the more convenient body of a lean, brown-haired white man. It was a good, strong body, but Doro knew better than to expect Anyanwu to appreciate it.

She said nothing when she saw him. She did not accuse him or curse him—did not seem hostile to him at all. On the other hand, she was hardly welcoming.

"You did take Susan, didn't you?" was all she said. When he said yes, she turned and walked away. He thought that if she had not been pregnant, she would have gone to sea and left him to deal with her not-quite-respectful children. She knew he would not harm them now.

Pregnancy kept her in human form, however. She was carrying a human child. She would almost certainly kill it by taking a nonhuman form. She had told him that during one of her early pregnancies by Isaac, and he had counted it a weakness. He had no doubt that she could abort any pregnancy without help or danger to herself. She could do anything with that body of hers that she wished. But she would not abort. Once a child was inside her, it would be born. During all the years he had known her, she had been as careful with her children before they were born as afterward. Doro decided to stay with her during this period of weakness. Once she accepted his two most recent changes, he did not think he would have trouble with her again.

It took him many long, uncommunicative days to find out how wrong he was. Finally, it was Anyanwu's young daughter Helen who made him understand. The girl sometimes seemed very much younger than her twelve years. She played with other children and fought with them and cried over trivial hurts. At other times, she was a woman wearing the body of a child. And she was very much her mother's daughter.

"She won't talk to me," the child told Doro. "She knows I know what she's going to do." She had come to sit beside him in the cool shade of a giant oak tree. For a time, they had watched in silence as Anyanwu weeded her herb garden. This garden was off limits to other gardeners and to helpful children, both of whom considered a great many of Anyanwu's plants nothing but weeds themselves. Now, though, Doro looked away from the garden and at Helen.

"What do you mean?" he asked her. "What is she going to do?"

She looked up at him, and he had no doubt that a woman looked out of those eyes. "She says Kane and Leah are going to come and live here. She says after the baby comes, she's going away."

"To sea?"

"No, Doro. Not to sea. Someday, she would have to come out of the sea. Then you would find her again, and she would have to watch you kill her friends, kill your own friends."

"What are you talking about?" He caught her by the arms, barely stopped himself from shaking her.

She glared at him, furious, clearly loathing him. Suddenly she lowered her head and bit his hand as hard as she could with her sharp little teeth.

Pain made Doro release her. She could not know how dangerous it was for her to cause him sudden unexpected pain. Had she done it just before he killed Susan, he would have taken her helplessly. But now, having fed recently, he had more control. He held his bloody hand and watched her run away.

Then, slowly, he got up and went over to Anyanwu. She had dug up several purple-stemmed, yellow-rooted weeds. He expected her to throw them away, but instead she cut the plants from their rootstocks, brushed the dirt from the stocks, and put the stocks in her gathering basket.

"What are those things?" he asked.

"A medicine," she said, "or a poison if people don't know what to do with it."

"What are you going to do with it?"

"Powder it, mix it with some other things, steep it in boiling water and give it to children who have worms."

Doro shook his head. "I'd think you could help them more easily by making medicine within your own body."

"This will work just as well. I'm going to teach some of the women to make it."

"Why?"

"So that they can heal themselves and their families without depending on what they see as my magic."

He reached down and tipped her head up so that she faced him. "And why shouldn't they depend on your magic? Your medicines are more efficient than any ground weed."

She shrugged. "They should learn to help themselves."

He picked up her basket and drew her to her feet. "Come into the house and talk with me."

"There is nothing to say."

"Come in anyway. Humor me." He put his arm around her and walked her back to the house.

He started to take her into the library, but a group of the younger children were being taught to read there. They sat scattered in a half circle on the rug looking up at one of Anyanwu's daughters. As Doro guided Anyanwu away from them, he could hear the voice of one of his sons by Susan reading a verse from the Bible: "Be of the same mind one toward another. Mind not high things, but condescend to men of low estate. Be not wise in your own conceits."

Doro glanced back. "That sounds as though it would be an unpopular scripture in this part of the country," he said.

"I see to it that they learn some of the less popular ones," Anyanwu answered. "There is another: 'Thou shalt not deliver unto his master the servant which is escaped from his master unto thee.' They live in a world that does not want them to hear such things."

"You're raising them as Christians, then?"

She shrugged. "Most of their parents are Christian. They want their children to read so they can read the Bible. Besides"—she glanced at him, the corners of her mouth turned down—"besides, this is a Christian country."

He ignored her sarcasm, took her into the back parlor. "Christians consider it a great sin to take one's own life," he said.

"They consider it a sin to take any life, yet they kill and kill."

"Anyanwu, why have you decided to die?" He would not have thought he could say the words so calmly. What would she think? That he did not care? Could she think that?

"It's the only way I can leave you," she said simply.

He digested that for a moment. "I thought staying with you now would help you get used to . . . to the things I have to do," he said.

"Do you think I'm not used to them?"

"You haven't accepted them. Why else should you want to die?"

"Because of what we have already said. Everything is temporary but you and me. You are all I have, perhaps all I would ever have." She shook her head slowly. "And you are an obscenity."

He frowned, staring at her. She had not said such things since their night together in the library. She had never said them this way, matter-of-factly, as though she were saying, "You are tall." He frowned that he could not even manufacture anger against her.

"Shall I go away?" he asked.

"No. Stay with me. I need you here."

"Even though I'm an obscenity."

"Even so."

She was as she had been after Luisa's death—uncharacteristically passive, ready to die. Then it was loneliness and grief pressing on her, weighing her down then. Now . . . what was it now, really?

"Is it Susan?" he asked. "I didn't think you had gotten that close to her."

"I hadn't. But you had. She gave you three children."

"But . . ."

"You did not need her life."

"There was no other way she could be of use to me. She had had enough children, and she could not care for them. What did you expect me to do with her?"

Anyanwu got up and walked out of the room.

Later, he tried to talk to her again. She would not listen. She would not argue with him or curse him. When he offered again to go, she asked him to stay. When he came to her room at night, she was strangely, quietly welcoming. And she was still planning to die. There was an obscenity. An immortal, a woman who could live through the millennia with him, yet she was intent on suicide—and he was not even certain why.

He became more desperate as her pregnancy advanced, because he could not reach her, he could not touch her. She admitted she needed him, said she loved him, but some part of her was closed away from him and nothing he said could reach it.

Finally, he did go away for a few weeks. He did not like what she was doing to him. He could not remember a time when his thoughts had been so confused, when he had wanted so badly, so painfully, something he could not have. He had done what Anyanwu had apparently done. He had allowed her to touch him as though he were an ordinary man. He had allowed her to awaken feelings in him that had been dormant for several times as long as even she had been alive. He had all but stripped himself before her. It amazed him that he could do such a thing—or that she could see him do it, and not care. She, of all people!

He went down to Baton Rouge to a woman he had once known. She was married now, but, as it happened, her husband was in Boston and she welcomed Doro. He stayed with her for a few days, always on the verge of telling her about Anyanwu, but never quite getting around to it.

He took a new body—that of a free black who owned several slaves and treated them brutally. Afterward, he wondered why he had killed the man. It was no concern of his how a slaveholder treated his chattels.

He shed the slaveholder body and took that of another free black—one who could have been a lighter-skinned brother to the one Anyanwu had liked, compact, handsome, red-brown. Perhaps she would reject it because it was too like the other one without being the other one. Perhaps she would reject it because it was too unlike the other one. Who knew which way her mind would turn. But perhaps she would accept it and talk to him and close the distance between them before she shut herself off like used machinery.

He went home to her.

Her belly got in the way when he hugged her in greeting. On any other occasion, he would have laughed and stroked it, thinking of his child inside. Now, he only looked at it, realized that she could give birth any time. How stupid he had been to go away and leave her, to give up any part of what might be their last days together.

She took his hand and led him into the house while her son Julien took his horse. Julien gave Doro a long, frightened, pleading look that Doro did not acknowledge. Clearly, the man knew.

Inside the house, he got the same kinds of looks from Leah and Kane, whom Anyanwu had sent for. Nobody said anything except in ordinary greeting, but the house was filled with tension. It was as though everyone felt it but Anyanwu. She seemed to feel nothing except solemn pleasure in having Doro home again.

Supper was quiet, almost grim, and everyone seemed to have something to do to keep from lingering at the table. Everyone but Doro. He coaxed Anyanwu to share wine and fruit and nuts and talk with him in the smaller, cooler back parlor. As it turned out, they shared wine and fruit and nuts and silence, but it did not matter. It was enough that she was with him.

*　　*　　*

Anyanwu's child, a tiny, sturdy boy, was born two weeks after Doro's return, and Doro became almost sick with desperation. He did not know how to deal with his feelings, could not recall ever having had such an intense confusion of feelings before. Sometimes he caught himself observing his own behavior as though from a distance and noticing with even greater confusion that there was nothing outwardly visible in him to show what he was suffering. He spent as much time as he could with Anyanwu, watching her prepare and mix her herbs; instruct several of her people at a time in their cultivation, appearance and use; tend those few who could not wait for this or that herb.

"What will they do when they have only the herbs?" he asked her.

"Live or die as best they can," she said. "Everything truly alive dies sooner or later."

She found a woman to nurse her baby and she gave calm instructions to a frightened Leah. She considered Leah the strangest and the brightest of her white daughters and the one most competent to succeed her. Kane did not want this. He felt threatened, even frightened, by the thought of suddenly greater visibility. He would become more noticeable to people of his father's class—people who might have known his father. Doro thought this too unlikely to worry about. He found himself trying to explain to the man that if Kane played his role as well as Doro had always seen him play it, and if also he clearly possessed all the trappings of a wealthy planter, it would never occur to people to assume that he was anything but a wealthy planter. Doro told the story of Frank's passing him off as a Christianized African prince, and he and Kane laughed together over it. There had not been much laughter in the house recently, and even this ended abruptly.

"You have to stop her," Kane said as though they had been discussing Anyanwu all along. "You have to. You're the only one who can."

"I don't know what to do," Doro admitted bleakly. Kane

would have no idea how unusual such an admission was from him.

"Talk to her! Does she want something? Give it to her!"

"I think she wants me not to kill," Doro said.

Kane blinked, then shook his head helplessly. Even he understood that it was impossible.

Leah came into the back parlor where they were talking and stood before Doro, hands on her hips. "I can't tell what you feel," she said. "I've never been able to somehow. But if you feel anything at all for her, go to her now!"

"Why?" Doro asked.

"Because she's going to do it. She's just about gotten herself to the brink. I don't think she plans to wake up tomorrow morning—like Luisa."

Doro stood up to go, but Kane stopped him with a question to Leah.

"Honey, what does she want? What does she really want from him?"

Leah looked from one man to another, saw that they were both awaiting her answer. "I asked her that myself," she said. "She just said she was tired. Tired to death."

She had seemed weary, Doro thought. But weary of what? Him? She had begged him not to go away again—not that he had planned to. "Tired of what?" he asked.

Leah held her hands in front of her and looked down at him. She opened and closed the fingers as though to grasp something, but she held only air. She gestured sometimes when receiving or remembering images and impressions no one else could see. In ordinary society, people would certainly have thought her demented.

"That's what I can feel," she said. "If I sit where she's recently sat or even more if I handle something she's worn. It's a reaching and reaching and grasping and then her hands are empty. There's nothing. She's so tired."

"Maybe it's just her age," Kane said. "Maybe it's finally caught up with her."

Leah shook her head. "I don't think so. She's not in any

pain, hasn't slowed down at all. She's just . . ." Leah made a sound of frustration and distress—almost a sob. "I'm no good at this," she said. "Things either come to me clear and sharp without my working and worrying at them or they never come clear. Mother used to be able to take something cloudy and make it clear for herself and for me. I'm just not good enough."

Doro said nothing, stood still, trying to make sense of the strange grasping, the weariness.

"Go to her, damn you!" Leah screamed. And then more softly, "Help her. She's been a healer since she was back in Africa. Now she needs somebody to heal her. Who could do it but you?"

He left them and went looking for Anyanwu. He had not thought in terms of healing her before. Let the tables be turned, then. Let him do what he could to heal the healer.

He found her in her bedroom, gowned for bed and hanging her dress up to air. She had begun wearing dresses exclusively when her pregnancy began to show. She smiled warmly as Doro came in, as though she were glad to see him.

"It's early," he said.

She nodded. "I know, but I'm tired."

"Yes. Leah has just been telling me that you were . . . tired."

She faced him for a moment, sighed. "Sometimes I long for only ordinary children."

"You were planning . . . tonight . . ."

"I still am."

"No!" He stepped to her, caught her by the shoulders as though his holding her could keep life in her.

She thrust him away with strength he had not felt in her since before Isaac's death. He was thrown back against the wall and would have fallen if there had not been a wall to stop him.

"Don't say no to me anymore," she said softly. "I don't want to hear you telling me what to do anymore."

He doused a reflexive flare of anger, stared at her as he

rubbed the shoulder that had struck the wall. "What is it?" he whispered. "Tell me what's wrong?"

"I've tried." She climbed onto the bed.

"Then try again!"

She did not get under her blanket, but sat on top of it, watching him. She said nothing, only watched. Finally he drew a deep, shuddering breath and sat down in the chair nearest her bed. He was shaking. His strong, perfectly good new body was shaking as though he had all but worn it out. He had to stop her. He had to.

He looked at her and thought he saw compassion in her eyes—as though in a moment, she could come to him, hold him not only as a lover, but as one of her children to be comforted. He would have permitted her to do this. He would have welcomed it.

She did not move.

"I've told you," she said softly, "that even when I hated you, I believed in what you were trying to do. I believed that we should have people more like ourselves, that we should not be alone. You had much less trouble with me than you could have because I believed that. I learned to turn my head and ignore the things you did to people. But, Doro, I could not ignore everything. You kill your best servants, people who obey you even when it means suffering for them. Killing gives you too much pleasure. Far too much."

"I would have to do it whether it gave me pleasure or not," he said. "You know what I am."

"You are less than you were."

"I . . ."

"The human part of you is dying, Doro. It is almost dead. Isaac saw that happening, and he told me. That is part of what he said to me on the night he persuaded me to marry him. He said someday you would not feel anything at all that was human, and he said he was glad he would not live to see that day. He said I must live so that I could save the human part of you. But he was wrong. I cannot save it. It's already dead."

"No." He closed his eyes, tried to still his trembling. Finally, he gave up, looked over at her. If he could only make her see. "It isn't dead, Anyanwu. I might have thought it was myself before I found you the second time, but it isn't. It will die, though, if you leave me." He wanted to touch her, but in his present state, he dared not risk being thrown across the room again. She must touch him. "I think my son was right," he said. "Parts of me can die little by little. What will I be when there is nothing left but hunger and feeding?"

"Someone will find a way to rid the world of you," she said tonelessly.

"How? The best people, the ones with the greatest potential power belong to me. I've been collecting them, protecting them, breeding them for nearly four millennia while ordinary people poisoned, tortured, hanged, or burned any that I missed."

"You are not infallible," she said. "For three centuries, you missed me." She sighed, shook her head. "It doesn't matter. I cannot say what will happen, but like Isaac, I'm glad I won't live to see it."

He stood up, furious with her, not knowing whether to curse or to plead. His legs were weak under him and he felt himself on the verge of obscene weeping. Why didn't she help him? She helped everyone else! He longed to get away from her—or kill her. Why should she be allowed to waste all her strength and power in suicide while he stood before her, his face wet with perspiration, his body trembling like a palsied old man.

But he could not leave or kill. It was impossible. "Anyanwu, you must not leave me!" He had control of his voice, at least. He did not have that half-in-and-half-out-of-his-body sound that frightened most people and that would have made Anyanwu think he was trying to frighten her.

Anyanwu pulled back the blanket and sheet and lay down. He knew suddenly that she would die now. Right in front of him, she would lie there and shut herself off.

"Anyanwu!" He was on the bed with her, pulling her up

again. "Please," he said, not hearing himself any longer. "Please, Anyanwu. Listen." She was still alive. "Listen to me. There isn't anything I wouldn't give to be able to lie down beside you and die when you die. You can't know how I've longed . . ." He swallowed. "Sun Woman, please don't leave me." His voice caught and broke. He wept. He choked out great sobs that shook his already shaking body almost beyond bearing. He wept as though for all the past times when no tears would come, when there was no relief. He could not stop. He did not know when she pulled off his boots and pulled the blanket up over him, when she bathed his face in cool water. He did know the comfort of her arms, the warmth of her body next to him. He slept, finally, exhausted, his head on her breast, and at sunrise when he awoke, that breast was still warm, still rising and falling gently with her breathing.

Epilogue

There had to be changes.

Anyanwu could not have all she wanted, and Doro could no longer have all that he had once considered his by right. She stopped him from destroying his breeders after they had served him. She could not stop him from killing altogether, but she could extract a promise from him that there be no more Susans, nor more Thomases. If anyone had earned the right to be safe from him, to have his protection, it was these people.

He did not command her any longer. She was no longer one of his breeders, nor even one of his people in the old proprietary way. He could ask her cooperation, her help, but he could no longer coerce her into giving it. There would be no more threats to her children.

He would not interfere with her children at all. There was disagreement here. She wanted him to promise that he would not interfere with any of her descendants, but he would not. "Do you have any idea how many descendants you have and how widely scattered they are?" he asked her. And, of course, she did not, though she thought by now they would no doubt make a fine nation. "I won't make you any promises I can't keep," he said. "And I won't wait to ask some stranger who interests me who his many-times-great-grandmother was."

Thus, uncomfortably, she settled for protecting her children and any grandchildren or even strangers who became members of her household. These were hers to protect, hers to teach, hers to move if she wished. When it became clear within a few years that there would be a war between the Northern and Southern states, she chose to move her people to California. The move displeased him. He thought she was leaving not only to get away from the coming war, but to make it more difficult for him to break his word regarding her children. Crossing the continent, sailing around the Horn, or crossing the Isthmus of Panama to reach her would not be quick or simple matters even for him.

He accused her of not trusting him, and she admitted it freely. "You are still the leopard," she said. "And we are still prey. Why should we tempt you?" Then she eased it all by kissing him and saying, "You will see me when you want to badly enough. You know that. When has distance ever really stopped you?"

It never had. He would see her. He stopped her cross-country plans by putting her and her people on one of his own clippers and returning to her one of the best of her descendants by Isaac to keep her safe from storms.

In California, she finally took a European name: Emma. She had heard that it meant grandmother or ancestress, and this amused her. She became Emma Anyanwu. "It will give people something to call me that they can pronounce," she told him on his first visit.

He laughed. He did not care what she called herself as long as she went on living. And she would do that. No matter where she went, she would live. She would not leave him.

Afterword

Sandra Y. Govan
Professor of English
Director, McNair Postbaccalaureate
Achievement Program
University of North Carolina at Charlotte

Wild Seed (1980) serves as the introduction to a long inter-locking tale that spans millennia. Penned as Octavia Butler's "prequel" to the four other books comprising the Patternist saga, *Wild Seed* introduces two of the most dominant characters in series fiction establishing the groundwork for the conflicts, tensions, and themes that will resound throughout the series. Successive books in the sequential narrative frame, *Mind of My Mind* (1978), *Clay's Ark* (1984), *Survivor* (1977), and *Pat-ternmaster* (1976), carry forward through the twentieth cen-tury and beyond strong, tightly knit, thematic threads Butler weaves in telling the absorbing tale of Anyanwu and Doro—two extremely powerful people. Hugely successful among the discrete constituent audiences that Butler's fiction has gained over time, the rich evocative tapestry that is *Wild Seed* offers something of substance to every interested reader.

Dedicated science fiction fans find that the novel pro-vides some of the most exciting traditional elements of the genre wrapped in innovative guises. While there are no an-droids, aliens, spaceships, or alternate worlds, Butler instead uses the sciences of biology and anthropology to examine ideas like the limitations of immortality, the evolution of a mutant species through selective breeding, the ethics of such genetic manipulation, and the development of community when people are scattered, gathered, and scattered again. In addition, *Wild Seed* allows Butler to explore the impact that having special "gifts" or unusual powers (longevity, telekinesis, telepathy, metamorphosing, superhuman strength, regeneration) imposes on those possessing these capacities, and the corresponding impact (admiration, awe, acceptance; or fear, pain, rage, and jealousy) on those around them. Cast Doro as an unusual variant of the "mad scientist" figure initially engaged in a selective breeding project for his own selfish ends; add to this mix the pseudo-utopian, isolated "seed villages" that first Doro, then Anyanwu, create; then factor in the notion that all these events occur as the novel moves from seventeenth-century Africa to mid-nineteenth-century antebellum America, throw in the drama of an African Holocaust and subsequent African Diaspora, and what emerges is a riveting novel that holds the speculative fiction fan's rapt attention from start to finish.

Readers of women's fiction or feminist fiction find *Wild Seed* equally engaging because of Butler's delineation of Anyanwu as a strong female character. Beyond Anyanwu's striking presence as the mythic wise woman, the shapeshifter, the nurturing healer, the wife to many men and the mother of generations, there is also her stature as the one human being who can oppose Doro. Because she consistently undermines and rejects patriarchal authority in whatever guise she finds it, whether it is the authority any of her African husbands sought to impose on her freedom or Doro's unlimited destructive power. Anyanwu symbolizes the heroic resisting woman. Her match against Doro involves not simply a contest of wills, or a battle of wits and philosophies, but a careful, learned, consideration of the strengths and weaknesses of her opponent. Once she understands that Doro's attraction to her is calculated and can prove fatal for her and her descendants if she is not careful, Anyanwu first plots her escape then struggles to reach an acceptable compromise that guarantees not just her life and freedom but the lives of those who come under her protection.

Early in the novel, Anyanwu's intuition tells her that "for her children's sake" she must go with Doro and stay with him. She speculates about what it would be like "to be married to a man she could neither escape nor outlive." This possibility makes her both "cautious and gentle. . . . She sought to make him value her and care for her" so that later, she might exert some "control" or "leverage" over Doro when such leverage might be required [33]. While she never gains any measure of control through feminine guile, Anyanwu eventually does attain some leverage with Doro; over time, she learns how to use it. When we remember that Doro has lived more than 3,700 years, and we consider how, or why, or when he destroys and consumes those who oppose him, Anyanwu's accomplishment in even surviving their very tense, yet at times very tender and loving relationship, stands as a tribute to her powers of endurance and adaptation. Hers are also the strengths of nurturing, community building, healing, and teaching—training the young to recognize danger to assure their survival in the future. Clearly, Anyanwu is a complex woman. She is by turns self-assured and fearful; self-sacrificing, courageous, yet cowardly; feminine and masculine; weak yet strong. Anyanwu illustrates the human capacity for growth and change, continually refining her unique abilities in a new country among different people with different customs, culture, and values. Their very names foretold that they were destined to meet—Doro means the east; Anyanwu means the sun; yet how they live out that destiny over time becomes the essential question.

Almost without question the initial appeal of *Wild Seed* for many African-American readers resides in Butler's lush and detailed yet credible descriptions of Anyanwu's African home. Butler's ability to make tangible the nuances of various communities, their respective cultures, customs, traditions, myths and beliefs in pre-colonial Africa through the medium of speculative fiction has garnered high praise. With carefully crafted anthropological renderings Butler creates vivid images that resonate with the central touchstones from African-American historical experience: the legacies of an Africa only dimly remembered; the horrific slave trade which included the Middle Passage; the brutality of American chattel slavery. Additionally, for many African-American readers, and others who possess wide reading experience within the African-American literary tradition, there is recognition of a kinship linking *Wild Seed* to that historical literary canon.

While readers obtain some glimpses of west African village life—the barter economy, the market women who did the trading, the farming practices, the religious traditions, the foods (yams, smoked fish, vegetables) they ate, Butler does not romanticize Africa. The people Anyanwu has lived among for centuries possess the same attributes and foibles of people the world over. They can be loving and kind; they can also be arrogant or jealous; they fear what they don't understand; they are hostile toward those manifesting difference. They often recast their fears and wonder at specific phenomena as powerful magic or religion; they sometimes sought Anyanwu's counsel as an oracle—one through whom a god spoke, and they sometimes attacked Anyanwu as a witch, forcing her to kill in order to save herself. In this regard Anyanwu and Doro exhibit some similarity; both can kill when threatened. Doro, however, after 3,700 years, cannot recall feelings of distress or pain when he has had to kill, while Anyanwu continues to feel a mixture of anger, shame, and regret when forced to defend herself by taking human life.

African village life is not idealized but seventeenth-century Africans are shown as various peoples with quite distinctive customs, values, sensibilities, and languages often different from those of their neighboring communities. However, these societal distinctions all but vanish—are suppressed, lost, or destroyed under the full destructive force of the slave trade. Only remnants remain. The beliefs, customs, values or sensibilities of the people captured and sold become immaterial when confronting the devastating and dehumanizing impact of Africa's Holocaust and Diaspora, the trade in human lives. Though *Wild Seed* does not aim to subject readers to the full horrors of the Middle Passage—what Robert Hayden called in his poem "Middle Passage" the "voyage through death/to life upon these shores"—Butler's more restrained and elliptical description of the hardships faced in transporting Africa's stolen people nonetheless proves moving and painful. What reader cannot empathize with Anyanwu's immediate recognition of evil upon her encounter with the Royal African Company and its sales preparation methods of the branding of new slaves? Who cannot understand her terrible feelings of isolation and loneliness as when contemplating the endless sea and the thought of leaving her homeland behind, Anyanwu feels called to seize control of her life. "She would leap into the sea. Its waters would take her home, or they would swallow her. Either way, she would find peace. Her loneliness hurt her like some sickness of the body, some pain that her special ability could not find and heal" [66]. Magnify Anyanwu's experience by the hundreds of thousands, by the millions, and the devastation to body and spirit the slave trade exacted on its black victims is abundantly clear. What Butler also makes abundantly clear is the negative consequences trading in human cargo exacted on whites as well. On seeing her first "slaver," Anyanwu notes his physical (and moral) condition: ". . . dirty and thin as though wasted by disease—which was likely. This land swallowed white men" [42].

The correspondences connecting the African-American literary canon to the novel came through most clearly in *Wild Seed*'s echo of characteristics embedded within the slave narrative and the earliest African-American fiction. In what is arguably the oldest and most original of American literary forms, narratives written by formerly enslaved people nearly always touch upon several key points. These narrators discuss the individual's introduction to slavery; the bonding among slave families, and the corresponding pain of forced separations of those families through slave sales; a catalog of the random violence and systematic brutality of the slave system; the reduction of human beings to the status of animals; the detrimental effects of slavery on black and white alike; an indictment of the hypocrisy among the so-called Christian slaveholders; the vulnerability of the slave woman as both servant and sex object; the slave mother's efforts to protect her children; ordinary life within slave communities; the value and importance placed on education; the desire for freedom and the escape North; and the insistence on the slave's status as a human being. The tenacity shown by enslaved people to demonstrate their humanity or force its recognition is recounted in hundreds of slave narratives.

While *Wild Seed* does not appropriate this entire list of tropes or common elements, aspects from it most certainly appear in the novel. To take just a few examples, Anyanwu's decision to leave her homeland with Doro is but one instance of her desire to shield and protect her offspring from a life of virtual enslavement. Throughout the novel, Doro repeatedly uses threats against her children to maintain his hold on her. The intensity of Anyanwu's desire for freedom comes early when she tries to jump overboard; at other points, Butler puts a distinctive, science fictional, spin on the escape motif. First, Anyanwu is able to shapeshift; in becoming another creature, albeit not a human being, she can elude Doro's control. Further, it is an ironic twist on the slave's escape to freedom in the North that Anyanwu flees further south, moving from upstate New York to the deep South. In Louisiana, Anyanwu establishes her own pseudo-plantation setting for her own people where she can both protect them from the outside world and prepare them for Doro's eventual arrival. Perhaps most powerfully analogous to the actual slave narratives is Anyanwu's continual insistence that the slave is a human being who, like every human being in any civilized community, must be allowed to live by some moral codes.

Some practices are an "abomination" within any human society. For instance, to Doro's repeated hints, suggestions, commands that his people marry each other despite ties of kinship, or his dictate that they have sexual relations with whomever he chooses, Anyanwu is quite firm. "Abomination! We are not animals here, Doro!" she says the first time she hears his suggestion that her children commit incest [15]. When Doro commands that she, too, violate the taboo against incest, she rejects the very premise vehemently. "How can I have the son when his father, my husband, still lives?" she demands. "That is abomination!" To Doro's response that disobedience is the only abomination, Anyanwu remains adamant. "I will not! Wrong is wrong! Some things change from place to place, but not this" [130]. What Anyanwu resists with all her might is what she perceives as dehumanization. She rejects Doro's desire to make her breed as an animal is bred; to do to her what ordinary slaveholders, in their desire to increase their stock, did to their slaves whenever they chose. She insists upon her humanity. That Anyanwu finally capitulates rather than destroy herself shows other dimensions of that humanity—fear of death, the desire to live, the burden of responsibility for those yet unborn.

Yet arguably, despite its large and seemingly dominant presence in the novel, chattel slavery is *not* the principal focus of *Wild Seed* nor is the book simply a meditation on American slavery. Rather, slavery can be seen as the speckled protective camouflage laid across the other issues Butler subtly underscores. Among those other issues are the human responses to fear, to difference, to greed and corruption, to anger and pride, to community and obligation. Other fundamental issues emerging from *Wild Seed* that will resurface in other Butler novels are her concerns regarding the uses of power and the human capacity for adaptation or change. Further, if we envision the novel as science fiction aligned to the period novel or historical romance, a fuller range of possibilities opens. In this alignment, slavery serves as an ancillary component; it is the backdrop against which Butler moves her characters. This narrative tactic allows her to inform, without being didactic, various audiences about slavery in its different phases or guises while depicting the customs and conventions, the mores and actions of a particular people in a particular society at a particular time and place.

Another complimentary narrative strategy subtly woven into the fabric of *Wild Seed* shows Butler illustrating inclusion or "diversity" on a distinctive scale—once again informing audiences, making them aware of the range of possibilities without seeming didactic or argumentative. Doro sought out people for his seed villages without regard to race or color but for whatever ability they could contribute to the gene pool. His people were African, European, or Indian; they were male and female; some were young while others were old; they were those with active gifts and those whose gifts were latent. What Doro valued was a distinctiveness based upon inner abilities, not outward appearances, outward professions of faith or goodness. What Doro cared about was not that his people maintain any allegiance to race but that they recognized the talent and power they had within, and of course, the power he exercised in controlling their lives. By contrast, in her own special community, Anyanwu teaches the people she collects, or those who find their way to her, the value of all human life regardless of any special ability. All are prized; all can make contributions to the whole community whatever their talents—some are the caregivers, others are the cared for. Those with special gifts are taught how to use them, how to control them. Anyanwu teaches her people, who come from different economic backgrounds, racial backgrounds, or cultural backgrounds, how to work together, to be compassionate to each other, to support, nurture, and rely upon each other. The only offenses she will not tolerate are malicious violence and wanton destructiveness. Everyone's life has value for her; this inherent value of all life is a trait she eventually helps Doro to recognize.

To return to a consideration of the larger issues encapsulated in *Wild Seed*, in depicting the arbitrary god-like Doro,

Butler paints an extremely determined, driven, obsessive, single-minded being with enormous unchecked creative and destructive capability. His abilities stem from the negative side of the power equation. Yet in creating Anyanwu, and having Doro seek and maintain a relationship with her, however strained and tense, Butler allows us to see that even powerful negative forces can be undermined; that indeed, everything must change; that there is a redeeming power in the human spirit, a redeeming power in the human capacity to give, to sacrifice, to love. Indeed, the power of love is a significant factor that should not be slighted in *Wild Seed*, for above all else, the story of Anyanwu and Doro is a taut love story spun out over time and space. By going back in time to establish the groundwork for the successive tales, Octavia Butler's *Wild Seed* has not only effectively set the stage for the rest of the Patternist saga, but it has also given her varied audiences a framing text that is simultaneously informative, innovative, evocative, exciting, and powerful.

About the Author

I'm a fifty-three-year-old writer who can remember being a ten-year-old writer and who expects someday to be an eighty-year-old writer. I'm also comfortably asocial—a hermit in the middle of a large city, a pessimist if I'm not careful, a feminist, a Black, a former Baptist, an oil-and-water combination of ambition, laziness, insecurity, certainty, and drive.

I've had eleven novels published so far: *Patternmaster, Mind of My Mind, Survivor, Kindred, Wild Seed, Clay's Ark, Dawn, Adulthood Rites, Imago, Parable of the Sower,* and *Parable of the Talents,* as well as a collection of my shorter work, entitled *Bloodchild. Bloodchild* includes short stories published in anthologies and magazines. One, "Speech Sounds," won a Hugo Award as best short story of 1984. The title story, "Bloodchild," won both the 1985 Hugo and the 1984 Nebula awards as best novelette.

—Octavia E. Butler

In 1995 Octavia E. Butler was awarded a MacArthur Grant. In what is popularly called the genius program, the John D. and Catherine T. MacArthur Foundation rewards creative people who push the boundaries of their fields.

In 2000 *Parable of the Talents* received the Nebula Award for Best Novel, and Ms. Butler was given the PEN Center West Lifetime Achievement Award.